SAVING ALICE

By David Lewis

*Sanctuary**
Coming Home
Saving Alice

*with Beverly Lewis

DAVID LEWIS

SAVING ALICE

a novel

BETHANYHOUSE
Minneapolis, Minnesota

Saving Alice

Cover design by Gearbox

Published by Bethany House Publishers
11400 Hampshire Avenue South
Bloomington, Minnesota 55438

Bethany House Publishers is a division of
Baker Publishing Group, Grand Rapids, Michigan.

Printed in the United States of America

Paperback:	ISBN-13: 978-0-7642-0051-9	ISBN-10: 0-7642-0051-8
Hardcover:	ISBN-13: 978-0-7642-0096-0	ISBN-10: 0-7642-0096-8
Large Print:	ISBN-13: 978-0-7642-0097-7	ISBN-10: 0-7642-0097-6

Library of Congress Cataloging-in-Publication Data

Lewis, David (David Gerald)
Saving Alice / by David Lewis.
p. cm.
Summary: "Stephen Whitaker has his whole life planned, but when he loses his true love—Alice—a gradual undetected spiral begins. When everything starts unraveling, whom will Stephen turn to?"—Provided by publisher.
ISBN 0-7642-0096-8 (alk. paper) — ISBN 0-7642-0051-8 (pbk.) — ISBN 0-7642-0097-6 (pbk. lg. print)
I. Title.

PS3612.E964S28 2006
813'.54—dc22

2005028050

To Jerry,
my father . . .
my friend.

"God works in mysterious ways."

Chapter One

Fourteen years later, I still dream of her. . . .

I find myself slipping back in time as if not a day has passed. The images are fragmented, not in any particular sequence, as if they are occurring at the same precise moment in time. But I can't miss the scents of vanilla and pizza . . . the sound of oldies playing in the background . . . the glisten of her brunette hair in the afternoon light. Then comes the relentless sense of dread, building into sudden panic, and the slippery feel of her silky blouse in my fingers . . . the momentary burst of relief . . . *she's safe* . . . and the final piercing echo of her scream.

Usually when I awaken, I'm gasping for breath and soaked in sweat. Donna wakes up beside me and touches my shoulder. "Are you okay, Stephen?"

I swallow hard, then nod. I'm sorry I've awakened her, and I hope she doesn't ask any further.

"The same dream?"

I'm tempted to fudge my answer: *a little different,* or *kinda*—just to spare her feelings. But Donna knows the truth, and although she pretends otherwise, my answer breaks her heart. I give her assurances which she accepts graciously, and then she strokes my back momentarily—*sleep tight, Stephen*—and turns over.

Later, as I feign sleep and as Donna slumbers beside me, I ponder the dream, and in spite of myself, I still wonder. . . .

What if I *had* saved Alice? Where would all of us be? Alice, Donna, and me.

I'm aware of my wife's gentle form beside me. In the stillness, I sense the rise and fall of her breathing. I gently place my hand on her hip, feel the warmth of her, and guilt consumes me.

When I think of our sleeping daughter, Alycia, I get up and wander my way downstairs to open her door quietly—my little girl hidden beneath a mound of pillows, blankets, and stuffed animals. I watch until I detect the rise and fall of her breathing.

Another shudder of relief washes over me, not unlike the dream, only this one is real.

She's safe.

Alycia was only ten when she came to me with a matter of life-and-death consequences. It was a Sunday afternoon, and I was relaxing on our secondhand pea green couch watching an exhibition game on our fuzzy TV. My spirits were bright because the Twins were pummeling the Rangers.

Wearing faded jeans and a pink Hello Kitty T-shirt, Alycia meandered into the living room and plopped herself onto a brown corduroy floor pillow.

I turned on my side and appraised her sudden melancholy. "What's the matter, Alley Cat?"

She looked away and sighed. "I throw like a girl."

This is as earthshaking as it normally gets for my melodramatic daughter, but rarely am I presented with such opportunities. "Maybe because you are one?"

"Da-ad," she whined. "It's not funny." She twisted on the floor to face me. "I want to make the team, okay?"

The team? "Surely you don't mean . . . the *boys'* softball team?"

"Yes," she said, her squint intended to nip my playful chauvinism in the bud. "They're letting girls try out."

"Really?"

Her squint turned into a frown. "So what am I supposed to do?"

I was reminded of my own childhood obsession with the sport—collecting cards and plastering my walls with pennants. I wasn't much younger than my daughter when our next-door neighbor gave me an old ball and mitt, and I remember bursting into our trailer, hoping to persuade my dad to throw with me. He did, lasting all of five minutes.

"Got an idea for you," he said, heading back in. "You're gonna love it, Stephen."

Next day after school I found a strange, beat-up apparatus in our side yard, resembling a sideways trampoline. My father introduced me to my new "friend."

"It bounces the ball back to you," he told me. "That way you don't need me." He tousled my hair and returned to the trailer as I proceeded to throw the ball against the canvas monstrosity. I lasted all of five minutes.

I now turned to my daughter, and with what I hoped was a twinkle in my eyes, said, "I'm afraid you'll have to accept your lot in life. You're a girl and girls don't—"

Wham! The brown pillow hit me squarely on the head. Gleefully Alycia leapt to her feet and began pelting me. My arms provided little protection, and my chortles only riled her further. Finally, with the pillow lodged against my important air cavities, we reached a truce.

Instead of our usual father-daughter activities—kite flying, bike riding, or library lurking—we commenced vigorous training sessions. For several hours each day after school, I taught her the rudiments of the game—how to throw and hit, how to catch grounders, and how to pitch. All that was missing was the theme from *Rocky.*

Six weeks later she tried out, and later that evening, I was the one who took the call from Coach Wolf: Alycia had made the team. I'd never seen her so psyched. By the end of summer, I was in the stands when my daughter, the only girl on the boys' team, hit a home run. She crossed home plate, turned and waved to me, and the catcher followed the direction of her gaze. My heart swelled with pride as I read her lips. *That's my dad!*

After the final game, she hung up her cap and never looked back. "Been there, done that."

"That's it?" I complained. "After all our hard work?"

"I'm a girl, remember?"

That retort inaugurated a spirited chase around our house—living room to kitchen to bedroom to hallway back to the living room, over and over again—followed by a visit to the Ice Cream Shoppe on Sixth Avenue, where we discussed my daughter's next big challenge.

"Sewing?" I suggested, licking my cone. "Cross-stitch, perhaps? Or . . ."

She narrowed her eyes.

" . . . basket weaving," I finished excitedly. "*There's* an idea worth exploring."

"I'm thinking brain surgery," Alycia replied, licking her own cone. "But I might need a few years to prepare."

"A few," I agreed.

As we sat in the frenetic atmosphere of an ice cream store, the casual observer would have seen the kind of father-daughter relationship that often takes decades to develop, if it ever materializes at all.

But things were different for Alycia and me. Her mother occasionally lamented that she felt like an outsider looking in on a private party, a perception I tried to dispel with little success. The truth was, Alycia and I had a special bond.

Alycia—pronounced *Ah lee see ah,* which she later shunned for the more traditional *Ah lish ah*—was a pretty brunette girl, waif thin, approximately five feet of pure energy. Graceful like a cat, she seemed destined to avoid the usual adolescent awkward stage, and yet, in spite of her athletic gifts, her heart-shaped face was almost doll-like—ivory soft with high cheekbones, expressive blue eyes, and the cutest little Minnie Mouse ears.

"She's all eyes," her mother liked to say, and sometimes Alycia, in the right light, seemed European, a reflection of my distant French ancestry. To me, Alycia's features were reminiscent of an adolescent Audrey Hepburn—only with wavy curls. When I first told her this, her face clouded with despair. "Audrey who?"

"You know. *My Fair Lady.*"

"Ugh."

"Just you wait, 'enry 'iggins!" I taunted her as only a father can, to which she covered her ears and moaned.

As with all pre-adolescent girls, "appearance" dominated Alycia's attention. About a year after her home run, she arrived home from school on the brink of tears. In spite of our persistent inquiries, she refused to open up. "It's just so . . . *terrible,*" she finally wailed. "It's *too* terrible to say."

I might have been more concerned if I hadn't been familiar with Alycia's tendency for theatrics. She slunk off to her downstairs room, closed the door, and turned off the lights. She sat in darkness for nearly two hours until I decided it was time to make another effort.

When I knocked, a quivering voice whispered back, "What does a girl have to do to get ice cream?"

At the Ice Cream Shoppe she finally fessed up. I'd been prepared for something earth-shattering: perhaps a popular boy had looked at her wrong, possibly one of her best girlfriends had dropped her, or maybe she'd blown a test.

Instead, she pointed to a bald man across the room, eating an ice cream sundae. As he did so, his unusually large ears twitched.

"That's it, Dad. That's my fate." Her voice carried the tone of deep regret.

I was confused. "You're losing your hair?"

"Da-a-d! Pay attention!"

I took another hard look and caught the man's eye. He smiled at me, and I returned it, then looked at my melancholy daughter for a much-needed explanation.

Alycia wilted. I was supposed to read her mind. She swallowed hard, and her eyes became circles of vulnerability. "Dad . . . my ears stick out."

I resisted the inclination to smile. "Yes, I know. It's cute . . . like Minnie—"

"No, Dad. My ears *really* stick out." Angrily she pulled back her chin-length hair. "Still think it's funny?"

I felt my eyebrows rise. She wasn't kidding. Somewhere between age ten and eleven they'd mushroomed.

"Jeff called me Shrek-a-lina."

I frowned. *Shrek-a-lina?*

"You know? Shrek? From the movie?"

I paused, then moved quickly to potential solutions. "So . . . try a new hairstyle."

"They'll just stick out no matter what I do," she whimpered. "And look even worse."

I leaned forward to analyze the situation. "Maybe it's temporary," I suggested. "Maybe in time they'll . . . flatten, or shrink, or . . . maybe your head will grow larger!"

"Dad . . ."

"What?"

Her eyes glistened. "Home-school me."

"How can I do that?" I asked. "Your mother and I both work."

A new wave of despondency fell over her.

"Why don't you try sleeping on them . . . you know, flatten 'em out?"

"I already sleep on my ears," she shot back. "C'mon, everyone sleeps on their ears!"

After driving back home, I brought Alycia into the brightly lit dining room. "Sit down," I said. "And hold still."

She frowned but complied. At the table, I examined her ears, pressing, pushing, prodding, and analyzing the intricate folds.

"No more jokes," she warned.

The next week, I promptly commenced research on the Web, and later, during the weekend, I spent three hours at Alexander Mitchell Library. Convinced I was on to something, I called several Ear, Nose, and Throat doctors, suffering through countless referrals for plastic surgeons. Since insurance wouldn't cover a penny, I finally settled on the plan we could afford. Having cautioned me to be extremely careful, Donna was still at work when I sat Alycia down in the living room, her expressive eyes wary but hopeful.

Without preamble, I announced my plan. "We'll pin 'em back."

A moment of incredulous silence passed. "You've *got* to be kidding."

"Why not?" I argued. "Your friends pierce everything else, don't they? Belly buttons? Eyebrows? Lips? Nostrils?"

Removing a textbook from my leather satchel, I turned to a middle page, showed her some ear diagrams, and explained the finer points of ear flesh and cartilage. The more we discussed it, the more animated she became. "We simply close these two folds with a skin-colored tightening pin."

"Show me in the mirror," she said.

We went into the bathroom, and I demonstrated by squeezing the two folds together. As I pinched, the ears twitched flat.

Her eyes widened. "What does Mom think?"

I gave her the modified version.

"You're kidding. Mom approves?"

I nodded. Although "approves" may have been a bit optimistic, I can say with assurance Donna did not disapprove.

She looked down, considering everything, then looked up. "So . . . who would actually do this for me?"

I took a deep breath. "I'll do it."

"You'll do it?"

"I've studied this," I explained. "I know exactly where to punch the holes."

Alycia raised her eyebrows. "*Exactly* where to punch the holes?"

I touched her right ear again. "If I do it right here and here, we're set. And if it doesn't work, we'll let the holes heal up and try again."

Alycia put her arms on my shoulders and peered into my eyes, as if searching into my very soul. I rubbed my hands together with ghoulish delight and spoke in my well-practiced Transylvanian accent. "So, my little princess . . . do you trust me?"

She grimaced, which I accepted as an affirmative gesture. Still rubbing my hands, I stood up, but she pulled me down again. "Dad . . . do you think God cares about stuff like this?"

I hesitated, taken off guard. Our eyes met as she waited for an answer. Truth was, as a kid, I did. These days if I so much as dared to send a prayer heavenward, I could all but hear the slamming of a door, the clicking of a lock, and a deep but muffled voice, *Go away, we're closed for business!*

I knew what Donna might say: *The hairs on your head are numbered, remember?* So I mentioned it.

"Oh yeah," Alycia said, brightening. "I forgot."

"I'm sure God has noticed your ears as well," I said, then surprised myself by adding, "The Bible also says, if you have faith the size of a mustard seed, you can say to this mountain, move, and it will."

The second it was out of my mouth, I felt like a fake. Who did I think I was, acting as an apologist for God? Besides, in a world of famine, disease, and death, I didn't think Shrek-a-lina ears qualified for God's overt attention.

"A mustard seed is pretty small, isn't it?" she asked.

"Tiny," I agreed.

Alycia's excitement grew. "And Jesus healed people all the time, didn't He?"

"You bet."

"Well . . . I think my faith is a little bigger than a mustard seed," she announced.

"There you go."

"So . . . can we pray about this?"

I cleared my throat. "Sure."

She scowled. "I'll pray, Dad. You just relax."

"I'll do it," I insisted, and she looked at me warily. I reached for her hands, and we closed our eyes. I whispered an awkward prayer, and when I finished, she seemed suddenly calm. "Okay. All set."

Ten minutes later, she sat on a bathroom chair as I proceeded to numb her ears, then disinfect them. Alycia kept her eyes closed, and breathed heavily. Her panic returned with the first punch. She grimaced and whined, "Dad, don't mess up! Don't scar me for life! Don't ruin my romantic future!"

"Sssshhhh. . . ." I whispered.

"I *can't* sssshhhh!"

"And don't talk about your romantic future to me, please."

"Face it, Dad, I'm blossoming."

I punched the last hole.

"Ouch!!"

"You couldn't feel that."

"It *felt* like I felt it!"

Finally . . . I installed the pins and stepped back. Sniffing tentatively, she stood up. Facing the mirror together, I braced myself as Alycia stared at her image in disbelief.

Amazing. Her ears were hardly distinguishable at the sides of her head.

Alycia burst into tears and hugged me tightly. "I love you, Dad."

I chuckled wryly and demurred her praise, but she shook my shoulders with wild abandon. "I'm serious! You saved my life."

I chuckled again. "Well . . . maybe not your life."

Wide-eyed, she shook her head adamantly. "I beg to differ, Daddy dearest." She looked at me with such adoration, it took my breath away. She hugged me again, so tightly, it would have required the Jaws of Life to peel her away.

"And thank you, God," she whispered into my chest. "Thank you for giving me the coolest, smartest Dad!"

While I didn't mind sharing the credit, it all seemed so melodramatic. Then again, my daughter was the ultimate drama queen. *You saved my life,* she'd said, and yet when I look back on that day, I tremble.

What I wouldn't give to have it all back.

Chapter Two

After I performed the miracle on Alycia's ears, dear ol' Dad could do no wrong.

She fixed me snacks on demand, retrieved the morning paper, and washed my car—no small feat—just to see my pleased expression. She even vacuumed the carpet in my office, and one day when I was studying the price and volume squiggles of the stock market on my home office computer, I caught her staring at me.

My chair squeaked as I turned around. "Something hanging out my nose?"

"Gross, Dad!" she exclaimed, leaning forward and resting her chin in her clasped hands. "I'm studying you."

"That's, well, comforting."

Alycia smiled innocently, a little too innocently. "I want to know what makes you tick."

"*I* don't even know that."

She was undeterred. What came next, during the following weeks and months, was what I call her curiosity phase, a time when she asked me countless questions and sat with rapt interest, palms on cheeks, while I told her stories from my childhood. I should have been honored; instead I was nervous.

While some of our discussions took place around the dining table, most of her interrogations occurred in the car as I played chauffeur—a captive, unable to escape. Of course, I respected her need for pure, undiluted honesty. "When I was a kid," I once began, watching the road, "we had no computers, no TVs, no cars, no beauty salons, and every morning I walked thirty miles to school—including Saturdays."

Out of the corner of my eye, I could tell Alycia was rolling her eyes. "For real, Dad."

"Okay, you caught me. The truth. After school my father locked me in a closet and fed me bits of bread under the—"

"Dad . . ."

Finally Alycia resorted to pointed questions, designed to penetrate my uncooperative behavior. *Speaking of your dad, why is Grandpa so weird? Was Larry your best friend? Or Paul? Did you get all A's? How old were you when you first dated?* And the big one: *When did you fall in love with Mom?*

I never gave the latter a straight answer, saving the whole truth for much later when hopefully she'd be old enough to understand, like age forty-five. Although my stories contained ample face-saving modifications, Alycia was good at putting two and two together.

I was driving her to the mall one day when she blurted out, "What aren't you telling me, Dad?"

"Say what?"

"You're dissembling."

"Am not!" I protested, then frowned. "What's 'dis—'?"

"Start over, and we'll see if your second version matches the first."

"Tell me again why you want to hear this?"

"Don't be so sensitive."

The more questions she asked me, the more evasive I became. Finally, she fixed me with a knowing smile. "You're hiding something. You have a secret, don't you?"

"A secret?"

"Everyone has secrets," Alycia declared. "Yeah, like a mystery. Hey, maybe I could even solve it for you!"

"That's clever."

Alycia brightened. "You do, don't you?"

I affected my best innocent expression, and then trudged up some rousing tale to distract her—like the day Larry and I threw firecrackers on the top of kid-adverse Mrs. Schumacher's aluminum trailer in the middle of the night, hastening to add that we apologized years later.

I stopped at the front entrance of the mall, and Alycia got out, then paused in the open car window. She winked. "You can run, Dad . . ."

"Yada, yada, yada," I replied intelligently.

For the moment, Alycia dropped the "secret" stuff, but I detected a knowing glint behind her eyes. Very annoying, but as usual she was right. I had a secret, and so did her mother. Actually, we had two, and while they weren't of the earthshaking variety, so far we'd done a pretty good job of keeping them under wraps.

"I don't want her to worry," Donna often told me. "You know how she is."

I agreed, but obviously we were only buying time. Unless I came clean soon, Alycia would discover the truth from her friends at school. In that event, my daughter would likely storm home and confront me, "Why didn't you tell me, Dad? I thought we talked about everything!"

The other secret, ironically, was hidden within Alycia's own name. If she'd just snooped through her mother's old pictures, she would have figured it out.

Sometimes Alycia's need for the truth skirted the edges of tact, especially since she had a nasty habit of calling a spade a spade. For better or worse, Alycia has always had an uncanny knack for sizing people up.

On the way to the "Y" where she was enrolled in a summer volleyball camp, she asked me, "How old were you when you realized Grandpa was a jerk?"

I gave her my parental scowl. "Grandpa deserves your respect."

"Sor-r-ry," she said melodramatically, as if *I'd* said something wrong. And yet guilt clouded her features.

She quickly transitioned to her next topic, but I was still contemplating her question. The answer was "age ten," and while there's a story involved, it's certainly not the kind you'd tell your pre-adolescent, post–Santa Claus daughter. Besides, Alycia wouldn't have been interested. It didn't contain a smidgen of romance.

On the other hand, it's also safe to say my entire caldron of simmering secrets—including the ones Alycia seemed so desperate to uncover—had originated the day I met Jim.

It all began after a long day in the fifth grade, when I spotted my father's car parked on the street across from the playground. Without smiling, he waved me over, striking terror into my young heart. I knew I was in trouble for something. But what did I do?

I got into the car, and my father proceeded to drive in the opposite direction of home. For several worried-filled minutes, I scrambled through my mind for my crime, hoping to figure it out and apologize long before he removed his belt. I remember staring at him out of the corner of my eyes—his long narrow face, pale and splotchy, was pinched in concentration. Several wisps of his slicked-back prematurely graying hair had broken free despite copious applications of Brylcreem. The smell always got to me. His large nose overpowered his face—especially from a side perspective—as if it had a personality all its own.

My father often joked, *When we hit it big, I'm getting a nose job,* and my mother would kiss his nose with her typical smooth-things-over approach, *It's your best feature, dear!*

Although I resembled my father, I'd acquired my mother's reasonable nose. She did, however, have giant feet for her size. For years I'd monitor my nose carefully every morning, going so far as to measure its length to settle my fears. Sometimes I measured my feet too, relieved when they seemed to be growing. If something had to stick out, I'd rather it be them. Later I wondered if perhaps my family's penchant for oversized appendages had found their way to Alycia's ears.

My father cleared his throat but remained silent.

"Everything okay, Dad?" I finally managed to squeak out.

He only grunted. Eventually, he turned into a gravel lot, the tires crunching as he pulled on the steering wheel and parked in front of a seedy storefront with bright neon signs. He told me to lock the door behind me, and I did. I followed him through the lingering clouds of our dust into a cavernous bar saturated with the scent of whiskey and rum and a lingering hazy smoke that stung my eyes.

The bartender, squinting into the doorway, was rubbing a tiny glass with a white towel. When he saw me, he cleared his throat and glared at my father. "C'mon, Lou, they can yank my license."

My father gestured helplessly and spoke in a woeful tone I rarely heard at home. "I'm stuck with 'im, Phil; the wife's got one of those doodad appointments, and I got a deal going with Sam. Is he here?" My dad looked around desperately, and I wondered how he could see anything in this dingy place.

Phil shook his head. "You're a piece a' work, Lou," he said, shaking his head. "Make it fast."

My father shrugged, throwing his briefcase on the counter. "Just tryin' to make a living."

I climbed up on the stool, relieved to learn this wasn't about me, and ran my fingers along the smooth wood finish.

"Thirsty?" Phil asked me, leaning over the counter with hunched shoulders.

I rustled around in my pockets. "I don't know if I've got enough—"

"Hey, Lou, your kid's thirsty," Phil said.

"Put it on my tab," my father said absently, pulling papers out of his briefcase. My father didn't drink, but he provided no end of drinks for his clients.

Phil's face clouded again. "I told you. No more credit."

I heard the sound of a flimsy door slamming behind me. My

father twisted in his seat, and his foul mood did a one-eighty. "Hey, Sammy, I'm bringing the office to you. . . ."

I looked up at Phil helplessly. "That's okay," I said. "I'm not that thir—"

"It's on me," someone said in a low, raspy voice, and for the first time, I noticed the guy sitting on my right, wearing a tan cowboy hat. His hair, which stuck out below, was silvery, his face grooved like an old tire, and his nose a misshapen lump of gray flesh, with tiny little spiderlike veins, to match the ones on his cheeks. With a cigarette nestled between two right fingers, he cradled a shot glass with the same hand, as if saving his left hand for something more important.

"Fair enough," Phil said to him, and then to me: "I got orange juice, 7-Up . . ."

"How much is the juice?" I asked, still searching my pockets.

"Don't worry about it," the old guy said, taking another sip. "Git 'im what he wants."

Phil nodded, walked away, and I sat there, embarrassed. By now I'd already been on the receiving end of more than my fair share of handouts, and I didn't like how they felt. "Thanks, mister, but you didn't have to."

The old man blew out smoke and gave me a sideways glance. "Don't mention it."

I should have left it at that. I'm not sure what I said next, but I probably rambled on about my growing independence.

The old codger cast me another look, a long one this time. "I pity you, kid."

I was snapped into silence, offended to the quick. For one thing, he didn't sound all that pitying, and besides, being pitied was the same as a handout. I was about to tell him so when I realized I didn't know what in particular he was pitying me for.

"I don't mind"—I shrugged nonchalantly—"As long as I get home for *Star Trek*."

"Ain't what I meant," he said with a hoarse chuckle. He brought the cigarette to his lips, his cheeks sucked in, and his eyes narrowed as he inhaled. The end of the cigarette glowed, nestled alongside the shot glass, and within the gloominess of that room, it had a hypnotic effect on me.

Again, I should have left it at that, but I had an insufferable curiosity and more than a little pride. "So what *did* you mean?"

"Forget it." He took a swig, stared at the glass, and gestured for another. Phil hunched over the counter again, regarding him warily. "You've had more'n enough, Jim."

"Wife's got the car," Jim said. "So it don't matter."

Phil sighed and shook his head with disgust. He placed a napkin in front of me, followed by the juice with a tiny red straw sticking out. I took a big, long, thirsty pull, then noticed Jim watching me out of the corner of his eye, as if sizing me up while Phil poured some amber liquid into the glass.

To my left, Dad broke into exaggerated laughter. I glanced over to see his hand on Sam's back, and suddenly leaning forward, speaking in hushed tones. "Seriously, Sam, this one's going to go straight up, like a wild dog, the moment they release it."

I looked back at Jim, and he was staring at my father as if little knives might come spurting out of his eyes at any moment.

"So what did you mean, already?" I repeated.

Jim looked away, took another drag, and when he exhaled his cheek popped out, like my father's when he was tired or fed up. "You just don't quit, do you?"

He looked at me again, and his eyes seemed bloodshot and vacant, and everything nice about him disappeared. I felt a cool shiver run down my back, and I wondered if he wouldn't rather strangle me than speak.

I was about to say his own words back to him, "Just forget it," when he spoke again, his voice gruff and low: "You ever been to a fortune-teller at the carnival? You know . . . the Gypsy lady that looks at the lines on your hand and tells your future?"

I thought for a moment. "Mom says it's of the devil. No one can tell the future."

His eyes narrowed to slits. "I can."

I frowned and stubbornly shook my head. "No, you can't."

He stubbed his cigarette in the charcoal-stained aluminum ashtray. "Hold out your hand, then, and I'll prove it to you."

"No, thanks," I said, pulling both hands to my lap.

"Suit yourself. This here's how it's done. . . ."

I watched wide-eyed as he laid down his drink and cigarette and picked up a shiny knife in his right hand. He held up his left hand, splayed open toward me, showing crevices nearly as deep as the ones on his face. Turning his hand back toward his face, he pressed the knife into his palm, then paused, meeting my eyes.

"Mister, what are you gonna—?"

Slowly, he pulled the knife down, pretending to make a cut several inches long. He did a good job of faking it because his lips were pulled down into a painful grimace.

It's just magic, I told myself. Behind my left shoulder I could hear my father's familiar setup and automatically braced myself for the inevitable father-son hug.

"It ain't the hand lines that predict your future," Jim was saying, turning his open palm toward me to reveal a drooling line of red liquid. "It's your *blood*line."

My mouth must have dropped open. The old codger was insane. At that point, my father leaned toward me, patting me on my back. "Take my boy here. I've already got him enrolled in a savings plan. By the time he gets to college . . ."

My father was reaching full crescendo with a sales pitch I'd heard so many times I could have repeated it word for word. The savings plan, of course, was a bald-faced lie.

Jim tossed the knife on the table, and it clattered against his glass. I waited for him to take a napkin or something to stop the bleeding, but instead he tightened his fist, causing small drops to leak out the bottom.

I wanted to say, *Are you okay? Do you need a Band-Aid? Are you crazy?* But settled on something akin to pretending what I saw hadn't actually happened. Besides, I was strangely captivated.

"So . . . what's a bloodline?" I croaked, my throat as dry as the smoke in the air.

Jim sniffed, still clenching his left fist. He extinguished the spent cigarette in the tray with his right. "It's your destiny, kid." And then he added with a ghoulish glint in his eyes, nodding toward my dad, "Your bloodline is your ol' man over there."

The way he said "your ol' man" shivered through me. His eyes gazed on me again, and his last words came out with a thud. "I ain't never seen something a Whitaker touched that didn't turn to dust." He gave a quick confirming nod of the head, lips drawn down deeply on the sides. "You never stood a chance, kid, and that's why I pity you."

"And that's enough, Jim." Phil emerged from the shadows, and I realized he'd been listening to the entire conversation. I felt guilty somehow, party to a betrayal.

Phil tossed the towel over his shoulder and leaned over the bar. "It ain't right to take it out on his kid."

"Fair warning, is all I'm givin 'im," Jim replied with another sniff.

"What you're doing is scaring 'im," Phil said. "Go home and sleep it off."

After a quick nod, Jim tossed back the final drop of his drink, stood to his feet, and considered his surroundings as if he'd forgotten where he was.

He glanced over at my father again, tipped his cowboy hat toward me, and headed for the door. I squinted at the light flooding my eyes, just before the door slammed shut.

My father, as if he'd finally awakened, turned to Sam, and thumbed toward the door. "Know that guy?"

I leaned over to catch Sam's reply: "Lost his farm couple years ago. Ain't been the same since." Sam made a twirling motion to the side of his ear.

"Well, that's not gonna happen to you," my father said, patting Sam on the back. "So . . . like I said, options will get you the biggest bang for your buck . . ."

Still staring at the door, I felt a tap on the shoulder. I turned halfway in my stool, and Phil leaned over the bar and whispered, "Just for your information, kid, Jim bought some worthless stock from your ol' man about three years ago. It ain't your fault. Just forget what he said."

I considered this for a moment. My father hadn't even recognized Jim. I turned toward my dad again, this time taking a real hard look. *Jim's right,* I realized.

But he's wrong about me.

Chapter Three

"Your father's behavior is incongruent with his words" is the closest Donna ever came to criticizing my dad. At the time, we were driving to see my folks in Frederick, a small town of barely three hundred, twenty miles north of our town, Aberdeen.

"You mean he's a fake," Alycia inserted from the backseat.

I glanced in the rearview mirror. Alycia cast me an *I'm-right-aren't-I?* look as if the truth was all that mattered.

"He's still your grandfather, Alycia," Donna said softly.

"Sor-r-ry. My *grandfather* is a fake," Alycia corrected herself.

Donna caught my eye, probably expecting something more than the shrug I gave her. She shook her head with thinly concealed frustration and turned to the window.

Much to his obvious annoyance, my father had never found any psychological weakness in Alycia. By the time she was five years old, she'd already gotten him figured out.

"Did Grandpa really lock you in a closet?" she asked as if she wouldn't have been surprised. We were sitting in the stuffy car at the end of that afternoon's visit, waiting for Donna to say good-bye to my mother. Sometimes their good-byes took longer than their actual visits. Dad had long since retired to his garage where he pretended handyman proficiency.

I gave the rearview mirror a knowing wink. "Rarely overnight."

Alycia made a face, then peppered me with follow-up questions. *Were you scared of him? Did he spank you? Did you have lots of chores? Why did Grandpa and Grandma get married anyway?* Which contained the hidden question: how could *anyone* marry Grandpa?

Then came the question that pierced my heart: "Were you poor then?"

I felt my face redden and sensed her unasked query: Have we *always* been poor?

"Yes," I replied.

I glanced out the car window to watch Donna give another quick hug and break free from my mom, and when I again looked in the rearview mirror, Alycia cast me another raised eyebrow as if to say: *To be continued, Dad. Don't think you're off the hook. In the meantime, please think about my questions, and consider offering more than one-word answers. . . .*

On the whole, Alycia's inquiries carried a not-so-hidden agenda: secret scavenging. When her questions got too direct, I gave her the evil-eye-dare, which she only returned. "Duck all you want, Dad, but you can't hide."

Frankly, I was more than happy to oblige since, fortunately, she was barking up the wrong tree. At the very least, telling her about my childhood served as an effective distraction. Besides, there wasn't anything inherently mysterious about my childhood. In spite of my father's natural-born salesmanship and my mother's housecleaning services, we were, as Alycia suspected, dirt poor. Over time, she heard the whole story.

We lived in a short, single-wide trailer on the good side of the tracks—if only by a few yards. Sometimes, after church, we'd eat out, which was the high point of my mother's week, and then take the back way home. Just before reaching the railroad tracks, my dad would point toward the right—to a small row of dilapidated homes—and mutter, *"Things could be worse, Maggie. We could be living in Uglyville."*

I came to believe that so-called Uglyville was the lowest rung on the ladder, much worse than a trailer, and yet it seemed so close to the rung we were already clinging to we seemed only inches away from its dismal destiny.

Although our financial situation was precarious, my mother did a pretty good job of pretending otherwise. She had a habit of finding the silver lining to every cloud, and if she struggled, she'd quote some Bible verse to make up the difference.

"There is no limit to God's miraculous power," she often said. "He'll supply all our needs. He will never forsake us." Even our living room pillows were stitched with biblical phrases: *Miracles happen to those who believe,* and so on.

The issue of whether or not to believe never even occurred to me, not then anyway, and there were times when I talked to God for hours, out in the ditch behind our trailer beneath the starry night. Usually I spent the time complaining, or asking for something, but in spite of my poor spiritual manners, the sense of God's closeness sometimes took my breath away. There were moments when I thought I could have reached out and shook His hand, but I never tried because the feel of God's hand in mine would have terrified me.

Raised in the same church, Mom and Dad had grown up in mutual poverty in Bowdle, about forty-five minutes to the west of Aberdeen. They'd married just out of high school, after which my father passed his brokerage test and hung a shingle in the "big city" of Aberdeen. My mother, positioned by my father's loud personality, existed in the mere background of our lives. Most people described her in terms of what she wasn't: She wasn't like my father—loud, boisterous, and opinionated, who had no end of compliments . . . for strangers.

I always wondered why people took him at face value, but later I realized they hadn't. Sure, there was a group of people who trusted him—the ever-present P. T. Barnum constituency, my father's bread and butter. But on the whole, most people had figured him out pretty quickly. Those who hadn't lost their savings, as I had first learned when I met Jim.

Larry Marshall and Paul Thompson were my best friends in elementary school. They were, and still are, the yin and yang of my life. After school, Larry, my "action" friend, would prevail upon me to race miniature gas cars and sometimes, on the weekends, fire model rockets.

For years Paul, my "thinking" friend, and I discussed stories from various editions of *Ripley's Believe It or Not:* stories such as the bearded lady, the man who'd been shot in the head and lived to tell about it, or the man who suddenly appeared out of the blue on the streets of London, confused and speaking a long-dead language.

Even then, Paul was interested in fringe physics—quantum mechanics, wormholes, super strings, multiple dimensions—the kind of extreme science that satisfied his attraction to the unexplainable.

As for me, the idea that the universe was not as it appeared held great appeal as well, and our discussions only increased my fascination with the idea of miracles—that on behalf of His creation, God sometimes exercised the power to act outside of time and space, and that sometimes He acted mysteriously.

In spite of Paul's interest in the unusual, he wearied of what he called my "increasing and disturbing religiosity."

"It's like oil and water," he told me, sounding like a pint-sized MIT professor. "Physics and religion don't mix."

I shouldn't have been surprised. His own family had never darkened the steps of church, and Paul's father reminded me of Jim, who spent most days and nights at the bar. In polite terms, he was an alcoholic, but in common vernacular, he was a mean drunk. Sometimes, late at night, Paul would show up on our doorstep, shivering. My mother would welcome him in as if receiving royalty, feed him a hearty meal, and get him settled on the couch for the night.

Briefly, my father and Paul's father had been friends, and although my father never drank, he frequented the bars for "sitting ducks." He liked that "sweet spot," the moment after the prospect had begun drinking, but long before he was too drunk to sign on the dotted line.

Although Larry's father, a deacon at the church, didn't drink either, he wasn't much nicer. Regardless of what Larry did, his father regarded him as a fat, lazy slouch whose backside needed the belt on a regular basis. For years Larry and I had a standing appointment. On report card day, I walked home with him, serving as a punishment buffer. That is unless his report card was full of A's—as in *all* A's, in which case his father expressed welcome lack of interest.

By the time we got to high school, however, my support wasn't needed—Larry never received less than an A. Unfortunately, his father kept raising the bar until even stellar work wasn't good enough. Finally, in his sophomore year, when Larry had reached six-two, he pushed his father, belt and all, through their flimsy living room wall.

Alycia frowned and sat up suddenly. She'd been lying on her side on the living room floor, picking at the strands of carpet. "Did Larry hurt him?"

I shook my head. "No, but his father never beat him again."

"I should say not!" Alycia exclaimed, obviously surprised at the notion of Larry's blatant disobedience. "Is that why he's so . . ."

"Intense?"

"Yeah," she agreed. "Serious."

I shrugged. "That's the only Larry I know."

She fixed me with a mischievous grin. "So, Dad, tell me. Who was your first date?"

I sighed.

"C'mon, no fudging."

"Your mother," I replied.

"Da-a-ad . . ."

Actually, it was true. Unbelievable perhaps . . . but true. However, since that wasn't going to fly, I told her about Cynthia Reiser, my junior high crush.

"Are there any secrets in this part?"

"Hmmm. Sorta."

"Real secrets?"

"You bet. Enigmas wrapped in riddles."

Alycia looked skeptical. "C'mon, Dad. You're supposed to throw the audience a bone once in a while just to keep 'em interested."

Cynthia Reiser was the prettiest, most popular girl in the seventh grade. Her father was a bank president, and they occupied the biggest house on Elm Avenue, where all the homes were large.

Cynthia reminded me of the "before" version of Sandy from the movie *Grease*, with straight blond locks and blue eyes. She also wore glasses, which seemed entirely appropriate, since something was needed to filter her beauty from common mortals.

For the longest time, I admired her from afar until, at age fourteen, I finally made my move during the dance at Holgate Junior High. It was a Saturday night, and since neither Paul nor Larry were into dances, I walked to school alone. Dusk slowly melted into dark as I prepared my battle plan and prayed for a miracle.

For two hours I lurked at the edges of the dance floor, enduring warbled high school renditions of "Smoke on the Water," and "Stairway to Heaven," squinting through the flashing strobe lights as a hundred junior high kids jived, thrashed, and flailed on the dance floor.

From across the gym floor, I watched Cynthia giggle with her friends and flirt with other boys. *Miracles happen to those who believe,* I reminded myself as I slowly worked up my courage. Since she was surrounded by an entourage, I had to plan my infiltration for just the right moment. Either that or the Almighty would have to part the rivers of junior high humanity.

Unfortunately, I planned wrong, or my faith was weak, because I was intercepted at the edges of the outer circle—but not before Cynthia's eyes met mine and not before she must surely have deduced my intentions.

"Her dance card is full," Mindy said in my ear with a humorous drawl, loud enough so several of the girls joined in a chorus of incredulous laughter. *Who did I think I was?* Cynthia's own grimace of disbelief settled it for me. I shrugged as if it were no big deal, then bid a nonchalant but hasty retreat to the side gym door, where the stoners and slackers were hanging out and sneaking cigarettes. Susan blocked my exit.

"I'll dance with you, Stephen," she offered, having witnessed the entire pitiful affair. Susan lived just north of the trailer court, in a neighborhood of two-bedroom, one-garage homes—a mere two rungs up from Uglyville. My father also had sold some stock to her father, a man who seemed to be everywhere but home.

She was wearing tight jeans with an even tighter sweater—probably hand-me-downs. Platinum blond and prematurely developed physically, Susan was a cheerleader for the football team. Word in the school was Susan would kiss any boy once and probably do other stuff if you asked nicely. Later in high school, we would refer to her as the "Queen of Hearts."

I glanced at my watch as if I had an appointment. "Thanks anyway, but . . . I gotta get home."

"We could make her jealous," Susan persisted, batting her eyelashes. I considered her offer, but it was the genuine pity in Susan's eyes that settled it for me.

I thanked her for the dubious invitation and walked home with newfound determination. *Who cares how pretty Cynthia Reiser is?* I thought. There were better-looking girls out there, nicer girls who didn't have to wear glasses. Besides, if I married Cynthia, I'd probably be stuck in Aberdeen for life. *No thanks.*

Soon after this, on a Sunday following church, my father took us out to Western Sizzler and my mother giggled like a schoolgirl, which is what she often did when nervous. Mom was a saint, but she wasn't perfect, and the tension of our poverty loomed over us like an ever-present cloud.

"We can afford it," my father announced, clearing his throat. "Because we're moving."

His reply didn't make sense.

"Where?" Mom asked, looking bewildered.

Grinning slyly, he didn't answer, but on the way home, we took the back way again, Roosevelt, and I felt a growing panic in my gut. Just before we reached the railroad tracks, he slowed the car—my heart skipped a beat—and thumbed toward our new house.

Uglyville?

"It's a rental. Already put a deposit on it. What do you think?"

I couldn't breathe. Mom was speechless. The rancher had been painted white once, perhaps sixty years ago. The clapboards were chipped and crooked, and the roof was a confusing mixture of wood and gray shingles. The yard contained approximately three green blades of grass, with the rest covered in dandelions and weeds. The crumbling cement sidewalk had experienced something akin to an earthquake. *Even the earth is ashamed,* I thought.

"It's just for a while," he added.

Later I would learn the truth: We'd lost the trailer. *How on earth do you lose a trailer?*

My mother found her voice. "Well . . . it needs a paint job."

It needs a bulldozer.

My father turned to me in the backseat. "Stephen's good at painting, aren't ya?"

I didn't reply. I felt my eyes watering but refused to sniffle. I was numb when we got out of the car, my legs tingly and weak, but Mom marched right up to the house and tested the screen door. Even from the street, I could see the torn screen mesh flapping in the breeze. She went inside anyway. I leaned against the car, crossed my arms across my chest.

"Wanna see your new room?" my father asked.

I wanna go home, I thought, recalling with a new fondness our sheet-metal trailer just a few blocks away—on the right side of the tracks.

Mom emerged from the shack and said, "Wonderful possibilities. Let's go meet the neighbors."

My father chuckled. "Now you're talking."

Later that night, my mother tiptoed into my room, her face shadowed in the dark. She sat at the edge of the bed. "Won't be for long," she whispered.

"That's what he always says."

She stroked my hair. "As soon as we can scrape up a down payment, we'll buy our own house."

How? I thought. *We can't even afford a trailer!*

"Let's pray about it," she said, leaning over and kissing my nose. She was putting on a brave face, but in the darkness I felt a tear on my cheek that wasn't mine.

"Sorry," she whispered and gently dried my face with her fingertips.

When she left, I censured myself for my foolish self-pity. My father had finally reduced my mother. That settled it for me. Poor or not, I was going to go to college, and someday I'd be rich enough to rescue my mother from her dismal life.

I knelt beside my bed. I whispered Scripture verses, reminding God of His promises: *All things are possible to him who believes.* And then I struck a deal with the Almighty. *Get me out of here and I'll help everyone I know. . . .*

The next day, I went to Larry and offered to take over his paper route. According to plan, the route would stay in his name, but since I'd be doing the work, I would keep the collection money. I didn't tell him that I'd already talked Kevin into his route just to the west of the trailer route. In order to complete two routes every afternoon, I'd have to be Super Boy.

No problem.

A few weeks later, Mom and I headed to the First National Bank and opened a bank account in my name. Since I was a minor, I needed her signature. My plan was to sock half my loot into the bank and give the other half to Mom.

She refused. "That's yours," she said firmly. "I won't steal my son's future."

Reluctantly, I agreed, but sometimes I would slip extra bucks into her purse when she wasn't looking—not so much that she could tell, but not so little that it wouldn't make a difference.

Not content with two paper routes, I made up flyers and passed them around the neighborhood, selling my services as a handy-boy. I offered to do anything: wash windows, mow lawns, rake leaves, shovel snow, detail cars—you name it, and before long I was busy from dawn until dusk. After sneaking a few bucks to Mom, and giving God ten percent, I put everything I made into that bank account.

By now, proving Jim wrong had become the obsession of my life, and I was determined to succeed in precisely the way my father had failed. When not working or studying, I read his stock-trading books, the ones he kept buying but didn't have the inclination to read. By the time I was fifteen, I'd already decided to make my millions as a world-class trader. The deck was stacked against me, but I had God on my side.

Convinced I had no time for dating, I never attended another dance. I could not imagine, not in my wildest fantasy, bringing a girl home to Uglyville, much less to meet my father.

As it was, I came home after dark and left before sunup, and *never* gave out our address. If asked, I gave out the area of town instead. "The northeast," I would say, which was bad enough, then quickly change the subject.

During this time, I read *God's Smuggler* by Brother Andrew and was impressed, not only with the amazing stories of missionary work in Russia, but with how God miraculously provided financial assistance for Brother Andrew during his schooling.

By now, I was praying nightly in the empty rabbit field behind our house, and despite those occasional glorious experiences of God's presence, I felt lonely in my quest to succeed. One night I remembered how God had led Brother Andrew to his future wife and with this anecdote in mind, and feeling rather bold, I unabashedly whispered my last rabbit-field request to the stars, as if God were my own private Celestial Dating Service. *She's out there somewhere,* I whispered.

By the time I graduated, I'd managed to capture good enough grades and scrape together enough cash for one year's worth of tuition, excluding room and board, to a good college in the East—far, far away from Uglyville and the Dakotas.

It was time for bed. Alycia frowned. "So when did Grandma and Grandpa finally move?"

I gave her the shortened version. Years ago, my financially disorganized father discovered that he'd purchased five hundred shares of Cisco at a rock-bottom price and promptly forgotten about it. Upon discovery, he subsequently sold the stock too soon but cleared enough to retire. He then bought my mother a house in Frederick, where few people knew him, and where, in effect, my father's haven became my mother's exile.

Alycia kissed me on the cheek. "Thanks for the stories, Dad. Keep 'em coming."

Just before heading off to the bathroom to brush her teeth, she gave me a sly look. "So . . . am I getting closer?"

"Cold as ice."

"Will you tell me when I'm getting warm?"

"Nope."

"So how will I know, then?"

"Listen to your inner Shrek."

"Dad . . ."

"Sorry."

She blew out an exasperated breath, then brightened. "I can't believe you prayed to meet Mom. That's so cool."

I smiled but didn't have the heart to correct her.

Chapter Four

A year later, the summer after Alycia turned twelve, the jig was up. Alycia's relentless questions were finally breaching my feeble security system. She fixed me with a knowing grin, placed her elbows on the table, clasped her hands, then opened Pandora's box with delicious triumph. "So Dad . . . tell me about . . ."

She paused for effect and dropped the bomb: *"Alice."*

"Alice who?"

"Nice try. She's the one in the picture—you know? In Mom's old albums?"

"Oh," I said. "*That* Alice."

Alycia gave me her patented *spare me* eye roll. Apparently she'd already interrogated her mother, after which Donna had referred her to me. The two of us were sitting in the Ice Cream Shoppe—which seemed an entirely appropriate venue for the forthcoming story. Surrounded by the buzz of a dozen excited conversations and the squeals of young children, I took my time. It wasn't a story that came easily and I'd hoped to have years, if not decades, to prepare.

Alycia prodded me. "Mom says you were going to marry Alice."

My stomach tensed. "Actually . . . she was your mother's best friend."

Alycia's eyes widened. *"Mom's?"*

I smiled. I'd opened with the clincher, and Alycia's impatient expression implored me to *Get on with it!!*

I relished my new power and wielded it with abandon. I started, then stopped, cleared my throat, and started again. "Well . . . uh . . . hmm . . . come on, you don't really want to hear this stuff, do you?"

"No fair!" Alycia's fingers darted out and pinched my arm.

"Ouch!"

Her expression promised further dire consequences. "I was named after her! Don't I have a right to know everything?"

We stared each other down, her militant sweetness against my good-natured frown, and then she giggled. "C'mon, Dad. Spill. If you don't, I'll just ask Mom again, and . . . and her stories are more juicy!"

I gave her my own skeptical eye—one eye half mast, the other cold and steely—and in the glare of my truth-gaze, she back-pedaled. "Okay, okay. Mom's stories are truly and dreadfully boring. But . . . c'mon, I'm dying here. I could always count on you before!"

The guilt trip coupled with an immediate threat: She poised her pinchers again and raised her eyebrows as fair warning.

"Fine," I replied. I took a deep breath and started at the very beginning, but I only told her a fraction of the story—the juvenile face-saving version. Nothing juicy. In spite of this, I should have known better. Although she'd finally worn me down, telling my daughter about Alice was not going to be a good idea.

I should have let her pinch me black and blue.

I was twenty when I met Alice. She was only eighteen, although she seemed older than her years. Her silky brunette hair was closely cropped around her face, and other than a slight dusting of powder, she used little makeup. Born into the upper crust of New England society, she wore fashionable clothes and displayed a fondness for expensive, but delicate, jewelry.

I eventually learned she had begun piano at age four, singing lessons at age five, and dance classes at age six. Later, her wealthy parents sent her to a finishing school and, to the disappointment of teen boys, forbade her to date until she was sixteen. I'm convinced she would have been plucked for a brilliant childhood career on stage or screen if a talent agent had been resourceful enough to discover her and if her parents had been foolish enough to consent.

If I were a poet, I would have described Alice as a wide-eyed, exuberant child seamlessly merged within the quiet soul of a confident woman, a woman utterly convinced of the inevitability of her dreams. And it was this—her magnetic aura of success—that mesmerized me from the moment I first glimpsed her "across that crowded room."

"You make her sound like a saint," Paul said when I first described her. But according to Larry, and before his enlightenment (divorce), women were necessary evils—practical bedroom accouterments at best, and at worst, glorified maids. If your woman liked football, well . . . you had yourself a live one. "She's only a dame," he once told me when I was back home during a rare visit and extolling Alice's gifts. "A garden-variety dame, like a fancy new Chevy truck, with a few bells and whistles thrown in. Don't lose your perspective."

I ignored him and returned to college and Alice. The romantic poets tell us that when you meet "the one," you'll know immediately. Well, I did. I knew from our very first date. And more important, I'd prayed—and God had answered.

But it was a May twelfth day that is emblazoned in my brain—the day I waited for her in our booth at the Soda Straw, our college hangout, with a diamond ring in my pocket and a proposal in my heart. While we hadn't talked about marriage specifically, we had talked of being together forever, and to me, that's the same thing.

I'd arrived an hour early to sip black coffee and gather my wits. We'd come a long way since a rather disastrous first date—saved only by her sense of humor—followed by a year of insufferably platonic friendship that included a threesome with Donna before Alice reached over the table, squeezed my hand, and said, "Stephen, I think I'm falling in love with you. Is that okay?"

Thinking back to that moment, I remember grinning like the village idiot. I'd actually done it. I'd shot for the moon and actually *reached* the moon—not just that proverbial lamppost. Successfully navigating an ivy-league college and the girl of my dreams—my prayers—across the table from me.

As far as school, the truth was that without Alice I would have dropped out before my junior year. Unable to qualify for a loan due to my father's poor credit, the school bills accelerated. Attending classes in the morning, working six hours in the afternoon, studying in the evening, sleeping two or three hours a night, my grades were falling precipitously.

Alice came to my rescue. "Hitch your wagon to my star."

I didn't understand.

"I'll lend you the money."

Dismayed, I shook my head, but she punched my shoulder playfully. "Snap out of your ego!"

"Alice—"

"I *believe* in you, Stephen. I'm making an investment in your future, nothing more. Pay me back later."

Reluctantly, I agreed, but only if we drew up loan papers. She chuckled at my silliness, but three days later, I quit my job. Two years later, I graduated with a cumulative GPA of 3.78, with a double major in Accounting and Finance, mere weeks after having received a lucrative offer with a Wall Street firm.

I was no longer the eleven-year-old boy who walked three miles downtown to buy his used comic books because his parents couldn't afford a bike. The days of macaroni and cheese for breakfast, lunch, and supper were a distant memory.

Waiting now for Alice to arrive for what I believed to be our most significant date yet, I bowed my head, oblivious to the noisy diner, and whispered my gratitude to the Almighty. In the end, my mother was right: With God all things *were* possible. Even for a kid from Uglyville.

Every detail of that day is etched on my brain—the stiff, lumpy feel of the red vinyl booth, initially cold to the touch, then growing warm and comfortable, the feel of my elbows resting on the sterile paint-flecked Formica table, the sound of oldies in the background—"Don't Be Cruel," "Time in a Bottle," and "Right Back Where We Started From."

I chain-sipped coffee and stared at the ring—soon to be hers—twirling the open box around in my fingers. Shafts of sunlight illuminated the afternoon dust through the slats of the window blinds. The walls echoed with the excited buzz of a roomful of college students. Most of all, I remember the smells: fragrant vanilla, grilled hamburger, and baked pizza.

Nina, our red-haired, jean-skirted waitress, sneaked up behind me. "Wow . . . nice rock!!"

Startled, I reflexively covered the box, but she was already stretching out her hand and wiggling her fingers invitingly. "Now that's gonna look good on my finger! It's my birthstone, Stephen! How did you know?"

I gave her a tense smile.

"C'mon. Let's see it again!"

I moved my hand from the white box, revealing the gold ring cushioned in purple velvet. The brilliance of the single diamond under the fluorescent lighting broadcast its authenticity, and the elegance of the setting, I felt, fit the recipient perfectly.

Nina whistled like a teakettle.

"I think your boyfriend might object," I joked.

After another quick glance about the room, she hurriedly sat across from me, placing her elbows on the table, and leaned over like a co-conspirator. "So am I right?"

I nodded, and Nina raised her eyebrows.

"What?" I asked.

"Who *is* it?" she asked, her eyes still darting about the room, alert for the next big tip to walk through the door.

"Who is who?"

"You know . . ." Nina replied with a leading tone and shaking her head. "Donna or Alice?"

"Oh," I said, hiding my annoyance. "Alice."

Nina's eyes widened. "Does she suspect?"

I assured her that she didn't.

"Good luck." Nina finally stood up, taking the hint. "I'll give you plenty of space. But you better leave a good tip." She looked back at me on her way to greet another table and whispered loudly, "Hide that box before she gets here!"

I glanced at my watch for the hundredth time.

It was 4:05. Alice was late.

"She was late?" Alycia exclaimed.

"Alice was *never* late," I added. "For her, punctuality was an obsession."

Alycia frowned. "Back up a sec . . . why didn't Nina know who you were dating?"

I shrugged. "The three of us were very close."

Alycia twisted her lips in concentration, then squinted. I knew what was coming next. "You left out some parts, Dad. I can tell, you know."

In response to this most grievous accusation, I delivered an eloquent and persuasive rebuttal: "Uh-uh."

"Yeah *huh.*"

"No sirree."

Alycia held out her pinky finger like a dare. "On your honor?"

I blew out an exasperated breath. "Okay, okay. But only the grown-up parts."

Alycia came uncorked. "Those are the very parts I want to hear! Now you have to start from the very beginning."

"Alycia—"

"Besides, I want to hear more about Mom!"

Feeling as if a dump truck had unloaded a ton of sand over my head, I started over, but with renewed determination to be even craftier in my elimination of those details Alycia would think juicy but I would label "too painful."

Alycia gave me another good-natured squint and flexed her pinchers. I proceeded to describe the day I'd first glimpsed Alice, at the beginning of my junior year.

Alice was on stage performing a solo vocal recital, ranging from highbrow Schubert and Mozart to the show tunes of Andrew Lloyd Webber, and Rodgers and Hammerstein. She projected an amazing command of the stage, dancing and gesturing like a professional, acting out the themes from the musicals.

I happened to be sitting next to fellow classmate Donna, a pretty, blond literature major I'd met in "American Novels of the Twentieth Century," which was a casual humanities elective for me but a required course for her. Without Donna I would have failed the course. We'd become friends three months earlier and had even gone on a few casual dates, though as busy as we both were, I can't imagine where we'd found the time.

Alycia interrupted me. "You're talking Mom, right?"

"How many Donnas do you know?"

"Just checking."

Halfway through the first song, Donna leaned over. "That's my roommate I was telling you about."

I nearly fell off my seat. "That's your roommate?"

Afterward, as Alice signed programs, Donna pulled me through the crowd, introduced us, and I proceeded to lose my voice.

Later, this would become a never-ending source of amusement for Alice. "You literally squeaked," she would giggle, squeezing my hand with reassurance while I blushed, taking her word for it, because to this day I can't remember what I'd actually said.

Of course, I adored her New England accent, which seemed exotic to me. And yet, strangely enough, during our first date, Alice interrupted one of my nervous ramblings. "Stephen . . . where you from?" Which, to me, sounded like, *Wahuh yohuh frawm?*

"Pardon me?"

"Your accent!" she exclaimed. (*Yohuh ahccint!*)

Imagine that—Alice considered *me* exotic.

Eventually, the three of us became inseparable, and while we attended musicals, museums, and fine restaurants, the Soda Straw became our weekly ritual, a celebration of the end of another grueling week of classes. It was here, the place of so many lively discussions and laughter, that Alice's regard for me finally evolved into romance.

Most fittingly, Donna witnessed it, the matchmaker becoming the overseer. While she refused to become a hindrance to our developing romance, we sincerely enjoyed her company and refused to let her simply wander off into the sunset. Sometimes we even succeeded in roping her into attending special events.

Unfortunately, and for someone so schooled in romantic literature, personal romance didn't seem to interest her. Devoted to her studies, she preferred to study the revisionary progression of Fitzgerald's tragedy *The Great Gatsby,* rather than attend a movie with a casual acquaintance. Much to our dismay, she regularly turned down dating opportunities, although occasionally Alice and I engaged in a little humorous matchmaking of our own . . . usually to disastrous results.

Of course, Fridays were set aside for the three of us. Alice and I insisted. Comfortable with our friendly humor, Donna preferred the backstage, more at ease as an observer than a participator. We often referred to her as "Scout" after her favorite novel, *To Kill a Mockingbird;* other times we called her "Dorothy" and inquired of her "pet Toto."

Although Donna met my family only once, my mother adored Donna. Raised in the church, and fervent in her faith, Donna had been born and bred in a small town in Kansas. And while our commonalities—hers and mine—were enough to build a good friendship, Donna reminded me of the life I'd so eagerly left behind, as if "Aberdeen" were still nipping at my heels.

During her junior year, Alice was accepted into Juilliard, an event which surprised none of us but didn't impress my mother one smidgen. Several weeks later, I called Mom in the morning and informed her of my intentions.

She was politely reserved, if not mildly patronizing, unwilling to spoil the moment but unable to give enthusiastic blessing. I shouldn't have expected better. From my mother's perspective, only one thing mattered, and it certainly wasn't Alice's significant natural gifts. While Alice had been raised in a respectable Methodist home, it wasn't enough, in my mother's humble estimation, to save her soul.

"She's a Christian," I argued.

"A *Sunday* Christian," she countered.

I sighed and made fruitless attempts to argue the point.

"I'm praying for you, honey," she said at last.

You'll see, I thought after hanging up. After I made my first million, I intended to buy my mother the biggest house in Aberdeen or, better yet, Mystic, Connecticut, a coastal fishing town close to the Rhode Island border—if I could convince my parents to abandon South Dakota, of course. My father would have the kind of Mercedes he'd always eyeballed in Danny's showroom floor. And Larry, who'd stayed home to attend Aberdeen's Northern State College, would have the kind of financial backing to ensure his own business success.

Everyone would share in the realization of my dreams, but no one more than Alice. She would continue to have the best of everything, the newest, the latest—whatever she wanted. We would travel to Europe in the summer, the Cayman Islands in the winter, and our children—what a delicious thought!—would be educated in the best institutions money could buy. In summer twilight, Alice and I would stand on the breezy balcony of our ocean-front Connecticut vacation home, and with my arms wrapped protectively around her, I would repeat my promises of undying love and devotion. Later, we would walk the beach hand in hand as the sunset gradually disappeared beyond purple skies.

Good ol' Donna helped me pick out the ring. After beseeching her with my ignorance, she agreed to forego Graham Greene's *The End of the Affair* and spend a Saturday afternoon with me. We cruised from jewelry shop to jewelry shop, ate lunch at famous Valentino's, a pizza place, and then meandered about for another two hours until Donna finally spotted the perfect ring.

"How do you know?" I'd asked, peering through the glass at her selection.

"It's so her," Donna replied, seemingly mesmerized by the diamond ring in the showcase. She paused, and her expression turned wistful. "She'll love it, Stephen."

I needed more reassurance. *Was it big enough? Fancy enough? Expensive enough?*

"She'll say yes to *you,* Stephen," Donna said. "Not the ring."

In jest I dramatically grasped Donna's hand, slipping the ring on her finger for a trial run: "Will you marry me?"

She blushed. Then playing along, she answered in similar style, putting the back of her hand to her forehead like Scarlett O'Hara, "Oh, Stephen, I thought you'd never ask. But I simply must refuse. You see . . . I have *nothing* to wear!"

"Then will you be my best man?" I asked, and she dropped the act.

"May I just say . . . I'm holding out for something more traditional—"

"What could be better than best man?"

"Maid of honor, perhaps?"

We laughed, and she gave me a congratulatory hug.

So there I was, sitting in our booth, wondering if Alice had stood me up. Beyond the windows, the annoying growl of a muscle car spiked my nerves and jiggled the restaurant windows, followed by the squeal of brakes as it negotiated the curve.

Finally, at four-fifteen, Alice arrived. Spotting her come in the door, I rose too quickly from the booth, bumping my thighs on the edge of the table.

"Clumsy!" she'd kidded me. "You okay, ol' sport?" an appellation originally bestowed upon me by Donna during her Gatsby period. With Alice's accent, it came out *ol' spo-huht.*

Dressed in a colorful skirt and silky blouse, she leaned over and gave me a lingering kiss, closing her eyes, then opening them slowly, as if the touch of our lips had melted her heart.

"I could get used to that," she said. Then after another quick peck on my nose, she slipped into the booth across from me, her hair shimmering in the overhead lights with an ethereal shade of dark blue.

But the moment she sat down, her eyes dimmed, and her expression fell, maybe not that noticeable to someone else but quite noticeable to me. Normally, her porcelain-smooth face carried the exuberance of a woman who harbored a never-ending fountain of good news with eagerness to share it.

I wiped nervous palms on my slacks and placed my elbows on the table, giving her my full attention. I asked her the usual questions, and slowly she relaxed to her normal self. When I placed my hands on the table, she grabbed them with both of hers and squeezed. "Oh, Stephen! We're *both* going to New York." But then her expression dimmed again, as if struggling against something bigger than either of us.

"Everything okay?" I finally asked. After another reflective moment, she shook her head as if she could hide it no longer. Her eyes watered and she sniffed softly.

"What is it?"

She shrugged. "Nothing." She glanced at her watch. "Where's Donna?"

"Donna's not coming."

She looked confused. Donna always joined us on Friday nights. Alice swallowed, then forced an unsuccessful smile.

I matched her smile, then foolishly proceeded with my original plans. While the words I'd rehearsed that morning seemed inappropriate in the glare of her current hesitant and distracted frame of mind, I took a deep breath anyway and stammered out with, "I have something for you."

That was my big line, about as romantic as a dish drainer. Her eyes widened as I removed the box from my pants pocket. Turning it toward her, I gently opened it. Her eyes settled on the ring, and then closed shut. "Oh, Stephen . . ."

I set the box down and reached for her hand. Her eyes glistened. Figuring she was moved by the imminent proposal, I uttered the fateful words. "Alice . . . will you marry me?"

For an eternity, I waited. Her gaze lingered on mine. She let go of my hand and taking the ring box in her hands, she turned it, examined the ring, then shut the box, and handed it back.

"I *wanted* to marry you, but . . ."

Her words trailed off into nothing.

I was confused. *Wanted?*

Alice pursed her lips. She looked miserable.

Of course, I thought. *I'm just a kid from Uglyville. How could I have been so stupid? Beautiful women don't marry hard-luck stories. . . .*

In the awkward silence that followed, memories of my past came roaring back—the disdain in Cynthia's eyes, the pity in Susan's, the glaring contempt in Jim's: *Ain't nothing a Whitaker touches that don't turn to dust.*

I sat back in the booth, my emotions reeling, unsure how to proceed. Alice swallowed again, appraising the obvious bewilderment in my eyes. She let out another long sigh, leaning back against the booth. I waited as she collected her thoughts. "Stephen . . ." She hesitated again, her eyes suddenly scrutinizing.

"What is it?"

"Do you love me?"

It was an absurd question. "I *adore* you," I whispered, grabbing her hand, but she pulled away as if I'd answered incorrectly, her face a turmoil of emotions I couldn't begin to understand. "Alice, why would you ask such a thing?"

She shrugged and looked away again. Biting her lower lip, she said, "I did something terrible."

Terrible? I was confused again, and then her expression shifted, as if coming to a tumultuous but important decision.

"I wasn't going to show you, but . . . now . . . now I can't keep this to myself."

She was already sliding out of the booth when a strange foreboding struck me. *Where was she going?* I lurched to the edge of the seat, and grabbed for her hand. Off-balance, she stumbled slightly, and I caught her as she practically fell into my arms.

"It's in the car," she said, pushing herself up and away from me.

"Don't go," I whispered.

"I'll be right back," she said, pulled away again, and this time I released her. My body still goes numb with the remembering. During my rising storm of whirling thoughts, she was already tugging the door open, twenty feet away. Turning back, she paused, and then she wound up and blew me a little kiss. My last glimpse of her face, chiseled on stone.

Nina was standing by the counter. She made a face as if to ask, *Didn't go so well?* just before full panic set in.

It happened the way I later saw it in my dreams: the blur of the room as I rushed to the door, bright western sunlight blinding me as I exploded across the sidewalk, frantically calling her name, followed by the sudden squeal of breaks, the muffled scream, Alice's well-trained, operatic voice filling my soul with terror, the sickening thump. Then it was as though she'd simply disappeared, followed by the sudden cessation of sound—the sound of time ceasing forever.

I found her lying against the curb, twenty feet away, her arms and limbs grotesquely twisted. People were screaming around me, but I barely heard them. A distant siren split the air. Alice was unconscious but breathing, and there was nothing to do but hold her broken, bleeding body and whisper frantic words of reassurance. By the time the ambulance arrived, she had slipped away.

During the days that followed, I was in shock, incapable of comprehending or accepting what had happened. *Alice is dead.* Though utterly grief-stricken, Donna made courageous attempts to console me, and I tried to be a comfort to her as well.

"She died quickly," the coroner told us. *"There was no pain. She wouldn't even have known what happened."*

Of course I blamed myself. If not for my inopportune proposal, Alice would never have rushed away. Besides, how could I forget those final moments, our last conversation?

Even Donna seemed consumed by guilt. "I feel responsible," she told me, which of course was ridiculous, but no amount of discussion would counter her belief. In the years since, however, I've grown accustomed to Donna's sense of unearned guilt.

Not until months later did I even consider the notion: What was in Alice's car that was so important? No one knew, not even Donna. A cursory examination of Alice's car had revealed nothing, but it hardly seemed important anymore.

I never showed up for my new job. I went home to the familiarity of family and friends, and stayed. During the following weeks, I spent sleepless nights praying foolish prayers—that God might somehow turn back time, that somehow the whole thing might turn out to be a terrible dream, that somehow I might have a second chance to save her.

Eventually reality sank in: There are some things that even God can't—or *won't*—do. There are rocks that even God can't lift. There are no second chances, no opportunities to make things right, no turning back the clock. As time passed, the veil between God and me grew darker and thicker, my prayers few and far between, until God seemed completely shut away from me. Not only had God betrayed me, He'd abandoned me as well. He'd played the part of a cosmic Lucy, jerking the football away at the last second.

Good riddance! I screamed one night in the field behind my home, then broke down in angry tears. My mother's faith, my *own* childhood faith, which had once seemed to be bigger than a mustard seed, now seemed nothing more than a big lie.

Three months after Alice's death, Donna paid me a visit in Aberdeen. Our meeting at the airport was an implosion of relief, and we hugged each other as if gasping for breath. For days afterward we reminisced about college and Alice, laughing and crying and, eventually, soothing our wounds in each other's arms.

I asked Donna to stay, and she did. She got a job at Walgreens downtown and shared a house on North Jay Street with two other women her age. In a few weeks we were engaged, and four months after that we were married. I'm sure Donna believed my struggles with faith were only temporary—a natural reaction to grief. She must have been convinced I would eventually regain my spiritual footing.

Ten months after our wedding, Alycia was born, and from the first moment I set eyes on her, I felt like the richest man on planet earth. I proceeded to bury my entire past—heartache, disappointment, and guilt—and devote myself to my little girl.

I'm going to do this right, I told myself.

When I'd finished, Alycia remained silent. I'd left out nearly half the story details, including most of the argument at the Soda Straw, and while I'd expected Alycia to complain, she did not.

"So that's why you married Mom," she murmured, more to herself than to me.

I gave her a regretful shrug.

"Not very romantic," she added, slumping back in her chair, and picking at her napkin.

"No," I agreed. "But your mother is a wonderful woman, and if I'd married Alice we wouldn't have had you. Not only that, but—"

"I get it, Dad," she interrupted me.

I should have foreseen her response. She now knew the truth: I'd married her mother because I couldn't have Alice.

"Did you ever figure it out?" she asked softly. "What Alice was going to show you?"

I shook my head and spoke wistfully. "We'll never know."

"Well . . . *I'm* going to figure it out," Alycia replied, but with little enthusiasm.

We drove home in awkward silence, and when it was time for bed, she didn't offer me her bubble cheek, much less say good night.

That was the turning point. The fateful moment. After Alycia learned about Alice, our relationship began its long decline. Except for please-pass-the-salt interactions, she didn't speak to me for weeks, and eventually, what had once seemed so unbreakable would shatter as if little more than fake party glass.

Chapter Five

Although living at those heights was somewhat dizzying and nerve-wracking, my brief sojourn on Alycia's pedestal was over, and while I found myself breathing a sigh of relief, my decline resembled the old cliché: The bigger they are, the harder they fall.

"Haven't seen any of Alycia's friends in a while," I commented to Donna in the kitchen about six months later.

"And you won't for a while," she'd replied absently, drying the silverware. "She's in her embarrassment phase."

I considered this, and Donna eyed me cautiously.

"I suppose her friends' parents live in big houses."

"Stephen, please . . ."

I slunk to my downstairs office and, as my daughter often did, sat in the dark for hours, pondering the passage of years, listening to a collection of my favorite childhood oldies, the kind of prehistoric tunes that offended my daughter's fine-tuned musical sensibilities. They never failed to bring me back to a time when the future seemed imbued with relentless possibilities.

After marrying Donna, I'd attempted—on a smaller stage—to reignite the old childhood determination, but trying harder only seemed to yield diminishing results, not to mention a catastrophic meltdown five years ago.

I was now in the midst of my third, maybe fourth, comeback.

But who was counting? By day, I performed routine business details, and by night, I buried myself in a renewed study of stock-market price data, preparing for yet another attempt. Unfortunately, research had taken on a life of its own, and the more I prepared, the less inclined I was to actually pull the trigger.

But someday soon, I told myself, *it'll happen, and I'll finally give my family the life they deserve.*

It was four forty-five on a Wednesday afternoon in late October, and I was dog-tired after a day of fielding difficult office calls. I closed my eyes, nearly fell asleep in my chair, and when I opened them again, my gaze fell on a smaller framed picture of Alycia. She was wearing the Minnesota Twins baseball cap she wouldn't be caught dead in today. *What a difference a year makes,* I thought. *It's a phase. It'll pass.* Other parents who have survived their children's adolescence often remark: *You lose them for a while, but they always come back.*

And yet, somehow, things weren't that simple for us. Our present problems seemed exacerbated by the memory and loss of our unusual closeness.

One of Donna's friends counseled her privately, "Stephen's problem was trying to be a buddy with his daughter."

I suppose she's right, but even that explanation seems too simple. Through the years, I'd never had a problem asserting my parental authority, and until the "moment of truth" Alycia had never had a problem responding to it.

At the office door, I flicked the switch and darkness fell. Omitting my usual good-bye to Larry, still shuttered away in a world of tax accounting, I headed across the empty reception room. When I reached the bottom of the stairs, I slowly pushed out into the cold world of streetlights and neon signs.

My breath mingled visibly with the scent of gasoline and oil, and I tightened my coat against the weather.

In the fourteen years since my college graduation, Aberdeen

hadn't changed. The landscape had received its first tumble of snow earlier in the month, signaling the beginning of a typically cold winter, something most Dakotans took in stride. I was thankful for the summery reprieve of the last few days, temperatures that thawed the snow during the day but froze into mud overnight.

I took Sixth Avenue to the east side of Aberdeen, stopped by Taco John, then parked my car in the mall lot. The retailers in SuperCity were geared up for Christmas. Tinseled evergreens with brightly lit red and green bulbs filled the store windows. "O Come All Ye Faithful" blared from the tinny mall speakers, confirming my belief that everything Midwest was a poor imitation of something original.

The mall was busy for a Friday night, considering the circumstances. According to the highway sign on the outskirts of the city, Aberdeen was clinging to a population of twenty-four thousand. When I was ten the population had been twenty-*five* thousand, which told me that for every child born, another got its wings.

I stopped by Tami's Gift Shop, intent on finding a birthday present for Donna. I labored over this for nearly fifteen minutes, lost in thought, until I finally settled on a pair of earrings with a card that said, *Happy 36th!*

"Excellent choice," the clerk said, a pretty brunette with dark circles under her eyes.

After I paid with a check, I checked the time. I had forty minutes left. As I headed back into the mall, I spotted an unattended youngster smiling placidly up at me, clutching a Big Gulp. The glimmer of his tousled flaxen hair reminded me of my own at his age. Instinctively, I dropped to my heels. "Hey there, little fella, where's your mother?"

He stared at my coat. I followed his eyes to the source of his fascination: the Mickey Mouse sticker attached to my lapel, a friendly offering from a potential client's daughter earlier today. I was about to remove it and offer it to him when a sudden flash to my left distracted me. I turned to see a woman's wrist encircle the boy's upper arm.

"You leave him alone!"

Stunned with her outburst, I jolted to my feet, coming face-to-face with a woman who clearly had misunderstood my intentions. Her face was a torment of disgust. "He doesn't have any money!"

Her son dropped his pop container, spilling it across the tiled floor, and immediately broke into tears.

"Now look at what you've done," she yelled, at which point I finally recognized her.

I scrambled for something diplomatic to say. "I'm . . . we're . . . involved in the restitution program."

"You think *that's* gonna put food on my grandmother's table?"

"No, but—"

"Fifty dollars a week?" she snarled.

"It's the best we can—"

"Well, do better!"

I nodded respectfully and began backing away. "We will, I promise you. . . ."

"Yeah, that's right," she hissed. "You run. That's all you Whitakers are good for. Take the money and run."

My heart beat against my chest as I retreated to a wooden bench just around the corner. I sank onto it, still shaking, clutching my wife's birthday present. Setting the bag down, I leaned over, put my face in my hands, and tried to forget what had just happened.

"Away in a Manger," another warped choral rendition, echoed off the simulated marble floors. Slowly, I breathed in and out and in my lap, I grasped my hands together, fighting the sense of despair that lately seemed to hover just out of reach.

I blew out an exasperated breath and tried a short prayer. *God, I need some help,* and then I stopped. How long had it been since I'd prayed? *Years.*

When I finally got up from the bench, the large marble hallway seemed surreal, my head felt blank, and my thoughts fuzzy.

One step at a time, I told myself.

My pocket rang. Fumbling through my coat, I found the cell phone and answered it.

"Stephen?"

I didn't recognize the voice.

"This is Jennifer at Joe's."

"Of course."

"Listen . . . Paul's got that look in his eyes again."

I cleared my throat, deciphering her choice of words. "Just . . . cut him off."

She hesitated. "You know how he gets."

I agreed to come immediately.

Chapter Six

I headed back out into the cold weather. In the car I noticed the forgotten burrito and briefly considered eating it cold.

Minutes after driving out of the mall parking lot, I reached a side street off Main and parked in front of a flickering neon sign. Turning off the ignition, I stared up through the windshield at the night sky. Even the brightness of neon couldn't hide the twinkling lights far above. But below, within this building, was a dingy room I'd come to despise. And if it wasn't for Paul, Susan, and a handful of high school friends, I'd never come at all.

"Why *do* you go?" Donna once asked me, especially since I didn't drink. It was hard to explain my reason—that if not for me, I feared Paul and Susan would lose their way entirely.

"Didn't Jesus frequent bars to save the lost?" I added feebly.

I almost expected her to reply, *That's interesting, coming from you,* but she didn't.

Instead she shook her head. "Go save your friends, Stephen."

When I got out of the car and entered the bar's darkness of lost time, the sound of laughter struck me, the clinking of glass, the buzz of conversation, the canned noise from the ESPN TV on the far wall. The room was long and narrow, consisting of a long counter occupied by a mixture of old farmers and younger white collars with beer mugs, their eyes glued to the football game.

Across the narrow aisle were several small tables in front of the windows, and toward the back, I detected the sound of a rowdy pool game mingled with the popping of a pool stick against the ball, with ricocheting clicks against the sides of the pool table. Sitting several yards away at a table by the street window, Paul lifted his glass and nodded.

"Didn't expect you tonight," he replied when I pulled out a scarred chair and sat down.

I glanced over to catch Joe's attention. Wiping the counter, Joe, a former math teacher from Central High, nodded back. I noticed Susan at the end of the counter, sitting on her perch. Wearing a short blue skirt, preposterous for these temperatures, she winked, then continued talking animatedly to the stranger beside her—a younger man with dark brown hair and a mustache.

"Lonely Hearts strikes again," Paul replied, having modified Susan's high school nickname to reflect current events.

"Know 'im?" I asked.

"Some loser," Paul said.

I appraised the alcoholic glaze in his eyes, the splotchy redness in his cheeks. I gestured for Jennifer, the brown-haired waitress and single mother of four who'd called me earlier. With an unneeded pencil behind her ear, dressed in jeans and a red shirt, she came and retrieved my usual order.

"Let me guess," Paul muttered. "Lemonade?"

I shrugged.

"Someday we're going to loosen you up."

Walking away, Jennifer cast me a furtive look: *Handle him!*

Susan, as animated and voluptuous as the day she asked me to dance, caught my eye again. I raised my eyebrows inquisitively. She held my gaze a second longer than normal, then narrowed them slightly, an unmistakable signal: *Butt out.*

Paul caught her expression. "Don't disturb a cat eating from her dish unless you wish to have your face accessorized." He took another chug of his beer, his eyes darting nervously about the room. Inebriation always seemed to increase Paul's natural paranoia, but he could keep his words sounding pretty normal. Jennifer returned with my lemonade, which Paul eyed derisively, adding a snort for good measure as he turned away.

Discreetly, I studied Susan's new guy. Tall and brawny and wrapped in blue denim, he seemed far too enamored with her, considering their obviously short acquaintance.

"Don't waste your time," Paul replied, as if reading my mind. He cleared his throat, then leaned over to his right, reaching for something on the floor.

"I need to rid myself of this albatross around my neck," he replied, placing a sophisticated black Nikon camera on the table. He glanced about the bar, pretending nonchalance. "Know anyone who wants to buy it cheap?"

"Have you advertised?"

"The paper," he said, shrugging.

"What about eBay?" I suggested, and he responded by biting his lip cautiously. "I suppose I could, but . . ." His voice trailed off.

I picked up the camera and studied it thoughtfully.

"How's the market?" he asked me, a nervous deflection from the embarrassing stare of my appraisal.

"Going up without me," I said, then added, "At least it's not going down *with* me."

"What's worse?"

Good question. I looked up and noticed a tinge of desperation in Paul's wolf gray eyes. His full head of thick red hair, slicked back, exposed his forehead, which accentuated his already too-narrow face, highlighting a pointy nose, crooked teeth, ending with a geometrically sharp chin. With his Benjamin Franklin style spectacles and pronounced cheeks, he projected a professorially debonair appearance—quirky perhaps, but not unsightly.

Jennifer wasn't kidding. His edgy mood reminded me of the time in high school when we were hanging out on a Friday night, my only night off. I was studying for a Monday test, while Paul trolled the

Peanut Gallery for a prom date, which required my moral support.

The *Peanut Gallery* had been a one-time-only experiment, a small school-sponsored booklet containing informal photos of nearly every student in Central. Apparently the administration thought it would lessen the cliquish nature of our school.

Within the sanctuary of my tiny room, Paul had begun making phone calls, inviting one girl after another to the prom, each one in turn asking for his *Peanut Gallery* page number. After a moment of silence, then a polite excuse, the girl terminated the call. Long about number ten, he gave up.

I still remember the sheer panic in his eyes. "It's a bad picture," I said. "And besides . . . these are cold calls. Most of the girls don't know you."

Days later he laughed it off, but I can't say he ever recovered. After that, Paul finished his ascent, or should I say descent, into the world of the mind. It was common knowledge that Paul was a genius, and the reason Larry hadn't achieved high school valedictorian was because Paul had already claimed that spot. And yet, deploring what he described as the hypocrisy of formal education, Paul declined the honor of addressing the graduating class. It then fell to Larry, class salutatorian, who didn't appreciate Paul's scraps. He declined the honor as well. I was on a short list, but it went to someone else.

Eventually, having achieved a scholarship to MIT, Paul recovered from his aversion to college and attended for a semester before washing out. Discovering the truth of the universe was more interesting to him than simply going to class.

Performing the small details of life—getting and keeping a job, taking showers, eating, and attending class—was excruciating for someone like Paul, who suffered from an extremely low boredom threshold. The great ponderings were easy for him, but the routine tasks of life rendered him pragmatically unfit for life. In response to his lack of responsibility, regardless of major or minor, Paul often trudged out his favorite quote: *It's no measure of health to be well-adjusted to a profoundly sick society.*

Worse yet, Paul had a near photographic memory, including the ability to remember conversations nearly verbatim. *A curse,* he'd once said, and I thought of his father's acerbic tongue.

A few years later he pulled it together enough to finish his bachelor's degree at a lesser college. On a roll, he continued to achieve a master's, followed by a doctorate, barely scraping by. His final grades were less than stellar, forcing him to accept an associate professorship of science at Northern State College. Having a job beneath his talent weighed heavily upon him.

I was still examining his camera. "I'll take it off your hands," I finally told him.

"But you already have one—"

Crash! The sound of Jennifer's dropped tray echoed through the room. "Better go plastic, Joe!" someone shouted, to the amused laughter of nearly half the bar. A mist of smoke seemed to hover above the room, mingled with the scent of whiskey and beer.

I turned to Paul and smiled. "I'll sell it myself on eBay. Make a profit on your foolishness."

Paul sighed nervously. "You could probably get, I don't know, two hundred, two twenty," he said. "But all I want, well, all I *need,* is one-fifty."

"I'll give you two hundred," I replied, and our eyes met. He blinked, then looked away. "That's too much," he said softly but didn't object as I wrote out the check. By then we were in need of a topic change. He looked at his watch, then squinted as if the numbers were hard to read. "Don't you need to get home?"

Susan broke into loud laughter across the room. We turned in time to see her reach over and slap the guy's knee.

This can only end badly, I thought.

I turned my attention to Paul's beer mug. Now his words *were* getting more slurred, which alarmed me, and his head seemed to list back and forth like a tall tree in a violent wind. Paul smiled crookedly, then gestured for Jennifer. He could barely raise his arm without shoving the rest of his upper torso off-balance. I found myself drifting off into my own thoughts, wondering when and if Jennifer was going to drop the bomb.

I took a breath and braced myself. "How many have you had?"

"Nonya."

"Maybe it's time to—"

"One more," he said, raising his voice. He flashed me a hideous grin. "For the road as they say."

"How 'bout *no* more," I insisted, but he pretended not to hear me.

Since we'd been down this road before, the progression of our conversation was predictable. Jennifer would just have to risk cutting him off. I caught her eye when Paul wasn't looking and quickly shrugged. She grimaced, then pursed her lips as if steeling her resolve.

"How are classes?" I asked.

He shrugged. "I don't like grading."

"Don't be so tough."

He snorted, took another drink.

"Read any good books lately?" I asked, hoping to distract him, but he barely shrugged. Apparently, he was drunker than I realized. Normally, the mere mention of his greatest passion—*metaphysical science*—was enough to rouse his enthusiasm.

I decided to pick up on our last discussion: wormholes, little tears in the fabric of reality, what Paul called "rabbit holes" in the space/time continuum. "So . . . how does one find a rabbit hole?" I said, smiling as engagingly as I could manage.

He shrugged with barely concealed disinterest. "You don't. It finds you."

I made several attempts to revive our previous conversation, but it wasn't easy, considering how often Paul now had to excuse himself for the bathroom. Eventually, I said something wrong and Paul's expression dimmed. He shrugged, took a sip of his beer, and glanced about the room again. "As usual, you missed the whole point."

"How so?"

"Ain't telling," Paul replied.

Out of the corner of my eye, I saw Susan rise from her stool. What's-his-name helped her with her coat. I caught her gaze again, and she shrugged me off. When her new boyfriend slapped several bills on the table and wandered to the bathroom beyond the pool table, she strolled over to us.

"I know what you're thinking," she said, buttoning up her pink sweater. "And you're both wrong."

"This one's true love?" Paul slurred.

She winked at him. "Yep. You're going to have to find me another nickname."

"How well do you know this guy?" I asked, but she never had a chance to respond, because the latest answer to her deepest romantic desires was emerging from the bathroom. Susan introduced him as simply "Brian," and he grunted his way through the introductions. Just before they left, Susan leaned over and whispered into my ear, "I'm through with this dump, Stephen. I'm getting out. But I'll send you a wedding invitation."

She stood up, reconsidered, then leaned over again, whispering so softly I could barely hear her. "By the way, Paul's had more 'n enough."

I nodded in agreement.

Later, as he and I watched the sports scores on the television screen and suffered through the explosive laughter of a now-crowded bar, Paul asked me what she'd said.

"'I'll see you in a few days, once this bozo dumps me,'" I replied.

"No, seriously," Paul persisted.

"Ain't telling."

A moment of silence passed.

"Okay, I'm sorry," Paul said. "I'm just touchy tonight. I'm also sorry that I'm so much smarter than you, but I'm mostly sorry that you overpaid for my camera."

"Could have stopped with 'touchy.'"

"I was on a roll," Paul garbled out. "Couldn't help myself."

When I finally told him her first comment, he only chuckled.

"Yeah. Me too." Then he leaned back, his head lobbing toward Susan's now-empty stool, and he almost lost his balance, nearly tipping his chair over backward.

"Why doesn't she ever learn?" he said when he'd recovered.

I ignored the irony and heard my name from behind me, near the door. I turned and noticed Larry walking briskly to our table. I was surprised to see him. In the darkened room, his kaleidoscope tie glowed like a neon sign in a field of pinstripe.

Larry towered over the two of us and glared at me. "I've been calling your cell phone for an hour."

"It's in my car," I replied, gesturing toward the end of the table. "Pull up a chair. Order a Coke or something."

"What are you doing here?" Larry persisted. "We were waiting for you."

A small sliver of panic edged into my gut. Larry glanced at Paul for the first time, and they exchanged obligatory nods, still unable, after all these years, to disguise their mutual disregard. Paul's eyes flickered at Larry's tie, and I could tell he was losing the battle. Even sober, Paul had difficulty curbing his acerbic tongue.

"Nice tie," he finally gave in, whispering it under his breath, then forcing a delicious smirk underground. Larry probably noticed it but wouldn't have given Paul the satisfaction of retorting.

In the meantime, I'd just put it together.

Donna's birthday party.

Paul raised his hand and, once again, snapped his fingers for Jennifer to refill his drink. I closed my eyes in self-disgust. *How could I have forgotten?*

Jennifer chose this moment, with big Larry hovering by, to cut Paul off.

Paul glared angrily at her. Suffering humiliation in front of Larry didn't help.

"Let it go, Paul," I said. I leaned forward over the sick feeling in my gut.

A suddenly riled Jennifer gave him a warning look, unwilling to budge an inch. "I think you'd better leave." She turned to me, caught my eye, and I immediately picked up on it.

Without further remarks, I grabbed my coat. "I'm driving you home."

Larry grinned down at him, but Paul made no effort to move. "No thanks. I'll stay until they throw me out."

I expelled an angry breath and bounded for the door. Larry called my name, but I ignored him. Outside in the cold, I jumped into the car, twisted the ignition key, then paused. What was my rush? Obviously, the party I'd forgotten to attend had long since disbanded.

I sighed into the excruciating silence, and it all came back to me. Two nights ago, Alycia had reminded me to pick up the cake after work and then hide it in the garage. "And don't forget, Dad." One of the few complete sentences she had sent my way in the recent past.

Who picked up the cake? I wondered.

I mentally retraced my steps back to the last minutes before leaving the office. I'd even gone to SuperCity to select Donna's last-minute gift. *How could I have forgotten?*

I imagined the entire party scenario—what Larry might have said to smooth things over and how Donna would have pretended nothing was wrong. At some point, Alycia would have begun sulking, and in a roomful of Donna's closest friends, the uncomfortable silences would have grown. "Where's Stephen?" someone would eventually ask as if they didn't know any better.

Perhaps Donna was relieved when I didn't show, I thought as pride gave way to the supremacy of rationalization. The last few months had been particularly difficult for us.

No, I corrected myself. *The last few years . . .*

I sighed again. *Face it, pal, the last fourteen years haven't been a picnic for either of you. . . .*

But the idea of my poor wife suffering through the embarrassment of my thoughtlessness crowded out every other self-serving excuse.

"You can't hurt me anymore," she'd told me three weeks ago, and

at the moment, I actually hoped this was true.

I was still sitting in the parked car when Paul finally shuffled outside, huddled within his winter gray parka. He didn't notice me. Larry followed shortly after, hunched within his long black overcoat, heading in the opposite direction to his own car. At last, I pulled out of the parking space, following Paul as he ambled down the sidewalk. When I honked to get his attention, he nearly fell over from the noise. Recovering his balance, he shuffled over. I thumbed toward my passenger seat. "Get in, and I'm not asking."

Removing keys from his pocket, Paul dangled them. His warm alcohol-saturated breath plumed into the frozen air. "I got my own car."

"You're in no condition."

He shook his head. "I'm only seven blocks away."

He tapped my car door, gave me a sloppy salute, and stumbled with the effort. When I opened my mouth to protest, he was already lurching away.

Sighing angrily, I briefly considered physically wrestling the keys from his possession. Instead, I shifted the car into drive and headed home.

Chapter Seven

We lived in a tiny three-bedroom shutterless rancher close to the corner of Twelfth Avenue and Northview Lane. Shortly after Donna and I married, we'd scoured the newspapers and found the newly built dark brown house advertised for a song. It was located a few blocks north of the trailer court, also just north of where Susan once lived, but less than a mile from Uglyville.

After the winter snow melted, we discovered that only one half of the yard had been sodded, lending a rather lopsided look to the front. We would also learn later that the house had been misbuilt, the plans erroneously flipped, which meant that not only was our side door a mere five feet from our neighbor's garage, but their property line actually went through the cement steps. The builder, acknowledging his mistake, threw in enough money to pay off the neighbor and push back the property line.

Across the street, to the east, the railroad tracks snaked behind similarly styled houses. It was a treeless neighborhood destined for more of the same, since few owners planted much more than the absolute minimum of marigolds and pansies, as if acknowledging the futility of improvement, or perhaps praying for temporary residence and refusing to think long-term. To the north, empty fields extended for miles.

Presently, I stopped in the vacant driveway in front of the

seven-year-old one-car garage, set back from the house. Parked inside the garage was our "good" car, Donna's Dodge minivan, a discolored navy blue scabbed with a cancerous rust, the interior light blue vinyl faded and dull. The windshield was pockmarked with tiny fractures no larger than a dime, yet destined to become long jagged slivers. When operated, the wipers gapped over half the windshield, and the lights to the radio display had long since extinguished. But the tires were relatively new, and the refurbished engine was still alive and kicking.

Noting the darkened house, I grabbed the earrings box and got out of the car. Pushing the car door closed instead of slamming it, I slinked up the sideways-sloping sidewalk. A sudden winter wind erupted, pelting granules of frozen snow against my face. Gripping my jacket tighter, I turned away from the offending gust.

I stamped my feet on the concrete step, then cringed at the noise I made, and opened the door to the living room. The Happy Birthday banners and party decorations Alycia had made on the printer in my downstairs office glared down at me. I slipped off my wet shoes, hung up my beige topcoat on a tree hanger, and placed Donna's gift on the dining room table.

Without further ado, I took a deep breath and headed down the short hallway to our master bedroom. The door was closed, so I steeled myself and turned the knob. *Locked.* I knocked softly but no answer.

"Donna?" I whispered.

I checked my watch. 9:30. Surely she wouldn't have retired so early. Instead of knocking again, I retreated to the kitchen, where dirty dishes were stacked on the counter. After thumbing through the mail, I discarded the junk and opened the bills. Then I rolled up my sleeves, filled the sink with hot water, and began a small measure of penitence, painstakingly avoiding any clanging of pots and pans.

Fifteen minutes later, when I could put it off no longer, I headed downstairs to the partially finished basement. The cement floor was cold and moist against my stockinged feet. At the far end of the room, a sliver of light was visible along the edge of Alycia's partially open bedroom door. No sounds.

Gingerly I pushed her door fully open. Hunched up on the carpeted floor, she leaned against her bed, surrounded by crumpled bed sheets. Although she must have seen me out of the corner of her eye, she refused to look up. She was wearing her headphones, something I had forbidden, then lectured, then pleaded, and now pretended didn't exist. Lately, those things I forbade only became her gauntlets.

According to her sixth-grade teacher, and in spite of the historic "Shrek-a-lina ear episode," Alycia had been the most popular girl in her class. On the other hand, seventh grade was now proving to be an adjustment. Her choice of friendships, not to mention her confidence, had deteriorated. Sometimes her melancholy—what her teachers and counselor have labeled as nothing more than pre-adolescent mood swings—seem to descend out of nowhere and last for weeks.

I stood in the doorway for a moment, waiting for her to acknowledge me, taking in her room décor: postmodern teenage rebellion. I looked for a place to sit, then gave up. Her clothes littered the floor, where "they're easier to find." The dresser was cluttered with bottles and sprays, potions and perfumes, and a menacing-looking blow dryer. One of the walls was covered with posters of rock groups—who looked more like axe murderers—and the opposite wall was covered with shirtless adolescent boys. I'm not sure which was worse.

Mixed among this devilish crowd were banners with slogans, irreverent statements of youthful defiance, including the poster of a gorilla holding his ears and closing his eyes: *Pardon me? Who you ARE speaks so loudly, I can't hear what you're SAYING.*

Catching her eye, I gestured "phone" to my ear.

"Sorry," I said, after she scowled the headphones from her head. "I meant . . . I wanted to talk to you."

"So you lied," she muttered.

"Guess I blew it," I said, hoping to slide over the first accusation. She frowned, probably wondering what I was referring to—either the tricky way I'd gotten her to remove her headphones or forgetting the party.

"I mean . . . about tonight," I clarified.

"Oh." She paused for a moment, and I could see the wheels turning. "So . . . you're assuming anyone actually thought you'd show up?"

Unsure how to respond to her sarcasm, I said nothing.

"Too bad you reminded me. I'd already forgotten." She put her headphones back on, giving me a quick headshake as if I was not worthy of consideration.

I hadn't expected her to make it easy for me, but I was surprised by the depth of her disrespect. Reaching over, I committed my second indiscretion within the space of one minute and pulled the headphone jack from her stereo, effectively removing a starving tiger from her mother's milk. The room was suddenly filled with screeching guitars. I frantically pressed the off button and stark silence replaced the musical anger.

Alycia came uncorked, ripping off her headphones and glaring at me.

"Alycia, I've asked you—"

She wound up, unfurled, and I flinched, but she wasn't throwing them at me. The headphones hit the wall above her sound system, disintegrating into an assortment of pieces, leaving a generous dent in the plaster. My first thought, following the shock, was to wonder if Donna had heard it.

Calmly, Alycia slapped her hands together as if removing residual dust, then gave me a mockingly innocent look. "All done, Dad. Sorry . . . I must have forgotten."

Let her get it out, I thought, deliberately choosing not to answer anger with anger. Frankly, I viewed it as a victory of sorts. The eardrum-puncturing headphones were gone. I suppose that's how skewed my parenting had become, how marginal and incomplete the victories.

Months ago I had lectured her with my own headphone horror

story—how I'd sacrificed twenty-five percent of my hearing on the altar of Sergeant Pepper. But instead of being horrified, she'd been impressed, viewing it as a symbol of commitment, a scar of dedication. I'd argued my point—*notice how I have to turn the TV so loud you always complain?*—but she was too busy estimating her own dedication. To lose one's hearing over music that defines your social alienation seemed the appropriate sacrifice. *The hearing doesn't come back,* I'd finally said, to which she'd presented her soundest argument: *"That's the point!"*

At a loss for anything else to say, I decided to cut to the chase and risk total alienation. "I love you, Alycia, and I certainly didn't mean to—"

She raised her index finger.

I sighed. "What do you want from me? I said I was sorry—"

"How 'bout the truth, Dad? See . . . what you should say is: 'I pretend parental affection when it's convenient.' "

That wasn't true and she knew it, but I let it go. This had reached an impasse far quicker than I'd hoped, but I continued the futility anyway, hoping to veer the subject back to its origin. "Listen, I made a mistake," I said. "I forgot . . ."

"You . . . forgot?" An incredulous snort. "I won't even dignify that, Dad. But, you know, if you came home once in while, you might have been here by accident. But like I said, no one noticed. You should have kept your mouth shut. I mean, do you think we even care anymore when you break your promises? It's expected. We plan our lives around it. It gives us a sense of stability knowing that you're so easy to predict."

Amazed again at her articulation, a trait she'd obviously inherited from her linguistically gifted mother, I had long since given up trying to compete with her verbally—like trying to fight a Samurai with a butter knife. I could have tried to argue that my late hours were usually spent at the office, hoping to make our lives better, but that wouldn't have set any better. And since no one understood my determination to remain friends with Paul and Susan, I didn't follow that route either.

As I began to back toward the door, Alycia leaned forward, adopting a more offensive posture. "So . . . have you talked to Mom yet?"

I hesitated.

"You didn't, did you?"

"Alycia—"

"You came here to complain about my headphones?" Another snort. "This isn't about me, you know? It's *Mom's* party you forgot."

"I understand, Alycia—"

"Actually . . . you know what I really told everyone?" She was just getting warmed up.

"No, I don't."

"I told everyone, while they were eating the cake, you know, the one you forgot to pick up, that you were in the hospital."

"I see," I whispered, waiting for the inevitable punch line.

"You should have seen the look on their faces, Dad. And then when I had their attention, I told them we had you committed for multiple personality disorder. You know what I'm talking about? This strange 'delusion of fatherhood' that overtakes you about five minutes a week?"

"Very clever," I whispered, resuming my retreat. Reaching back for the doorknob, I glanced back at her and glimpsed her on the bed, startled to see that her eyes had suddenly melted into tears, her thick mascara creating black streaks down her cheeks. When our eyes locked, her face contorted suddenly as if acutely disappointed in herself.

In spite of all that had just happened, I was tempted to rush to her side, take her into my arms, and make the hurt go away as if she were five and had merely scraped her toe.

"I'm very sorry, Alycia," I repeated for the third time, my voice hoarse.

"You're *always* sorry, Dad." The tone of her voice was as anguished as the glossy look in her eyes. "I'm not giving you a clean slate anymore. This one stays up there."

I made a small step forward, but she twisted her head sharply, her suddenly furious eyes boring a hole into me, giving me the unspoken warning that I had better stop in my tracks. When I did, she brushed her face clumsily with her sleeve.

With newfound flatness in her voice, she said: "Please lock my door on your way out."

I complied, setting the lock. Pulling her door closed behind me, I headed for the stairs.

Shaking from the encounter, a small glimmer of hope broke through. *She was waiting for me,* I realized. *She would have locked the door otherwise.*

Upstairs, at the edge of the living room, I gazed down the hallway toward the closed bedroom door, wondering if Donna was asleep. I wandered down the hall and knocked on the door again. Still no answer. I checked the door. Still locked. I paused for a few minutes, then decided against trying again.

I turned out the lights to the house, then headed back downstairs, but instead of going straight toward Alycia's room, I turned left into the furnace room area. My study was toward the back, bordering Alycia's wall.

I'd spent nearly a year finishing this room, doing the work myself: framing the walls, wiring the electric, installing and texturing the sheetrock, even installing and seaming together the overstocked remnants of cut Berber carpet.

Opening the door to my inner sanctum, I smelled the musty dampness and closed the door behind me. Sitting at the desk, I looked at my metal bookshelf—an entire library dedicated to stock and futures trading.

Some of my trading books were new, others decades old. Some were reissues of the philosophies and strategies of long-dead market wizards; others contained ideas culled from recent analysis, complete with elaborate computer back testing. Some extolled the virtues of fundamental analysis, the study of company performance; others taught the art of technical analysis, the practice of interpreting stock behavior.

Although new indicators were created every day, all the old standbys were here: moving averages, stochastic systems, relative strength indicators, trend lines, support and resistance, etc.

Lately, I'd preferred to combine an old concept, buying stocks on dips—what I called my divergence system—with a relatively new concept: the fractal, something derived from chaos theory, which, ironically, gave Paul and me another topic to discuss.

All told, my shelves contained reams of information, and more information is what every trader is looking for—that final piece that will make all the difference: the unerring indicator. The magic bullet. The Holy Grail.

We'll be fine, I told myself, thinking of my plans for my family. Once I pulled it together financially, we'd all look back on these days and laugh.

The other walls were covered with cheap posters of serene landscapes—places far from here: the giant boulders on the Oregon Coast, spring flowers in the Colorado Mountains, autumn hills in Vermont. And my favorite: a sunset pewter bay in Mystic, Connecticut. The tiny basement window, just below the ceiling, was covered with a heavy curtain, designed to eliminate not only any proof of local surroundings but also the annoying webs of spiders who built them faster than I could brush them out.

Finally, my tired gaze fell to the burnt orange couch, sagging and desprung from Alycia's preschool need to jump for hours on end. My pajamas had been neatly placed on the arm of the couch. At least Donna had been calm enough to plan our sleeping arrangement.

I switched on the computer, navigated to eBay, and listed Paul's camera. Briefly, I had considered giving it back to him sometime in the future, maybe as a gift, then thought better of it. We needed the two hundred dollars as much as he did.

Chapter Eight

I awakened at four in the morning with my back hurting and my neck feeling like a pretzel. Upstairs in the kitchen, I fixed a quick cup of instant coffee, then drove to Kesslers on Sixth Avenue, an all-night grocery store. In the florist section, I considered the refrigerated contents. An array of carnations and daisies stood in buckets of water.

Bought flowers seemed little more than rubbing sand into a festering wound, and yet, with Donna not speaking to me, my only options were to do nothing or do something, regardless of how feeble it seemed.

Opening the glass door, I grabbed a dozen roses, assorted colors, and winced at the price. When I finally paid at the register, the clerk smirked between yawns.

At home again, I arranged eleven roses on the table, propping the birthday card against the vase. Next to the vase, I placed the white box containing the earrings, then stepped back to appraise my hopeless gesture.

Downstairs on Alycia's door, I taped a pink rose. Then, with a hopeful heart, I got into my twelve-year-old rust-bucket Ford sedan—a rattletrap with spongy suspension, metal-on-metal brakes, and failing heater—and headed off to work. I parked several blocks away, on a side street, noticing Larry's Buick on Main Street itself, positioned in front of our third-floor offices. It took arriving at five o'clock to park that close.

Climbing the stairs to the top floor, I pushed into the reception area, a sterile-looking room with a single desk and computer. The walls were covered with prints and ego plaques. A woman's touch would have added a sense of female efficiency to the office, but without our receptionist, we were clueless.

Standing there, I realized it was still dark enough to see my reflection in the window. Within the lit corner office, a windowed room with the door closed, Larry was already deep into it, hunched over his desk. Electing not to bother him, I spent an hour nursing a warm cup of coffee, completing some billing and updating our Web site.

Larry wandered out just as I was sealing a few envelopes addressed to several of our former investment clients. "You're in early."

"Never-ending details," I replied.

Larry leaned against the wall and took a sip from his own coffee mug. A conservative but impeccable dresser, six foot five with thinning blond hair, Larry was a model of restrained propriety. In keeping with his size, he reminded me of a heavyweight boxer with a flattened pug nose, ample cheeks, and double chin—all of which seemed to belie his quick mind. But when it came to ties, he was fashionably oblivious.

Today's tie resembled a sordid mixture of Van Gogh and Monet. And like the rest of his ties, it seemed to betray the entire package of the rest of him. At least he wore them loose about his collars, as if lacking commitment, which also helped when making quick changes before more serious appointments.

He noticed me staring. "Too bright?"

I shrugged.

"Too loud?"

"Too too," I said.

He considered this before nodding. "You okay?"

"Breathing."

"That bad?"

"Been worse," I replied.

Larry paused, took another sip of deep roast, then smiled. "Maybe you should burn in hell for a few days."

"I don't think Alycia would be satisfied with only a few days," I replied, then described my encounter with her last night.

Larry shook his head. "Why do you let her talk to you like that?"

I rubbed the fatigue from my eyes and didn't answer. Alycia's rebellion and disrespect was a recent development, and since it was primarily directed toward me, I ignored it—mostly.

The phone rang, and we simply stared at it. I checked the caller ID and shook my head. If I didn't recognize the name, or if the ID was blocked, I didn't answer the phone. After countless angry phone calls, we'd learned our lesson the hard way.

"Besides, that's not what really happened," Larry said, picking up on the discussion and sliding his thumb down his tie, checking it for splatters, as if he could have found one.

"Sorry?"

"The multiple personality joke? Alycia didn't actually say that. She told everyone you had an unexpected emergency meeting with an important client." Larry shrugged, taking another sip. "Everyone bought it, Stephen. It wasn't as bad as you thought."

That's strange, I thought. Alycia rarely ever lied.

Larry sat in the chair across from me. It groaned under his weight. "We have an important interview today." He gave me a mischievous grin. "Remember Cynthia Reiser?"

I frowned carefully. "Sorry, the name doesn't ring a bell."

Larry chuckled. "Nice try."

Obviously, her name conjured up an entire litany of memories, including not only the junior high dance, but also Homecoming Queen. Mark, who she later married, had been starting quarterback for the Golden Eagles.

"I thought they moved away."

Larry shrugged. "Mark is setting up a sheet-metal manufacturing plant here and needs an accountant." He paused before adding,

"Apparently they haven't heard yet, so we've got a real shot at this."

Lately, much of our local business had come down to that simple question: *Had they heard or not?*

Five years ago, after a series of bad trading decisions, I'd lost thirty percent of our entire investment capital, all clients' money. That wasn't the worst part of it. Desperate to recover, like a gambling addict determined to get back to even, I'd foolishly placed the remainder in S&P futures, betting the entire sum on a single direction of the market.

But I bet wrong. The market exploded on the upside, and before I could pull out, three million had evaporated to a mere three hundred thousand. All told, I'd lost ninety percent.

Lawsuits quickly followed, claiming the equivalent of *financial malpractice. Marshall and Whitaker* was sued by thirty-plus former clients, most of them senior retirees. We'd lost and were ordered to make restitution. If our homes hadn't been mortgaged to the hairline, the court would have taken them too. Our smartest option had been bankruptcy, but we'd decided against it. To his credit, Larry stood by me when it would have been easier to jump ship. At the present rate of our payments, which was all we could manage, we'd be finished with restitution by the time I was seventy.

Fortunately, at the time Larry had been transitioning to a Web-based tax consultant and asset-protection business for national clients. Having mastered the detailed nuances of the IRS code, Larry's acumen kept us from going under.

After we let our receptionist go, I handled everything, not only the secretarial details but payroll, billing, and Web-site management, including marketing and design. The next years were touch-and-go as Larry began traveling on a regular basis, giving lectures, acquiring countless new clients not familiar with our local meltdown. Eventually his national consulting overshadowed our local reputation.

Shortly after my trading disaster, I convinced myself that the itch was gone, but that didn't last long. And today as I prepared for the appointment, I couldn't help noticing the computer screen, watching as the market continued to hit new highs. Billions of dollars were being made. None of them by me.

Ten minutes before the appointment, I knocked on Larry's door, holding an array of ties I kept in my lower drawer for these occasions. Having crossed this bridge countless times before, he sighed and acquiesced to powder gray with a checkered design.

"Tie it tight," I told him, and he did so, grunting with annoyance.

I'd hoped that Mark would be alone when he arrived for the appointment, but they came in together, Cynthia wearing Ralph Lauren blue jeans and a yellow designer sweater. Her youthful face was still cherubic, with blond bangs covering her forehead and the power of her beautiful eyes now unrepressed, due to either laser surgery or contacts.

"Hi, Stephen," she said demurely.

"Welcome back," I replied, wondering whether to hug her. In the awkward moment of indecision, I didn't even shake her hand. I was relieved when Larry didn't hug her either, although Larry wasn't much of a hugger anyway.

After the initial handshakes with Mark, the four of us moved to Larry's office where the window overlooked Main Street. I sat closest to the wall while Mark and Cynthia sat near Larry. After further formalities, including a healthy dose of high school nostalgia, Mark leaned forward. "Larry, I have to be honest, here. I almost canceled the appointment. . . ."

So he *had* heard. I had a sinking feeling, but to his credit, Larry continued the sales pitch undaunted. He described the current situation, emphasizing its freedom from "our" investing mistakes. On several occasions, I could feel Cynthia's eyes on me.

"We've learned our lesson," Larry said. "We're paying everyone back, and we're sticking to what we do best. Most important, I can structure your business for maximum tax savings."

Larry went on to describe a few elements of his tax plan and how it would apply to Mark's situation. "You won't find that kind of in-depth tax planning with any other accountant. And most lawyers are too specialized to grasp the latest asset-protection techniques."

Mark was sold.

"I promise you," Larry finished, with a wink and a nod, "I won't let Stephen touch your account."

Cynthia looked my way again. Mark laughed and shook Larry's hand. We walked them both to the door, and they headed down the stairs for Main Street.

Larry turned to me immediately. "Sorry. I took it too far."

"You did what you had to do," I said with a shrug.

Larry squeezed my shoulder, then headed for his office. It was four in the afternoon, but our day was just getting started. Larry continued his tax work, and I transitioned from payroll to market study. While Larry worked sunup to sundown, he found *my* long office hours just short of deplorable.

"Don't make my mistake," he'd often told me. "Your wife is waiting for you at home," which wasn't true anymore. Most evenings, Donna worked two blocks away at a clothing store as a sales clerk, a part-time job she'd acquired shortly after the court judgment.

I put in another two hours, and just before leaving, about seven, I checked the market only to discover another record-breaking day: a two-percent rise for the NASDAQ while our minimal family account was safely tucked away in Main Street's Dacotah Bank—eking out a "safe" money-market return.

Grabbing my suit jacket off the door, I paused by Larry's office. Poring over documents, he looked up.

"We're coming back, Stephen," he said with little emotion. "Mark is well-respected in this community. High school quarterback. Millionaire before forty. Didn't he take us to state?"

I nodded. Larry was right about the business. After five years in financial purgatory, things were in fact looking up. Eventually, we might even afford to pay ourselves livable wages.

"Thanks for not quitting on me," I said.

He leaned back in his squeaky chair and frowned. "We're partners, man. Better or worse, right? Through thick and thin?" He chuckled at our private joke.

I bid him good night and headed out. Since it was Friday night, Donna would be off early, and given that Alycia wouldn't get home till late, we'd be alone together.

For better or worse, I thought to myself, wondering how Donna had responded to the flowers. If her reaction was anything like the last time, the vase of flowers would be waiting for me on the sidewalk, the glass crushed to pieces, the roses mangled, making the entire neighborhood privy to our failing marriage.

However, upon arriving home, the sidewalk was free of debris and Donna was nowhere to be seen. Inside, the roses remained on the table, the envelope, unopened. I went downstairs and found the rose I'd taped on Alycia's door early this morning now taped upside down to my own office door, with a small note scrawled on a Post-it memo: *Pathetic, Dad.*

At least I'm still "Dad," I thought.

I lingered for an hour, nervously pacing the living room, until I gave up. When I arrived at Joe's, Paul waved me over, his mood seemingly improved over the night before.

"This is only my first," he announced before I could ask. "I'm stopping at two."

"Wonderful," I said, hoping my constant badgering was finally taking effect. We discussed the Vikings for an hour. Susan didn't show up. I glanced at the date on my watch, hoping she wouldn't be back. Maybe she'd finally found her true love.

Hours later, after Paul's early and miraculous departure, I was still sipping lemonade and sketching trading notes in the dark, variations on the stock-trading ideas I'd developed years ago, tested ad infinitum, but hadn't implemented yet. The trading itch was growing stronger.

When I got home, our bedroom door was closed. I heard dull, rhythmic thuds emanating from downstairs and breathed a sigh of relief. Alycia was home safe. Three months ago, after finding evidence that she was sneaking out the tiny basement window in her room, I'd nailed it shut from the outside. It was like putting a Band-Aid on a broken leg. The following morning she'd glared at me over the breakfast table but said nothing.

Sinking into the living room recliner, I stared across the room, expecting to fall asleep immediately. Instead, my mind wandered, and I found myself recalling better days. Back when Alycia and I were still talking—and laughing, and cutting up. . . .

After I'd pronounced her the spitting image of a juvenile, curly-haired Audrey Hepburn, Alycia had made her own comparison. We'd been watching a series of old movies on the Classic Movie Channel, and we'd just finished *High Noon.*

"I think Mom looks a little like Grace Kelly," she announced.

"Grace Kelly?" I muttered, grabbing Alycia around the neck from behind. I rubbed my knuckles across her head and tortured her with the theme song, *"Do not forsake me, oh, my darling . . ."*

She wailed in mock pain. When I let her go, she persisted, "But don't you think she does? And don't you think Grace Kelly was pretty?"

"Marilyn Monroe was pretty," I said, playfully contrary.

"That ditzy chick?" Alycia objected. "No way. Mom is royal, and graceful, and . . . demure!"

"You mean finicky."

"Da-a-d!" She frowned, and then grinned. "Mom can't be that finicky. She married *you,* didn't she?"

That did it. I chased her around the room before catching her and tossing her on the couch, subjecting her to a full minute of unrelenting tickling. She squealed like Daffy Duck, "You're dethpicable, Dad, dethpicable!"

By the time I was done, we both had tears of exhaustion running down our faces.

"Are those days gone forever?" I now whispered into the gloomy silence.

Slivers of moonlight, reflected from the snow, slipped between the cracks of the curtain, the fabric moving from the breezy heat vent just beneath the front windows. The living room hummed and rattled with the sound of our twenty-year-old furnace.

It reminded me of our summers in Uglyville. Since we couldn't afford air-conditioning, my mother accumulated old fans instead, most of them purchased from garage sales, a few from the thrift store. Eventually every room contained at least three fans, creating a kind of inner windstorm, so noisy that Dad had to take his business calls outside. I remember him stretching the phone cord out the side door, shouting over his shoulder, "I can't hear over those idiotic fans!"

At one o'clock in the morning, I was still awake when Donna wandered out of the bedroom heading to the main bathroom. Wearing a terry cloth robe, she hesitated in the hallway as if peering out into the shadowy room. When I twitched, she spoke softly. "You're home."

I pulled the lever on the recliner and leaned forward. Across the room, her dark blond hair seemed to glow in the light from the hallway in spite of the premature strands of gray hair she no longer tried to hide.

"Been home for a while," I said pleasantly, then added, "I'm really sorry I forgot the party."

Her face was partially hidden in the shadows, so I couldn't tell if she was looking at me or beyond me.

"Shall I sleep downstairs again?" I asked, hoping to sound conciliatory. "Or perhaps—"

"Wouldn't that be best?"

I opened my mouth to reply, but she had already slipped into the bathroom. I sighed. At least we were talking. Swallowing my nerves, I pushed out of the chair. The space across the room seemed endless, but I was compelled to make some kind of bridge, a down payment on the reconciliation I hoped would emerge after a few days.

When she opened the door, I was standing in the hallway. She was tightening her robe when I reached for her, intending to hug her, nothing more, but she moved away from me, backing up. She crossed her arms defensively, visibly shaken, her eyes wounded. I felt the blood drain from my face, and her own cheeks turned crimson red.

"My emotions are written on my face," she'd often lamented. Donna couldn't so much as feel mild disappointment without clearly signaling it. We stood there for an awkward moment, regarding each other. Nervously, she looked down, then brushed at her hair, pushing the strands behind her ears, a gesture which I knew betrayed her lack of composure.

"You just . . . scared me, Stephen. I didn't expect to find you here."

She gestured apologetically to the light switch, and I stepped back. When she flicked the bathroom light off, I stepped back further, allowing her to pass, hoping for further conversation. But she headed down the hall and closed the bedroom door without so much as saying good night.

Chapter Nine

The next morning I awakened to the sound of rushing water. At first I didn't recognize it, since both Alycia and Donna usually slept in on Saturdays. Pulling myself up to a sitting position, I glimpsed the clock above my desk. 6:21.

I wondered if Alycia had planned a day with her friends and was showering early in preparation. *But the mall isn't open at this hour.* Besides, getting out of bed was normally a three-snooze-alarm affair for my morning-averse daughter. The last time I'd awakened her this early, she'd stared up at me in delusional wonder before tugging the covers over her head.

Slipping into my ratty blue robe, I made my way upstairs to the kitchen, boiled water in the microwave, and spooned myself a cup of instant coffee. In the back room I heard thuds emanating from our bedroom. Apparently, Donna was also up.

Strange.

I was still puzzling over this when Alycia emerged from the bathroom in her own bathrobe, her hair wet and stringy. She stepped gingerly into the kitchen, head bowed, her face half covered in dark dampness.

"You're up early, kiddo," I said to her back as she walked to the fridge. "Going somewhere?"

I waited, expecting nothing more than, *Do you have to control every detail of my life?* Instead she shrugged, opened the door, and leaned in. Pushing the wet strands from her eyes, she considered the refrigerator contents while I pretended interest in the bottom of my coffee cup.

She shut the door without removing anything. When she headed back, she lingered by the table, again pushing her hair away from her eyes. I looked up to see her staring down at me.

"What is it, Alley Cat?" I asked, forcing a nervous smile.

Her head dropped slightly, causing the hair to crowd around her soft pink cheeks like a closing curtain. She sniffed softly, then whispered, "I'm sorry, Dad . . . about the other night."

I was taken aback. She'd said, *"This one stays up there,"* and I couldn't remember the last time she'd apologized.

"I'm sorry too, Alycia," I said.

She took another quick sniff and hesitated, atypically unsure of herself. After another moment, her eyes glistened, and she breathed out a sigh.

"Want to do something today?" I asked, wincing at the absurdity of my suggestion. She hadn't wanted to be seen outside the house with me in months.

She looked sheepish. "I can't do it anymore, Dad. Okay? Nothing personal? And not to be rude, but I just . . . can't." The last word came out scratchy and pinched. I opened my mouth to speak, but she seemed so troubled I thought better of it. She bit her bottom lip, paused for a moment, and then proceeded to descend the stairs, not in her old hopping fashion, but ploddingly, one slow step at a time.

I continued drinking my coffee, trying to piece together the mystery of what had just happened. Five minutes later, I glimpsed movement beyond the sheer window curtains and heard the soft thud of the *Aberdeen News* hitting our sidewalk. After a squeal of frenetic pedaling, I heard another distant thud at the neighbor's house.

I went to the front door, descended the coarse steps in my bare feet, and snatched the paper. Heading back, clutching the paper under my arm, I heard the putter of a car engine. Peeking around the corner of our house, I noticed the garage door raised a foot from the ground. Beneath it, a soft curl of smoke sputtered into the cold morning air.

Stepping gingerly, I went to the side door and opened it. I pushed the opener mounted on the wall, and the door slipped down. I pushed it again and the door began to rise until fully open. Staring into Donna's minivan, I made out the shadowy outlines of boxes and suitcases. My entire body went numb with the realization.

I was still standing on the sidewalk, between the garage and the house, when Donna came out, carrying an armful of dresses. Her blond hair was tied back in a kerchief. When she saw me, she stopped in her tracks.

Our eyes met, and I read the flicker of guilt behind her eyes. She seemed to steel herself before continuing past me into the garage.

"You're up early," I said, at a loss for anything significant to say. "Can I help you with anything?"

"No, Stephen," she replied curtly, shoving the box on top of another and slamming the door shut.

"Are you going somewhere . . ." I started. "Vacation or . . ."

"A well-deserved vacation," she answered. Her chest heaved slightly as she took a slow, deep breath.

"Do you want to talk—"

"No," she said, walking past me. Her voice seemed stronger, as if she was gathering her courage. She poked a thumb toward the front. "There's more . . ."

She took a few indecisive steps, then whirled around. Her eyes flashed with anger. "I want a divorce, Stephen."

The first utterance of those words brought a deep chill to my bones. Even in the worst of our years together, she'd never used the D word, not even in anger.

Heading back in, she gave me no time to reply. I followed her, my formerly cold feet now numb. Further discussion outside would be broadcast to the neighbors.

Entering the house, I saw Donna turn the corner quickly, heading back to the bedroom. I stood just inside the doorway and waited for her to emerge. When she did, she was carrying a cardboard box.

I stepped aside, hoping to appear reasonable. "Can we talk about this?"

She bit her lip again, but shook her head. "No, Stephen. I'm done talking."

"Is this about your party?"

Seemingly confused, Donna set the box down, and folded her arms over her blouse. Her voice contained an incredulous whisper. "Do you think I'd actually leave you just because you forgot my birthday?"

"I'm really sorry, Donna."

Her face flushed red. "Are you *really,* Stephen?"

"Yes."

"No, Stephen. *I'm* the one who's sorry," she said. "For you, 'sorry' is just a word, but for me it means something."

Her eyes were filling with tears, and her breath was coming in heaves. "I wasn't going to do this . . ."

I lowered my voice to a whisper, hoping she'd do the same. "We don't have to, Donna. We can talk later if you want."

Ignoring me, she took a deep, heart-wrenching breath. When she blinked, the tears finally streaked down her face. "You know what I'm most sorry for?"

I tried to breathe.

"I'm sorry I ruined your life. I'm sorry I was such a poor replacement for the best thing that ever happened to you."

"Donna, that's not—"

"Please, Stephen." She exhaled sharply. "I'm sorry I wasted so many years believing in *us.*" She said "us" as if it was a four-letter word.

I stood there, waiting for her to finish.

"And I'm sorry we wasted a decade, Stephen."

"We had Alycia," I whispered lamely, and I was foolishly tempted to remind her of the good times, something our counselor had once advised us to keep in mind.

Donna's eyes darted to the basement door. Finally, she lowered her voice. "And look what we've done to her."

Dropping to her heels, she picked up the box and pushed out through the door, then propped it open with her leg, letting the box rest on her bended knee. She nodded toward the kitchen. "I'm leaving the papers on the table."

I glanced toward the kitchen and saw the documents. She must have put them there when I'd slipped outside to get the paper.

"It's pretty simple," she said. "I don't want the savings. But I get sole custody of Alycia."

I felt like she'd physically slapped me. How did we get to this so quickly?

"Shouldn't we consider . . . a temporary separation?"

She shook her head. "What's the point, Stephen?"

"Then take the house, Donna. I'll leave instead. You and Alycia belong—"

"No," she said, looking about the living room. "I can't deal with the memories. This was more your house than mine. All I want is my daughter."

"But what about joint—"

"Don't even go there, Stephen."

"But—"

"She needs stability."

The knot in my gut twisted further. The thought of losing Alycia completely struck terror to my heart. I'd always harbored the hope that Alycia and I would get back on an even keel, but if she didn't live here, what were our chances? It was an irrational fear, but I wasn't thinking clearly at this point. One minute Donna and I are married, the next minute we're negotiating visiting rights.

"It's only for a while," she continued. "Till Alycia can find her way . . . half a year, a year."

A year? "Just give me two hours a week."

"That's two hours more than you're doing now." Her eyes blazed. "Stephen, please. You're always at the office, and when you're not, you're with your friends. Don't torture her. And don't you dare get her hopes up again. If you care for her at all, you'll leave her alone for a while. She's more fragile than you think."

"Two hours," I repeated weakly, but Donna had lifted the box and was already pushing through the screen door. Over her shoulder, she called back. "I have a few more things, and then we'll be gone."

I heard the creak of a door, and Alycia appeared from the downstairs, still looking awkward and sheepish, and carrying a single backpack. Her hair remained damp, and she was wearing white slacks and a brown sweater, considerably more drab than her normal attire.

"Can I help you, honey?"

"I'll get the rest later," she said without meeting my gaze. She headed outside.

Donna returned and handed me a piece of paper. "Here's where we'll be staying."

It was the address and phone number for Sally, her best friend, who lived in a tiny apartment two blocks from the library.

"I need a moment with Alycia," I said, faltering.

Donna glared at me.

"Please, Donna."

"No more promises, Stephen."

Without agreeing, I headed outside again, my pulse pounding. In the garage, I knocked on the passenger window. Alycia looked up at me through the window, then rolled it down. Her eyes were red, her face pale.

"I'm really sorry, honey," I said.

"That's okay, Dad."

"I want to pick you up this Friday night for dinner," I said, crouching down. "We can go to one of those fancy places you like. We need to talk about this."

Alycia frowned. "You're kidding. Friday night?"

"Uh . . . okay . . . how 'bout Saturday? Saturday morning. Brunch."

She shook her head in disbelief. "I'm not waiting all day for you to show up."

"I'll be there."

"You won't show. . . ."

"I promise, Alycia."

"Take an aspirin, Dad. It'll pass."

"I *promise.*"

"No, Dad. I promise *you.* I won't be there. And I happen to keep my promises."

"Ten o'clock," I said firmly, and my insides were shaking.

Alycia's eyes filled with tears. "Please, Dad. Just leave me alone." And with that she rolled up her window. She turned forward, dismissing me, wiping her eyes. I stood there longer, staring at her, wishing for her to roll the window down again, but she refused to acknowledge me. I even reached up and touched the window, remembering a time when she would have matched my fingers with her own.

I'm making a fool of myself, I realized. I kissed my finger and touched the window again, but Alycia only closed her eyes and leaned back.

When I entered the house again, I suddenly realized how frantic I felt. I heard Donna rummaging around in the bedroom. I stared down at my trembling hands.

I've finally lost everything—my wife, my little girl. . . .

I couldn't let Donna see me like this. I headed straight downstairs, feeling dizzy, gripping the railing. When I reached my office, I closed the door and leaned against it, trying to compose my emotions. I noticed the clock. 7:31.

Pushing off from the door, I sat on the couch, and lowered my head to my hands. I hadn't truly prayed in years, but the words seemed to materialize out of thin air. *Lord, don't take them away from me. Please give me a second chance. . . .*

My forehead felt hot, but the rest of my body shivered. The vibration of the terror, the panic, was beginning to fill every part of my body. I was puzzled by it. I took several deep breaths until slowly the emotional turmoil began to subside, and then suddenly the strangest sensation fell over me. The room began spinning, I felt suddenly exhausted, and everything went black.

I "awakened" seconds later and shook my head quickly, marveling at the disturbing effects of stress. I rose to my feet, steadying myself. My insides still churned, but the overwhelming panic had left me.

I peered at the clock again. 7:41. A question flickered across my mind, but I dismissed it. Taking one last deep breath, I twisted the knob on the door and headed back upstairs. Ducking my head at the last minute to avoid the low spot in the ceiling, I grabbed the doorknob to the kitchen, then hesitated before going through. Surely they were gone by now.

When I walked into the kitchen and peeked around the corner, Donna was standing in the hallway looking at the pictures on the wall.

"I thought you'd left," I whispered.

Donna sighed. "Poor Alycia's still in the car waiting for me."

She was evidently calmer now. While Donna's anger had always been quick to fire, it was just as quick to diminish. Arms again folded across her chest defensively, she appraised the photos as if she would never see them again. Her expression turned wistful. "My favorite isn't even up here anymore."

Approaching the wall, I followed her gaze.

"I took it down years ago," Donna said, turning to me. "Remember?"

I squinted at the wall, then remembered how, following an argument, Donna had removed a picture, but I couldn't place it now.

"You don't, do you?" she said now.

"No," I admitted, wishing I could have said yes.

Another sigh escaped her, and she shook her head mournfully. "It seems you've forgotten everything."

Turning from me, she appraised the entire wall again, like a final good-bye, then turned back with a piercing gaze. I simply stood there, waiting for her to speak.

"It was all my fault, Stephen."

"No, it wasn't," I said.

She nodded. "I knew in my heart why you were marrying me. . . ."

I shook my head to object, but she didn't stop.

"I ignored my head and followed my heart," she said.

"But it doesn't matter how it started," I said.

She only smiled sadly. "We both tried to keep her memory alive." She blew out another breath. "We even named our daughter after her, Stephen. What on earth were we thinking?"

We heard a click from the front door. "Mom . . . are we going? I have to meet Denise at—"

"Just a minute, honey," Donna replied softly, and we traded glances, wondering if Alycia had heard the last comment. I tried to catch Alycia's eye, but she was already on her way back to the car.

I turned to Donna. She looked away and bit her lip as though trying not to cry.

I reached for her but she pulled away.

"Don't go, Donna," I whispered, but her face turned stony again.

"I don't blame you for leaving," I added. "I've been . . ." I stopped, then started again. "I've been a terrible provider."

Donna blew out an incredulous breath. "Oh, Stephen . . ."

"Are you sure there's nothing I can do for you? We've got a little savings. At least half is yours."

She shook her head and let out one long sigh, then slowly walked to the door.

With her hand on the knob, she paused again, then turned to me. "I failed you, didn't I?"

"Don't be silly."

"But I promised."

"It was an impossible promise," I replied.

Our eyes met, and she seemed to accept this. There was nothing left to say. After fourteen years, we'd exhausted our supply. And with that, Donna slipped out the door.

Chapter Ten

I didn't budge from the hallway wall for the longest time, as if lingering at the scene of an accident, gawking at the carnage. Donna's words echoed in my mind: *"My favorite isn't up here anymore. . . . You've forgotten everything."*

Most of the pictures were posed studio photography: a family portrait, taken two years ago when Turbo, our misshapen Labrador, was still alive. Grasping Turbo's neck like an oversized fuzzy black lollipop, ten-year-old Alycia smiled enthusiastically for the camera. Donna's pose was proud and motherly, and mine, formal and professional.

Alycia's brown hair was lighter, more curly, her freckles more prominent, and the glint in her eyes as yet undiminished. But when I looked closer, I saw the spark of something to come and felt another twinge of regret.

Next to this was another taken of us at the Mall of America in Minneapolis during a weekend trip, an automatic digital photo of us on the roller coaster—Alycia with her hands in the air, Donna, grinning wide-eyed, and me, holding on for dear life.

"I want a divorce" rang over and over in my head.

The walls were closing in on me. I went to the kitchen, ignored the papers on the table, and grabbed my car keys. Closing the door, I locked up the house, then sat down on the concrete step for a moment, taking in the neighborhood. Except for the clouds of moisture from my lips, the air seemed frozen. Above me, the sun struggled through a restraining gray cloud.

I idly wondered if any of our neighbors had observed Donna's departure. Across the street, Mrs. Saabe, the sweet elderly widow, was wandering around her yard with a watering can, hydrating her collection of marigolds along the sidewalk, for their one last gasp before winter took full control. Apparently, she hadn't figured anything out yet, because she gave me an enthusiastic wave before continuing her gardening, now leaning over and pulling a few bedraggled weeds.

Regardless, I knew I soon would have a series of unpleasant questions to face: *"How is Donna? I haven't seen her around lately."* Then again, news travels fast in a small town. If they didn't already know, they'd know by tonight.

I took a drive, heading south to Eighth Street, then east to Roosevelt, winding my way to Sixth Avenue, which ultimately became Highway 12. Eventually the trees disappeared, revealing a broad horizon of mind-numbingly flat farmland, where all roads intersect at unimaginative right angles.

Farther out of town, a gentle wind blew a dusty white sheet of snow across the icy highway, wispy and ghostlike, like the sands of time slithering before me. Little bristles of tan weeds jutted above the recent snowfall.

A few miles later, I passed a half-frozen small pond on the left, where shivering mallards, taken by surprise with this early winter weather, bobbed their heads into the water, flapping for balance.

Before my cell phone signal could fade out, I called my mom and gave her the news. Although acutely disappointed, she didn't seem surprised. Perhaps Donna had already briefed her.

"Are you okay, Stephen?"

"I'm sorry, Mom," I said, recalling my mother's fondness for Donna.

"Is there any hope, Stephen?"

I took a breath and considered Donna's determination. "Yes," I replied weakly. "There's always hope."

"Good for you, Stephen." She wondered where Donna would be staying and I told her. We talked a bit longer, and I voiced my concern for Alycia.

"Kids are resilient," she said. "But don't give up on her. She's a moody one."

I smiled at my mother's interesting choice of words. When it was time to hang up, I told her I loved her. "I don't think it's hit you, Stephen," she said. "I'm so sorry. I'm praying for you. I'm praying for all three of you."

I called Larry next.

"Need some time off?" he asked, and I declined.

"Wanna talk about it?"

"Need time to think," I told him.

"Mmm-hmm," he replied, and I could read his mind. In his opinion, expressed in countless conversations over the years: thinking—or *over* thinking—was at the heart of my problem.

"I'll see you tomorrow," he said and hung up.

I tossed the phone onto the passenger seat and vaguely remembered a time when Larry wouldn't have taken *no* for an answer. He would have insisted on getting together to offer support.

Driving into the snow-covered fields, beneath the cloud-trapped sun, surrounded by the harshness of winter air, vivid images came out of nowhere—things I hadn't thought about in years—and most of the memories depressed me, not because our marriage had been all sad but because if this was the end, even the good memories would always contain an underlying tinge of hopelessness.

Some memories were hopeless by definition, like the time when Donna's parents stayed a week when Alycia was only seven. Donna's mother had cornered me in the kitchen. "You've ruined my daughter," she said urgently. "I don't even recognize her."

At first, I was taken aback by the harshness of her word choice. *Ruined* her daughter? But instead of arguing, I stood there like a guilty man, unable to answer, which only fueled her flame of indignation. I tried to think of what I had done to hurt Donna. In the early years, we rarely fought, and I never berated her, but her mother was quick to fill in the blanks. "She's not the same girl we raised."

"What has changed?" I finally managed to ask.

"You drink."

"Not anymore," I replied.

Donna's mother scowled at me. "Don't lie to me, Stephen Whitaker. I know you go to that bar."

"But—"

"And now she sees movies!" her mother exclaimed, and I wondered how she knew. In anticipation of her parents' visit, we'd even hidden the television set in a closet.

"Disney," I replied, which was a half truth.

"Doesn't matter," her mother countered, lips firm. "She knows better."

After Donna had seen her first movie in college—*The Computer Who Wore Tennis Shoes*—she'd promptly rushed back to the dorm in tears, thoroughly repentant.

Paradoxically, she and her parents didn't view literature in the same way, leading me to wonder if Donna compensated for her strict upbringing by reading everything she could get her hands on. And while I couldn't argue with her mother's points, they didn't add up to marital abuse, at least in my mind.

Didn't matter. According to Donna's parents, she'd left the straight and narrow, and it wasn't Donna's fault. It was mine.

As I drove and dusk descended, the growing darkness seemed almost sinister.

Surely our marriage wasn't for nothing, I rationalized, as if I needed it to have meant something. And yet all the struggles, all the tears, all the good old-fashioned hard work and compromises seemed pointless unless you could achieve the blessed "till death do us part."

We wasted a decade, she'd said, because for her, the good times weren't enough to redeem the bad.

It's not over yet, I thought, as if trying to convince myself.

Eventually, I turned the car around and headed toward home. When I reentered our neighborhood, I parked on the street before remembering the empty garage. Had Donna left the remote? Doubtful. Most likely, it was still attached to her visor.

I gripped the steering wheel. In the stillness of my car, I took several deep breaths, leaning back in the bucket seat, unsure of what to do next.

I finally got out of the car and walked to the garage, unlocked the door, and pressed the opener. Although I was prepared for it, the mechanical sound startled me, and in that split-second space between dark and light, her car reappeared in its usual spot only to disappear again.

Turning on the light, my movements seemed suddenly imbued with hyper self-awareness, as if I were watching myself, studying my reactions, wondering if I might at last be coming undone.

Shaking my head, I went inside the house and puttered around in the kitchen for a few minutes. On the dining room table lay the garage remote.

I sighed and felt myself drawn back to the pictures again, as if unable to stop beating my head against the wall. I removed the photo of Alycia at age eight, and I sat at the sofa facing the front window, studying it.

The first tears slipped down my face. *Our marriage wasn't for nothing,* I told myself, tracing the outline of Alycia's eyes with my fingers.

"She's more fragile than you think," Donna had insisted.

Losing my battle with self-pity, I clutched my daughter's photo tightly to my chest and leaned back.

Surely there's still a chance, I thought.

As twilight deepened into darkness, I headed downstairs to my office. The walls seemed to echo with the latest memories, including a tense exchange with my daughter nearly a year ago. Rarely have I walked into my office without a tiny flicker of recollection. Before, the memories seemed painful, but now I welcomed anything that reminded me of my little girl.

"Let me get this straight." Alycia's words were clipped and incredulous. "You're building . . . an office . . . right next door . . . to my room?"

"I don't mind your music," I'd said. "We can coexist peaceably."

She wasn't amused and turned to her mother. "Can I have the upstairs room?"

"That's Mom's sewing room," I intervened.

"So?" Alycia exclaimed. "She doesn't sew anymore."

I switched gears. "It's storage now."

"She can use mine for that."

"I'm not going to spy on you," I interjected.

"Spying on me will be the inevitable result," she countered.

Inevitable result?

Donna broke in, "Take my room, Alycia. I don't mind."

Alycia threw me an eye dagger and stormed out of the kitchen. From across the living room door she yelled: "Just forget it! I don't even care. From now on, I won't come home unless I absolutely have to."

"Perhaps to collect your allowance?" I retorted.

Donna cast me a disapproving glare just before Alycia huffed out of the house.

Memories of my selfishness now repulsed me, and in the complete darkness of the room—where I was finally hidden—I put my hands to my face and let it all out. I wept for Alycia. And I wept for what I'd done to her mother, who had deserved far better.

Hours later, I awakened to a strange vibration. Opening my eyes, I saw my phone blinking, its buzz muffled on the carpet. I must have turned off the sound.

"Need some company?" Larry asked. "I'm hungry. My treat."

I hesitated, knowing Larry well enough. He wasn't just hungry.

Bone tired, and against my better judgment, I agreed to meet him at the Pizza Inn on Sixth Avenue.

Twenty minutes later, I found Larry standing outside the white-brick building, blowing into his hands and rubbing them together. He looked like a menacing Mafia figure in his black overcoat.

I parked and met him at the door. Once inside, we ordered pepperoni and sausage, and I sequenced the gory details. When I finished, he gave me a serious look. "Sounds to me like she didn't want to leave."

I frowned, wondering what part of my story he'd missed.

"I know what she said," Larry continued. "But maybe she's just trying to get your attention."

Only a lifelong friend is that pointed, although Larry never let something as small as tactlessness get in the way of his opinions.

Larry continued to probe. "Did you ask her to stay?"

"Of course."

"Just call her. See how she's doing."

"Maybe she needs some time."

"You aren't gonna fight for her?" Larry shook his head, and expelled an impatient breath.

"C'mon, Larry. We've been through this."

"Is it our finances?" Larry asked, raising his eyebrows.

I shrugged. *How could it not be?*

"Did you tell her things are looking up?"

I nodded. I'd been telling her this for years.

Larry gestured to the waitress across the room, then leaned forward. "Passion doesn't last, Stephen. Not for anyone. You have to settle for mutual regard. You have to embrace practicality, and appreciate convenience."

Larry viewed life in black-and-white, either-or terms. In his universe, shades of color didn't exist, and neither did ambiguity or imprecision. His remarks to me often contained the words, *In the final analysis,* which rarely followed with *any* analysis on his part—instead spoken as a way of cutting through mine.

There had been times when I'd wondered how we'd stayed friends so long. But in high school, we were more alike: He was a bit more reflective, I was much more optimistic, and somehow we met in the middle.

"That's not what Donna wants," I said. "She wants . . ." I stopped, unable to continue.

Larry frowned. "Just give her what she wants."

I did, I thought. No, that wasn't true. I tried. And sometimes I probably didn't try hard enough.

It was pointless to continue. The waitress brought the check, and Larry, without looking at the bill, handed her his credit card. It was his turn to pay. Larry frowned at the bill, then looked up, his expression sober. "I'm not sure I ever loved Megan. Until she left, that is. I learned my lesson the hard way, after it was too late. But it's still not too late for you." He studied me for a moment. "Don't you miss Donna?"

"Of course," I replied.

The waitress returned his credit card, and Larry signed the credit slip. I could tell he was disgusted with me. As far as he was concerned, I should have been serenading her from the street, wooing her back.

"You'll regret letting her go so easily," he said, putting his wallet away. "You'll wake up one day, it'll be too late, and you'll wonder why I didn't talk sense to you, and I'll say I did, but you didn't listen. And then I'll have to talk you out of doing something really stupid like starting your car in a closed garage." He cleared his throat. "Take her to Hawaii. Borrow the money if you have to. Maybe something will happen, you know?"

I cringed. For Larry, Hawaii was the answer to all relational ills.

"Which island?" I asked, letting my annoyance show.

"Who cares?" he retorted. "Pick an island. Any island."

I tossed a couple of dollars on the table for the tip and got to my feet. Larry followed suit. Standing, he shrugged into his black overcoat. "I suppose you think I'm a hypocrite," he said, brushing the sleeves.

"Never crossed my mind," I said, watching his ritual. I'd once asked him, *"What are you brushing off?"* And he'd replied with a lecture intended to put an exclamation point on his previous exhortations: *"The past! Stephen! It weighs me down!"*

Tossing a wave to the waitress, I followed Larry through the first set of glass doors. He stood in front of the second set for a moment, rubbing his hands together once more as if preparing to tackle the arctic temperatures single-handedly, just as he'd once tackled quarterbacks in high school. He reached over and squeezed my shoulder, his trademark older-brother routine, patronizing yet comforting. "Call me if you need to talk."

I shrugged, then reminded myself that Larry's straight-shooting comments, while simplistic, were a shadow of a much better attribute: his rock-steady loyalty. If you were Larry's friend, you were a friend for life. If you asked for his shirt, he'd begin untying his tie without so much as asking why. And despite our recent drift, and regardless of my continuing friendship with Paul—which he considered my biggest foolishness, at least till now—we remained bonded by the past, connected by countless shared events and emotions.

Zipping up my parka, I followed my friend into the unfriendliness of a South Dakota winter.

Chapter Eleven

I sleep-walked through the next week, ran the washer and dryer, folded up the "couch sheets" every morning after a restless few hours, and washed the dishes in the sink.

At Kesslers, I bought enough oatmeal and prepackaged macaroni and cheese to last a month. TV dinners would have been easier but more expensive. I skipped the meat aisle altogether, but rationalized produce. Although more expensive, I knew enough about nutrition not to eliminate apples and oranges. One a day wouldn't break me.

After a brief weather reprieve, we experienced another winter sleet, turning the trees along Eighth Street into skeletal icicles. Temperatures descended precipitously, and the windless atmosphere of the past few days carried the hushed quality of an impending storm. Eventually it came and went, but not until dumping a new blanket of snow. Its fluffy whiteness covered our landscape like mounds of newly spaded dirt over a freshly dug gravesite. My fingers went numb after a few minutes of shoveling our crooked sidewalk.

Each night after work, I noticed a growing absence of Donna's belongings. One day it was Donna's remaining clothes, the next day it was the contents of Alycia's room, until eventually, what remained was what I expected Donna to take first—her books. Her personal shelf contained various volumes of Shakespeare, Mark Twain, Henry James, Ernest Hemingway, John Steinbeck, Scott Fitzgerald, Graham

Greene, and Jane Austen, not to mention dozens of other literary notables.

On Tuesday, more than a week since Donna had left, I sat numbly on the floor in front of her bookshelf and removed her old copy of *The Great Gatsby.* I thumbed through it, noting the underlined passages and scribbled notes from her college days.

"I prefer tragedies," she'd told me in college. "I love the inexorable descent into hopelessness."

I'd thought she was joking. "Why?" I'd asked. "If it's all so hopeless, and the end is so obvious, why keep reading?"

She gave me several justifications for the tragedy before offering her own perspective. "But for me?" she asked as if wondering whether I really wanted to know.

"For you?"

She'd smiled wryly. "I love tragedies because I never stop believing that somehow everything can be solved. Even at the worst of moments, I imagine the characters finally coming to their senses, imploring God to save them from their foolish thoughts and choices, and then I imagine the Almighty . . . in His brilliant power and majesty snapping His fingers: Poof! All solved!"

I must have looked at her as if she was insane. "*That's* what you get out of tragic literature?"

She laughed. "Why not?"

Donna eventually persuaded Alice and me to read certain classics for the purpose of discussing them, and while initially I balked out of time constraints, Alice was enthralled with the idea. "C'mon, Stephen, it'll be fun!"

"We'll do the short books," Donna suggested, and since *Gatsby* contained a mere one hundred eighty-nine pages—her favorite tragedy—we settled on that one first. After we read the others, *Gatsby* remained our group favorite as well, although for different reasons. Alice liked *Gatsby* because of his chivalrous, albeit unrequited, love. Donna argued against Alice's simplistic evaluation, insisting that

Gatsby, born to a poor family, was reaching for a woman he could never have.

Personally—and perhaps obviously—while I enjoyed Fitzgerald's command of language, I didn't appreciate the book's apparent theme, that financial and romantic overreaching leads to tragedy. *"What's wrong with ambition?"* I asked out loud. As far as I was concerned, Fitzgerald had unrealistically manipulated story events to foster an erroneous conclusion.

In the course of the following year, we read five additional novels, most hand-selected by Donna: *Mockingbird,* of course, *The Old Man and the Sea, Lord of the Flies, Animal Farm,* and my only contribution to the list: *Ender's Game.* Donna argued for *Anna Karenina,* but Alice and I put our feet down. *Too long!*

I closed the book and placed it back in the shelf. Sitting there, it occurred to me I would have preferred she had taken all her belongings at once. Resting against the wood footboard of the bed, I closed my eyes and tried to imagine the next days and weeks ahead. So far I had managed to shrug off the impolite questions, "What happened, man?" with deft humor.

By now, Donna's version of the story would be circulating from one end of the town to the other, although not from her own lips. Knowing Donna, she would answer inquiries with respectful diplomacy. But knowing her friends, they would distribute the "true" version behind her back.

I stood up, went to the closet doors, and peered inside. Everything else was gone except for the box of photo albums at the top of the shelf. I considered them, wondering if Donna planned eventually to take them at some point with the books.

Removing the box, I grabbed the top album and perused the contents. Mingled with the family photo albums were a few individual albums, and one of college. I removed it and flipped to the first page of our college memories. I recognized it immediately. The three of us huddled awkwardly for the camera, our smiles somewhat forced, taken the night after Alice's first vocal performance. I smiled wistfully, knowing the end from the beginning. Eventually, hugging each other would become second nature. *Let it go,* I thought, closing the cover like the lid on a coffin.

I removed the family album and flipped through the pages. The photos of Alycia's first seven years contained an inordinate collection of just Alycia and me—beautiful memories mingled with not so happy ones, like the time Donna hurt her back and was laid up in bed. For a week, I brought her breakfast in bed, and to the amazement of a wide-eyed five-year-old, one evening I presented Donna chocolate pudding for dessert.

Alycia came to me the next day. "My back hurts, Daddy."

At first I was concerned until she screwed up her face and declared, "I think I need chocolate. That would really help."

I smiled at the memory, and remembered another, when she'd frowned at me for some indiscretion I couldn't recall now. "I'm *sad* at you, Daddy."

The next three years of photos featured a balanced assortment of Donna, Alycia, and me, until the last year when my presence diminished considerably—my financial obsession recorded for posterity. I was somewhat surprised that Donna had continued collecting photos and placing them in the album.

I flipped back to the beginning, to the first pictures taken shortly after our wedding. Even from the earliest moment, it was apparent to me now that Donna and I had made a terrible mistake. You could see it in our eyes—if not panic, at least uncertainty. There was no denying that I had married on the rebound, nor was there any denying that Donna had betrayed her own long-term dream of doing something with her literature major. And yet here we were, smiling for the camera, determined to make the best of it.

Not too long before our wedding, Larry had come to me with a business proposal to form a partnership. Paul was still in school, and Mom and Donna were becoming fast friends. I'd never seen my mother so animated as when Donna was in the room. They were like sisters, twenty years removed in age. "We have so much in common," Donna once exclaimed to me.

For the first three months Donna and I traded love notes written on yellow Post-its attached to the bathroom mirror, but, in retrospect, it seemed like we were trying too hard. Trying to prove we hadn't married for the wrong reasons.

All I ever wanted was you, Donna said to me shortly after our first anniversary. We were making up after an argument, and I must have looked visibly shaken by her declaration, because I couldn't answer in kind. I tried to think of an equal declaration to make, but the moment passed. "I love you too, Donna," I replied, and truly meant it.

She seemed to have a hazy view of our history, including a strange, continued guilt over Alice's death. Again, I viewed this as normal for Donna. After all, she seemed to feel guilty about everything. I figured she felt guilty over marrying the man Alice loved, nothing more, and if I attempted to question her regarding this, she simply froze up. "You wouldn't understand, Stephen."

I suppose if I'd truly examined it, I might have realized that Donna's guilt was an indication of something much bigger. It was Alycia, a regular bloodhound for veracity, who would eventually uncover the truth about her mother's participation in Alice's death.

In our second year of marriage, Donna poignantly asked, "Why do you always push me away? Are you afraid you might love me after all?"

"I do love you!" I declared earnestly, unaware of "pushing her away," but my assertion only elicited another round of silent tears. Then one day, it came to her like a flash of insight. "You're afraid of losing me, Stephen. Just like you lost Alice. That's what it is."

I remember holding her near and kissing her repeatedly. "I don't *want* to lose you."

"And you won't," she replied firmly. "I'll prove it to you." And that's what she'd meant on the day she left, when she'd said, *"I failed you."*

Like many women, Donna was an incurable romantic, and I truly enjoyed buying her flowers, and chocolate, and little cards. In keeping with this, *Somewhere in Time* was one of Donna's favorite movies. I thought it was corny but kept my opinion to myself. Christopher Reeve, so enamored with a woman from the past, *thinks* himself back in time. *Yeah, right.*

If only changing the past were that easy, I remembering thinking. Reeve falls in love with Jane Seymour, only to lose her forever when something from the future breaks the spell. The resolution? They are united in heaven. When I saw the ending, I thought, *That's all there is??*

Donna and Alycia, however, wept lakes of tears.

Later Donna cautioned Alycia regarding certain unsavory aspects to the movie. "They obviously didn't save themselves for marriage," she said. "So don't take any cues from that, Alycia."

Alycia only rolled her eyes. "I get it, Mom."

"You don't want to ruin your life," Donna cautioned. "Teenage pregnancy would be a lifetime curse."

"I *get* it, Mom."

Of course Donna kicked herself for letting Alycia see the movie at all.

Through much of our struggles, our love for Alycia was the glue that kept us together, and for years, I never watched a lick of evening TV. Instead, I came home and spent time with Alycia until it was time for bed. We played board games, made up story scenarios with her dolls, and read nearly every picture book in the library together. As she grew up, the sophistication of her toys and games grew as well. In the evenings, I read from various classics for youth.

Alycia had always waited for me to come home. When I pulled into our driveway, without fail I would spot a dark silhouette in the living room window. Moments later, the silhouette emerged into focus, a little girl pressing her nose to the window. Then suddenly, the front door would burst open, and Alycia would come running down the steps to explode into my arms.

She was no less enthusiastic on birthdays, her favorite "holidays," and as much as she loved her own birthday celebrations, she preferred planning them for others. I remember the night of my thirtieth birthday when she was only seven. I arrived home, and as usual she came sprinting out the door.

I pressed the power button to the window, and she leaned in grinning. "It's about time. Mom's waiting."

"What for?" I pretended.

I had become the proud recipient of her fast-developing state-of-the-art eye roll. "Dad, you'd forget your own head if it wasn't attached."

"Maybe that's why it is," I said. "Attached heads are for people like me who really need them to be attached."

She grinned, then suppressed a giggle. "Happy old age," she announced, and then, "As if!"

I glanced toward the front window of the house. "Alycia?"

"What?"

"There ain't no people in them thar hills, are there?"

Her face went blank. "Would you like there to be?"

"Nope," I replied.

A wry smile emerged. "What if there were *little* people in them thar hills?"

"No little or big people, please."

She nodded quickly—a little too quickly. "Cool. You have your wish, Kemo Sabe."

I affected a comically stern face. "Tonto . . ."

"I mean it!" she protested, and then quickly covered her mouth, spurting a giggle into her hand. "Oops!" She cleared her throat and blanked her face again. "That didn't mean anything, Dad. Pay no attention to the giggle behind the curtain!"

I squeezed my eyes shut and sighed.

"C'mon, Dad. Get some guts." She opened my car door and pulled on my arm. "This is how it works. One foot goes in front of the other. It's called 'walking.'"

I didn't budge. Instead, I held out my left hand and extended my pinky finger. "Pinky swear," I insisted, evoking the solemn pledge. "Pinky swear there are no people in there."

"In where?"

"In the house."

She extended her pinky, locking it with mine. "I pinky swear there are no people in our house. Now, c'mon, Dad!"

"All right, all right," I replied. "I'm coming."

She'd tricked me with a technicality. The people in "them thar hills," which included Paul, Larry, and John, had been hiding in the garage all along. At age seven, she'd planned the entire thing, including the Daffy Duck cake. *Dethpicable!*

In the truest sense, my marriage to Donna was imbued with our daughter's incessant energy. The older she got, the slower she rose in the morning, but once she did rise, resting was impossible until she finally fell asleep under duress. She never could understand how I could relax on Sunday afternoons when the "entire world was our oyster!"

"C'mon, Dad, let's take a drive! Let's see the world! Let's explore! Let's eat grasshoppers!"

I grimaced. "Explore what?" I asked. "Have you forgotten where we live?"

"Let's pretend we're in an exotic world!"

Her pleas fell on deaf ears, especially during football season, which she considered a crime against humanity. Undaunted, Alycia would wander into the room, lean over me—standing in front of the TV, no less—and whisper, "Defy the couch."

Then she'd sit on the floor, and with all the subtlety of a TV evangelist, say, "You're bigger than the couch, Dad. It has no power over you that you don't give it."

"You've got it all wrong," I told her, leaning on my side and employing the appropriate sports cliché. "The couch is my friend. I say: *Be* the couch. In fact, keep your eye *on* the couch."

"The couch has destroyed your will to live," she countered. "It's not your friend. It's your enemy."

"Then I invoke the rule of Julius Caesar . . ."

She frowned in anticipation.

"'Keep your friends close, but keep your enemies closer.'"

She rolled her eyes.

I could have written a book and called it *Adolescent Facial Gestures,* along with the subtitle: *And How to Interpret Them,* filling the pages with a hundred photos depicting the subtleties and variations of eye rolling alone, such as, the look-away eye roll, the blink-and-you-miss-it eye roll, the cross-your-arms-deliberate eye roll, the slow-motion eye roll, the nod-your-head eye roll, and Alycia's all-time favorite: the quick you're-crazy-shake-of-the-head eye roll. Sometimes, to preserve its effectiveness, the eye roll was dispensed with altogether, replaced by the delicate one eyebrow raised.

In keeping with our modified form of communication, Alycia and I would often reinvent the words to Donna's favorite show tunes, such as, "I've grown disgusted with your face," from *My Fair Lady,* or my own favorite: "How do you solve a problem like Alycia?" from *The Sound of Music,* and while Donna didn't participate in our remake of Broadway classics, every May she would break out her nostalgic records, including *Camelot,* and sing along: "It's May, it's May, the lusty month of May." Which elicited the proper retort: "That's gross, Mom."

And if we were really bored, Alycia and I tortured Donna by singing her favorite Broadway tunes in "Elmer Fudd." "If I wuh a wich man. Ya ha deedle deedle, bubba bubba deedle deedle dum. All day long I'd biddy biddy bum. If I wuh a wealthy man."

For most of Alycia's elementary years, Donna and I were treated to explicit and elaborate descriptions of classroom life and politics—who hated whom, who liked whom, who wore what—including her teachers' countless foibles. Mrs. Morrison had a beak like an eagle; Mrs. Shumaker shook the tables when she walked; and Mr. Wolf, her old gym teacher, looked like one.

We were also treated to elaborate descriptions of the social fabric of elementary school, including the sophisticated caste system. And then, one day, all commentary disappeared. In one fell swoop, we became the enemy, no longer trusted with her inner observations and conclusions.

Alycia was right about her mother, of course, although I'd never noticed before. Donna did have a "Grace Kelly" thing about her, perhaps more so in college. But what I remembered most about Donna was what seemed to me her spiritual naïvety. She had a rosy optimism, as if everyone would become a Christian if they just listened to reason. When they didn't, it puzzled her to no end. "Don't they get it?" she would exclaim.

And yet mingled within her optimistic Christian faith was her unrelenting disposition to guilt. She was forever repenting of thoughts and actions that had seemed to Alice and me utterly innocuous.

And yet, paradoxically, Donna's personal navigation between the seemingly contrary worlds of literature and religion, at least in college, came effortlessly. However, with the passage of time and approaching middle age, it seemed to become difficult, as if she'd suddenly awakened to the irreconcilable differences, then struggled in vain to find a truce between her heart and mind.

C.S. Lewis wrote that if a child is taught something as harmless as standing on a chair is wrong, then later, even as an adult, they will never stand on a chair without guilt. In fact, it seemed to me that Donna had been taught that nearly everything in life was wrong *except* standing on a chair. As a youngster, she never attended dances, never listened to pop music, never set foot in a movie theatre, and never ever watched TV. Her folks didn't even own one.

Unfortunately, the slow dissolution of her childhood faith accompanied the gradual erosion of our marriage. In keeping with this, I remember the day she threw a Christian novel across the room. Considering her literary tastes, I was surprised she was reading it at all.

"It doesn't ring true," she complained, and when I quizzed her further, she replied, "I can't relate to it. It doesn't reflect how Christians really live their lives. . . ."

I was curious at her seeming overreaction, and she shrugged. "Their miniscule struggles. Their laughable temptations. Their near-perfect lives. And no one makes unredeemable mistakes. I mean . . . no one even swears in those books. The characters are plastic!" And then she scoffed, "I don't know anyone who doesn't let a word slip now and then."

I considered this, tempted to dispute her claim. After all, I hadn't heard Paul swear in years, mainly because he viewed profanity as anti-intellectual. Larry rarely swore, because he viewed it as lazy and undisciplined. Despite this, and although I never read fiction, it seemed perfectly reasonable that Christians would prefer to read sanitized stories.

Donna was undeterred. "Besides . . . people don't just sit around having religious discussions."

I had to smile. "*We* do."

She only stared at me.

"We discuss religion all the time," I said. "And don't you remember your argument with Paul?"

She closed her eyes, exasperated. "Please don't remind me."

Chapter Twelve

At the time I wasn't aware that Donna was already in a process of spiritual reevaluation. Despite this, I should have known better.

We'd invited Paul over for dinner. Donna had prepared chicken and rice, green beans, and apple cobbler for dessert, and by the time Paul showed up, six-year-old Alycia had already been tucked into bed. The meal itself progressed uneventfully, but after discussing an assortment of benign topics, Donna naïvely asked, "So, Paul, where do you attend church?"

Stunned by Donna's question, I gave Paul a warning glance, hoping he'd temper his famous cynical intellectualism or dispense with it altogether.

Paul ignored me. "Why would I go to church?"

I was about to interrupt with something sports-related, but Donna was already speaking, "Why wouldn't you?"

"Church is for people who believe in God," Paul replied simply, shoving a spoonful of beans into his mouth.

I sucked in my breath, hoping Donna would transition to another topic. I knew for a fact that Paul would have loved to discuss literature with my wife. I opened my mouth to suggest it, but Donna was already saying, "You *don't*?"

"You *do*?"

"Of course."

"How?" Paul asked, and we were off to the races. The entire discussion turned into a great debate regarding religion versus science, and I wondered if Donna, despite her educated articulation, knew what she was up against. As for myself, I became a bystander to a verbal Ping-Pong match.

Donna seemed undaunted. "Do you really think we just evolved, that somehow matter created mind?"

Paul was all over it. "Quantum physics proves that we create our reality by observing it. God is us, looking back at ourselves."

I wanted to crawl under the rug, but Donna didn't skip a beat. "Physicists are like the blind boys touching the elephant. Each one touches a different part—the trunk, the tail, the legs, the stomach, then declares to know the truth of the elephant. Not only do they miss the big picture, but they forget that the elephant is *alive.* Defining parts of His creation doesn't define God himself. There's a Person behind the pieces of your universe."

"A personal God is self-refuting," Paul said. "It reflects our anthropomorphic tendencies to personalize everything."

"Personality is what this universe is all about," Donna countered. She cited the anthropic principle—the well-accepted scientific theory that our earth had been meticulously designed for human inhabitation. While I'd heard of it, I was surprised that she had too. Then I reminded myself that Donna was a voracious reader.

"It takes a Personality to design a world for other personalities," she added. "Look at our human body. The details of our scientific functioning are still beyond our ability to fully grasp, and yet the parts aren't what we're about. We were made to think, to be human, to have personality."

Paul shook his head, but Donna continued undaunted. "Our Creator knows us intimately. In fact, He became human, Paul, and died for you."

Paul nearly came uncorked. "How did we get to this point? First we're discussing the nature of the universe, and now you're referring to a myth."

"Myth became true," Donna countered. She glanced at me for a moment, then continued. "Sure . . . God first revealed himself in the myths of mankind, but the myth of a God becoming human and then dying was ultimately revealed in history."

Paul snorted. "You can't believe that's literally true?"

"Of course," she replied.

"That's just fundamentalism," he replied, as if identifying it thus closed the argument. "They've stolen your religion. The fundamentalists are literal about everything."

Donna was quick on the draw. "And the Liberals, New Agers, and Humanists mythologize everything. Christianity offers answers to the deepest longings and questions of mankind," she replied steadily. "Even if you have a problem with Christian fundamentalism, as you call it, the core of Christianity still rings true."

Paul scoffed and reached for his water glass. "Believe me, the god I can conceive of is better than the god Christians have created. For one thing, my god doesn't send people to hell."

"Neither does mine," Donna replied.

"My God . . ." Paul stopped, suddenly unwilling to finish the statement.

"Your God is my God," she replied with confidence. "And *our* God is the truest realization of all our fondest ambitions, hopes, and dreams. When we meet God, our greatest expectations will not only be fulfilled, they'll be surpassed. When we go home to heaven we'll never, ever again wonder: *Is this all there is?*"

By now Donna's face was flushed, but Paul's face had become a dark cloud of exasperation. In spite of her escalating emotion, Donna persisted. "Imagine having the complete, undivided attention of the God of the universe," she said, eyes bright. "All the pleasures on earth are mere metaphors for our eventual experience of God. All the joys are an intimation of the ultimate Joy. Everything good on earth is a metaphor for our personal relationship with God."

Paul shook his head again.

"How could you possibly disagree with that?"

"Because it's not true," Paul said. "It's wishful thinking."

"And where did wishful thinking come from?"

"Huh?"

"I mean . . . how could we wish for something that doesn't exist?"

Paul frowned again, then smiled wryly. "What about time travel? I've always wished for that."

"Maybe time travel exists!" Donna exclaimed, then added, "In heaven we won't be constrained by time. Everything in your world of physics fits nicely within the logical framework of a personal God."

Paul only laughed. "If Christianity is true, how do you explain the church?"

Donna frowned.

Paul continued. "Talk all you want about God's love, but you won't find it in the church. You want to quote the Bible? The Bible says, 'You'll know them by their fruits,' but there aren't any to be found! Case closed!"

Paul smiled as if he'd just scored the big one, but Donna wasn't to be deterred. "Don't reject God just because you reject the church, Paul. God is bigger than the church."

The conversation took a different turn as Paul began to describe his own personal experiences with Christians and their inability to live up to their own countless rules. Slowly, the wind evaporated from Donna's sails. She listened but now seemed lost. The red splotches in her face turned pale. The whole thing petered out once Paul realized Donna was no longer arguing.

The evening never recovered. Later that night, I awakened at one o'clock to find Donna sitting up in bed. When I turned on the lights, I saw tears streaming down her face. Her eyes were closed, and she was hugging herself tightly.

"Too bright," she whispered.

I switched off the light. "What's wrong?"

I detected a shadowy shrug.

"Try me."

"You don't need God to love you, Stephen. And you don't even believe anymore, so you wouldn't understand."

I stroked her leg. "I'm sorry I invited Paul over," I said.

She shook her head. "It's not his fault."

"You were right, you know," I said.

She sniffed. "About what?"

"The wishful thinking stuff."

She shrugged. "Does it matter?"

Days later, Donna received Paul's note in the mail, thanking her for the meal and apologizing for the argument. While she figured I'd put him up to it, she wrote him a thoughtful letter back anyway. Although Donna was one of the few who truly accepted Paul, I never invited him back. In turn, this became another in a long line of rejections for Paul, especially painful because of his enormous respect for Donna. As of now, other than Susan, I was his only remaining friend.

In all truth, and in spite of her disagreement with Paul, I turned out to be the greater thorn in Donna's faith. While I didn't discourage her, I gave her zero support. The most I did was smile politely as she talked about her love for Jesus and agree too vociferously with her own frustrations with the church.

As for my own faith, Donna never accepted why I'd "given up."

"I didn't let go of God," I replied. "He let go of me. God can't be trusted."

She smiled wryly, but her eyes held bitterness. "Why? Because He took Alice away?"

I opened my mouth to object.

"You quit believing at the very time when you should have persisted, Stephen. Did Job quit believing when God allowed everything to be taken from him?"

"The story of Job doesn't count," I argued. "God gave it all back to him!"

"He didn't *know* God was going to do that," Donna insisted. "He believed without knowing the outcome. Maybe God would have restored everything to you if you hadn't quit."

I was frustrated with her silly notion. "Impossible."

"You should have persisted, Stephen, like Jacob wrestled with the angel, or the importune widow, or the woman whom Jesus seemingly scorned, telling her, 'I've only come for the lost children of Israel.' But later, after she persisted, He marveled at her persistent faith and gave her what she believed."

I decided to puncture her argument. "So," I said, "you're saying God would have brought Alice back to life?"

"It's not like He *couldn't*!"

"You're kidding," I exclaimed. "You don't even believe that yourself, do you?"

Her eyes glistened. "God can do anything."

"Except make you feel loved," I replied, my voice tinged with my own bitterness.

Her eyes welled up with tears. "But I won't stop believing that He does. I don't care if I don't feel it. I still believe it."

And to prove my point, a few weeks later Donna did something very foolish. She took up smoking.

I wouldn't have believed that someone like Donna could do this if I hadn't seen it firsthand. Initially, I wondered if maybe she didn't start as a way to help our marriage, as if to further align herself with my antifundamentalism the only way she could. She already was going to movies and watching occasional TV.

"Why does Mom smoke?" six-year-old Alycia once asked me.

Because she can't quit, I almost said. Instead, I struggled to come up with a decent reason. "Your mother's not perfect," was my feeble reply. "She's trying to prove something to herself."

My little daughter swept her right hand over the top of her head in her unmistakable gesture: *I don't get it!*

I laughed and kissed her on the forehead.

"Are you angry with my smoking?" Donna once asked, implying that I should be.

Of course I wasn't, which puzzled her. "It's not a good habit, but it's your choice." Such a reply was foreign to her, and I suppose she used it to question my love for her, because, according to her warped childhood view, if I had loved her, I would have berated her personal failings. Eventually Donna did quit smoking, six months after she started, although it took several attempts.

Our last year of marriage was a disaster. "You touch me like I'm your sister," she once said, a reference to our uninspired bedroom life, and I remember taking her in my arms and giving her the most passionate kiss I could muster. But when I released her, she glared at me, her eyes glistening, "See?"

Of course Donna was like any other woman. Surely as a young girl she'd yearned to find her own knight in shining armor, her own handsome Prince Charming. Surely she longed for someone to carry her away to his protective castle. Perhaps she'd even longed for her own Gatsby—her own romantic fool.

While I couldn't lie and pretend I hadn't adored Alice, I truly loved Donna, but despite our college friendship, we never recovered from our dubious beginning. The loneliness and grief we'd quenched in each other's arms wasn't a legitimate reason to marry, and my financial failures, my obsessed distraction, and my loss of faith only exacerbated our difficulties.

Three months before she left, Donna had whispered into the silence of our estranged bedroom, "You win, Stephen."

Win what? I thought, recognizing the beginning of yet another futile argument. I kept silent, but she continued in a flat and unemotional voice, "I can't wait any longer. I can't compete with your imagination of what might have been. I can't wait to see the same look in your eyes, the way you once looked at her. I can't wait for you to love me."

I remember sitting up, putting my hand on her shoulder. "Donna, I *do* love you."

She shook her head. "Not like you loved Alice."

"But I'm glad I married *you*."

She glared at me. "Then why do you still dream of her?"

I wanted to say the content of my dreams was outside of my control, but instead I said something even worse. "If we hadn't married, we wouldn't have had Alycia."

She swallowed. "So that's the only reason you love me? Because I gave you Alycia?"

I tried to reply, but she had already turned her back to me.

Chapter Thirteen

On Wednesday I worked later than usual, but Larry still outlasted me. It was nine-thirty when I got into my car, reluctantly shedding the protective world of work. I started the engine, considering my options. I hadn't yet returned to Joe's. Paul hadn't heard about Donna's and my marriage separation, at least not from my lips, and Susan, if she was back by now, would be full of consolations, conclusions, and exhortations. In the end, she'd probably throw up her hands with, "Men! Can't live with them, can't kill 'em."

I sighed into the darkness of my vibrating rattletrap and thought about Alycia. *"Leave her alone,"* Donna had said.

"I can't," I whispered above the annoying buzz of the car heater.

I put the car into gear and took the long way home, then backtracked, driving around and around the back streets of Aberdeen, until I found myself on the street leading to Sally's one-room apartment. As I drove slowly past the window, I peered up at the dark and uninviting curtains. Where was Donna sleeping? On the couch? Where was Alycia? On the floor? Or in the sleeping bag I now recalled seeing in the backseat of the car?

I'm sorry, I whispered, words they'd grown tired of hearing, words they no longer believed. I stopped the car in the middle of the street where Donna or Alycia, or even Sally for that matter, could peek out the window and recognize me. I considered calling Donna and begging her again to take the house. But as quickly as the thought came, I knew Donna would reject it as she had our bank account. Besides, she'd already moved everything.

Back during the humiliating court proceedings related to my trading fiasco, during which Donna had loyally stood by my side, I'd never felt like this, as if I were falling through a black cloud, searching for any kind of silver lining.

Go home, I told myself. *Go through the motions. Prepare for bed. Wash the dishes. You're not the only one who's staring at a divorce. Tomorrow's another day.*

I gazed at the window again and imagined Donna behind the curtains. I pictured Alycia talking on the phone, probably in the bathroom where no one could eavesdrop. I put the car in drive, released the brake, and headed back home.

Later that evening, I pulled on my pajamas, then reconsidered the bedroom. I hadn't slept in our bed in nearly a week and hadn't turned on the TV because I couldn't bear the superficiality of canned lives.

I trudged out to the living room and threw a clean sheet over the couch. I stared at the phone on the floor and resisted the temptation. How easy it would be just to call her.

Come home! I'd be tempted to beg her. But why? So I could torture her with another fourteen years of my insidious poverty, not to mention the emotional vacuum we seemed to have created? Maybe she'd be better off without me. Maybe Alycia would as well.

I sighed with frustration at my own descending self-pity.

"I'll be praying for you," my mother said recently. "Are you praying, too, Stephen?"

"Sure," I said, but she knew better.

Reclining on the couch, I reached over to the lamp table and turned out the light. As usual, I lay awake for hours. I played the memories over and over in my mind, and my mother's words seemed to echo in the back of everything: *Miracles happen to those who pray and believe.*

For a moment, I even considered trying again. I stared up at the ceiling, felt the words forming in my mind, then gave up before they crossed my lips. I turned over on my side and doubled my efforts to fall asleep. *Trusting God is a recipe for disaster.*

That settled it, but it didn't bring sleep. About two o'clock, the notion crossed my mind: *The least you can do is win your daughter back.*

I sighed into the listless darkness and shrugged it off, but the thought persisted, growing larger until I finally entertained it: What would it take?

"She's in her embarrassment phase," Donna had said.

Money, I thought. *It would take more money.*

"I keep my promises," Alycia had declared.

I modified my appraisal. *Money and dependability.*

That thought jumped the curb and landed in the strangest place: Maybe I could finally begin trading again. The idea was ridiculous . . . and yet tremendously appealing. Trading is how I lost it all; trading is how I had to find it again.

I turned on my side and tried to mentally force sleep to overtake me.

"Leave her alone!" Donna had implored me.

Would it be so hard? I knew what to do, didn't I? I knew all the methods, the systems, and the process. I'd been studying it for years, methodically searching for the magic indicator, but didn't it all come down to one truth? Hadn't I already found the magic bullet? The perfect system wasn't a system at all: It was *me*—consistent and disciplined.

Bottom line: I'd been afraid to pull the trigger again. That's all. This time I could do it right. I could ride out the inevitable losses without losing my head.

I sat up and smiled into the darkness. *I can win her back.*

My body shivered with the thought. Hours earlier, I'd been at my darkest moment, and now I was suddenly exhilarated with the possibilities. I thought of poor Donna living in her friend's tiny place, living below poverty level. She deserved a decent alimony. In fact—

and by now my brain was blazing—I could pay them *all* back—every single investor I'd wronged.

The small flame became a fire. I could redeem the last fourteen years of my life. I could parlay a life of failure—like a magician creating a rabbit out of thin air—into a life of success. I could fulfill a lifetime of broken promises. I could finally finish the journey I began in college.

There I was, wide awake in the middle of the night, days after losing my wife and daughter, and suddenly I was beginning to believe again.

I can pay them all back, I said into the darkness.

The fire became an inferno. I burst from the living room couch and headed downstairs to my cave. I already had the system, didn't I? It wasn't perfect, but if implemented consistently, it was good enough.

I turned on the computer, pulled up a recent spreadsheet file, and began reviewing my old data, thousands upon thousands of past instances, proving to myself yet again that my divergence trading system could work. I studied for hours, examining screen after screen of stock charts until I was too bleary-eyed to continue, and then at dawn it hit me, and suddenly I flicked the computer off. The monitor's light buzzed into oblivion. I pushed away from the desk and stared at the blackened screen with newfound disgust.

"Enough!" I whispered.

I picked up the second Market Wizard book and read one of the passages I'd underlined years ago. "All the great traders gained and lost small fortunes before finally succeeding."

It's time to act, I thought. I felt another surge of adrenalin and considered my resources. At the moment I had seven thousand in the bank that I had intended to split with Donna, in spite of her refusal.

What if I traded with it instead?

I continued reading: "Most of the great traders turned small sums into millions—not doubling, or tripling, or even quadrupling their money, but multiplying their money *one hundred to one thousand times.*"

My mind was ricocheting like an aimless bottle rocket. Forget the seven thousand. What if I had *thirty* thousand? And then . . . what if I employed derivatives? With options or futures, I could turn it into a million bucks in a few months.

I felt the first pinprick. *It's not the knowing, Stevie boy. It's the doing. And the doing has always been the devil.*

Even Larry didn't believe in the possibilities. He didn't even believe in a predictable market. Years earlier, he'd admonished me: "You're bending the historical data to match the trading system. Your results are bogus. The stock market is haphazard, Stephen. You're finding patterns where they don't exist. It's like an ink-blot test: You're seeing what you want to see."

Wrong, I now told myself. *Hundreds of successful traders have proven him wrong.*

My heart beating like a galloping elephant, I lay down on my cave couch and closed the cover of my book. I repeated to myself over and over: *I can do this. I can do this.*

I went to my CD player and inserted the cheesiest collection of tunes I could find.

"For you, Dad . . ." Alycia had once exclaimed, "cheesy is a way of life."

"Slipping Through My Fingers" broke the silence. I sat back down on the couch, my hands laced behind my neck. The song reminded me not only of my childhood but of one year ago.

I'd played the song three times, raising the volume with each repeat, and finally elicited a response from my next-door neighbor. Alycia pounded on the door, then entered the inner sanctum of my cheesy empire, her hands over her ears, her eyes full of mock anguish. "Please make the bad music go away."

"What's wrong?"

"Do you have to ask?"

She stood there, hands over her ears, but listening to the words in spite of herself. Her expression changed. "Tell me that isn't about me."

I shrugged. "Why would you think that?"

"It *is* about me."

"C'mon, it's a sweet song about how kids grow up too fast."

She sighed with exaggeration. "If I hugged you, would you make it stop?"

I shrugged nonchalantly. "It's negotiable, I suppose."

"I need some commitment here."

"Okay, I suppose if you hugged me I'd shut it off."

She closed her eyes and sighed again as if she were making a deal with the devil. Lately, variations of sighing had replaced her elaborate eye rolling. I turned in my chair, faced toward the wall, and folded my arms to indicate the strength of my position. "Slipping . . ." continued to play. After a moment, I sensed movement behind me, and then a kiss on the back of my neck.

Alycia stepped back as if I was harboring parasites. "There. Now shut it off. We had a deal."

"We never shook on it."

"Dad . . ."

"Besides, no one said anything about a 'kiss.' Wasn't there something in the Bible about a betrayal 'kiss'?"

"Dad . . ." She raised her eyebrows and twitched her pinchers, but the usual mirth in her eyes was missing.

"Okay, okay," I replied. "I suppose for a kiss I can turn it down."

She harrumphed loudly—another variation of sighing—and stormed out. That might have been our last civil conversation.

That's the past, I thought, smiling tentatively. *I can do this. I can win her back.*

My smile broadened. *And maybe I can win Donna back too.*

Chapter Fourteen

Five long years ago, at the behest of John, another high school buddy, I had accepted an invitation to the business department of Northern State College. John was an assistant professor at the time and needed someone in the arena of investing to give a one-hour lecture to the Investments 101 class. Unfortunately, the class began at seven-thirty in the morning.

Taking my place in front, I looked out at the twenty-five or so sleepy, indifferent students. I had contemplated how I might get their attention. John, in his professorial bow tie and white shirt, took his seat in the far corner and gave me a halfhearted *do-the-best-you-can* shrug.

I'd considered opening with a general philosophy of money. *Right or wrong, making money is how most Americans live their lives. Opportunity and wealth are on every side of us, like apples ripe for the picking. There's no reason to be poor in America. . . .*

Instead, I came prepared with something more dramatic. In spite of possibly overplaying it, I removed a fake one-thousand-dollar bill from my pocket.

I held it up. "Mr. Robbins asked me to talk to you about the world of investing."

Waiting for everyone's attention, I didn't say anything more.

Slowly, the room awakened. Their eyes expressed their thought: *What's with the big bill?*

When I pulled out the cigarette lighter I'd picked up at the local 7-Eleven, their eyes widened further. I now had everyone's attention.

"Is it real, Dude?" A spike-haired surfer-type asked from the back.

"Investing is boring," I said. "Let's talk about trading." I placed the thousand-dollar bill and the lighter on the table on a front desk where it would tantalize them further.

A serious-looking brunette in the front row frowned. "What's the difference?"

"Good point," I replied. "The only difference between trading and investing is the time frame. Instead of months, or even years, you're dealing with days, hours, even minutes."

The brunette seemed fascinated.

"Everyone is an investor," I continued. "For example, everyone will eventually buy a house and hope to sell it later at a higher price. Short-term trading is the equivalent of buying a house at one in the afternoon for fifty thousand dollars and selling it three hours later for fifty-five thousand."

"People do that?" someone exclaimed.

I nodded, then asked, "How much did I make on the house sale?"

"Five thousand dollars," the brunette replied. "Ten percent on your money."

"Ten percent in three hours," I confirmed. "Pretty good return."

Everyone nodded.

"It gets better," I added. "What if I purchased that fifty-thousand-dollar house for only five thousand?"

The brunette smirked. "It's called a down payment."

I smiled back. "In the trading world it's called an option." I opened my hands in a questioning manner. "So now how much did I make?"

A red-haired girl with blue-tinted braids frowned. "The same."

The brunette broke in again. "Well, not exactly . . ."

"Actually . . . I doubled my money," I finished. "With just five thousand invested, I made another five thousand. That means . . . one hundred percent . . ."

" . . . in three hours," someone else finished.

"Dude!" the surfer said in an awestruck voice.

The brunette flashed him a look: *How ignorant can you be?*

"Happens every day," I said. "But that's only the beginning."

Unbelief moved across the roomful of faces.

"Good traders are making one *thousand* percent on their money."

More incredulous frowns.

"Trading is the gold rush of today," I continued. "It's the final financial frontier, but unlike the old days when commissions were high and access was difficult, today anyone can trade. Because of the Internet, everyone has a place at the table. All of us can put our pan into the water, sift out the rocks . . . and find gold!"

"Keep talking," another boy with a crew cut said.

"The trader is the gunslinger of today," I said, mixing my metaphors. "Independent. Beholden to no one. No boss, no employees. You and you alone decide how much to pay yourself." I paused. "But there's a catch."

Several narrowed their eyes. They'd been expecting this. "Imagine with me," I said, "that you've got a thousand dollars in the bank." I picked up the bill from the table. "Think of all the things you could do with that thousand dollars—down payment on a car, new shoes, fancy watch . . ."

"Shopping spree!" one girl giggled.

That was the perfect moment. I picked up the lighter, flicked it, and set fire to the bill. Mouths opened wide. Gasps escaped their lips. Gloom and frowns descended upon their faces. I held it up as it disintegrated into ashes, then placed it on a saucer of water I had ready. "How did that feel?" I asked.

"Painful," the brunette replied, her face ashen. "Hope that wasn't real."

"That's trading," I told her.

Another hush of silence before someone squeaked: "But I thought you made money?"

"You have to burn money first."

Their chagrined faces turned confused.

"It's like counting cards in blackjack," I continued. "For every hand you win, you lose a hand. Same with trading. For every thousand you make, you'll burn another thousand. For every good day, you'll have a bad day, but sometimes you might not burn any. And that's how you get rich. The key is knowing when to bet and how much to bet. And if you get attached to your money, if you start counting it before the day is finished, you are finished. The inevitable bad days will so debilitate you that you'll have nothing left for the good days."

Sitting in the corner with his arms crossed, my buddy John grinned.

"Only those with stellar character survive. Only the most courageous persist. Trading is the purest form of psychotherapy known to man."

I pointed to the surfer dude. "Want to know what you're made of?"

He shrugged with a smile.

"Then trade," I said.

"Want to test your limits of emotional fortitude?" I asked the brunette.

"Date?" she asked slyly, and the room filled with laughter again.

I grinned, then asked the entire room: "If you want to determine the extent of your mental pain threshold? Trade. When it comes to fear, skydiving is easy. When it comes to risk, surfing is easy. Trading is the scariest activity ever created by humankind."

You could have heard a pin drop.

"Take a man or a woman of towering self-confidence, yet inexperienced in the world of trading," I suggested. "Lock them in a trading room. Make them trade their own money. In a few hours, they'll be sweating. They'll turn red. Panic will be leaking out of their very pores, and they won't be able to hide it. Eventually, they'll ask—no, they'll *beg*—to be allowed to stop. In a matter of hours a person who seems to have total confidence and inner strength will have been turned into a quivering fool."

"Why?" someone ventured.

"Because the market will cause you, force you, intimidate you, into doing the opposite of what you should do. It will play you like a fool, then spit you out. It will take your money and give you nothing in return."

"So what's it take?" someone asked.

"Faith," I replied, slightly noting my own irony. "Faith in your ability to withstand pressure. Faith in your market research. Faith in yourself." I dropped the final bombshell. "The truth is: only one percent of one percent succeed."

"It's that hard?" the surfer asked.

"Not technically," I said. "This isn't rocket science. You don't need a college degree to figure out the mechanics."

"So . . . how much do the good traders make?" someone asked, getting down to brass tacks.

"What is your major?" I asked him.

He shrugged. "Accounting."

"As an accountant, you'll make, in today's dollars, about two million dollars . . ."

He seemed intrigued.

" . . . by the time you die," I finished, and his face fell.

"You'll spend most of it on your house mortgage, on your wife's hobbies, and your daughter's shopping sprees."

"Hey!" the lover-of-shopping-sprees objected, then smiled. But the accounting major wasn't pleased.

I finished my comment. "But a good trader can make a million every year."

"Just by sitting in front of the computer?" a blond girl asked.

"In your bathrobe," I added. "In fact, if you wanted, you could live anywhere in the world. You could drive the nicest cars, live in the biggest houses, and attract maintenance-free men!"

The brunette flushed.

"So how does it work?" someone else asked, and a few others nodded in agreement. I smiled with approval. Now that I had their attention, it was time to get on with the fundamentals of how Wall Street operated—as if anyone in the world really knew.

I began with the bottom line: "The value of all things in life, especially stocks, is based solely, and exclusively, upon perception. . . ."

My lecture went over so well that John invited me back the next month, but I never made it.

Two weeks after my classroom lecture, I burned three million dollars.

Chapter Fifteen

The digital display showed 4:30 A.M. when I finally gave up trying to sleep. After showering, I grabbed a cup of caffeine and headed for the office. I arrived just before five and parked on Main.

The early bird gets the parking spot, I mused. Getting out of the car, my shoes crunched the old snow. A slight breeze nipped at my exposed collar, but the day promised higher temperatures—maybe as high as thirty degrees.

Climbing the stairs, I opened the rickety door and hung up my coat on the hanger in the reception area. In my office, I turned on the computer, then glanced over at Alycia's photo.

"Hi, sweetie," I whispered.

I sat at my clutter-free desk, empty but for the keyboard, screen, and phone. I accessed the computer, navigated through a few Web sites, and within minutes, renewed my old data service accounts. Much had changed in the last three years, so I purchased and downloaded new software—albeit nothing expensive or elaborate. I accessed my online broker and discovered yet more services—company research, analyst opinions, stock ratings. *More distractions,* I told myself. *More voices whispering in my ear.*

I reminded myself of what I'd forgotten during the past year, that most traders, including myself, are looking for the next idea, the next complex variable method, the newest software, the next sure thing. Amateur traders, desperate to quantify every conceivable variable, confuse complexity for improvement. Yet, according to the great traders, the best methods are so simple they can be written on an index card.

I prepared morning coffee for Larry and looked out at the growing dawn. Main Street had a new sparkle to it, welcoming the first cars of the day with their frost-covered windows and pluming blue-gray exhaust smoke, which dissolved into the humid cold.

After last night's deliberation, I'd decided to go with S&P futures—a leveraged approach to trading the S&P 500. *Less to monitor.*

A quick examination of the latest price charts confirmed for me what I'd already suspected. Considering yesterday's high, and with the market at such lofty heights, I needed to wait for prices to dip—enough of a dip to trip my divergence indicator, which was nothing more than a short-term moving average juxtaposed against a longer one. So when the market resumed its upward move, I would be automatically stopped in at the safest place, statistically speaking.

However, if the market continued to dip after I was on board, I would be automatically stopped out below the price bar of the previous day. Sure, I would have lost some money, but I also would have saved enough money to fight another day. Just as I'd told those students five years before, the disciplined approach to this system would yield a profit, but only if I could weather the occasional losses.

When asked why she posted her secrets of swing trading for the whole world to see, multimillionaire Market Wizard and accomplished violinist to boot Sarah Taylor only laughed. "I could disclose all my secrets—publish them in the *New York Times* for that matter—and it wouldn't make a difference. Knowing what to do is worthless. It takes the emotions of Spock to compete in this world."

Larry arrived at six o'clock, stood in my doorway for a moment, wearing a sophisticated charcoal suit with a silly tie that appeared to have been finger painted by toddlers. I leaned back in my squeaky office chair and grinned at my dazed partner.

He shrugged, yawned casually, and headed for his own office. As usual, we performed most of our duties with the minimum of interaction. Larry remained knee-deep in tax consulting while I carefully screened phone calls, sold our tax services to new wealthy clients, answered e-mails, and monitored the Web site.

At eleven, I called Dacotah Bank, talked to Matt Goeman, an old high school acquaintance, and arranged for a two-o'clock meeting.

"I'm taking a late lunch," I informed Larry without explaining further. He grunted with indifference. When the mail arrived, I sifted through it and discovered another round of letters from the IRS. The hazard of operating a tax service turned out to be getting very familiar with the tax enforcers.

I placed all the letters on Larry's desk.

"What do you need the money for?" Matt asked me, after we'd dispensed with a minute's worth of informalities. He was my age, thirty-six, and while he'd lost most of his dusty brown hair, he was still in denial, carefully combing it over the thinning area on top.

His office was starkly decorated with sheer white curtains on the windows, shiny veneer coating the desk, and industrial blue carpet covering the floors. Against one wall was a small bookshelf. His expansive desk, like mine, was nearly empty of pencils, pens, or paper.

"Business capitalization," I replied. Technically, it was true.

"For the company?"

"Not the partnership."

"So, it's . . . for you personally?"

"A side business," I replied calmly without expounding further.

Matt stared blankly at me. And then, in the absence of any forthcoming explanation, his gaze dimmed. "Stephen . . ."

I swallowed and plunged forward. "I'm providing my house as collateral."

"After your second refinance, there's not much left."

"All I need is twenty thousand dollars."

Matt leaned back in his chair, but not so far back he couldn't tap a pencil eraser on the edge of his desk. The chair squeaked as he adjusted his position. He regarded me curiously: "Are you going to trade with this money, Stephen?"

That's the problem with a small town. Everyone knows your past and assumes your future. Your personal mistakes are etched upon the stone of their memories.

"Short-term investing," I told him.

"I see," he said with a note of finality.

"There's plenty of equity in my house," I repeated. "I'm good for it, Matt."

"I know you are," he replied. "And we're pleased with your loan history, but we're also familiar with your personal history. I can't do this loan, Stephen. I'd lose my job."

Just like that, the meeting was over. He walked me to the door and patted me on the shoulder. I expected him to say: *Get some help, Stephen.* Instead, he said, "I was sorry to hear about you and Donna."

I repeated my pat answer. "She's a wonderful woman. We're working it out."

Matt nodded patronizingly. Most likely he'd heard a different story.

Hugging myself against the cold, I walked the three blocks back to the office. Undaunted and seated behind my desk again, I proceeded with Plan B. I picked up the phone and dialed my credit card company. Despite the bank experience, I figured my chances were modest to good. When I reached a customer service rep, I presented my request for a home equity line of credit.

They put me on hold. Two minutes later, the rep returned with good news. Although the interest rate and fees were ridiculous, the loan was readily approved. I downloaded the documents, then scanned in my signature. According to the rep, I'd have access to thirty thousand dollars in a matter of days, deposited automatically in my bank account. From there, I'd wire it to my broker. That, plus the margin—another fifty percent of account total—would bring my total trading capital to forty-five thousand. More than enough to begin.

It was seven when I left Larry at the office and headed for Joe's, promising myself an hour and no more. Paul was sitting at our usual table, staring up at the TV, watching ESPN scores scroll across the bottom of the screen. When he saw me, his face lit up. "Buddy!"

Sitting down, I felt a roomful of eyes on my back. Paul cleared his throat. "So . . . was it forgetting the party?"

I sighed, then recited my now oft-repeated speech. After nearly half an hour of Paul's inebriated responses to the collapse of my marriage, he finally gave it a rest.

Bracing myself, I nodded toward his glass. "How're we doing here?"

I felt like a parent monitoring a child, but Paul only grinned. "I'm stopping at three."

I asked about Susan.

"Haven't seen her," Paul said.

"Maybe it's true love?"

Paul smiled sluggishly. "And maybe statistical probability doesn't exist."

After that comment, I debated whether to tell Paul about my new stock-market activities. Since I hadn't even told Larry yet, I decided against it. Instead, we discussed the latest sports news.

Half an hour later, I stood to my feet. "Gotta go, Mr. Mole."

Paul's eyes looked pained. "So soon, Mr. Loon?"

I hesitated. "Three, right?"

"I promise! Relax, Dad."

I grinned and headed out. On the way home, I thought of Susan again and her last remarks. *"I'm getting out."* Maybe she'd finally found the true romance she'd been seeking for twenty years. I sincerely hoped so.

Later that evening, in front of a cable sports recap, I was eating a TV dinner—something chickenlike in texture but without the familiar taste—when Donna finally called. It had been a week and a half since she'd left.

At first, hearing her voice on the phone startled me. "Is everything okay?" I asked.

"Fine," she said, and then asked about me.

"Same," I replied, trying to read the tone in her voice. I asked about her job and about Sally and we made small talk for a few minutes as if she'd never left, as if she were sitting across the table from me.

I wish you'd come home, I was tempted to blurt.

"How is Alycia?" I asked instead.

"Still navigating through the maze of junior high society," she replied. "Stephen . . ."

"I miss you, Donna."

The line went silent. I heard her clear her throat. "Stephen . . . I'm going through with it. I'm filing for divorce."

I felt a shudder go through my soul. "So soon?"

"I'm sorry, but . . . isn't it pointless to drag this out further?"

I began to gently argue. I asked her to take more time, but she refused. I told her I still loved her, but her voice only turned cold. I asked her to consider Alycia's situation, but she told me she had.

"You've talked to her?"

"I don't have to, Stephen."

While harboring a small hope in my heart, I finally gave in.

We proceeded to discuss the fair division of our property, which, considering our impoverished state, progressed without argument. I mentioned the seven thousand again. After acquiring the loan, I'd decided to follow through with my original intention of giving

Donna half of our savings. Her response was different than I'd expected. Apparently, a few days in Sally's apartment had registered. She softly acquiesced. "I guess that's only fair. . . ."

"Good," I said. "And don't you want child support?"

She sighed into the phone. "No."

We had carefully avoided the topic of custody, saving it for last. And then something occurred to me. Maybe she planned to move out of state, perhaps back to Kansas, hoping to avoid any judicial prohibition. Maybe that's why she'd been so eager to move out. I voiced the question as tactfully as possible.

A moment of silence passed. "I haven't ruled it out. But I'd discuss it with you first."

"I'm sure you've reviewed child custody law."

"So, let me get this straight. The moment I leave, you suddenly decide to become a father again?"

Her choice of words stung, and she apologized immediately. "I'm sorry, I didn't mean—"

"Give me another chance, Donna."

"Another chance . . ." Her words trailed off, but I detected some confusion in her tone.

"I meant . . . with Alycia."

"I know what you meant," she said, her voice rising.

I tried to sound as reasonable as possible, with no trace of defensiveness. "If I were a good father would you be taking her away?"

"I never said we were moving away."

"But . . . *would* you?"

She didn't answer, and I hoped she was thinking it through and not just getting angry.

"Give me a chance to prove myself," I repeated. "I don't care about joint custody, but I want to see my daughter."

"And I want you to see her, but she needs some time."

"One more chance," I repeated. "Just one more, and if I blow it, you can do what you want." As I said this, I felt a small shiver but dismissed it. *I can do this,* I reminded myself.

"Oh, Stephen . . ."

"Then you agree?" I asked, hoping she'd sensed a sure thing.

"I would never deny you the right to see your daughter."

"But you might move, right?"

She hesitated, and I repeated my offer.

After another pause, her tone turned conciliatory, "Okay, then."

I sighed with relief. The deal was done. If I blew it again, Donna had my permission to leave the state.

"One promise broken," she reminded me as we finished our discussion, and my heart constricted.

"I'll be there this Saturday," I said. "Will you have Alycia ready?"

"That's up to Alycia," Donna replied firmly. "She's already given you her answer."

"So, you're not—"

"I'm not going to make her. Have you seen how well that works?"

I had, and it wasn't pretty. Forcing Alycia to do something was like the old cliché about dragging a horse to water without getting the horse to drink. Only in Alycia's case, you couldn't drag her to the water or get her to drink it. Sometimes the mere suggestion would polarize her into the opposite course. On a regular basis, we employed reverse-reverse psychology, and even that was "iffy" at best.

I affected as polite a tone as I could muster. "Would you at least remind her?"

Donna paused. "I'll remind her, but that's it."

"Then I'll be there," I said cheerfully, as if Donna had actually agreed to something difficult.

"And if you're not?" she asked, driving the point home.

"We have a deal."

I hung up, and my spirits wavered. Donna's resolve seemed steely and determined, and she sounded more testy than I remembered. It was a side to her I couldn't recall, and I wondered if she needed to stay angry in order to pull this off. I also knew that in spite of my own determination, the odds were against me. One mistake, and Alycia would be moving to Kansas—the land of Dorothy, Toto, and the Cowardly Lion.

Down in my cave, I turned on the computer and pulled up some old trading files for further review. Now that I'd actually pulled the trigger, I decided to grant myself an exception, if for no other reason than to maintain confidence in my system.

According to my notes, thirty percent of the divergence instances resulted in significant profit while ten percent resulted in small yet positive outcomes. However, *sixty* percent of the instances resulted in losses, some small, some big, but not enough to derail the forty-percent profits—but only if the losses were taken quickly, according to plan.

It was two o'clock when I collapsed on the downstairs couch in my clothes.

Chapter Sixteen

By Friday midmorning, the market appeared set for another down day. Combined with the previous down days, yet still within the long-term rising moving average, another S&P dip would be significant enough to trigger my signal.

Larry and I ate our weekly lunch together, this time at the Sirloin Pit, just off Sixth Avenue. As usual, my steak-and-potatoes friend ordered . . . just that. I ordered a salad and a side of corn.

"Have you talked to your wife?" Larry asked, placing the cloth napkin in his lap.

I informed him of last night's divorce discussion, and he seemed shocked. "Already? What about a trial separation? More counseling, perhaps?"

Despite my attempts to explain, for the duration of the meal, I subjected myself to Larry's gentle tirade—everything I was doing wrong, and everything I should be doing right. If he knew I was trading, he would have coughed his steak across the room.

I was surprised at his scorn, and tried several times to change the subject, to no avail. He acted as if he had something personally at stake in our marriage. I suppose his attitude might have been a clue for what would happen next, but looking back on the whole thing, Larry was the last person I would have suspected.

At the end of the meal, we drove back to the office in silence.

Settling back in my office, I put the lunch encounter behind me and tackled the meticulous tasks of accounting with gusto. By the end of the day, the market had indeed dropped enough to trigger an entry signal. Placing a stop above the day's high, I was now ready for Monday's opening, back in the probability business at last, heady with anticipation, but dog-tired.

On Saturday morning, with yet another night on the couch behind me, I awoke early. After showering and shaving, I took a morning drive to Richmond Lake, inflicting myself with a worst-case-scenario talk in preparation for the humiliation of sitting in front of Sally's apartment waiting for an absent Alycia. *Pay your dues,* I thought, adjusting my expectations to zero.

Driving back, I stopped at McDonald's and ordered a breakfast sandwich. When I asked the clerk to hold the egg and sausage, she stared at me.

"Like a grilled cheese sandwich," I said, smiling.

They held them but included a hash-brown wafer by mistake, which I discarded. I'd long since developed an intolerance for fried foods, and I'd never liked eggs. Besides, it was the coffee I was after, and while Donna had always ignored my nutritional hypocrisy, Alycia was all over it—especially when I'd conveniently forget to order French fries on family vacations. "So Dad . . . when did coffee become a health food?"

I arrived at nine-fifty, pulled into a fortuitously empty parking space in front of Sally's apartment, several cars to the south of Donna's minivan, and debated whether to buzz the apartment. The streets had received a dusting of snow the night before, creating a nostalgic winter wonderland. The stark tree branches were fuzzy white, as if someone had tossed white cotton at sticks coated with honey.

If Alycia showed up today, I would be amazed. I wasn't even prepared for the possibility. What would we do? Where would we go?

At ten o'clock, I walked up the sidewalk to the rust-stained stucco building. I read the old apartment list, then buzzed Sally's apartment intercom.

Donna's voice came on immediately. "I'm sorry, Stephen. She's not here."

"I'll wait, then."

"In the cold?"

I shrugged as if she could see me. "In the car," I replied. "Did you remind her?"

A moment passed, then "Yes," and a static click.

Back in the car, I settled in for what I assumed would be an hour of uninterrupted study. Pushing my seat back, I began rereading *Reminiscences of a Stock Market Operator,* the classic story of one man's stock-trading adventures. An occasional turn of the key to start the engine and heater kept me from turning into an ice block.

Thirty minutes later, I was interrupted by a soft rapping on the window. It was Donna, wearing gray sweats beneath a long maroon coat.

I pressed the power button to lower the window, and Donna leaned in. The interior of my car was immediately graced with the scent of lavender cologne, her favorite, with a touch of apple shampoo. I was startled by her appearance. She must have lost ten pounds. Her damp blond hair was tied back, and her lips looked ashen.

"I'm sorry," she said. "But I warned you."

"I'm not complaining." I reached in my back pocket, removed my wallet, and pulled out the check for thirty-five hundred dollars. I handed it to her. She examined it without expression, then folded it and shoved it into her coat pocket. Our eyes locked for a moment, and she looked away.

"Would you give her a message for me?" I said, squelching the lump in my throat.

Donna raised her eyebrows skeptically, and that gesture alone surprised me. Not because I hadn't seen it before, but because I could see myself already forgetting her mannerisms.

"Just tell her I'll be back next week at the same time."

Donna gave me a feeble smile and nodded, then pushed away from the car. I watched her walk up the sidewalk and even that seemed new to me somehow, as if I hadn't seen her in years, not days.

I went home and read the afternoon away—one of Donna's favorite classics: *The Pearl.* In the evening, Larry called. "Doing anything?"

"Licking my wounds from our last encounter."

Larry cleared his throat and rambled something about working too long and getting irritable. Even his apology had a lecturing tone.

"Truce?" I asked.

"Truce," he agreed.

We went to a movie, a comedy. While I found it amusing, and while other people on all sides of us were in stitches, Larry never laughed once. The prospect of ordering his favorite snack, popcorn, failed to cut through his gruffness.

When I got back home, my phone light was blinking. I answered it and found a message from my mother, inviting me out for lunch tomorrow. "Better yet, Stephen. Come to church. Your father is pinch-hitting for Tom Northrup."

I knew Tom as the Sunday school teacher at the local Lutheran church, but I was surprised they had begun attending there on a regular basis.

Just thinking about it raised my ire. My mother adored the Pentecostal church in Aberdeen, and it represented one more example of how Mom's entire life had become subservient to my father's self-centered agenda.

Grandpa's church isn't as painful as Mom's, Alycia once muttered from the backseat on a rare Sunday visit to Frederick. Donna had glanced at me accusingly, saying nothing, but the message was obvious: Alycia's lukewarm spiritual state was my fault.

It was still early when I called Mom back. She responded to my voice as if the president was on the line. "Hello, Stephen!"

"When does the service begin?"

"Eleven," she answered hopefully. I hadn't attended church with my parents in several years, mostly due to Donna's participation in the choir at her own church, a handy excuse for me. "Your father is teaching the Sunday school at nine," my mother said, repeating her phone message.

"I won't make it to that," I said. Listening to my father teach would have been unbearably over the top for me.

"That's fine," she said.

Years ago, I'd come partially clean with my mother. "I'm not much into institutional Christianity."

She'd smiled quickly. "Neither was Jesus."

I decided to quit while I was ahead, especially since she seemed to forgive my haphazard church attendance. Perhaps she preferred to overlook the obvious, seeing only what she wanted to see.

After hanging up, I considered my apparel options, which meant traipsing back into the bedroom Donna had completely vacated—the books were now gone.

In the closet, I discovered a gray suit, then considered my collection of ties. I've rarely met the man who didn't depend on his wife for specific clothing guidance, and while I wasn't half bad in helping Larry with his tie selection, choosing one for myself revealed a glaring blind spot. Even now, Donna's instructive voice echoed in my ear: *"Wear the blue tie with your white shirt. Wear the gold-and-silver tie with your cream color."*

I couldn't recall how many times Donna remarked to me, at least during the early years: "You're going out in public dressed like that?"

"Of course not," I'd reply,. grinning. "Just testing you."

Donna would lead me back to the closet, and with a supportive pat on my arm, help me pick out some combination that would "dazzle my prospects."

"Maybe I'm cutting my own throat here," she told me after I had redressed, "but you look positively delicious in those slacks, ol' sport!" Then she laughed. "Just don't look any woman in the eyes!"

"Yeah," I replied wryly. "Real danger there."

Donna grabbed my tie, tightening it to my neck. "You don't think women notice you?"

I raised a skeptical eyebrow.

"We women are surreptitious about our 'noticing,'" she explained. "On the other hand, you guys practically foam at the mouth in the presence of long hair and legs."

She patted my chest and pecked my cheek. "But that's okay," she added, brushing my shoulders. "As long as you don't know you're cute, we're safe."

Despite our fair share of arguments over the years, we never quarreled about money. *"It's the most corruptive force on the planet,"* Donna once told me, a feeble attempt to console me over my trading failures. She'd lost two of her local friends defending my reputation, but she never looked back.

"Good riddance," she said, referring to them. "You made a mistake. You're paying it back. You could have declared bankruptcy, but you didn't, and I'm proud of you."

Eventually, Alycia discovered the secret. And while she'd heard rumors about her father at school, she hadn't stormed in the house and confronted me. Perhaps by that point, bad news about her father didn't surprise her, especially since my pedestal days were long gone. Could I blame her? It's no wonder Alycia had lost admiration for dear old Dad—what with learning about Alice, living with insidious poverty, and experiencing the slow disintegration of her family's reputation.

While the financial court judgment weighed on our shoulders, Donna had carried on with courage, taking a second job without complaining.

"Don't we have plenty of food?" she once asked. "A roof over our head? Loyal friends?" She snuggled up beside me on the couch. "And don't we have each other?"

I remembered pulling her closer, kissing her cheek, immensely grateful for her loyalty and determined to become a better man for it.

At the time, I think Donna saw my failure as an opportunity, not a tragedy—a chance to draw closer, to gain strength from each other, and maybe even save our marriage.

Instead, it seemed to take what little we had left and tear it all apart.

Chapter Seventeen

The following day, Sunday, I awakened at five o'clock, my stomach in knots. I completed my morning routine, eating Alycia's three-month-old stale Cheerios, and absorbing three cups of coffee.

At ten-thirty I headed north to Frederick, on Highway 20, slowing my pace when it appeared I was ahead of schedule. My parents lived next to the parsonage across from a weed-infested former football field. The white wooden church raised its traditional steeple only a few blocks away.

I parked in the side parking lot, along with twenty or so older sedans. A handful of new cars stood out like a bald spot on a teenager. Pastor Neall, a brown-haired young man wearing the standard vestments, greeted the parishioners as they entered the sanctuary.

"You must be Stephen," he said to me, shaking my hand firmly. Apparently he'd snoozed our previous meetings, at least three of them by my count, and my mother must have alerted him to this one. Next he introduced me to an usher who closed the door behind me as I entered the sanctuary. I was surprised by the attendance. The small room was packed. *Where do they all come from?*

My mother, sitting next to my father on an oak pew in the second row, discreetly twisted in her seat and waved me up. "You made it just in time," she whispered enthusiastically after I'd squeezed in between several seated parishioners, feeling their eyes on my back.

Dad nodded in my direction. After we sang an assortment of hymns and echoed a few responsive readings, my mother leaned over. "For some reason, I thought you might bring Alycia," she whispered.

I was tempted to retort, *Last time I checked, hell hadn't frozen over,* but Mom wouldn't have appreciated it. *In that context, Stephen, "hell" is a swearword,* she would say primly.

Recently, when I had mentioned that Alycia had developed a "bit of disdain" for good ol' Dad, she'd only laughed. "Oh, Stephen, that's normal for a teen girl. It'll pass." Of course, I'd left out clarifying details, mainly that Alycia and her mom were as close as ever.

After the sermon, the congregation began filing out, and my father's patented smile made its first appearance. He moved ahead of us, slapping one back after another. My mother grabbed my arm and introduced me to several older ladies in elaborate hats. By now the entire room had acquired a pre-nursing-home aroma. Eventually, we worked our way outside.

"We're going out," Mom broadcast to everyone within earshot. "My son is here."

I suppressed a smile. To Mom "going out" meant visiting the café on Main Street. She couldn't have appeared pretentious if she tried. On the other hand, my father suppressed a growing scowl behind his glistening good ol' boy smile, frustrated with my mother's social naïvety.

We drove in Dad's blue LeSabre Buick. He took a circuitous route, pointing out nearly every house along the way, making idle commentary I'd heard countless times. Six blocks later, we parked on Main.

"I've been trying to get your father to go to the doctor," Mom said as I held open the car door. Entering the restaurant, I stood at the door while Dad ambled by, and Mom squeezed my arm on the way in, affectionately reinforcing her appreciation for my company. "Last time he went to the doctor, Nixon was president," she murmured to me.

Sliding into a booth by the window overlooking the street, Dad grunted and grabbed the white canister of salt.

"I think this is someone else's booth," I said, noticing a bowl of hard-boiled eggs.

"I have no use for those Me Deities," Dad said, his tag for medical doctors. He grabbed an egg and sprinkled a generous portion of salt over it.

"Dad, that's—"

Mom patted my shoulder. "Standing order, honey."

I stepped back as she slipped into my side of the booth.

"We're here every Sunday. Twelve-thirty on the dot. Finally got 'em trained," Dad mumbled through a mouthful. He pushed the bowl toward me. "Here, try one."

I smiled, shook my head, and glanced at my watch. No wonder we'd taken the long route. It was exactly twelve thirty-one.

"C'mon, ain't gonna hurt you."

Mom, wearing the kind of floral pattern outfit I'd always associated with ancient spinsters and kindly grandmothers, leaned her elbows on the Formica table. "Stephen doesn't eat eggs."

Dad frowned. "Since when?"

Since age five, I thought.

Dad shook another aggressive layer of salt over the half-eaten egg, and Mom rolled her eyes. "Can't get him to eat my rhubarb pie, but don't take away his salt!"

"That's because it's sour rhubarb," I said, accidentally aligning myself with Dad. He grunted his approval, and I was forgiven for my personal eating preferences.

Dad bit into another egg. "Ever call a doctor by his first name?"

I resigned myself to another retelling.

"He gets this offended look, as if I slapped 'im or something."

"Some doctors are women," my mother replied.

Dad leveled a finger at her, the one still grasping the beveled white saltshaker. "They ain't sticking nothin' up my—"

"There's a reason for that," my mother interrupted.

Dad snorted. "It's symbolic of what they're doing to this entire country."

Mom forced a smile, but her sweet sensibilities were being stretched to the limit. "Don't be crude, dear."

Dad chuckled, catching my eye.

Mom patted her upper stomach area. "He has pain in his . . ." She stopped when she caught his warning glance.

Dad grimaced. "I got pain, all right. I was born into pain."

"So what was your Sunday school lesson?" I asked, not caring in the least but hoping to stem the inevitable outcome of his previous thought.

Mom answered for him. "Romans something."

"'I do what I wish I didn't,'" he said, paraphrasing it. "The only verse in the Bible that makes complete sense to me."

Mom sighed, and our conversation meandered along similar lines. Dad had a penchant for biblical paraphrasing. As far as he was concerned, the apostle Paul had it right: Women should keep quiet in church, not to mention everywhere else. He also launched in on his theory regarding Paul's thorn in the flesh.

Mom fidgeted nervously, then patted my hand. "Just for the record, Stephen, Pastor Neall does not agree."

"What does he know?" Dad asked derisively. "He only went to Bible college, not seminary."

When our waitress arrived, Dad ordered ham and scrambled eggs. Mom settled on a salad, and I ordered a turkey sandwich.

"You'll like it," Dad assured me.

Halfway through our meal, we were interrupted by an older gentleman pausing by our table.

"Wally, you ol' duffer," my dad exclaimed. "Whadya know? Anything?"

Wally chuckled slyly, brushing our table with his knuckles. My dad grabbed his hand, and you would have thought Wally was a visiting VIP. I waited for the inevitable transition to the stock market, followed by the deft handing over of his business card, *How's your investment portfolio working for you?* before I remembered my father was retired.

"How's that looker of yours?" Dad asked Wally.

"Getting hitched," Wally replied proudly, adjusting imaginary lapels.

"She finally picked someone out of the dozen or so trying to court her?"

Wally laughed. "I was gettin' tired of loading the shotgun. First thing ya know, one gets through the fence, and another into the chicken house, and it's all over."

After another ten minutes of this kind of repartee, Wally tipped his Amoco cap. "Y'all have a good one," he said before turning away.

Dad's expression soured immediately and he took another bite. "Food's cold, thanks to that blowhard." He snorted. "Have you seen his daughter?"

I shook my head.

"Let's put it this way," Dad said, shoving a piece of ham into his mouth. "I'd rather marry a horse!"

"Be nice, dear," Mom said.

"An ugly horse at that!" He laughed. "There's only one reason guys were hanging around, if you catch my drift." He winked at me as if I needed the signal.

"Jesus loved Mary Magdalene," my mother replied.

"But he didn't have to marry her!" Dad said, breaking into a guffaw. And then he winked again.

Mom's face fell. Still chuckling, Dad caught her expression. "C'mon, it's a joke."

"It isn't funny," she replied. "It's irreverent."

"Okay, okay," he said, coaxing her smile back.

Mom gave me a *what-can-you-do* face.

Dad nodded at me. "So . . . how you doin'?"

"I'm fine," I replied.

"Probably better'n ever," he said. "Free and easy, and on the prowl!"

Another loud guffaw as my mother closed her eyes and shook her head with chagrin. I remembered when Dad had congratulated me on our tenth anniversary. *"Ten is the cutoff,"* he'd proclaimed. *"Your marriage is now a success, no matter what happens next."*

Mom touched my hand. "How's Alycia?"

"Spunky," I replied.

"Divorce is very hard on the kids," she said, shaking her head.

"You got a while?" Dad asked between chews.

"He wants to show you his new toy," Mom replied.

"I have to get back."

He nodded quickly. "Sure you do. Of course. My son is a busy man."

"It's a computer," she added. "An IBM."

"Welcome to the future, Dad."

"He could use a few pointers," Mom said, eyeing me conspiratorially.

"He's got to get back," Dad said, his voice rising. "There's always tomorrow."

"Not if you don't see the doctor," Mom said.

Dad grimaced at me. "If it ain't one thing, it's—"

"Tell him, Stephen," Mom said.

"Don't bother, Dad," I said. "They only want your money."

"That's what I think!"

"Oh, Stephen," Mom said. "You and your father could be twins."

Dad gave her a sideways grin. "But I'm the better-lookin' one."

A rare and momentary lull fell over us, and I resisted glancing at my watch. Dad fixed me with a pointed look. "You ain't tradin', are you, Stephen?"

I hesitated. "Stick a fork in me, Dad."

Dad frowned. "Wha—?"

Mom leaned over. "He means he's done."

"Good for you," he replied. "Ain't no one makes money trading. Only idiots trade. Worse'n gambling. Or drinking. They're all 'tradaholics.' I say, know your limitations. Buy and hold, son. Stick with mutual funds."

He launched off on the glory days of his stock brokering, and I braced myself for his revision of history. Maybe it's what he had to believe in order to sleep at night. "I helped many a soul prepare for retirement," he declared.

I couldn't remember a single one.

"I knew I had a winner when I found Cisco . . ." he said, then launched off on another diatribe. "Trading is for suckers, Stephen. People who want a fast buck and don't have the discipline for long-term investing."

We'd been talking over empty plates for ten minutes when Dad stood up and left for the bathroom.

I rubbed at the exhaustion in my eyes.

"Your father talks about you all the time, Stephen," Mom said. "You should come by. He'd be on cloud nine for days."

"I'll try to find the time."

"Is it so hard?" Her gaze was unflinching.

I sighed and stood up. Mom's eyes wilted with disappointment. Dad was already out, tucking his shirt in. He extended his hand. "So soon?"

I shrugged, smiling pleasantly, shaking his hand.

"Well, don't be such a stranger. Keep your chin up."

"I'll try."

He put an arm on my shoulder, and I resisted the urge to tense up. He whispered what he must have thought was an encouraging word. "Your failures don't matter to me, son."

When I walked out, I felt my entire body decompress. I could only imagine what he was telling Mom. *Ungrateful idiot, losing a wonderful woman like that! Does he think he can do better? And that daughter of his? What a grouch!*

When I reached sunny Main Street, I realized my car was parked three blocks away, back at the church.

No matter. I needed the exercise.

On the way back to Aberdeen, I pushed in a Bill Douglas CD, another of Donna's favorites. She'd always ignored its pagan flavor, once declaring: "All good music is an intimation of the Divine," to which Alycia had perked up in the backseat. "Does that mean *Eczema* is of God?"

"Eczema?" Donna asked. "You mean . . . the rash?"

"Mom!" Alycia was hurt. "The band!"

"Oh."

Alycia harrumphed in the backseat.

I winked at her in the rearview mirror. "Besides, we were talking about good music."

She gave me a squinty smirk, the one that meant, *The gloves are off, Dad, and considering the musical cheese reeking from in your office, you don't stand a chance. You're a sitting duck for my superior talents.* She even flexed her pincher fingers to reinforce the point.

Now I smiled wistfully. As the first piece, "Feast," filled the silence, I felt my nerves decompress and my optimism return. A hybrid of classical, improvisational jazz, choir, with a touch of New Age, *Songs of Earth and Sky* filled my occasional need for contemporary highbrow. Even Alycia enjoyed these pieces—although she wouldn't have admitted it to save her soul.

Chapter Eighteen

On Monday, the market nudged upward, hitting my entry stop. I was now in, but it didn't last long. On Tuesday, the employment report was released, the numbers fell short of expectations, and the market overreacted. By noon, the Dow had dropped one hundred fifty points, the NASDAQ thirty, and the S&P ten. By one o'clock, I was sitting on a loss of fifteen thousand dollars, hovering close to my stop loss.

My hands were clammy and my heart thudded as if I were walking along the edge of a skyscraper.

I vacillated all morning. One moment: *Pull the plug!*

The next: *Follow the system.*

Back and forth it went: *You can't afford to start out with a loss. Just get out and clear your head!*

No! Stay in! Forget the profit. Do the right thing. Go down with the ship if you have to.

According to Michael Wiggins, another famous Market Wizard: *Great traders know when to deviate from their system.*

Was it already time to change course? Surely not. Finally, out of desperation, I disconnected from my real-time data feed and tried to bury the impending disaster with correspondence and report preparation. I muddled through until 5:00 P.M. when I couldn't resist any longer. I navigated to the Web site, pulled up the day's close, and waited for a ton of bricks to bury me.

I was stunned. The market had done a complete reversal. The DOW was *up* one hundred points, and the NASDAQ and S&P were sitting on modest increases. I sat back and pondered this. Either the latest media guru had reassured the market, or cooler heads had prevailed.

Despite my better judgment, I pulled up my personal account and counted my money. I was back to even. A profound wave of well-being permeated every cell of my body. I'd dodged a bullet, and although I hadn't made a cent yet, I felt flush. I'd stayed the course. Not quite the nerves of Spock, but close enough.

That evening, at home, I watched the business news. "The market appears more resilient to bad news than we thought," the anchor announced. "According to the prevailing consensus, the market is poised to go higher."

As it turned out, the pundits were right. During each of the next three days, the NASDAQ, the Dow, and the S&P closed higher, all on higher volume. By the end of the week, due to the miracle of leverage, I was sitting on eighty thousand, having nearly doubled my account in two weeks. Better yet, according to the statistical patterns of market volume acceleration, a reliable indicator of institutional conviction, the market was bound to go higher. A lot higher.

Eighty thousand was nothing to sneeze at, but it wasn't a million dollars, and it wouldn't pay off my debts. Still, there was no denying it: my plan of redemption had kicked into gear.

Friday evening, I went to Joe's for the first time in a week.

"Welcome, stranger," Paul said as I sat down. "Thought we'd lost you."

"Busy," I replied, noticing his right hand's strangle grip on the beer mug, as if he was afraid someone might abscond with it. As usual, I wondered how many he'd had.

Paul either read my mind or my inquiry had become habitual. "This is my first. So chill."

I wanted to ask, *Would Jennifer corroborate your story?* but decided against it. No point starting out on the wrong foot.

"So. Seriously," he said, grinning. "What have you really been doing?"

"Fielding calls from George Soros," I said.

Paul looked surprised. "You in the market?"

"Hand over fist."

He blew out a quick, "Hmmm."

Then, "Guess who's back?" he said, nodding his head toward the counter. Nestled within a row of regulars was Susan's usual stool—empty at the moment, but I got the message.

"Walked in just before you got here," he said. "Probably in the bathroom."

My spirits fell. I'd been hoping for a wedding invitation. "She okay?"

He shrugged.

"Let's invite her over."

Paul raised an eyebrow. "I'm not paying for her drinks."

"Fine," I said. "I will."

"Oh, great. I'll look cheap."

I removed a twenty-dollar bill, folded it into my hand, and stealthily slipped it to him. "Here."

He grimaced, his eyes glancing furtively around the room. "Yep, not a soul saw that little exchange."

"Don't call her Lonely Hearts," I said.

"Why not?"

"Her name is Susan."

Paul considered this. "How 'bout 'Suzer Loser'?"

"It's your nose."

"You must be sitting on a loss," Paul retorted. "You go short again?"

Susan accepted our invitation, surrendering her prime spot at the bar. The three of us made casual conversation for an hour, during which no one mentioned her unexpected return nor my impending divorce, but the overly flirtatious, high-energy Susan had disappeared. Instead, we saw the lonely, vulnerable version of our eternal cheerleader. The most animated remark came when I made a solidarity comment regarding the overall unreliability of the male species. "Tell me about it!" she shot back.

I couldn't help noticing the lingering vacancy in her eyes. These days, it seemed to take longer and longer for her to recover from romantic disaster. To me, she seemed caught between two worlds. Because of her physical beauty, women didn't trust her, and yet because of her ditzy demeanor, most men saw her as little more than a sex object.

"I'm still a virgin," she'd once said to me several years ago. "Emotionally, I've never been touched."

The three of us were a regular lonely hearts club, retelling stories from the past, gossiping about the present, ignoring the future. Eventually, Paul stood up and shuffled to the men's room, leaving us alone.

"You know what I've always wanted to do?" she said.

I smiled, encouraging her to continue.

"Run a restaurant, or something. Maybe catering." She said it almost dreamily, as if searching for anything to improve her sense of hope. "I'm sorry to hear about you and Donna," she finally said. I gave her the shortened version, unprepared for her response. Her eyes glistened. "If you and Donna can't make it, there's not much hope for me."

I found myself wondering how Donna would have counseled Susan. Obviously, Donna's stringent rules forbade her to ever set foot in a place like this. Because of that, the kind of encouragement Donna might have shared would never have reached Susan's ears.

"You're too good for this dump, Susan," I finally said, a feeble attempt to play Donna. "You're fishing on the wrong side of the tracks."

Susan blew out a breath. "That's where you're wrong, Stephen, cuz I'm done with fishing."

After a few moments, she sighed heavily, reached down, and grabbed her purse. "Say good-bye to Paul, okay?" Her voice was tear-stricken.

"Where are you going?"

She shrugged. "Home."

"Will you be okay?"

"I'm a rock, Stephen," she said, patting the top of my head as a good-bye. I grabbed her hand, stopping her progress, and she gave me an unconvincing smile.

"Tell me the truth."

"I mean it," she said. "I'll be fine."

"Promise me."

Another grin, this one convincing. "I *promise.*"

I let her go. When Paul came out he confronted the empty chair. "Gone?"

I nodded.

He sat down and pondered her absence.

"Any change left?" I asked.

"What about the holder's fee?"

"Fine," I said, narrowing my eyes. "Keep it, but—"

"I'll apply it to rent," he said, reading my suspicions.

On Saturday, I was parked in front of Sally's apartment by nine-fifty-five, sipping coffee from a large Styrofoam-enclosed container, and reading the IBD newspaper. Beside me on the passenger seat rested three market books and a blue spiral notebook. A recent warm spell had melted the snow, but the weather report called for another blizzard. I walked up to the building and pushed the buzzer.

"She's not here," Donna replied over the tinny intercom.

"Just checking in," I said and wandered back to the car.

At ten-thirty, Donna strolled out, wearing jeans that seemed too baggy on her thinning frame, and a blue sweater. Her arms were crossed defensively across her chest. I rolled down the window, and she peeked in, holding her blond hair away from her eyes. I smelled lavender again, the scent I'd long taken for granted.

"I've been thinking, Stephen," she began. "This is silly. Why don't I just call you when she's ready?"

I gave her a knowing grin. "Nice try."

"Forget the deal, Stephen," she said. "We're not moving away."

"I don't have anything better to do on a Saturday morning," I said.

She pursed her lips. "Did you get the legal papers in the mail?"

I nodded. I hadn't read them yet, but they waited for me on the kitchen counter. Donna pushed away from the car, and our eyes locked again. She seemed suddenly lost. She opened her mouth to speak, then seemed to think better of it. She forced a smile instead, and I gave her a little wave.

At eleven, I pulled away from the curb and headed home.

The market hit yet another high on Monday. On Tuesday it erased most of the previous day's gains, but on Wednesday it opened with an upside gap. By noon, all told, I was sitting on two hundred thousand dollars—a one-hundred-fifty-five-thousand-dollar profit.

I sat spellbound for nearly half an hour, examining my account. I was actually doing it. I was getting rich. Mentally, I pinched myself. *Hold on, big boy,* I cautioned myself. *You've got a LONG ways to go.*

One of a trader's biggest dangers was to become complacent, to take success for granted and to forget to take precautions. I'd done that once. I couldn't let it happen again.

At four, Larry's head bobbed in. "Busy?"

I shrugged. He closed the door behind him and sat in the rarely occupied chair by my desk. He seemed worried.

"What's wrong?" I asked.

His gaze flickered. "Alycia's here to see you."

"She's *here*?"

He nodded. "But, uh . . . she, uh . . . looks a little different. I'm just preparing you, okay? Don't freak."

Taking a deep breath, I followed Larry out of my office. Alycia was standing in the reception area, and I had to physically restrain my mouth from dropping open. In fact, I wasn't even sure it was my daughter.

Her face was powder white, with heavy black eye makeup and dark lipstick. She was wearing black nail polish, and her normally tight curls were needle straight.

This is December, I reminded myself. *Too late for Halloween.*

Her partial black T-shirt was covered by a black fishnet blouse, and I detected a flash of metal near her navel above a black miniskirt. Her normally tennis-shoe-clad feet were adorned with high black boots, and on top of everything else, she was wearing a long black trench coat hanging open, its silver clasps glinting on either side all the way down.

I recalled her recent plea to paint her room black. *"Gothic is in, Dad."*

I wasn't sure where to look, so I focused on her eyes. I was tempted to ask her if school had dropped its makeup code, then quickly realized she must have applied the makeup after classes.

"I forgot which office was yours," she said flatly, meeting my eyes with a trace of defiance.

My mind sorted through a multitude of different replies. Larry hovered by the window, looking out onto Main Street as if interested in the traffic.

"What's up?" I asked bravely.

She affected a casual expression, but her continuing eye contact was almost unsettling, as if she were scrutinizing me.

She cleared her throat, belying her nerves for the first time, and I noticed the dog tag around her neck. She stepped forward, extending her fist. Reflexively, I extended my own, and she dropped a key ring with a single key into my open palm.

"That was yours," she replied simply.

"Oh . . ." I said, realizing it was a key for the house. "Don't you want it anymore?"

"I don't need it, remember?"

I nodded, my spirits sinking. *She never intends to visit me?*

"How's school?" I asked.

She shrugged. "School's a bore."

My mind shifted through another dozen possible replies and questions, thinking better of each one, navigating carefully through the eggshells that seemed scattered in front of us.

"So . . ." I started, hoping something verbal would follow, like: *Will I see you this Saturday?* But nothing emerged.

"I have to go," she said, taking several small steps backward.

"Sure good to see you, kiddo," I said, then cringed. *Did I just say kiddo?*

She smirked, the first intimation of a smile since she'd arrived. Before I knew it, she was pushing through the glass door. Just like that, a wonderful opportunity slipped away. She started hopping down the steps, then, as if realizing hopping didn't quite mesh with the attire, slowed to a sauntering descent.

I turned around just as Larry exhaled. "That was a close one. I thought you were going to have a coronary."

"I did," I replied, opening my hand again, staring at the ring.

Larry chuckled. "She didn't come to give you that key."

I considered his statement. "So . . . did I pass?" I asked, still trying to erase the image of my ghoulish daughter.

"I'm not sure," Larry said, looking out the window. "There's always the possibility that she just wanted to see how you're doing."

He peered down toward the street again and then gestured for me to join him at the window. I moved to him and followed his gaze. What appeared to be a young man, equally black-attired, had his arms around Alycia.

"Apparently, she needed moral support," Larry said. "Know the guy?"

"Haven't a clue."

"So . . . she's dating."

"Apparently."

"He looks at least sixteen," Larry added. "Almost a foot taller than her."

"Thanks for the analysis," I muttered.

"Could be eighteen," Larry added. "Of course, Alycia herself looks four years older than her age."

Especially now, I thought.

Larry patted me on the shoulder before returning to his office. "Wake up and smell the hormones."

I stood at the window a moment longer before retreating to my own office.

That evening, I summoned the courage and called the apartment. Sally answered and I asked for Alycia. Minutes later, Donna came on the phone. "Stephen?"

"Sorry to bother you. I was trying to get Alycia."

"She won't come to the phone," Donna said coldly. "Why don't you give it a rest? You're accomplishing the opposite of what you want."

No kidding, I thought. "I need to talk to her."

"I'm not going to force her."

"Would you ask her again?"

I'd intended to talk to Alycia first, elicit some kind of assurances or promises regarding this boyfriend before I informed her mother. If I didn't, Alycia was likely to say, *No fair, Dad. You told on me. You broke our deal.*

According to Alycia, not coming to her first was tantamount to betrayal. Although I always told Donna in the end, it was usually after the fact, after the situation had been discussed and solved by us first. *"Mom always overreacts!"* Alycia had told me countless times. *"She gets mad, but you and I can talk about stuff."*

But since I couldn't get Alycia, I had to change course. Unfortunately, Donna didn't give me a chance. "I'm hanging up, Stephen. We've already had this discussion."

"Donna we need to tal—"

Click.

I stared at the phone. I couldn't believe it. Donna had never hung up on me before. In fact, she wasn't the type to hang up on anyone. Her deeply ingrained sense of courtesy and ethics prevented her from being rude, even to solicitors. Through the years, we'd often joked about her inability to freeze out a sales call.

I decided against trying again tonight. That evening, I fell asleep in front of the TV, an old boxing replay of Ali versus Foreman.

Chapter Nineteen

When I awakened on Saturday, I considered briefly throwing in the towel. Maybe Donna was right. Maybe my weekly vigil was accomplishing exactly the opposite of what I intended. What was to be gained by further alienating my daughter?

And yet, regardless of my frustration, I needed to talk to Donna about Alycia's boyfriend, dire consequences aside: *Thanks for telling on me, Dad! You certainly have a knack for ruining my life!*

I arrived at nine fifty-two, pulling up to the curb. By now the routine was starting to feel very familiar. I'd brought my usual books, including the IBD newspaper featuring the weekend market report.

I sipped my coffee, read the news, then about ten-thirty heard a rapping at the passenger window. It was Donna, wearing her maroon coat. Her eyes were shadowed, and I couldn't read her expression. I rolled down the window.

"Alycia's not here," she said, her voice flat.

She pushed off from my car, but I called after her, "Alycia has a boyfriend, Donna."

She wheeled around, shoving her hands into the pockets of her coat. "What are you talking about?"

She approached the car again, and I recounted Alycia's appearance at my office. In spite of the boyfriend news, Donna seemed just as shocked to hear that Alycia had stopped by to see me.

"He looks pretty old," I commented.

"They *all* look old," she countered, sniffing softly. The cold did that to her—it made her sniffle endlessly. *I'm allergic to winter,* she often joked. *Who isn't?* Alycia usually muttered.

"Did you know about him?" I asked her.

"No," she admitted.

"Donna . . ." I gestured to the passenger seat, "just get in the car, okay, so we can talk about this?"

Expelling a frustrated sigh, she opened the door, settling in. When she pulled the door shut, it didn't click fully. The scent of lavender was muted.

"So . . . what are we going to do?" I asked.

She crossed her arms quickly and glared at me. "Who's *we*?"

I hadn't expected her to make this easy. She had never been good at enforcing rules, and our separation obviously wasn't making it any easier. She stared straight ahead before putting her hand on the door handle. "I'll handle it."

"She'll lie, you know."

She released the door handle and glared at me. "Alycia doesn't lie."

"You'll need to forbid her to see him, Donna," I said.

"She'll defy me."

"Then I'll talk to her."

"Yep. That'll work." She expelled another sigh. Her eyes glistened in the reflection of sunlight off my windshield.

"She's only thirteen," I said.

"She had a training bra at eleven," Donna countered. "She looks, and acts, like a sixteen-year-old. Besides, I'm not the disciplinarian you were."

"Much good it did us," I muttered.

"It worked when you two were . . ." Donna's voice trailed off. She leaned back, closing her eyes. A moment passed before she spoke. "Is it so surprising, Stephen, that she would be looking for older male attention?"

Touché. "Is she home now?"

"No," she replied. "Alycia leaves the apartment just before you arrive."

I whispered the obvious. "To avoid me?"

Donna shrugged. "Maybe to avoid knowing whether you showed up or not."

My heart sank. What was the point? Donna was right. I was accomplishing the exact opposite of what I intended.

Donna reached toward the handle again, then hesitated. "But she asks me the moment she gets in, so that couldn't be it."

I could tell she was dying to get out. She turned again and gave me a piercing look. "I don't approve of this game of yours. Have I told you that?"

"Yes," I replied.

"I asked for a few months, that's all."

"You asked for a year," I said.

"Maybe a year is what she needs."

"By then, I'll have lost her."

Donna expelled an exasperated breath. "You should know better than that."

"I can do this," I insisted.

She narrowed her eyes, "Oh, really? Why now? What will make the difference this time?"

I didn't answer. As if sensing my struggle, Donna sniffed softly again.

"How's church?" I asked, hoping to veer our conversation to less stressful topics. My change of subject was clunky and obvious, and I expected her to answer, *None of your business,* or to ignore my question altogether. Instead, she gave me a dubious glance. "Loraine has dismissed me from the choir."

I was taken aback. Singing in the choir was one of Donna's few genuine enjoyments.

"Why?" I asked.

She gave me an incredulous expression. "You have to ask?"

Of course, I realized. *Divorce. The cardinal sin.* According to the official evangelical line, the church was filled with sinners saved by grace, but in reality, some Christians eat their own.

"It's the platform, Stephen," she continued. "We're being observed by others."

"So what are you going to do?" I asked.

"I deserve whatever I get," Donna said.

"No, you don't."

"I would expect you, a nonbeliever, to say that."

Neither of us spoke for a moment, and then she forced a chuckle. "But it's really absurd, you know. One half of the church can hardly stand to look at me anymore, and the other half, mainly the guys, have suddenly decided I exist. Even some married men are paying attention."

I looked at her, and she gazed back at me. I experienced a strange flutter of jealousy. "I don't blame them," I said. "I mean . . . you're an attractive woman."

It was, perhaps, the most patronizing thing I could have said, inappropriate to our discussion, and I half expected her to lay into me. Instead, she made a halfhearted pull on the knob, then stopped. The tone in her voice was full of subtle wonder. "I don't think you've ever said that to me." She looked away after she said it, perhaps embarrassed, but I touched her arm, and she visibly bristled.

I could think of dozens of times I'd marveled—aloud—at her attractiveness. Had she never heard, or had she refused to believe me? Unsure of what to say, and hoping to avoid another argument, I said nothing and removed my hand.

"Never mind." Donna opened the door and got out. Before pushing it closed, she placed her hand on the doorframe. "I'll talk to Alycia."

She granted me a small smile, and I watched as she put her hands in her pockets again and slowly trudged up the sidewalk.

I drove home in a fog as pieces of our conversation played over in my mind. *What will make the difference this time, Stephen?*

Hadn't I been asking myself the same question? If there was one thing I had learned in college Psych, it was that the river of human behavior reverts to its habitual groove.

At the moment I was sitting on one hundred fifty-thousand dollars in profit. So far, so good. Maybe I'd learned my lesson after all. Maybe the passage of time had eliminated my bad habits. *Sometimes an overflowing river cuts another furrow!*

But rarely, I admitted ruefully.

Even now that couldn't discourage me. Donna and I had actually conducted a reasonably civil conversation. I'd paid her a compliment, to which she'd responded favorably, but most important: *The moment she gets home, she asks if you came.*

By the end of market hours on Tuesday, the S&P was sitting at a record high above the fifty-day moving average, and according to the prognosticators, *The market is careening out of control.*

Obviously we were due for a significant slow-down. I reminded myself that while great traders let their profits run, they also know when to cash in their chips. So, according to my trading rules, I initiated a protective stop based upon a five-day moving average.

If and when the price closed below this average, I'd be stopped out. In addition, once the market hit my stop, it would indicate another divergence, setting up another potential entry point in spite of the fact that such an elevated position would be risky at best. The market needed to tread water for a while. Breathe a bit. And frankly, so did I. But regardless of my emotions, I planned to follow my rules to the T.

That evening, Donna called me. "I talked to her, Stephen. And you were right."

"How old is he?"

"Sixteen."

I winced. "Should be a crime."

"She'll be fourteen in April."

"Still."

"I don't think she told him her age."

"Did you tell her she can't see him?"

Donna cleared her throat. "Of course I did. But she wasn't happy with me—"

"Doesn't matter. You still have to—"

"I don't need your lectures on parenting, Stephen."

I paused, then asked, "Did she agree?"

Donna sighed. "Stephen, please . . ."

"What's his name?"

"What are you going to do?"

"Never mind," I replied. "Just tell me."

"You'll embarrass her, Stephen."

What do I have to lose? I thought. "Have you ever talked to her about, you know . . ."

"Sex?"

I exhaled again.

"Yes, I have," she said, sounding annoyed. "And we don't need to have this conversation. She's not having sex, okay? I know my daughter."

Well enough to know she was dating? I thought but didn't say. Before hanging up, I assured Donna I wouldn't embarrass Alycia. Reluctantly, Donna finally gave me the boy's name.

The next morning I called the principal and informed him of the situation. He was no help. "We can't be responsible for your children after school hours. That's your job."

On Wednesday, I borrowed Larry's car and drove over to Holgate Middle School, parking on a cross street near the entrance so only the front end of the car was visible. Like a spy, I donned sunglasses and ball cap and waited for my daughter to appear.

At three-twenty, she emerged from the front door wearing black again, this time without the face paint. She walked down the sidewalk with a Gothic girlfriend on each side, then stepped into a waiting car. I caught a glimpse of the young man in the backseat.

I considered stalking the car, then decided against it.

That evening, I called Donna again.

"It didn't take," I told her.

"How do you know?"

"Trust me," I said. "Do you want me to talk to her this time?"

"In what galaxy do you live?"

A moment of silence passed before she spoke again, her voice pinched. "I'm not good at this, Stephen. You should know that, but I'll do it because I have to. This is the kind of stuff that makes me very angry with you."

I tried to imagine the conversation. Alycia would probably fly off the handle if Donna didn't get it right.

"I'd help if you just let me."

She ignored my offer. "I wouldn't come this Saturday, if you catch my drift."

"Why?"

"Because you're liable to lose a car window."

"But—"

"She'll figure it out, Stephen."

For the next few days, the market ignored the prognosticators and continued its upward tear. My anxiety grew in direct proportion to its acceleration. My leveraged account had now ballooned to just over three hundred thousand dollars. Daily, I adjusted my trailing stop along the five-day moving average, determined to squeeze everything possible from this significant trend.

I had just finished plugging in my new price point when it suddenly hit me: I'd gone the distance. I had tamed the wild bull. I'd created a small fortune in a ridiculously short period of time.

On Saturday, once again, I waited in front of Sally's apartment. Remembering Donna's warning, I stayed wide awake, just in case

Alycia needed to express her anger in a physical fashion, although I couldn't imagine my little girl throwing a rock at my car.

I smiled to myself. *Maybe a rotten egg.*

However, as usual Alycia didn't show. Instead, Donna wandered out five minutes to eleven. She looked tired, even crabby. I rolled down the window, and she leaned in. "She's agreed not to see him anymore." Her voice was cold and stony.

"Is she okay?" I asked.

Donna shrugged. "Let's just say neither you or I walk on water anymore."

On Monday, my suspicions were confirmed. An extremely large-volume day resulted in minimal upward movement, a sign of impending doom for the present trend. I double-checked my stop. At some point in the following weeks, I was likely to see a downward break, also on higher volume. Then, after a couple of sell-off days, I might see a frantic return to the previous highs, only by that time the volume will have, in all likelihood, diminished considerably.

During the rest of the week, the market followed my prediction exactly, and on Wednesday, I was finally stopped out with three hundred thirty thousand dollars.

Suddenly financially liquid again, I called my broker and requested a small portion, a few thousand dollars, to be deposited in my bank. Considering my family's living conditions, I hoped Donna wouldn't refuse it. And just maybe, she'd get the message: *Things have changed.* There was still plenty left in my account to parlay into my ultimate goal: Millions! Enough to pay back everyone I'd wronged.

On Thursday and Friday the market came roaring back—on lower volume, just as I had foreseen. This part was tricky. While the market might resume its upward trajectory, thus popping my divergence stop, the odds of further trending at this lofty elevation above the fifty-day moving average was unlikely. If I did get stopped in, I needed to be prepared for a sudden precipitous drop.

Either way, I was ready, and since the market was significantly above the fifty-day moving average, I ruled out going short, betting on the market's decline. The probabilities were against it. Shorting would remain an option for much later, once the bull market had ended, but only when the price had closed significantly below the moving average.

As for short term, the market would probably range a bit. Most likely, the following weeks would be volatile, followed by a series of quiet weeks. If and when the market decided to resume its bull market run, I would be waiting for the next uptrend, setting my stop just above the fractal high of the slowly building price base.

Regardless of my predictive analysis, however, I set my present buy stop above the latest divergence, precisely following my system, just in case my speculative evaluation was wrong.

If I handled it correctly, I could ride the next wild bull into the stratosphere and get off just before it fell to earth.

Chapter Twenty

I sent another check to Donna, but she sent it back. Across the top, she wrote, *Where did this come from?* and below that: *We're making it fine, Stephen. Please don't go in debt just to help us.* She'd misunderstood, but could I blame her? I considered picking up the phone and telling her the truth, then reconsidered. I wasn't ready to go public with my trading activities—considering my last meltdown. Better to bide my time.

Through the remainder of December, the market merely churned in a narrow price range. I drove to Sally's every Saturday morning, waiting in my car for a full hour. While to others it might have seemed an exercise in futility, I considered it a test of my resolve and some small message to Alycia, hopefully to Donna as well. *I've changed.* I reframed it in my mind, continued to set my expectations to zilch, and eventually Saturday mornings simply became a relaxed time to read the paper . . . in the car with the engine running occasionally.

Donna didn't come down as often, although, a week before Christmas, she retrieved my gift for Alycia. After I had quizzed Donna regarding various gift options, she'd informed me, "Don't try to buy her something cool. Cool changes from week to week." So I purchased a gift certificate to Alycia's favorite clothing shop—at least her current favorite.

Two weeks before Christmas Day, my mother called, requesting my company. I agreed and arranged to spend half the day with my parents and the other half with Larry.

My time in Frederick went as expected. My mother fixed Christmas lunch, and my father complained about the toughness of the meat. Later, we opened presents and Dad complained about the color of his new sweater. "I said 'blue,'" he muttered. "Not *navy* blue."

"We'll exchange it," Mom said graciously.

I gave my father an expensive tie clip and some computer software. When he opened the package, his face fell.

Mom filled me in. "Your father gave away the computer."

"Oh," I replied.

"Too danged complicated," he muttered. "You got the receipt, right?"

I nodded.

"Good boy."

After we'd finished unwrapping our presents and Dad was momentarily out of the room, Mom pulled me aside. "Your father still won't see the doctor."

"'Nixon administration,'" I reminded her.

"He'll go if you go with him."

I wondered what Mom had been smoking. "I doubt it."

"Try."

Dad walked into the room. "My ears are burning." He stared at the Christmas tree. "That thing look crooked to you?"

Before either of us could answer, he'd crouched below the tree and begun adjusting the stand.

"Hey, Dad, let's go see the doctor."

Mom grimaced, obviously thinking my timing was off.

Without looking up, Dad replied, "I'll go to the doctor when Linda Svenson wears an A cup. And not a minute sooner."

"Lou!"

"There's your answer," I said to Mom, wondering who Linda Svenson was.

"Don't even ask, Stephen," she said quietly, reading my mind.

That afternoon, when I called to wish Alycia *Merry Christmas* on the phone, she was, as always, "unavailable." It was beginning to wear on me. The likelihood of regaining my daughter's trust or at least some kind of civility between us seemed unlikely, if not futile. At this point, I could only hope I would be invited to her high school graduation.

A month after the mini-correction, including several weeks of high volatility, the market began to settle down. Twice, it had charged like a bull at the old high, each time either falling short or gasping just after breaking the high. Since low-volume breakouts were suspect, I tightened my stops. I lost a little money during these ranging days—about ten thousand—but nothing to worry about. All normal, and all according to plan.

On February fifth, the thirteenth Saturday since I'd begun waiting for Alycia, I arrived by nine forty-five, reclined my seat, and promptly fell asleep. I awakened to the sound of soft rapping and peered through the condensation-clouded passenger window, expecting to see Donna. Instead, it was Alycia.

I turned on the engine in order to power the windows, bracing myself for the worst: *Would you just leave me alone! You're ruining my life!*

I glanced at my watch. It was eleven-thirty. I'd overslept my usual departure time. As the window lowered, I took in the sight of my daughter, hidden within her parka. The thick white face paint was gone, despite a rather heavy application of eyeliner and eye shadow.

She simply stood there, glancing about, her attention seemingly preoccupied with something in the neighborhood.

"Hey there," I said, smiling like a fool.

"I'm hungry," she finally replied. "There's nothing here except crackers and peanut butter."

I pounced. "Wanna grab something?"

She shrugged, and cast a quick look toward the apartment. Turning back to me, she added with a reluctant casualness, "Why not?" and pulled open the car door.

Sure, I thought. *Why not?* Plopping into the seat, she pulled the door closed and clasped her hands together on her lap. She was wearing jeans and purple tennis shoes. Then remembering my car rules, she reached back, grabbed the seat belt, pulled it over her chest, and clicked it into place.

I was as nervous as a pimply-faced adolescent on his first date.

"Taco John?" I asked.

"Cool."

Heading down the street, I was reminded of the last time she'd been in my car. Driving her to the mall, she'd spent most of the time scrunched down in her seat. Three blocks away, we'd approached a group of junior high students. Peeking just above the window, Alycia had shuddered and collapsed into the seat, flat as a pancake. When they were directly across from us, my annoyance got the best of me.

"It's safe," I'd said.

Alycia sat up, only to crumple like a reverse Pop-Goes-the-Weasel. "Da-ad! You lied!"

I never heard the end of it. My driving privileges were instantly revoked, and Donna did the escorting after that.

As we drove in silence, I tried to gather my thoughts, searching for something uncontroversial to say. I thought of her sixteen-year-old boyfriend, and hoped it was over, although I couldn't imagine using the word "over" in reference to such a thing.

Don't bring it up now, I decided.

"I got an A in Algebra," she finally volunteered.

"Wow," I exclaimed softly. "And it's not even English."

"I know," she chuckled. "Pigs fly."

I resisted the typical parental reply: *I knew you could do it.*

When I turned in, I parked at the side of the tiny fast-food restaurant and switched off the engine. Alycia seemed suddenly tentative.

I'd blown it. She'd intended for us to drive through, not sit in. All kinds of respectable folk might see us.

"Hey, let's just go through the drive-through," I announced casually, inserting the keys back into the ignition. "Then we can drive around while we eat."

"No, that's okay," she said bravely, reaching for the door and pushing it open. Once outside, she closed the door and stood like a sentry, furtively searching into the glass of the building, and then turning to survey the parking lot, her eyes darting left and right. I waited until she seemed to relax and caught my eye through the car window.

I raised my eyebrows: *All clear?*

She smiled tentatively, then shrugged as if to say, *Why would I care anyway?*

Inside at the counter, Alycia ordered three hard-shell tacos from a teenager in a white uniform, with bed hair and what looked like braces on his nose and lips, then wandered toward the booths in the back of room. I gave my order to the same boy, waited for a few minutes, then followed in her direction with the food tray. Halfway back, I stopped. Alycia was nowhere to be seen.

Well, it was a start, I thought, figuring she'd ditched me. I settled down to eat a rather large lunch for a man who'd suddenly lost his appetite.

A few minutes later, Alycia emerged from the rest room, her face flushed. I was relieved, but tense. *This is killing her,* I thought, now wondering if Donna had talked her into coming today.

As she settled into her seat, facing away from the front door, I reconfirmed my decision to avoid anything remotely controversial. *Stick to small talk. Inconsequential minutiae.*

I asked her about her Christmas without mentioning my gift. She hadn't acknowledged receiving it, much less thanked me for it. Another can of worms.

"Well, don't you want to know how Mom is?" she asked.

"I talk to her nearly every week."

"Oh," she replied, taking a small self-conscious bite. The hard shell crunched between her teeth, and she seemed embarrassed by the sound.

"How's her job?"

"She's working all the time," Alycia shrugged. "I don't see her much anymore."

I decided to change the subject, and searched my memory for the name of one of her friends. "So, um . . . how's . . . uh . . . Leesa?"

She frowned. "Leesa? We haven't been friends for a year."

"Oh, yeah, that's right," I said, but Alycia seemed annoyed with my feeble attempt to hide my ignorance.

"Actually, I didn't know," I added. The tension was excruciating. Obviously she felt it too, because she stopped eating after half a taco. "Guess I wasn't that hungry."

Finally I decided to go for broke. I couldn't think of anything nonparental to say, and this little reunion was bordering on disaster. "It's sure good to see you, Alley Cat."

She forced a smile.

"I've missed you."

She looked away as if she hadn't heard me.

Okay, I thought. *That went reasonably well.*

"You don't have to say that stuff," she said, clearing her throat.

"I'm just following the rules in the Obnoxious Parental Guide Book."

A smile crossed her face, then quickly disappeared. She looked at me for what seemed like the first time. "That's so dumb, Dad."

"Yeah, I know, but did you expect anything better?"

"No."

"So, I didn't disappoint you."

"What are some of the other rules?" she asked, with a familiar but fleeting grin.

I thought for a moment, then nodded as if I remembered one. "Always remember that no matter what you say, no matter how brilliant, it will be perceived by your son or daughter as either stupid or embarrassing—or both."

She chuckled reluctantly, as if agreeing. Then she frowned. "But that's not really a rule."

"Oh yeah," I agreed, looking across the room toward the front windows. I saw a white minivan pull up. Seconds later, five young girls popped out. I vaguely recognized a couple of them. The driver got out as well, a young man, probably an older brother of one of the girls.

I leaned forward. "Rule number thirty-two: Never take your daughter to a taco place, because you're liable to bump into her friends and consequently destroy her life."

I gestured forward with my eyes, and her expression froze. Her eyes flashed in panic, and her face flushed again. You would have thought we were on the sinking *Titanic.* I smiled reassuringly. "Don't worry. Your secret is safe."

Eyes wide, she nodded hopefully. I quickly grabbed my trash and stood up. Her school friends had just reached the front door. The high school kid was pulling it open.

"Bye," I said, touching her shoulder briefly. Heading for the back door, I slipped out just as her omnipotent peer group slipped in.

Walking to my car, I watched the ensuing scene out of the corner of my eye as the entire party converged upon Alycia with surprised smiles and dramatic gestures. When the group giggled back to the counter to order their food, leaving her alone for a moment, Alycia looked out the window and gave a subtle wave. The sunlight reflecting off the window masked the visibility, but I'm reasonably sure she mouthed the words, *Thank you.*

I got into my car, started the engine, every neuron in my brain firing with triumph. I'd done it. I'd bridged the first gap. Maybe after another month, I'd see her again.

Halfway home, my cell phone rang. It was Alycia and she sounded ecstatic. "They didn't suspect a thing!"

"Living on the edge," I laughed.

"Thanks for the tacos," she said softly. "But next week, just to be safe, we should eat them in the car."

"Yeah," I replied. "So . . . should I come at eleven, then?"

"Probably," she answered, and then hung up.

I rode the rest of the way home on a cloud. *Unbelievable.*

Three months of sitting in front of that apartment with nothing to show for it, and suddenly my daughter appears out of nowhere.

Wanna grab something? I'd asked.

Why not? she'd said.

Simple as that.

I cringed. *Hold on, Kemo Sabe,* I told myself. *You've only crossed the first bridge. Don't be counting none of those proverbial chickens.*

There was still plenty of time and opportunity to blow it, and blow it bad. First things first.

When I pulled into the garage, I took a quick look at my surroundings, and as the garage door rattled down behind me, I kicked myself. Why was I still driving around this rattletrap? I had the money, didn't I? No wonder Alycia could barely stand to be seen with me.

I needed to prove to Alycia that dear ol' dad wasn't a bum. I pressed the remote and the garage door rattled up again. I drove all the way downtown to the Ford dealership, where I promptly traded in my bucket of bolts for a new convertible fire engine red Mustang.

Wait'll Alycia sees me in this!

Chapter Twenty-One

During the next week, the market continued to settle down. The breakout fractals were getting closer together, and I continued placing stops just above them. Within this narrow range, however, there occurred a series of high-volume days with little market movement. This indicated a volatile standoff between the bears and the bulls, an ominous sign. The market was poised to explode—either higher or lower.

On Wednesday, I redoubled my resolve. If Donna wouldn't accept child support, maybe she'd accept a house. Somehow, at the time, the inconsistency of this new line of reasoning didn't strike me. Sure, I could have bought a nice big fancy house for myself and impressed my daughter's friends and increased Donna's respect, but I couldn't see it, not with Donna and Alycia living just above squalor.

Secretly, I hoped that after a reasonable separation—whatever time Donna needed—she'd invite me back. And then, we'd sell the Northview Lane house, and be done with the past. It seemed like the perfect plan. Excitedly, I called a Realtor acquaintance, Ned Glazer. Over the phone, he clued me in on several areas and offered his services. "I can take you out looking tomorrow."

The next day, it didn't take us long to find something that fit my specifications: an attractive eighteen-hundred square foot trilevel recently refurbished—new windows, carpeting, and kitchen appliances—in the southeast part of town, a well-established neighborhood. Most important of all, it had four bedrooms, three up and a private one on the lower level for Alycia.

I wired myself a ten-thousand-dollar check from the trading account, enough for a down payment, and on Saturday I arrived for Alycia at ten forty-five. While I tried to modify my expectations again, my insides were bursting with anticipation. Alycia came out five minutes later, her petite form lost in her giant gray parka. I shouldn't have been so surprised to see her—after all, Alycia never broke her word.

Halfway down the sidewalk, she stopped in her tracks. She frowned. I leaned over and smiled through the passenger window. A confused smile erupted on her face. I pushed the door open. "You're not dreaming. Get in."

Hopping into my Mustang, she pulled her hood off, and glanced about the interior. She wiggled in the leather seats. "Cool!" She ran her fingers across the glove compartment. "Cool!" She stared up at the sunroof. "*Too* cool!"

My plan was working to a T. Like the Trojan horse, my car had melted her heart. Inside the Trojan horse was dear ol' dad, waiting to pop out and reclaim his daughter's affections.

"You like?"

"Can I have it?"

"Sure. When you're sixteen."

"Too cool!" She put on her seat belt. "Where to, James?"

"McCromwell's, for a slice of cayke, and a spoh a' teh."

She wrinkled her nose. "A spoh' of teh, you sahy?"

So we drove to a burger joint. Before turning in, I handed her a pair of sunglasses. "You might feel safer in these."

She giggled, taking them into her hands, trying them on. She modeled them for me.

I laughed. "As cool as my car."

She removed them and placed them on the dashboard. "You know what?"

"What?"

"Everyone has parents, right?"

"Technically."

She turned to me with a mischievous expression. "I mean, were you afraid to be seen with *your* dad?"

"Deathly," I replied. "Still am."

"Then maybe you need counseling," she giggled again.

At the drive-through window, she ordered a burger with extra pickles and a strawberry shake.

"We're out of strawberry," said the voice over the intercom.

"Oh, man," Alycia announced. "I had my mouth shaped for strawberry." She ordered chocolate instead. "Do you like pickles?" she asked me as we turned back onto Sixth Avenue.

"Only with vinegar."

"Here," she said, leaning over and stuffing three into my mouth. "They all come with vinegar, and I have too many."

"Fwank woo."

"Don't talk with your mouth full."

"Sworry . . ."

We drove into the country, and the farther away from town we were, the more relaxed she became. I revved the engine at the appropriate times, took a couple of hairpin curves, looked around, and pushed it to ninety on a straightaway.

The difference between last week and this week was like the difference between winter and summer.

"Too cool!" Alycia exclaimed.

Later, after the demonstration was over, I made my only error and accidentally pushed an oldies CD into the player. "Waterloo" broke the silence.

Alycia wrinkled her nose. "Ick."

I pressed the eject button. "Sorry. Wasn't thinking."

"Dad, you display an alarming predilection for prehistoric bubble-gum pop."

"And the problem with that is?"

"Self-explanatory."

"Is predilection even a word?" I asked.

"You've damaged the car."

"Huh?"

"It's been tainted by your music." She giggled. "Hey wait! You know what we should do?"

"Before you speak, remember I'm a grown-up. I don't tee-pee houses anymore."

"Oh, man," she said with mock disappointment. "I know! We should see one of those movies my friends wouldn't be caught dead in."

"Surely, you don't mean . . ." I lowered my voice to a conspiratorial whisper, ". . . a *Disney* movie?"

Her eyes widened in silly horror, and she suddenly reached out, covering my mouth with her hand. "You must never, ever, use the 'D' word in teenage company."

"I pwomise ne'er to ou i' a'in." I muttered through her hand.

"What?" she asked, removing her hand.

I repeated it.

"That'll do, Pig," she laughed.

"Pig?"

"Yeah. Don't you remember *Babe*?"

"Oh."

On the way back into town, she picked up the sunglasses from the crevice in the dash. "Just in case."

"Chi-cken," I taunted.

"Daa-aad," she whined good-naturedly. "Please don't enumerate my inconsistencies."

"Sorry."

Half incognito, my daughter and I attended an afternoon Disney film. She thoroughly enjoyed it. While she had removed the sunglasses when the lights went out, she put them on the moment we hit the lobby.

Afterward, we rode home in contented silence. When I pulled up to the apartment, I touched her shoulder. "I have another surprise for you, Piglet."

Her eyes lit up. "Another one? Piglet *loves* surprises."

I considered unleashing the house surprise but suddenly lost my nerve. *Take it slower,* I thought. I'd just startled Alycia with my new car. Next week was soon enough for the house. "But you have to wait till next week."

"Huh?"

"I have to wrap it up, or something."

She crossed her arms and harrumphed. "I gotta wait a whole week?"

I shrugged, affecting my best apologetic expression.

"I'm thinking it doesn't come in a package, does it?"

"How did you get so smart?"

"Hours and hours of mind-numbing, life-wasting, social life-destroying homework."

Our eyes met, and for a moment the old knowing passed between us. I'd forgotten what it was like.

"Did you have a good time with your annoying, prehistoric father?" I asked.

She turned contemplative for a moment, putting a reflective finger to her temple as if to ponder an impossibly difficult question. "Hmmmm. Can I get back to you on that?"

"Ouch."

"I'm kidding!!" she exclaimed, leaning over, puffing out her cheek. I kissed it gently. Then she jumped out of the car and headed up the icy sidewalk, twirling once to wave. She appraised the car again and gave me the thumbs-up. My heart swelled with pride. Alycia no longer considered me on the same level with pond scum.

For the second time in a week, I drove home on a cloud. I breathed out a sigh—my daughter still loved me—and I mentally counted my money again. I was now sitting on over a quarter of a million dollars.

I'd clawed my way to success, little by little, but just as surely, and in the end, all I'd needed was a little kick in the pants. Of course, I had Donna to thank for that.

And if you'd said to me, "Hold on a minute, pal, something doesn't smell right," I would have said, "Sure, I'm familiar with the old saw: Money can't buy you happiness, but let me tell you from personal experience, the lack of money can make you miserable."

On Sunday afternoon, Donna called me. "What have you done to our daughter?"

A small stutter caught in my throat. "Come again?"

"Alycia actually smiled at me today. You know how long it's been since she actually looked at me without disdain?"

I breathed out a sigh of relief. "We went to a movie, that's all."

"Well, whatever it was, please keep doing it. Things are a lot easier around here."

After I described our visit in generalities, she chuckled softly. "Stephen?"

"Yes?"

"Please be careful with her."

I promised and Donna accepted my reassurance.

Thinking of the money sitting in my brokerage account, and the house I was about to spring on them, I decided to break the ground with another attempt.

"Child support?" she asked, hesitation creeping into her voice. "Oh . . . that's right. Alycia told me about the car."

"It's paid for," I volunteered, feeling like a fool. "I mean . . . I can afford it now."

Donna went silent. I was about to fill it, when she spoke: "I appreciate the offer, Stephen. Perhaps we might talk about it later?"

"Well, I just wanted you to know, I'm willing."

From what I could pick up over the phone, I thought she seemed both pleased and tentative. I couldn't wait to show her the house.

That evening my father called. "Your mother is convinced I have to see a doctor."

"Then see one," I said.

"I'd rather poke my eye out."

"Then *don't* go."

Dad paused. "Why don't you come with me?"

"I can't," I fudged. "I'm—"

"Busy. Of course you are," he said agreeably. "Dumb idea."

"Have Mom go with you," I added.

"You bet," he said.

We made excruciating small talk for a few minutes.

"Hey, you know what?" Dad exclaimed.

"What?"

"We should hang out sometime, you know, watch some ball on TV, maybe play catch like we used to."

Hang out? I almost smiled at my father's clumsy attempt at hip lingo. Then a lifetime of annoyance got the best of me. "When exactly did we do that?"

"Do what?"

"Play catch?"

My father hesitated, then chuckled softly. "Oh yeah, good one. Got me there."

I swallowed my frustration and another lull filled the silence. My father finally broke it. "Well . . . don't be a stranger, Stevie."

Just before we said good-bye, I said, "See the doctor, Dad. Make Mom feel better."

"I heard ya there."

On Saturday, Alycia came bouncing down the sidewalk. "Where to, James?" she said, getting in and slamming the door shut. "Did I tell you how much I love this car, and by the way, where's that-them-there surprise of yors, pardner?"

"You're mixing your accents," I said.

"Cough it up." She held out her hand. "Don't make me hurt you. I can, you know. Pay no attention to my size. I can hurt you *bad*."

"Get your mom," I said, smiling.

"Huh?"

"This surprise is for her too."

She looked at me carefully, trying to read my expression.

"Don't worry," I said. "It's fine."

She jumped out of the car and scampered up the sidewalk. I should have known what she was presuming, but my ever-present mental myopia had reached groundbreaking levels.

Minutes later, Donna came wandering down without Alycia.

She stopped and stared at my car. I smiled broadly.

"Hop in," I exclaimed through the open window.

She recovered from the shock. "Alycia said you wanted to see—"

"I want to show you something. Where's Alycia?"

"I told her to wait a sec." Donna crouched beside the door. "Stephen—"

"C'mon," I said, trying to infuse the moment with the sheer blaze of my own excitement. "Just hop in."

After giving me another scrutinizing gaze, Donna turned and waved toward the second-floor window. I reached over and opened the door from the inside.

"I hope you know what you're doing," Donna said, pushing the front seat forward and squeezing into the backseat. "If you have something important to discuss, you should say it in private."

I rubbed my hands together like a little kid. "You're going to love this."

She sighed.

When Alycia jumped in, I pulled away from the curb and headed to the house where the Realtor would be waiting.

Donna tried again. "Where are we going?"

"You'll see," I replied cheerily.

"Chill, Mom," Alycia said, twisting in her seat to face her mother. "Don't you like surprises?"

I smiled into the rearview window. Donna was a wreck. A pathetic smile was superimposed over an expression of dread. *Of course she doesn't like surprises,* I thought.

"Did you eat, Mom?"

Donna didn't answer. She sat there with her hand frozen to the armrest. She hadn't even buckled in. In spite of all this—*hello-o-o, big red truck!*—I was still oblivious. "Obliviosity is a guy thing," Alycia once told me. "And since you're technically a guy, you're clue-challenged."

I didn't know which insult to address first. "Technically a guy?"

"Yeah . . . all guys over thirty are morphing into geezer."

When we reached the neighborhood, Alycia's excitement peaked. She became an absolute flutterbug. I parked across from the tri-level and, without further tantalization, poked a proud thumb toward the house. "Thar she blows."

Peering out my window, Alycia leaned forward as I leaned back. "What kind of ship is that?"

"It's a houseboat," I said. "With the kind of floor plan your mother has always admired. Remember? Anyway . . . it set sale three weeks ago."

I smiled into the rearview mirror again. Donna's face was aghast.

"It's big," Alycia announced. "Much bigger than ours—er . . . uh . . . the old one."

I suppressed a proud smile. It wasn't that big, but compared to Sally's apartment and my house, it was a Beverly Hills mansion.

Alycia couldn't stop staring. I could only imagine what she was thinking. Her friends might actually visit her here.

"Wow, Dad," she said, her voice hushed to a solemn whisper. "You must be rich."

Beaming, I opened my door and smiled back at Donna. "Let's take a look."

She glanced away, reaching for her own door. Her persistent reluctance was beginning to puzzle me. She got out, and Alycia followed suit. Like a happy family, the three of us crossed the street. I introduced them to the Realtor, and Ned Glazer shook Donna's hand, and winked at Alycia. "You're going to love your new room."

Donna tugged on my jacket at the precise moment Ned and Alycia walked in the front door. Her words came out in a desperate whisper, "Tell me now, Stephen. What're you doing? No more beating around the bush, okay?"

I shrugged proudly. "It's for you and Alycia."

Her eyes flickered. "Me and Alycia? The *two* of us?"

"The two of you," I repeated. "And maybe—"

Donna locked eyes with me. "Maybe what?"

I hesitated.

"Did you explain this to Alycia?"

I shrugged no, and Donna shook her head in disbelief. Alycia burst out of the house. She jumped down the front cement steps and grabbed her mother's arm. "You've got to see the fireplace!"

"Alycia—"

"C'mon!" Alycia said, pulling her mother up the steps. Donna's eyes briefly lingered on mine as she allowed herself to be dragged into the house.

I was still standing on the porch, poised to enter with Donna's words echoing in my mind, when Alycia poked her head out. "Dad, my stuff would disappear into that room. I've got to get more stuff!"

"Bummer," I replied.

Stepping over the threshold, I saw Donna at the back window, in the dining room, staring out into the yard full of mature trees. Apparently, Alycia, caught up in the excitement of the moment, had already scampered off.

I walked up to my wife. "You've never had a real dining room, Donna."

She hugged herself, as if the temperature had suddenly dropped.

"And I know how you love maples."

She let out a small sigh, staring out at the beautifully landscaped backyard. "What are you doing, Stephen?"

"This is for you," I said.

"Can we go now?" She turned to me, her eyes glistening. At that precise moment, Alycia came running up the steps from downstairs. "So, Dad, which one's your office?"

Donna's gaze drilled a hole into my face. *Get it now?*

I was too stunned to speak. Alycia assumed I planned to move in with them immediately, but I couldn't say, "Maybe someday." Not with Donna glaring at me. She waited for me to respond, and when I didn't, she forged ahead. "Your father wouldn't be living here, honey."

The words dissipated into the sudden silence. Alycia stood frozen. Her gaze flickered from Donna to me, then back to Donna again, then back to me as if waiting for a full rebuttal.

I tried to rescue the moment by reinserting enthusiasm into my voice. "I'm buying this for you and your mother."

Alycia's response was immediate, her next words clipped and angry. "No, Dad. You're not." She stormed across the living room to the entryway and slammed the door behind her.

I stood there dumbfounded.

"Next time talk to me first," Donna whispered.

Oblivious to the drama, Ned walked into the living room. "S'what do you think?"

My brain was buzzing. "I need a moment with my . . . uh . . . with Donna, Ned."

"No problem," he said, his smile unfazed. He excused himself to the next room.

I lowered my voice to a whisper and tried to explain. Donna listened, and now that we'd weathered Alycia's explosion, her manner was softer. "This isn't for you to decide anymore, Stephen. We're separated, remember?"

"But *you* would own it. I'd pay the mortgage. I know you've always loved this part of town."

She shook her head. "But I can't accept this from you."

Exasperated, I pulled out my checkbook. "Then accept this on Alycia's behalf, and you can live anywhere you want." I scribbled out a check and extended it to her. "I made some money recently, and since we're still married, half is yours. You can do what you want with it."

I expected Donna to be impressed, to suddenly look at me with new eyes. And in the back of my mind, I actually thought the money would change everything.

Instead, she reached for it, scrutinizing my writing. Our eyes met and I realized what she was thinking: *You're trading again.*

With a regretful expression, she began tearing it up into tiny pieces. "I never wanted your money, Stephen. And I never wanted a fancy house. I followed you to Aberdeen with no complaints, didn't I?"

"Donna—"

"Stephen . . . please." She paused, biting her lip. She handed me the check pieces, and her voice wavered. "I'll try to smooth things over with Alycia. Give me a few minutes."

Moments after Donna walked out the front door, Ned walked into the room once again, this time rubbing his hands together. He seemed puzzled with Donna's absence. "She's out looking at the yard?"

I pulled Ned into the kitchen just in case Donna came in again. I spoke barely above a whisper. "We'll take it."

"Wonderful choice!" he exclaimed. "Congratulations!"

Confused and embarrassed, I drove them home. I attempted conversation, but neither seemed interested. When I dropped them off, Donna got out first—"Bye, Stephen"—and headed up the sidewalk.

Alycia sat stock-still, looking forward. "Man, I had my mouth shaped for that room."

I turned to her, "Are you kidding?"

She shrugged and still wouldn't look at me.

"We could still talk to your mo—"

"Dad?"

"What?"

"Mom would say 'no' regardless."

She leaned over with her balloon cheek.

I kissed it.

"I have to go." She pushed the door open, but I gently reached for her coat. She turned back with a question in her eyes. "So . . . will I see you again, Dad?"

"Try to get rid of me."

"I like the sound of that," she said.

I playfully punched her shoulder, and she punched me back. Her smile a bit wobbly, she jumped out of the car, turned around halfway up the sidewalk, waved again, then headed into the building.

Her step had lost its jauntiness, and I berated myself for being so dense. I needed to give Donna time and not jump the gun.

Chapter Twenty-Two

My daughter and I were finding each other again. What we once had now seemed within reach again, and I was determined not to blow it. Lost in my own little fantasy world of hopes and dreams, and hoping to impress my family, I'd all but forgotten the reality of the divorce filing.

On Monday the finalized documents arrived. Our court date had been set for two weeks from today. As I thumbed through each sheet and evaluated the mind-numbing legalese, it slowly sank in: Our marriage was almost over.

At work, Larry and I barely spoke anymore, not because of any personal issues but because he rarely emerged from his office. Lately I had become little more than his secretary, clearing his office of Styrofoam cups, plastic plates, half-eaten donuts, and broken pretzels, dusting the flat surfaces, filing and mailing documents. Although I purchased the junk food, from the amount I discarded, he didn't seem to have his old appetite.

The IRS notices also increased, but as usual I simply passed them on to Larry. "Business must be picking up," I remarked. "Information requests?"

"They can't even keep up with their own Tax Court decisions," he mumbled.

At Joe's, Susan was now sitting with Paul and me on a regular basis unless there were new guys in the arena of play. In that case, she sat at the bar with an empty buffer seat between her and anyone else, flirting with foolish abandon.

We tortured her with our pestering glances until she made *leave-me-alone* faces in return. One night, when the pickings were slim, she hung out at our table, and she and Paul initiated a "top-this" version of Whose Father Is Worse?

My heart wasn't in it, but Paul hit his stride immediately, dredging up story after story of his alcoholic father, joking casually as if growing up hadn't been such a painful experience. Susan did the same, regaling us with tales of her father's philandering. When my turn came, I tried to decline, but they would hear nothing of it. After further coercion, I reluctantly rehashed my Uglyville story.

"Not even close," Susan remarked with playful disdain. "So what? You were poor. We were all poor."

Paul agreed. "Doesn't even register on the universally accepted scale of family dysfunction."

"There's a scale?" Susan asked, amused.

"There is now," Paul insisted, eyes glazed over. "I just made it up."

Out of friendly regard—present company excepted—they granted me a distant third place, which I accepted with a shrug. After all, compared to their fathers, my father was a saint.

I considered their stories and remembered Dad's recent call, *"Let's hang out!"* And I now regretted not giving him a chance, despite the old resentments which hovered just below the surface. *Maybe someday,* I thought.

Unfortunately, when Susan told Paul six drinks in the space of one hour was plenty, he stormed out, leaving a bad taste to an overall fun evening.

The next Saturday, Alycia came out to the car and plopped into her place. "What's on the agenda?"

"Let's go to the mall," I suggested. "Buy you some new shoes or something."

She gave me her best eyelash flutter. "New shoes?"

I nodded eagerly. "I've got money burning a hole in my pocket. The question is: Are you feeling dangerous? We're talking mall exposure here." I opened my eyes ghoulishly wide, then narrowed them in a feeble attempt to appear humorously frightening.

She pursed her lips. "I don't even care about that anymore, Dad."

"Since when?"

"Popularity isn't what it's cracked up to be."

I resisted the impulse to raise my eyebrows again. "Do you want to talk about it?"

She frowned: *What planet are you from?*

"Just something I'm required to say."

"Anyway, if you have to buy me shoes, fine."

"Me pleasure, me lady. Allow me the honor of transporting you aboard me carriage."

"Technically, it's a horseless carriage," she said.

"Technically, it's a Mustang," I argued. "So that makes it . . ." I pondered this for a second, then declared, ". . . a carriageless *horse.*"

She giggled. "You're getting good at this talking stuff."

"I should be. I've been practicing longer than you."

As we drove to the mall, I could sense something building within her. While we hadn't yet discussed anything delicate, I knew we were overdue for an honest heart-to-heart talk about the impending divorce. I could only hope she'd still be speaking to me afterward.

When we arrived at the mall, I parked as close to the entrance as I could. Getting out, we headed across the parking lot, and although I was tempted to walk a few paces behind her, Alycia refused my magnanimous gesture, so we wandered in side by side, unprotected and vulnerable to observation. I grinned. Maybe she was actually proud to be seen with me. At the very least, being seen with my daughter filled *me* with pride.

In Fannie's Footwear, she tried on several pairs of shoes, until she eventually unearthed a few possibilities. She even considered a few of my own lame suggestions until she saw the price. "Too expensive, Dad."

"Since when?"

"Du-uh."

"C'mon, the fire is spreading beyond the pocket. My whole leg is starting to burn."

"I'm not walking into the apartment with those shoes," she said with a sharp look.

Of course.

"Just buy me another milkshake," she added.

"That won't even touch the fire."

"Then buy Mom a ring. A real one this time."

Our eyes met and she apologized immediately. "Sorry, Dad. That was low."

"S'okay." I shrugged, knowing her humorous jab was Alycia's way of getting the ball rolling for the discussion that was sure to follow.

Alycia finally settled on some ridiculously cheap shoes, although not half bad in style.

"You have your mother's good fashion sense," I told her.

"Mmm-hmmm," she said thoughtfully. "I'm not sure how to take that."

"I meant it well," I said.

"I'm being annoying, huh?" she said as we finally walked out of the mall, shoe box in a stylish plastic bag.

"Wanna talk about it?"

"Is that your favorite expression?"

I shrugged off her pretense, but in the car, she nodded thoughtfully. "Okay, let's talk, Dad."

I blew out a quick *oh boy.* But inwardly I was relieved.

"Called your bluff, eh?" she noted perkily.

"You're not allowed to use 'eh' unless you're from New England."

"They say it in Ohio," she protested. "And Canada. It's working its way across the country. 'Eh' is in." She smiled knowingly at me.

"What?"

"Nice deflection, Dad. Now, about that talk. Did you mean it, and what's off limits? Let's talk boundaries, ground rules, and penalties for infractions."

I sighed with a surrendering chuckle.

She laced her fingers and turned them inside out, cracking them. "I'll go easy on you."

"Please do." I cleared my throat, and she sniffed slightly, glancing out her side of the window as if what was to follow would be too painful for eye contact. "So . . . I take it you and Mom aren't getting back together?"

I hesitated. Whatever I said would find its way back to Donna in some form or another. "Your mother is determined to proceed," I said.

Alycia's eyes flickered on mine, seemingly surprised by my lack of hedging. "And you're not?"

I paused again.

Alycia's eyes widened. "Don't you miss her?"

"Of course I do."

Alycia came uncorked. "Then talk to her!"

I let out a breath. "Alycia, marriage wasn't easy for your mother and me. We tried hard to make it work."

"So . . . try harder next time," she replied. "It's mostly your fault, you know."

I nodded.

"So talk to her."

I took another deep breath and let it out softly. "Talking isn't a cure-all. It's just a start. You have to be able to agree."

Alycia bit her lip. "I can't believe I'm giving my dad marital advice." She fixed me with another *no-fudging* stare. "Do you love Mom?"

"Yes, of course."

Her eyes scrutinized mine, and she seemed to wilt a little. "Talk to her, Dad."

I put the car into drive, and we drove a few blocks in silence. I could sense her continuing inner debate. She wasn't finished with me yet. She turned, commanding full eye contact. "Next topic."

I braced myself, grimacing humorously.

"Are you still in love with Alice?"

I blew out another breath. This honesty stuff was getting close to the edge. I wondered if I shouldn't plead the fifth or something.

"Cuz everyone says you are."

I hesitated.

"You can handle it, Dad. You just say the first thing that comes to mind and let me separate the chaff from the wheat."

"I *was* in love with Alice," I replied. "But she's gone, and we moved on."

"Did you really?"

"Alycia . . ."

"Are you in love with Mom?"

"I love your mother very much."

"Not the same thing, Dad."

I cleared my throat. "Your mother was my best friend. And we should have had a wonderful marriage, but I made a few mistakes—"

Alycia gave her head a quick dismissive shake. "Back up. Your *friend*?" She shook her head again. "Guys are *so* oblivious." She paused as if gathering steam. "You remind me of Fred, Dad."

I resisted the inclination to smile. Fred had been Alycia's pet turtle in the second grade. "This should be good."

"Do you remember how I kept putting him in mud, he'd get stuck, and I had to pull him out?"

I winced. "Ouch."

"You're just like Fred," Alycia announced. "And you need to get *un*stuck. Someone needs to pull you out."

"And that would be whom?"

She made a triumphant face. "Moi."

When we pulled up in front of the apartments, we sat there for a moment. Alycia looked at me again, and I must have looked deathly worried because she broke into a grin. "Cheer up. You can't get rid of me that easy." She jumped out and closed the door. I lowered the window and she leaned in. "Next week, Bat Dad?"

"Same Bat channel."

"Same Bat time?"

"Same Bat car."

Stepping back, she looked my car over. "Not the right color, but close enough!"

We shared a laugh, and all seemed forgiven. Then the mood changed again, and she paused reflectively, staring down at my floor mats. "Can I say one more thing?"

I smiled, and could see her face growing pink from the cold. "You can always say one more thing."

"Okay," she agreed, her words creating puffs of moisture. "You don't have to buy me expensive stuff, okay?"

I shrugged. "Resistance is futile."

She flashed me a defiant smile. It seemed the perfect good-bye, but neither of us budged. The earlier conversation seemed unfinished, and both of us sensed it.

"I never wanted to hurt your mother, honey."

"I know, Dad," she replied, unflinching.

"Please don't take this the wrong way," I continued, hoping she'd understand. "But you're the best thing that's ever happened to me."

Her eyes blinked, and I wondered if I'd blown it again. While I'd been trying to temper our "Alice" comments, I'd just devalued her mother again.

"What I meant was—"

"I get it, Dad." She sniffed softly, then tapped the edge of the car door. "I appreciate it. And even though you're a loon, I still love you, okay?"

"I love you too, honey."

She gave my car a final tap—"*Talk* to her!"—then skipped up the sidewalk as if she were eight, not thirteen, then suddenly came rushing back. I stepped on the brake and lowered the window again.

"Almost forgot! Mom and I are going to Brookings next Saturday. Remember Madison?"

I nodded, although the name seemed only remotely familiar.

"First grade, Dad."

"Okay," I replied.

She snorted. "Anyway, you have the week off, so plan it wisely!"

And then she was gone. I drove home exhausted. I'd endured the Verbal Inquisition of Alycia Whitaker and lived to tell about it.

Chapter Twenty-three

A week later on Saturday night Alycia called and left a message on my voice mail.

"We're back from Brookings! Well . . . I can't believe we drove so far just to see Madison. Her nose is sticking straight up. Her attitude is like a wind tunnel—know what I mean? Anyway, call me, okay?"

She paused. "Dad? Now's a good time. Mom seems upset."

After I finished listening to the message, I stared at the phone. I reached for it again, then stopped.

Most likely, Donna was just fine, and Alycia was attempting a last-ditch effort to stop the divorce. I didn't blame her.

But I went for it. I dialed Donna's number, and got Alycia. "Honey . . ."

"Wanna talk to Mom?"

A little hesitation was all she needed. I heard her cover the receiver and call, "Mo-o-o-om!"

What was I doing? Obviously, Donna was determined to go through with this.

When she answered, I mumbled a few things until Donna interrupted me. "Are you okay?"

I cleared my throat. "Just . . . uh . . . wanted to know how you think Alycia's doing."

"Oh . . . well . . . great, I think."

We continued along that line for a moment, meandering into other related topics. I asked her if she'd reconsidered the child support issue, but she hadn't. I asked about her church, and she seemed confused, but answered anyway. Finally, it was time to either hit the ball or quit the game. "Are you sure you want this? I mean . . . the divorce. Shouldn't we . . . uh . . . take more time? Not rush into it?"

She paused. "Haven't we had enough time, Stephen?"

Of course. We'd had plenty of time. And we'd wasted it—wasn't that what she'd said the day she'd left?

"Stephen . . . are you there?"

"I only want the best for you, Donna."

Silence again. It lasted so long I wondered if we'd lost our connection.

She sniffed softly. "I need to go."

Without protesting, I let her hang up.

That night I had the dream again in the same disjointed fragments. The smell of pizza and vanilla filled my senses. The oldies played in the background. I waited for her, my heart beating with dread, but she never arrived. Suddenly I spotted her across the room, her shimmering brunette hair unmistakable. She blew me a kiss and opened the door. I tore out of the booth, but she was already gone. Screaming her name, I burst through the door and glimpsed her just as she stepped into the street. I practically leapt across the sidewalk just as the sound of screeching filled my ears, and with my fingers outstretched, brushed her silky blouse . . . and then she was gone.

I awakened, gasping for breath, soaked in sweat. I looked for Donna beside me, but she was gone too. I thought of the impending divorce, the recurring dream, and realized Donna was right. How many more nights would I torture her by awakening from the same dream?

Around six o'clock on Monday, the morning of the court day, I drove to Sixth Avenue for a quick cup of coffee. Since I hadn't planned to go to work until after the divorce was final, I had a few hours to kill.

I was just leaving the drive-through when my cell phone rang.

"Stephen?" It was Donna, and her voice sounded tentative. "Where are you? I mean . . . what are you doing?"

When I told her, she chuckled nervously. "McDonald's? For coffee? Why am I not surprised?"

The tone in her voice heartened me, and we made small talk as if we were about to go out for dinner, not to divorce court. But the more we talked, the more labored her words became.

Suddenly, she took a deep breath and said quietly, "I've been thinking about what you said and . . . I think you're right. I mean . . . I made a mistake. I shouldn't have left you."

Her statement hit me like a thunderclap in the middle of a sunshiny day. I didn't know what to say. Donna wasn't the type to vacillate, and it never occurred to me that she would simply change her mind. I was reminded of Alycia's phone message. Perhaps, Donna had been contemplating this for a while.

When I didn't reply, she continued. "Are you seeing someone, Stephen? I mean . . . are you . . ." Her voice lowered, ". . . well, interested in someone else?"

I was surprised by the frankness of her question. "No."

"Me neither," she said, as if we'd just compared notes and found a brilliant commonality. "So, really . . . I had no reason, no basis. I was selfish, Stephen. Maybe I just needed some time to sort things out. I'm sorry to wait until the last minute . . ."

I still didn't know how to respond. For the second time since she'd left—hanging up on me when we were on the phone being the first—she'd totally surprised me.

"Stephen? Are you there?"

I assured her I was still on the line.

"I'm thinking of withdrawing the petition," she said. "Besides, we've been getting along, haven't we? We haven't fought in months.

It's like the old days, you know, like when we first married? Do you remember?"

They seemed hazy to me, but I answered, "Yes."

"So . . . what do you think?"

This is where I was supposed to say, *I'm so glad. Please come home!* Hadn't I just called her with the same idea? Instead I heard myself saying, "I'm just . . . surprised."

"I know. It is rather sudden. I'm sorry. But I have been thinking about it for a while."

I hesitated. Larry would have slapped me. *Snap out of it! She wants to come home! Roll out the red carpet, Stevie boy!*

"I've missed you, Stephen. I've never stopped loving you."

Holding the phone to my ear, I closed my eyes. "Donna . . ."

"Yes, Stephen?"

"Maybe you just have cold feet," I said, wincing at my own words.

"Cold feet?"

"Are you sure—"

"But you asked for more time, didn't you? I mean . . . you called me. What has changed?"

"I didn't want to push you—"

"Can we talk in person, Stephen? I hate to do this on the phone."

I agreed.

When I arrived at the apartment building, Donna was standing by the curb, her hands sheltered within her winter coat, her breath creating cold puffs of moisture. When she saw me, she came to the car immediately and quickly got in. Closing the door, she exhaled and shivered, rubbing her hands together. Immediately I caught the odor of *Charlie,* her college perfume. I'd always loved the scent, and she'd always known it. She smiled at me, but her eyes were pained. "Where can we go?"

The implication was obvious. We lived in a small town. Anyone might see us.

"Let's just drive," I said, and she nodded agreeably—eagerly, in fact.

I looked at my watch. We had two hours before we had to appear in court. We drove into the country for several miles without returning to our previous conversation. Instead, we made inane small talk about the weather, about Sally, about her work hours.

Off to the right, I saw a herd of deer, and it reminded me of a family vacation a few years back and a similar sight. I'd pointed and exclaimed, "Look, a gaggle of deer."

Alycia had spurt Coke over the front seat. "No," she exclaimed. "It's a flock."

Donna had chimed in with, "It's a school of deer!"

I now reminded Donna of the memory, and she chuckled. It seemed to break the ice. "I can't believe what you've done with Alycia, Stephen. She's so different." She turned in her seat, reached out and touched my shoulder, and without any kind of preparatory remarks, whispered, "Can you forgive me, Stephen?"

I spotted an empty office building, pointed to it. It served the purpose of buying time. She nodded, "Good idea. We can talk more easily there."

I turned left into the deserted parking lot. When I brought the car to a stop, we were surrounded by white fields with little straws of wheat sticking out. The landscape was empty and desolate. The car rocked as the wind blew little grains of snow against the glass.

I turned to her, and she looked at me earnestly, her eyes hopeful. I struggled for words—and the way to say them—but before I could speak, she said, "You're not interested, are you?"

"Donna—"

"I was a fool for believing again, wasn't I?"

"I didn't say that."

"You didn't have to." She blew a sorrowful and exasperated sigh and closed her eyes. "What was I thinking?"

Then she turned to me. "You're questioning my timing, aren't you?"

"No."

"You thought I was impressed with your sudden money."

I shook my head. "I know you don't care about that."

She bit her lip. "But money's important to you, isn't it?"

"Donna—"

"And that's why you loved Alice."

I was too startled to speak.

"I didn't want her money."

"No, of course not," Donna replied, shaking her head. "But you wanted her life."

I opened my mouth to respond, but nothing came out.

Donna let her hands fall lonely-like to her lap. She swallowed, then crossed her arms defensively and looked out her window for a moment. "I'm sorry, Stephen. I didn't mean it the way it came out. I meant . . . she was so . . . so what can we say? Exotic."

She reached over again—as if she couldn't stop touching me—and gently grasped my arm. Her gaze was scrutinizing but vulnerable. "Did you ever love me, Stephen?"

It was a simple question. But instead of leaning toward her, instead of squeezing her hand, instead of answering immediately and vehemently in the affirmative, I hesitated, and one moment's hesitation was all it took. When I finally attempted an answer, Donna smiled sadly. It was a painful smile, tinged with heartache, and her face turned splotchy red. "That's not the kind of question you have to think about." She blinked and the tears slipped down her face, but I resisted the inclination to reach over and wipe her cheeks.

Stillness overcame us, and I looked down at my fidgeting hands. The wind was blowing harder against the edge of the car, rocking it gently. The snowflakes pelted the car like sand pebbles.

"You caught me by surprise," I managed weakly.

"You were right, though. We were best friends once," she continued wistfully. "Isn't that what you told Alycia?"

I nodded. So they *had* talked.

Donna sniffed softly and wiped her cheeks. "After years of trying to live together, we forgot what it was like," she continued. "But since you seem convinced that we're truly over, and you have every right to feel that way—I mean . . . after how I left you and all . . . then I'm willing to try for what we once had. Are you willing?"

I considered her generous offer and felt another wave of regret. It was unlikely that we could ever return to the friendship we had in college. Most likely marriage had ruined that as well. But Donna, in her sweet naïvety, wasn't ready to let it go.

"I'm not a fool, Stephen. I've learned to accept your limitations." She bit her lip. "Well, I don't mean you are the only one who has them—I sure do." She turned and seemed to appraise me again. Her next words came out haltingly. "You know, I never thought I'd get married in the first place. You of all people should remember that. I was afraid of my own voice. How many times did you and Alice try to fix me up?" She blew out a humorous breath and started again. "I never intended to marry, unless . . ." And then she stopped again.

Unless what? I thought, waiting for her to finish, but she didn't.

The windshield was filling with windblown snow, almost completely eliminating visibility. She pursed her lips regretfully. "It doesn't matter anymore. You're right. We just took the wrong road. We were lonely, but that wasn't a good reason to marry. Sometimes it's not too late, you know, to go back and take the right road, the one we should have taken in the first place."

I shrugged and now reached for her hand. Our conversation was coming to a close, and she allowed me a gentle squeeze before pulling away. It was time to go. We drove back to town in silence. When I pulled up in front of the apartment, she drew the parka closer around her, peering out her window toward the building. She blew into her hands in preparation of getting out into the cold.

And then she turned to me, meeting my gaze before speaking. "Do you think God will forgive us for what we're about to do?"

I opened my mouth to say something reassuring, but stopped. No matter what I said, she wouldn't believe it, and then it occurred to me. Hadn't I refused her request for reconciliation?

I told her this and she shook her head sadly. "It's still my fault," she whispered, and slipped out into the cold.

In the end, we took separate cars so as not to mislead the court into believing that our marriage was reparable. I met her at the courthouse, and it only took another ten minutes, a slam of the gavel, and a loud announcement, *Next case!* to dissolve our marriage.

In the hallway afterward, we paused awkwardly. I was tempted to hug her but didn't. I was also tempted to ask her out to lunch—to celebrate? To soothe her damaged feelings?—but quickly dismissed it. Lunch at this time would be awkward and counterproductive. But maybe someday we might get together and . . . reminisce?

Of course not, I realized.

In the end, we said good-bye as if nothing had happened, ignoring that we'd considered changing our minds, ignoring the fact that Donna still loved me, and the ultimate irony, I still loved her.

Later I strolled through the judicial building, procrastinating my return to work. After peeking in on several proceedings, I sat in on a hearing and watched as the accused man pled guilty to stalking his ex-wife. In a matter of minutes, he agreed to counseling, signed up with a parole officer, paid a fine, and was released.

I didn't last much beyond that. Later at the office, Larry didn't even pretend interest in the details of my morning.

"Buried?" I asked him, standing at the edge of his papered abyss.

"Drowning," he replied.

"Need some help?"

He took a sip of coffee. "Give me a week or so."

I went to my office, closed the door behind me, and flicked off the lights. I took the phone off the hook and sat for half an hour. *It's over,* I thought, letting it sink in again, replaying Donna's and my morning conversation.

Very soon I'd begin paying a generous alimony despite Donna's refusal. Maybe I could finally persuade her to live in the house. Certainly, she would never have to work again, not if she didn't want to. Financially, I was on my way to complete solvency. But most important, Alycia and I had reconciled.

In spite of all this, I couldn't shake the lingering apprehension.

Chapter Twenty-Four

There's a tired old expression that truth is stranger than fiction. Sometimes I've read stories that seemed unbelievable, only to wonder later: Were they really that untrue to life? Or did they lack credibility because they were even *truer* to life?

Another expression: Tragedies happen in threes. Usually, though, three tragedies don't happen to the same person. But, again, occasionally the unbelievable happens. Consider a copy of *Ripley's Believe It or Not* or something by Shakespeare. Or an even better example, the Bible.

Why do you like tragedies? I'd once asked Donna. *What's the point of reading when you know the story won't end happily?*

I should have paid more attention to her answer. As for my own story, I suppose if someone had written a novel with what would happen next, I wouldn't have believed it. Then again, if I'd read it in a newspaper, I might have.

On Tuesday, the market broke its fractal on higher volume. Having waited nearly two months for a buy signal, I shifted the entire account into a long S&P futures position.

On Wednesday, the market sputtered. Several unexpected earnings disappointments were announced, and the market plunged one percent in the space of thirty minutes. I was stopped out with a loss of twenty thousand.

On Thursday, I set a buy stop at a new divergence point.

The market rallied through, retrieving my twenty thousand, then sputtered again, dropping below my stop loss. All told, I was down thirty thousand plus since the first fractal.

On Friday, the market continued its recovery threat, but this time, instead of setting a buy stop according to my system, I hesitated.

Recover your nerve, I told myself. *Take a break.*

On Saturday, Alycia and I took another drive into the country. She seemed more reserved, which I'd expected following the finality of the divorce. I knew she was angry with me but was fighting hard not to give me the silent treatment. I also knew she would forgive me. We both seemed determined not to let things deteriorate again.

When I dropped her off, she bubbled her cheek, and when I kissed it, she let it pop. I jumped, startled, and she giggled.

"Still love me, sweetie?"

"Yes, Dad. Even though you've really blown it this time."

I let this settle in. "Is your mom okay?"

She forced a smile. "She's breathing."

She'll be fine, I almost said but decided against it. I also wanted to tell her that her mother deserved a chance at true happiness, but that would be a conversation for another day.

Next Monday, the market roared back without me. By Wednesday, I panicked for a completely different reason. I was missing the entire move. I set a buy stop at the next fractal point, which was way beyond the base and a clear violation of my system, but at least I'd get on board. One little deviation wouldn't matter, would it?

The next day, I was stopped in—but scared to death. At this elevation, I closed my charts and refused to look down. Unfortunately, more earnings disappointments rang through the halls of Wall Street, followed by a disappointing inflation report. Then, when the Fed chairman made disparaging remarks about the state of the economy, the market went into a freefall.

I'd been suckered in. That evening, I mentally calculated my "paper" losses. Seventy thousand. Operating my brain was like thinking underwater. Pure emotion—fear and impending doom—had taken over. I shut down my computer again, determined to take a long break from the market and let my sell-stop handle the rest.

On Friday, by the time I arrived at Joe's, Paul had been there for three hours. Considering his inebriated state, making intelligent conversation became such an effort, I quit after five minutes. When I suggested he might slow down a bit, Paul came uncorked. "Mind your own business."

Our argument took a predictable course until I sputtered, "Fine. It's your life."

He caught Jennifer's eye across the room and gestured for another, but she only shook her head. He began seething again. "If you hadn't come, she wouldn't have had the guts."

At that point, Susan walked in, wearing her usual tight jeans and even tighter blue sweater. She placed her hands on her hips and declared: "Well look-ee here! Is it . . . no, it can't be . . . *Stephen*?"

I pulled out a chair, but Susan shook her head. "Sorry, hanging with you guys ain't good for a young lady's prospects."

I shrugged, guiding the chair back under the table. Susan patted Paul's shoulder. He only grunted. She cast me a look—*what's wrong with Cheerful?*—and went to sit at her end of the bar and begin flashing her eyelids, smiling at nearly everything in pants, methodically unreeling her net.

Paul remained silent. In spite of his relentless mood descent and Susan's latest prowl, I was preoccupied with my own graying cloud. *I'm still up eighty thousand,* I told myself. *Nothing but a temporary setback.* I glanced over at the counter and noticed that Spider Woman had already snagged a new guy. Minutes later, she was hanging over him as if he were a long-lost friend.

I stared at the man for a moment, wondering why he seemed familiar. I couldn't put my finger on it. Dismissing this, I turned to Paul and made another attempt. "You okay?" I asked.

He shrugged morosely.

"How're classes?"

"How would I know?"

I probed further and, despite his surly attitude, Paul threw me enough clues to figure it out. Apparently, he'd been fired, and while he didn't volunteer the reason, it wasn't hard to determine. Colleges prefer their teachers to show up sober to their classes.

"I'll drive you home."

"When I'm finished," he replied tersely.

I assured him he was.

His jaw clenched.

I turned to the TV, hoping to avoid another argument. My attention was distracted by Susan getting to her feet. She and her new guy were already blowing the joint. Paul followed my gaze as I watched her slip into the back rest room.

"Leave her alone," he grouched. "It's her life."

"So now you care?"

He expelled an angry breath. "You two are just alike . . ." And I braced myself for another drunken onslaught.

"She has everything she wants," Paul said. "She's got looks and a great personality. But she thinks she's got nothing." He practically spit out the last word. "Look at me. At least, I know I've got nothing, and I'm tired of you two moping around as if your lives were so miserable."

Several patrons tossed us curious glances.

"Careful, fella," I said, lowering my voice. "You're wearing your dissonance on your sleeve."

Paul wasn't finished. "Most guys would give anything to have a woman like Donna. But you . . . you just throw her away. And then you come in here and tell me *I'm* messed up."

My stomach clenched as if he'd slugged me. I lowered my voice. "We're just trying to help, Paul. You're addicted—"

"*I'm* addicted? *Moi?*" Paul scowled. "You're just as addicted as I am, my friend, only your addiction is socially acceptable."

My addiction? I refused to get sucked in.

But he stared at me, his eyebrows raised. "Care to play?"

"No," I muttered.

"Aaaagh!" Paul whined like a game show buzzer. "Wrong answer. Wanna try again?"

"Paul . . ."

"Aaaagh!" he whined again. "Sorry. Studio audience says . . . you're addicted to the past. Wow, there's a shocker."

My face flushed angrily. "You finished?"

"What was that chick's name?"

I frowned. "Who?"

Paul leered crookedly, his eyes scarcely able to focus. "The one you keep dreaming about?"

Years ago, I'd told him about my infrequent but predictable dream of Alice, the one where I'm trying to save her but never reach her in time. He'd replied in typical Paul fashion. "Imagine what might happen if you did?"

"Sorry?"

He'd smiled wryly. "I meant. . . what if you actually saved her?" He'd leaned forward, his face suddenly pensive, as if poised to dispense a profound metaphysical truth. "Seriously. Maybe by changing the dream past, we can change the present future. In fact, maybe you'd wake up and find yourself married to her."

I laughed off his comment as silly conjecture, but he'd only shrugged. "Stranger things have happened, Stephen."

"She wasn't a 'chick,'" I now said. "Her name was Alice."

"Ooooh," he said, his tone mocking. "Of course. Alice. My mistake."

I looked up at the TV again, hoping he'd drop his little rant. We sat stewing in silence for a few minutes, avoiding each other's gaze.

Toward the back, beyond the pool tables, the bathroom door opened, and despite my stupid argument with Paul, my emotions switched gears. A shudder of dread gripped me as Susan and her new guy walked by. She glanced at me out of the corner of her eye. I nodded toward our table. She shook her head no and continued walking toward the door. I turned to watch her go, and she looked my way one last time, narrowing her eyes.

"Leave her alone," Paul repeated.

Ignoring him, I rose to my feet. Susan was adjusting her coat when I approached her. She turned quickly to the guy. He leaned over. She whispered something in his ear. Looking up, he quickly scrutinized me. Satisfied with my lack of threat, he sauntered out the door.

"Can I talk to you a sec?" I asked, then without waiting for an answer, I grabbed her arm and pulled her over to the wood-paneled wall where we could talk in private.

She jerked her arm away. "What is it now, Stephen?"

"This guy gives me a creepy feeling."

She smirked. "You don't even know him."

"Neither do you."

"Better'n you do."

I sighed. "Susan, I've got a bad feeling about this one."

"Stop trying to run my life, Stephen."

"Since when—"

"You can't even run your own."

I opened my mouth to speak, then stopped. She crossed her arms, looking over my shoulder toward the darkened exterior of the barroom. I gazed at Susan and for a split second saw the desperate seventh-grade girl who only wanted her father to love her. And because she grew up blocks from me, and once tried to rescue me from humiliation during a silly junior high dance, I'd felt forever determined to help her. I followed her gaze to where Paul leered at us from his usual table, where he slowly drank himself to death.

Was I so different from Susan and Paul?

When I looked back at Susan, her gaze had intensified, her eyes suddenly desperate and vulnerable. "May I go, please?"

She was right, and so was Paul. I'd made a mess of my own life. Hadn't I let a wonderful woman walk away?

I searched my memory one last time, trying to place the guy. When nothing came to me, I stepped aside. Without saying goodbye, Susan headed for the door, pushing out into the cold without looking back. I turned to see Paul rambling toward me, adjusting his woolen scarf. He could barely walk. His eyes settled on me disdainfully just before he followed Susan out.

When I arrived home, I found a message on the recorder. It was Alycia. "Call me, okay? Tell me what we're doing tomorrow."

It was too late, so I didn't, but later that night while I made up the couch for bed, I finally placed Susan's new guy: He was the man from the courthouse who'd pled guilty to stalking. I picked up the phone and dialed her number, but no answer. Next, I dialed the police, and they promised to follow up. But what could they do? I was operating on a hunch—no crime had yet been committed.

The next morning my stomach threatened to convulse everything I'd eaten in the last twenty-four hours. I sat at the edge of the couch and tried to reclaim my bearings. Memories of last night's argument with Susan and Paul spun around in my brain. I tried calling Susan again, to no avail.

I attempted to stand, and the room shifted. I sat back down, frozen with inexplicable fear. An hour later I called Alycia and canceled our visit. I expected her to protest, but she didn't skip a beat. "That's okay," she said cheerfully. "Next week?"

The rest of the day was spent coming to grips with my trading mistake. I had plenty of money left—much more than I'd started with—but I couldn't shake the pervasive worry.

Sure enough, the following week, the market continued to sink. I tried soothing myself with the usual rationalizations: I wasn't the only one who'd lost money. I was already out, thanks to the miracle of automatic stops. At least I'd done *that* right, although I had yet to access my account to view the damage firsthand. I simply needed time to clear my head, that's all.

The next Saturday morning, the phone rang. I pried my eyes open and looked up at the digital clock. The numbers were fuzzy. By squinting I could barely make out something elevenish. What day was it anyway?

Saturday?

I answered the phone and my heart was pounding. "Hi, sweetie."

"Coming, Dad?"

I took a breath, cleared my throat, and put it together. "Sorry, honey, but . . . I overslept."

"Are you sick?" she asked, sounding concerned.

"No, I'm fine."

Her voice was crisper now. "So . . . you're not coming?"

"I'll be there in a few minutes," I said.

"Okay," she said and hung up.

I dressed, tossed on a baseball cap, and headed out the door. The winter wind stung my eyes, but the rest of my body felt hot and feverish. When I arrived, Alycia greeted me as if nothing had happened.

"I like the hat," she said, getting in the car. "You're a grunge-rabbit today."

We stopped by a burger joint, and then took a short drive east. She talked nonstop, catching me up on the previous two weeks. Neither of us mentioned the divorce or our last discussion, but despite her chatty nature, I detected some reservation in her manner. Unspoken between us lurked the suspicion that the past was starting all over again.

When I dropped her off, she wrinkled her nose playfully. "Take a shower!"

I laughed, but a serious expression covered her cherubic face, and then her eyes turned triumphant. "I forgot to tell you. I finally figured it out, Dad."

I frowned. "Figured what out?"

"Why Alice went back to her car."

I grinned. "You're kidding. I thought you'd forgotten all about that."

"I had, but last week it just came to me. Like, out of nowhere. I told Mom, and she didn't completely fess up, but she came close."

"So . . . what was it?" I asked, playing along. If Donna knew, that would mean she'd lied to me.

Alycia's smile turned mischievous. "It's my turn to keep a secret."

"Oh brother."

"But at least, *I* give clues," she said. "It's in something Mom forgot at the house."

I was confused. *At the house?*

"She wants it back too." Alycia opened the door. "So . . . will I see you next week?"

I smiled at her determination to pique my curiosity. "Of course."

She nodded as if it were a done deal, then headed up the sidewalk.

I called her name, and she turned. I gestured for her to come back, and she did. When she reached the car door, I sighed. "I never apologized, Alycia."

She smiled graciously. "I forgive you, Dad. Okay? I don't expect you to be perfect."

"Actually . . . I was talking about the divorce."

She shrugged. "So was I."

When she reached the door, she turned back and waved again. She blew me a kiss, and a shudder passed through me. It reminded me of Alice's last gesture to me. I blew her a kiss back, then headed home, and gave no further thought to her little clue.

Chapter Twenty-Five

I spent nearly the entire Sunday at Joe's watching ESPN, eating lunch and then dinner without ever budging from my spot. I kept my back to the door, expecting Paul to walk in as if nothing had happened, wondering if he'd been too drunk to remember our last interchange. Any minute, he would poke my shoulder. *Dude, you got started without me!*

I looked for Susan as well, but she didn't show. Yesterday, I had called her apartment at least five times. By now I figured she'd simply had enough of my interfering.

About eight o'clock, my cell phone buzzed. I didn't recognize the number and hesitated before answering.

"Stephen?" An older woman's voice, ragged and desperate.

"Yes?" I answered, and then placed the voice: Clare Thompson, Paul's mother.

Her voice broke, and I heard the soft clearing of her throat. "Paul's been taken to the hospital."

My eyes darted to the empty seat.

"Just come," she said. "Please come quickly."

I arrived at St. Luke's Hospital ten minutes later, and after a moment of indecision and frantic sign reading, ended up in the pediatric ward. The nurses aimed me in the opposite direction toward the emergency room. There I found Mrs. Thompson standing alone in the waiting room, peering outside through the foggy glass windows. She was shaking. When she turned to me, her face was pale, eyes red.

"He was in an accident," she said, gesturing toward a closed door. Moments later a nurse came rushing out the door, and in the temporary gap, I saw several blue-green coats leaning over a helpless form.

A shudder of dread passed through me. I grabbed Clare's shoulder and pulled her to me, and whispered what I hoped was true. "He's in good hands. He'll be fine."

She broke down and wept on my shoulder. "They called me at home," she cried, her voice hitching. "I guess he hit a parked car." She took a deep breath and let it out slowly. "He'd been . . ."

She couldn't finish.

I squeezed her tighter, leading her away from the door, back to the waiting room.

"He'll be fine," I assured her again.

After further minutes of tortured waiting, the doctor came out with a poorly composed poker face. He stood in front of us, and Clare looked up at him hopefully.

"He's stable for the moment . . ."

Clare nodded, her face suddenly optimistic.

"But he's showing extremely erratic brain activity. . . ."

Clare put her hand to her mouth.

"We're going to continue to monitor him, but . . ."

"Will he. . . ?" Clare couldn't finish.

"We don't know," the doctor said. He smiled apologetically, then slipped away. Once again, I hugged Clare tightly as she burst into tears.

"You were his only friend, Stephen," she cried into my shoulder, as if he were already gone.

I didn't arrive home until early next morning. Clare's friends had come quickly following the doctor's urging. Most of them were from her church; others were family members who lived in surrounding rural communities, people I might have met if Paul were a different sort. They scrutinized me carefully, as if suspecting my association with Paul had somehow contributed to this tragedy.

Eventually, we had been allowed to enter the room, where Paul, scratched and bandaged beyond recognition, was attached to an assortment of machines and tubes. The irregular brain wave on the monitor confirmed the doctor's grim diagnosis. I sat in a chair for hours, surrounded by the usual hospital fare: the obligatory crucifix over the bed. The required pastel scenic painting. The sterile smell of disinfectant, like a thousand Band-Aids. The IV pole. Oxygen tubes. The heart monitor.

Donna called early evening to offer her sympathy. I did my best to explain what happened, but she seemed more concerned with my own personal state.

"You tried to get him to quit, didn't you?"

I wasn't up for guilt alleviation. "Not hard enough."

That evening, I finally reached Susan on her cell phone. She hadn't heard and became immediately distraught. "Is Paul going to die?"

I wanted to tell her what I believed, that if he didn't die now, someday we might wish he had. The more we talked, the more distressed she seemed.

"I've been trying to reach you," I said. "You okay?"

She ignored my question. "Which room?"

I told her.

"I'll meet you there tomorrow," she said, hanging up.

The next day, Tuesday, I went to the hospital early and found Clare lying on a small couch in the waiting room. I went to peek into Paul's room, then heard her ragged voice behind me, "No word, Stephen."

I sat down with her for a while and once again offered my assistance, but she declined. "I've got friends staying with me."

Midmorning, I went to work. When I arrived at the office, I

realized I hadn't even told Larry. He responded with exaggerated shock, his demeanor initially apologetic. But within minutes, he was preoccupied again.

It was one o'clock in the afternoon when Judy, one of Clare's friends, called me—at the office. The doctors couldn't agree as to the degree of Paul's brain activity. Most tests indicated significant and permanent damage, so a follow-up CT scan had been scheduled.

After work I stopped by the hospital again, and once more waited for several hours in the outer room with Clare. Susan showed mid-evening, and the reason for her earlier avoidance was obvious. Her face was a mask of bruises, and a bandage was over her nose.

"Oh, Susan," I whispered, reaching for her. Her eyes scrunched together, and she seemed to fight the tears but finally gave in. She wept in my arms, whispering, "You were right, you were right."

I sat her down, and she started from the beginning. At some point, Mr. Right had transformed into Mr. Hyde. What had begun as a silly argument inexplicably transitioned into a fight, and then Mr. Hyde slapped her around, breaking her nose in the process. Frightened for her life, Susan had finally bolted out the front door.

"Did you call the cops?" I asked—a silly question.

She nodded, then shrugged. "They picked him up this morning."

Together we crept to the edge of Paul's room. Looking in through the glass, Susan began weeping again. "He looks so peaceful," she cried, burying her face in my shoulder. I knew what she meant. Under normal circumstances, neither of us would have described Paul as a peaceful person.

Later I followed her home in my car. She stood at my car window and thanked me. I watched her walk up the steps to her house, insert the key, wave once more, and slip inside.

I sat there for a moment longer, suddenly struck by the foolishness of our lives, and if it hadn't been so tragic, it would have been ironically funny. It's almost as if the three of us, Susan, Paul and myself, had been cursed somehow, bound and determined to play out a record that had been broken in childhood.

Snap out of it, Larry would have said ironically, unaware of his own chains to the past. Larry simply plodded along, determined to channel another groove.

I dismissed my pointless conjecture and headed home.

On Wednesday, I went to the office early and received a phone call. While I didn't recognize the ID, I picked up anyway. I wasn't in the mood to be yelled at by a former disgruntled customer, but in the glare of recent events, it didn't seem so daunting anymore. The man identified himself as my online broker, and the room went blurry the moment he spoke. "Do you want to meet your margin call?"

Margin call?

"There must be some mistake," I said. "What is the value of my account?"

"We're at five thousand," he said.

Five thousand? "You must have the wrong party."

"Are you Stephen Whitaker?"

The room seemed to spin. "Don't understand . . ."

The voice on the phone began the explanation, but his words barely registered.

"But . . . I set a stop . . . didn't I?"

I heard the distant clicking on a keyboard. "We have no record of a stop-loss order."

Impossible, I thought. Without a stop, my entire account would have followed the market's recent decline. A three-percent market drop in itself was nothing, but magnified by the leverage of my account, it was enormous. Not only would I have lost my profit, but I would have lost nearly every cent of my credit-line money. I was worse than broke. I was in debt with nothing to show for it.

Unable to catch my breath, I stammered into the phone, "Please close my position."

When I hung up, the room began to spin. *How could I possibly have forgotten?*

Moments later, without thinking, without pausing to consider the consequences, I picked up the phone and called Donna. Sally answered on the third ring.

"I need to talk to my wife." I stopped. "I mean, uh . . ."

"Donna's not here," Sally said coldly.

"Will you . . . have her return my call?"

"Sure—"

"Never mind," I replied as evenly as I could. "I'll contact her later."

I hung up. What was I doing? Calling my ex-wife for comfort? I turned off my own cell phone, removing the temptation, and sat there, allowing the reality to wash over me.

Maybe it's simply a mistake, I thought. *Maybe they lost my stop order.*

Of course they hadn't. There was no mistake. In the moments of self-reproach that followed, the truth slipped into my consciousness, like a snake slithering through the weeds.

Had I *really* forgotten? Why had I been so anxious during the past weeks? The answer was obvious. *Traders are as successful as they want to be.*

My defeat had been inevitable long before I'd opened my first position, and now I was finished. There was no recovery. This was the end of the line. There wasn't enough money to begin again. There wasn't even enough equity to repay the debt. Only one option: bankruptcy, the selling off of every asset I owned, the final submission to my failure.

Chapter Twenty-six

During the following week, I visited Paul in the hospital twice daily, a few hours in the morning, a few more in the evening. Susan and I alternated "visiting" duty. She was a shadow of her former self, as if she'd finally crossed the point of no return. Her own prognosis was dim, although not life-threatening. Her nose, so badly damaged, probably would never look the same again.

I tried consoling her, to no avail. Slowly, she closed herself up, devastated not only by the physical abuse and the betrayal of yet another fervent wish, but with the diminishment of what she had seen as her only asset. Her own "trading" account was now down to zero.

Eventually they moved Paul to another room, upgraded his status to serious, and continued to watch his progress. He hadn't regained consciousness since the accident, and his brain monitor continued to show erratic signs.

Waiting there, sitting with Paul's mother in the sterility of the waiting room, had a disconnecting effect on me. With Paul lying there unaware of his surroundings, I felt nearly jealous of his oblivion.

At work I muddled through, and as usual Larry never noticed. *One foot in front of another,* I repeated to myself. Eating and drinking lost their appeal, and I lost five pounds in seven days.

Monitoring the caller ID, I ignored all but the most pertinent of calls. Donna called several times and left a couple of messages: "Sally told me you called." Later: "Did you get my message, Stephen?" And finally: "I'm worried about you, Stephen."

By Wednesday, the initial panic gave way to something akin to mental anesthesia. By Friday, further removed yet, I felt something akin to relief, as though divorced from the "pressure" of seeking success.

Friday afternoon, my mother called. Suddenly, we were in the land of stranger-than-fiction.

"Your father has been admitted," she said.

She told me Dad had doubled over with a terrible case of heartburn while tooling around in his garage. The doctors had commenced a series of tests, but the initial consensus was positive. Gallbladder attack was the initial prognosis, and most likely surgery would be scheduled to remove it.

"Stephen, he wants to see you."

"What room?" I asked. She told me—and the number was a mere three hospital doors down from Paul.

I dashed down the steps to Main Street, jumped in my car, and ten minutes later I was climbing the hospital steps to the second floor. Reaching my father's room, I knocked softly and heard my mother's voice. "It's open."

I pushed the door open, slowly crossing the threshold. My mother, wearing a flowery blue dress, was sitting on the heat register at the end of the room, her back against the windows, her arms braced against the vent. My father's room was a carbon copy of Paul's—same speckled linoleum tile, sky blue walls, pastel prints hanging, and warped plastic chairs, issued in bright primary colors.

Lying in a bed surrounded by chest-high aluminum bars, my father's eyes were closed, his mouth partially open. He had clear plastic tubes in his nostrils, which crossed his cheeks, looped over his ears, and connected under his chin. From there they extended to a hole in the wall. Another tube snaked from his arm to a bag of fluid hanging from a pole, and I recognized a blood pressure cuff. Little wires were connected to adhesive patches on his chest, which ran to a heart rate monitor. I watched the EKG line flicker—squiggly marks, line, squiggly marks, line. Another number indicated his heart rate. He looked terribly vulnerable.

Mom rose from her perch, leaned over him, and passed a gentle hand across his forehead, then smoothed his silvery hair. She'd always been so proud of his full mane, and Dad wore it—and preened it—like a peacock.

You got that from me, he once said, appraising my own hair.

"Mom's father is bald, so the verdict is still out," I'd told him, determined to deny him the right to pass anything of value to me.

I sat in the flimsy chair. "Is he in pain?"

Mom bit her lip and nodded. "This came out of nowhere."

I leaned forward, reaching for her hand. "How are you holding up?"

She nodded again, and her eyes blinked as she did so. "He was asking for you," she said. "On the way here."

I requested further medical clarification, and she gave it to me. They'd scheduled him for an abdominal ultrasound. I inquired of the garage episode, and she indicated that he'd been popping antacids like candy. "But you know how your father is. . . ."

Yes, I thought, wondering how many times I'd heard her defend him with those words.

She sequenced the details for me, then fell silent. I remained with her for several hours as the nurses traipsed in and out with overly cheerful countenances. *Don't they know where they are?* I thought, and yet, at that point, it hadn't even occurred to me, or anyone, that my father's hours could be numbered.

Just after seven o'clock my father finally opened his eyes half mast. His gaze lingered on me, and his words came out in a raspy whisper, "Well, I'll be the court jester."

Mom echoed the sentiment, which seemed to hearken back to an earlier conversation. "I told you he'd come."

I didn't know what to do—rise to my feet, approach the bed, or stay sitting. My father's gesture solved it for me. "Let me get a look at ya."

I rose and went to stand beside the bed.

"I got heartburn, that's all. I shouldn't even be here anymore."

"Let 'em finish their tests, Dad."

He shook his head. "So I gotta get sick to see my own son?"

My mother stifled an angry snort. "Lou . . ."

I smiled at Mom to assure her and looked down upon this man I'd spent my life trying to avoid. In that moment, I came face-to-face with the truth of my emotions—the fact that for years, I hadn't cared whether he lived or died.

My father cleared his throat. "I got a will, you know."

"Lou!" my mother exclaimed. "That's unnecessary. You're going to be fine."

"It's routine, Dad," I added.

My dad was nothing if not stubborn. He stopped, swallowed, then gazed up at me. "I left you something."

I shook my head, and Mom jumped to her feet. "Lou, you can give it to him yourself, if it's so all-fired important."

All-fired? That's the closest my mother had ever come to swearing.

"Dad, you're just like Alycia. You're a drama king."

Still looking up at me, he winked, and then his eyes drooped shut again. He didn't awaken again that evening, and around ten o'clock, I bid my mother farewell, promising to stop by again tomorrow.

"Morning?"

I nodded, pursing my lips as I did so.

"He wanted to talk to you," she said.

"And he did."

She shook her head adamantly. "No, Stephen. He really wanted to talk."

I shrugged *okay,* wondering if the stress was getting to her.

"I'm sleeping here tonight," she continued. "Maybe I'll stop at Ruth's for a little while in the morning."

Ruth Westerly was my mother's best friend from church. I reached out for her and hugged her tightly. She hugged me back. "Promise?" she whispered again.

"I promise, Mom."

She patted my back. "It felt so good to have you here."

"He's fine, Mom. Relax."

As I drove home, and as I pondered the last few hours, I realized I'd forgotten to look in on Paul. Only a few rooms away. *Bizarre,* I thought, struck again by the absurdity. First Paul, then my father . . . *what next?* Like a page out my childhood *Ripley's.*

In the driveway, I shut off the engine and gripped the steering wheel, impressed with the impulse to pray, to say something—*anything*—to God.

I racked my brain, started *O God,* and came up with nothing else.

Chapter Twenty-seven

The next day, Saturday, I awakened at four o'clock, my head pounding again. I stumbled to the bathroom, and the mirror revealed the results of my fitful night. I went back to the couch, hoping for another hour or two, but sleep eluded me.

At ten, I finally dragged myself up and called Donna. When I gave her the news about Dad, she was concerned.

"Apparently . . . it's just routine. But—"

"But what?"

I shrugged as though she could see me. "Nothing."

"Are you worried?" she asked, her voice just above a whisper.

I had difficulty putting it into words. My father had looked worse than his diagnosis.

"Oh, Stephen, Alycia will want to see him."

I didn't question Donna's assessment, regardless of Alycia's low opinion of her grandfather. I suggested stopping by to pick her up.

"No," Donna said. "We'll meet you there."

We agreed to meet at the hospital in thirty minutes. When I arrived, Donna, in light slacks and striped blouse, and Alycia, in jeans and T-shirt, were waiting for me in the main-floor reception area. The moment I walked in through the doors, Alycia rushed to me. We hugged beneath the crucifix. "Is Grandpa gonna die?" she asked.

I smiled down at her and wiped the tears from her eyes. "No, honey."

I hugged her again. Moments later, the three of us rode the elevator to the second floor, where I led them across the linoleum floor to room 252.

Donna paused before entering. "Where's Paul?"

I nodded down the hallway.

Donna shook her head in disbelief. I shrugged to acknowledge what she must have been thinking. She asked me the prognosis, and I shrugged again. "No one knows yet. But it doesn't look promising."

Donna put her hand to her mouth.

"We're hoping for the best," I said, the kind of trite remark that comes way too easily in the midst of disaster.

She reached out and touched my shoulder before realizing what she'd done. When she retracted it, I smiled, and she smiled back. An innocent mistake. We walked in.

My father's eyes were still closed, and his expression seemed coffinlike. The moment my mother spotted Donna, she burst into tears. With arms wide open, she practically ran across the room.

"I've missed you," Donna exclaimed, and my mother echoed the sentiment. They collapsed into each other's embrace.

Alycia moseyed over next to me. Before I knew it, she was leaning against me so heavily I had to step back with one leg in order to stay upright.

"It's okay, sweetie."

"I know, Dad. I'm just . . . sensitive, okay?"

I chuckled. "No kidding."

She elbowed me in the ribs.

"Ouch."

While my mother laid out the chronology of the entire sorry situation for Donna, Alycia remained buried in my arms. I squeezed her even tighter, kissing the top of her head, and she sniffed.

Donna and Alycia stayed for another two hours, during which time my father remained asleep, but they were present, at least, for the verdict, and it wasn't what we expected. Dr. Parmele came in, friendly but professional, holding a folder. "I need to talk to the family."

Donna stepped closer to me, giving me a look that said, in no uncertain terms, she still qualified. Speaking softly and compassionately, the doctor, nevertheless, stated the unvarnished truth. "I'm afraid we've made another discovery. It was difficult to spot at first but . . ."

I could sense Mom bracing herself. Donna frowned in anticipation.

"I'm afraid we've found a large aortic aneurism," the doctor finished. She looked at my mother. "We need to schedule immediate surgery."

At first none of us said a word, reading instead the doctor's grim demeanor.

"When?" I asked, and Dr. Parmele looked at her folder again. "No later than tomorrow, but there's no need for ICU. He'll be in good care here."

When she walked out, my mother nearly collapsed into her seat, and Donna rushed to grab her arm. Alycia leaned against me again and burst into tears.

Early afternoon, when it was time to take Alycia home, Donna wanted to talk. She paused at the door, nodding for Alycia to go on ahead. "I'll meet you just outside the downstairs elevator, honey."

In the hallway, Donna and I compared impressions, and we both agreed: Something besides my father's situation was bothering Alycia. Normally, she was a rock of courage during tragic events, determined to be strong for everyone else.

"I'll call her later," I said.

Donna began to move down the hall again, but I touched her arm. She turned, her eyes inquisitive. I heard my mother's voice muffled from within the room, then my father's husky tone. Apparently, he was awake.

I took another breath. We stood there awkwardly until she bridged the gap and hugged me. She smelled just as I remembered, but it seemed terribly different. She was here because she wanted to be, not because she had to come out of a sense of responsibility. I resisted the inclination to linger within her arms. She felt comfortable, warm and safe, and when I let her go, she kissed me on the cheek and smiled into my eyes as though we hadn't been divorced just a few weeks earlier.

Minutes later, Larry came by, carrying a bouquet of flowers.

My father rasped out humorously. "I ain't no female, son."

"Flowers are for men too," my mother assured him.

Larry didn't skip a beat. "Actually . . . I was hoping to impress the nurses. Maybe . . . get a date or something . . ."

"Well, then," my father exclaimed, gesturing to his fold-out table. "Put 'em front and center. I'll put in a good word with that cute brunette down the hall."

Larry sat down and bantered with my father while my mother left the room to compose herself. When she returned, her face splotchy, Larry offered to bring supper for her, as though playing the dutiful son she supposedly never had. She politely accepted his offer.

"Bring me some ice cream," my father said, tongue-in-cheek.

Larry laughed and left the room.

It was early evening when my father, after taking another nap, decided it was time for our talk. Larry had left hours before, having punched my shoulder on the way out. Hard. It still smarted.

My mother rose. "I'll be down the hall."

"Stay, Mom."

Dad shook his head. "I need to talk to Stephen alone."

Hidden from my father's view, Mom lingered at the doorway. *Be careful,* her eyes said, and I nodded, which seemed to reassure her.

Once Mom had left, my father's eyes closed again. At first I wondered if he'd suddenly fallen asleep again. Then, without looking at me, he said, "I don't blame you at all, Stephen."

I was prepared to head him off at the pass. I didn't want to hear his premature deathbed confessions. "You're going to be fine, Dad. Let's not do this, today."

He opened his eyes. "Do what?!"

"Anything that will needlessly rile you," I said. "You need to stay calm."

"Stephen, please," he said, shaking his head vigorously. "May I have five minutes of your time?"

I sighed. My father swallowed, then started again. "I don't blame you for hating me."

I looked down at the floor. "I don't hate you."

My father licked his lips and considered my dubious reply. "What kind of idiot do you think I am?"

"Dad, please—"

"I can't make up for being a lousy father, but I *can* apologize, and if you don't want to accept it, then don't, but at this point, that's all I got."

I expelled an exasperated breath, still looking at the floor. When he didn't continue, I looked up. His eyes were closed again. I waited for another minute before he spoke again.

"I never intended to cheat anyone, but there's a whole lotta folks who'll tell you otherwise. I was trying to help, Stephen. I just . . . wasn't very good at it."

"You were a good salesman," I said, for lack of something better to say.

He blew out an exasperated breath. "That'n' a quarter will get you a cup a coffee."

"Dad—"

"I don't want to rehearse the past, Stephen. There comes a time when you just chuck the whole thing and hope that God sorts it out." My father took a deep long breath and sighed. He opened his eyes again and fixed me with a piercing gaze. "I kept 'em," he said.

"You were only twelve when I realized the game was over, but I kept 'em anyway."

I tried to make sense of his seeming incoherence.

"They're in a box," he said. "Your mother knows what they are, and when you see them, you'll understand. I wanted it all back, Stephen, but by the time I woke up, it was too late."

My father struggled with his composure. "I wanted it back . . ."

"Dad, get some sleep. We'll talk tomorrow."

He snorted. "I got all eternity to sleep."

I resisted the inclination to chide him. "I'm going to get Mom."

Dad reached out and grabbed my arm. I was startled by his strength, like a vise grip, and his eyes pierced my own. He opened his mouth, then closed it. "If not for her, I'd die with nothing."

I forced a smile. "Mom's special. We all know that."

Closing his eyes, he sighed, and I gently pulled away from his grip. "I'll get her for you, Dad."

After I had found Mom and we returned to the room, Dad lay very still. I assumed he'd dozed off again, but his face lacked color. *He's tired,* I told myself, ignoring the queasy feeling in my gut. For the next few hours, Mom and I shared few words, and Dad didn't awaken. Mom thumbed through a gardening magazine, if for no other reason than to stay occupied, and I caught a few winks in the chair, thinking about the upcoming scheduled surgery.

Snippets of our conversation flickered through my mind. *I got all eternity to sleep.* And I cringed at the memory of our last phone call. *Come with me,* he'd said.

I was suddenly awakened to the sound of a continuous shrill beep. *Code blue 252* echoed over the intercom system. I glanced up at the heart monitor and to my horror, realized the EKG had flatlined. Before I could react, several nurses burst into the room, pulling what appeared to be a big red toolbox. In a flash, our room became the center of frenetic activity.

I hugged my trembling mother, who prayed under her breath.

One nurse opened the box and pulled out two paddles, and another nurse ushered us out of the room. As the door closed behind us, I heard the words, "Charge! Clear!"

For thirty minutes, Mom and I hovered by the door, waiting for any word. Finally, a doctor came out, his face glistening with sweat. I recognized the truth in his grim expression. So did my mother. "He's with Jesus," she whispered, closing her eyes. "Dear Lord, watch over my husband."

The doctor continued speaking. "His aneurism must have ruptured. We don't know for sure, but an autopsy would confirm this."

As I tried to listen, my thoughts were as incoherent and rambling as my father's speech. *He was perfectly fine a few hours ago.*

They allowed us to visit Dad one last time, to say our good-byes. I did my best to simply hold Mom as tightly as I could, until she'd said everything she'd needed to say and the nurse gently lifted the sheet over Dad's face.

A few minutes later, two men in blue hospital gowns gently lifted my father's body to a gurney. As Mom and I followed, they took him downstairs. The mortuary had already been notified.

The next few hours were a blur. Larry came back. Ruth was there. Eventually, all the arrangements had been made, and when my mother hugged me good-bye, just before getting into Ruth's car, she whispered what I would have expected: "You're in shock, Stephen. Please don't worry about me. Take care of yourself."

My throat closed. My dear mother. Her husband had just died, and she was worried about me. Dazed, I drove home in the dark, through a world that had changed suddenly. Inside the house, and alone again, I tried to embrace the reality of it. My father was dead. I slept fitfully that night, trying to erase the last images of my father's life.

The next morning, I drove up to Frederick to attend Sunday church with my mother. She'd insisted on seeing her friends again, regardless of the timing.

When we entered the church, the entire congregation converged upon us. People I'd never met before hugged me, offering condolences.

"Your father talked about you nonstop," someone said to me. "His death was so sudden!"

"You look just like him," someone else whispered in my ear, and for once it didn't seem like such a blight.

We sat up front again, like privileged guests. The pastor acknowledged my mother from the pulpit, then announced the plans for a Wednesday funeral. I reached over and patted Mom's hand.

"He's in a better place," she said, smiling through the anguish in her eyes.

On Wednesday, during the funeral, Donna and Alycia sat on one side of me, Mom and Larry on the other side, while the minister spoke of a gentle man who didn't resemble my father. Alycia sobbed nonstop, and I wondered if our divorce hadn't contributed to her newfound vulnerability.

"She's more fragile than you think," Donna had said to me.

It's natural, I told myself. *No one handles funerals well.* But in my heart, I knew there was something else going on.

Thursday my mother invited me out to the house. I drove the twenty miles in radio silence, and was relieved to see her surrounded by friends, seemingly in good care.

When I came in the door, her friends greeted me, and I lingered for as long as seemed appropriate, listening as the others engaged in painful reminiscing.

Excusing myself, I wandered around the house until I noticed, in the living room, a cardboard box resting on an old ottoman.

When it was time to go, Mom handed it to me. "Open it at home."

I was tempted to protest, to buy some time, but instead placed it in the trunk of my car. When I got back, I pulled into the garage and shut off the engine. I pressed the remote and the garage door lumbered down.

In the dimness of the garage, I opened the trunk and stared at the box. Bracing myself, I lifted the lid and found my old softball and mitt, given to me by neighbors I'd long forgotten.

Slowly, I closed the box again, folding the flaps. Carrying it inside, I buried it in a corner of the basement, hoping I'd never see it again. When I ascended the stairs, it finally hit me. Strangely exhausted, my legs stiffening, my arms suddenly weak, I allowed myself to sink to the stairwell.

I'd already spent a foolish lifetime lamenting what might have been, and as I sat in the middle of the stairs, I now wept for what could never be.

Chapter Twenty-Eight

On Friday morning, the doctor provided a preliminary diagnosis for Paul's situation. What seemed to be a coma, they said, wasn't a coma at all. "It's severe brain damage," the doctor said in his now-familiar clinical tone. "He'll need to relearn how to talk, how to walk, how to eat." A lifetime of physical therapy would be required, not to regain his former life, but to function merely like a five-year-old. "Even that's somewhat optimistic," the doctor told Clare, who was visibly shaken. We all had expected, hoped for, something far better.

Susan wasn't around to hear the report. She'd already left for Minnesota to stay with her sister. She hadn't even said good-bye, and I didn't expect to see her for a long time.

In the meantime, I'd called my attorney to begin the bankruptcy proceedings, and while I waited for a court date, he suggested I attend Gamblers Anonymous. I looked for one, but the closest chapter was Sioux Falls, two hundred miles away.

Late morning, Alycia phoned me from school, and her mood was more dark than at the funeral. I tried to conduct a normal conversation, but getting her to open up was like extracting teeth.

"What a pair we are," I cracked a fake chuckle, but she didn't chuckle back.

"Let's get some ice cream," I suggested.

"I hate ice cream," she said. "Always have."

During the course of our remaining conversation, I continued to probe gently, but the more I did, the more distant she became. Finally, I asked, "Is there someone else you'd rather talk to?"

I meant it well, but she must have taken it wrong and hung up on me. An hour later, Alycia called back. She sounded as if she'd been crying again.

"Okay. Fine. I need to talk to you—in person," she said.

"Of course, honey," I replied. "But have you tried talking to Mom?"

"I *can't* tell Mom," she cried. "I need to talk to *you.*"

"Okay," I agreed. "Whatever it is, honey, we'll get through it."

I promised to pick her up after work, and once again, she hung up without saying good-bye.

Unfortunately, Larry had picked this day to release the bombshell I'd been anticipating for months. When he poked his head in the office, I nearly dropped my teeth. The patented affluent suit and incongruent tie had been replaced with jeans, a long-sleeve plaid shirt, and tennis shoes.

"What are you doing for lunch?" he asked in an offhand manner.

My initial inquiries were met with a hokey smile. We locked the office and took his car to Sixth Avenue. On the way, I tried to read his cheerful behavior.

"Going on vacation?" I asked him, sizing up his attire.

He turned to me and granted me another puzzling smile. "I'll tell you everything in a few minutes."

The Steak House was a semi-fine restaurant with no windows and plenty of private booths. A young man in a white jacket confirmed Larry's reservation and then led us to the back, to what seemed like a padded cubbyhole.

Larry ordered wine, another first, and after perusing a selection of steaks, we ordered lunch.

He leaned on the table and swished the wine in his goblet. "I know you've been trading, Stephen."

He said it as if I'd done something illegal, but I didn't deny his accusation; at this point, admitting it would have been a mere formality. Besides, my poker face wasn't up to par.

"That's what you brought me here for?" I asked.

"I knew you would lose it all." He took a sip of his chardonnay and continued. "It was inevitable, wasn't it?"

I bit my lip and braced myself for what now appeared to be a rather abysmal lunch, but he switched gears. He asked about Donna and Alycia, as if he and I were mere acquaintances, not best friends, as if he had suddenly come to earth after having been gone for months.

When the waiter brought the food, my appetite had long since disappeared into a quagmire of irritation. I fixed Larry with a confused frown. "What's going on, Larry? Surely, you didn't bring me here to give me a lecture."

This time he didn't hedge. "We're about to be indicted, Stephen, and I'm not sticking around for it." Larry casually finished cutting off a piece of steak, stuck it in his mouth, and began chewing.

That simple.

"Indicted?"

Again, that goofy smile emerged as he chewed his food. He seemed to enjoy eating in a way I hadn't seen in months. "Tax fraud," he mumbled through a full mouth.

"Tax fraud," I repeated. *Of course.*

In an exaggerated casual manner, so casual I wondered if he wasn't just making the whole thing up, he explained the situation. The more he talked, the more flabbergasted I became. Offshore trusts. Fraudulent charitable foundations. Diverted income to nonexistent foreign corporations.

He finished by confirming the obvious. "We're ruined, Stephen. There's no partnership anymore. Once they arrive, and I figure they'll be here in days, no later than Monday, our assets will be frozen—what's left of them, that is—and eventually the business will be dissolved."

I leaned back in my chair and fixed him with a bewildered frown. Monday was only four days away. "Am I missing the punch line?"

He laughed, nodding proudly. With a dramatic flair, he reached into his shirt pocket, pulled out an envelope, and handed it to me. "You beat me to it."

I stared at it, confused. Opening the flap, I pulled out a small paper. It contained what seemed to be an account number, a random array of letters, and the name of a bank.

"Remember how you once walked me home after school because I was too scared to face my dad alone?" Larry's expression bordered on the nostalgic, a new emotion for him. " 'For better or worse,' remember?" Larry chuckled. "Your half, partner."

"Half of what?" I asked.

"Just don't lose the number *or* the password," he said. "It's your ticket out, Stephen."

I stared at the number. "How much?"

"Two point four," he replied without blinking.

I stared at him. "Thousand?"

He laughed. "Get serious."

"Who does it belong to?"

"You."

"Where did you get it?"

"Multi-multi-millionaires. All of 'em rich enough to absorb my fee without batting an eyelash. Thirty thousand a pop. And for that, I saved them millions."

"You stole it."

He shook his head with irritation. "Of course not. They paid us fair and square. They knew the risks. For my advice and expertise they took a chance. Most of them will survive unscathed."

"Most?"

Larry nodded. "I've burned the paper trail. The files have been shredded. The hard drive has been wiped clean. Tax returns are all they have."

It was all so glib. Another walk in the park. Another day at the zoo. Two million dollars. Finders keepers, losers weepers.

"Where is it?" I asked. "What country?"

Larry grinned proudly. "Guess."

"Switzerland."

Larry laughed. "Grand Cayman."

I considered this. "So . . . what's next?"

"I told you," he replied, cutting the last piece of charcoaled steak, forking it into his mouth. "I'm leaving." He finished chewing, dabbed his mouth with the linen white napkin, and wiped off his hands. Apparently, he was leaving now.

"Where?"

Larry tossed the napkin on the table and abruptly stood up. "Deniability, partner. I can't tell you."

"So . . . you're leaving me here to answer the questions."

"I'm paying you well for it."

I looked at the paper again.

"Check it out," Larry said. "They have an online Web site. Plug in the number, but erase your footprints once you're finished."

"I have to lie?"

Larry snorted. "Is that a problem?"

"They'll give me a lie detector test."

"So . . . fail it. Lie detector results are not admissible evidence." He chuckled. "Besides, they can't torture you."

He'd thought of everything. Larry extended his hand. He looked me squarely in the eye, and I felt as if I was shaking with a stranger. After all these years, I suddenly marveled at how little I knew my own business partner.

Larry cleared his throat. "Sometimes, you've got to take care of yourself. I wish you all the best, Stephen. I'm sorry it came down to this. But we won, you know."

He strolled out the door, left me with the meal tab for twenty-seven dollars and ninety-three cents and the number for an account containing nearly two and a half million dollars. I sat there dazed.

"We won," he'd said.

I paid the bill, left a generous tip, and wandered out into sunshine. I walked the two miles back to the office, my mind racing. The idea of keeping or not keeping the money hadn't yet entered into the equation.

Slow down, I finally told myself. *Start over.*

I started with the fundamental question: *What if I did keep it?*

I'd have to leave town. My reputation couldn't survive another hit, not like this. The newspapers would have a field day. *Stephen Whitaker has done it again!*

I could give Donna a decent share, and I could help Alycia through college, but they'd have to leave town as well.

I pondered this all the way back. When I got to our building, I climbed the stairs slowly, lost in thought. Walking through our reception area, I went to Larry's office, peeked in and discovered a near-empty room. The filing cabinet was bare, and the CPU unit to his computer had been opened. Obviously, as a precaution, he'd removed the hard drive.

I closed the door to his office and paused in the middle of the reception area. If everything he'd told me was true, the only point to returning here would be to close the books and send our clients on their way.

After taking another look around, I turned out the lights. The answering machine would handle the calls. For now.

I left the office, locked the door again, and flipped the sign—*gone until . . .* —to read: *gone until . . . tomorrow*—and began walking aimlessly along Main Street. *By Monday, at least,* he'd told me.

We haven't personally defrauded anyone, I told myself. And we certainly hadn't defrauded anyone locally.

I never knew would be my standard reply. *Larry kept me in the dark.*

How is that possible? They would ask me. *He was your partner.*

I recalled Larry's countless overseas trips. Sure, it had crossed my mind to wonder what he must have been doing, but I'd dismissed the suspicion. Straight-arrow Larry didn't engage in illegal activities. *I provided the cover,* I thought. *My distraction provided the means.*

"Thirty thousand a pop," he'd said. I added it up in my head, and it came out to a mere one hundred sixty clients. One hundred sixty wealthy clients tired of paying exorbitant taxes and willing to take risks they did not fully understand.

In an effort to determine my degree of complicity, the IRS agents would ask me a series of questions, leading to the obvious: *Where did he go?* That would be easy. *I don't know.*

Where is the money? Just imagining the question caused me to break out in a cold sweat. *What money?* I practiced.

From this moment forward, everything I did would be back-tracked and analyzed. My phone records would be dissected. Every-one I knew would be interviewed. And yet, even now, I had no direct evidence of a crime, only Larry's word for it. There was no aiding and abetting. No complicity. For all I knew, Larry had made it all up. I didn't even know for sure if the Cayman account existed.

When did you know? the police would ask.

I never knew for sure, I could honestly answer. *Not until you showed up.*

So what did you do after he told you he was leaving?

I waited, I would tell them.

I made my way back to my car. I stood for a moment at its open door, looking up at the now-dark office windows. I shook my head, sighed, and climbed into the car. The piece of paper in my shirt pocket seemed to come alive.

Chapter Twenty-nine

With Paul and Susan gone, I couldn't bear to spend another minute in Joe's dingy establishment. Instead, I wandered to a corner greasy spoon and ordered a ginger ale. I sat there for hours, trying the money on for size, playing different scenarios over and over in my mind. *Two point four,* I repeated over and over. *I could begin again.* Again.

Long about ten-thirty, I slipped out of my chair and headed home. I discovered three messages from Alycia, one at seven: *Dad, are you coming?* One at seven-thirty: *Dad, I'm waiting, how could you forget?* And a tearful one at ten: *Call me, Dad.*

I kicked myself mentally and sighed into the darkness of the living room. *No excuse,* I whispered. I put my hand on the phone, but after some mental debate decided against it. By now Alycia would be in bed.

Tomorrow, I told myself. *First thing.*

I sat on the couch and took another mental swipe at the money.

Two point four.

Sleep was out of the question. I began walking through the house, mentally organizing it, planning for the near future—what to take, what to toss.

Two point four echoed in my brain.

Eventually, I rolled up my sleeves and began sorting through the house, putting odds and ends into the few boxes Donna had left behind. Starting with the kitchen, I worked my way through the living room.

In the bedroom, I opened the closet and spied the box of photo albums on the shelf. I remembered Alycia's gleeful pronouncement: *I figured it out, Dad!*

I smiled. She'd thought she had solved the mystery of the ages. Reaching for the box, I pulled it down and set it on the floor. The last of Donna's things. *Mom left it at the house . . . she wants it back . . . she all but admitted it.*

So was the secret contained in this box? Was it a photo? A letter? Fitting with Alycia's *modus operandi*, her mother's "admitting it" could have been nothing more than, "Honey, stop asking so many questions!"

Kneeling, I pushed the large albums from one side to another, examining the contents. Nestled on one section of the box were some of Donna's college memories, her graduation tassel, a childhood music box that played "Moon River," a beige leather diary, a first-place award plaque she'd received for a short story she'd written. Ironically, it was after writing that story that she'd decided she didn't like writing. She preferred to read literature, not try to emulate it.

Mashed between everything else were several stuffed animals scented with *Charlie* perfume, smaller picture frames, a couple of necklaces, and a few other knickknacks.

Even Sherlock was wrong once in a while. I was placing the box back on the shelf when something struck me. I brought the box down again, placed it on the floor, and retrieved one of the framed photos.

A shiver shot down my spine. I'd forgotten this one. In the photo, the Three Musketeers were standing in front of the clock tower in the middle of campus, close to dusk. I'd arranged to have white rose corsages professionally dyed blue for the occasion. I was on the left, smiling like a puppy dog, wearing a tuxedo. Donna was on the far right side, her own blue rose corsage pinned to an elegant powder blue gown and Alice, photogenic and charismatic, was in the middle, holding her miniature blue rose corsage against her white gown.

The blue rose—a botanical impossibility—had become our metaphor, a symbol of our goals, especially since the three of us had aspirations that seemed unreachable. Alice's goal was, of course, to star on Broadway. Mine was to trade on Wall Street, and Donna's goal was to teach American literature at the college level.

I turned the frame over and removed the backing. There it was in Alice's handwriting: *Remember our favorite song?*

A melody slipped across my memory: . . . *sun is shining in the sky, there's not a cloud in sight . . .*

I smiled wistfully and traced her handwriting with my finger. How could I forget? "Mr. Blue Sky," by Electric Light Orchestra. If the blue rose was a symbol of our dreams, "Mr. Blue Sky" was our anthem.

I carried the photo downstairs and scrambled through my old CDs until I found it. I placed it in my stereo, pressed *Play,* and sat down on the couch.

A static-charged radio signal, out of range, followed by the sounds of a repeated piano chord, rhythmic clapping, and a staccato drum rhythm filled the silence. I hadn't heard this song in over a decade.

As the music played, I gazed at the picture. Donna smiled back at me, still full of hope. And Alice . . . dear Alice remained locked in time, forever beautiful, forever witty, and forever young.

For a moment it seemed as if I had gone back in time. The song finally transcended into a chorus, and then after ending on a final note, another reprise . . . a full-blown symphonic ending, with a final electronic utterance, barely perceptible.

I expelled a breath, physically spent, suddenly weak and tired. Overwhelmed with a strange sleepiness, I huddled into the couch and began giving in to the pull of unconsciousness.

I closed my eyes, thinking not about the money. Instead, for the first time in over a decade I let myself fully remember Alice, lost to me forever—*somewhere in time.*

When I fell asleep, I . . .

. . . I was back in my dorm room, staring into the mirror, frantically tying my tie. Chris Marino, my roommate, came wandering in.

"What time is it?" I asked him.

He laughed. "You're late, lover boy."

After starting over three times, I finally achieved the tie's proper length.

Chris lounged on his bed, flipping through a magazine. "How do you rate?"

I stared at the mirror, checking my teeth. "Say what?"

"Two beautiful women. Lavish banquet. What's the occasion again?"

I didn't remember. Instead of answering, I searched for my phone.

"What are you looking for?"

I told him, and Chris looked at me incredulously. "*What* phone?"

Oh yeah. We didn't have phones in our dorm rooms—certainly no cell phones. There was one phone per floor, located at the end of the hall.

That's when I knew I was dreaming.

Chris looked at his watch again. "It's five, partner."

I hesitated. "Where did I tell you again?'

Chris laughed and shook his head. "At the Clock Tower?"

I suddenly realized what I was about to do, and it didn't seem like just a dream anymore.

It seemed . . . *real.*

I muttered good-bye, left the room, and began running down the hall, navigating my way to the first floor. I raced through the lobby, out the double glass doors, and began sprinting across the campus.

At the Clock Tower, a one-hundred-foot three-legged cast-iron structure, I slowed down, sweating profusely in the tux. *Where are they?*

Emerging from the girls' dorm, Donna's blond hair caught me by surprise. And then Alice followed, as if stepping out of the shadows.

Approaching me, both women broke into smiles.

"At last," Alice said, smiling. "Our date has arrived."

I lost my ability to speak. *Alice?* She was standing in front of me, as physically real as the day I'd lost her, and I couldn't help myself—I couldn't stop staring at her. *She hasn't aged,* I thought.

Of course not! She's as young as the day I lost her. Then I realized that in this dream world we were all the same age.

I swallowed the lump in my throat, struggling with the emotions that welled up within me.

Donna broke my reverie. "Where are the corsages?"

The corsages?

"Oh . . ." I stammered and slapped my shirt pockets, as if I might have found them in there. "I guess . . . uh . . . I forgot them."

"Where?" Alice asked.

I didn't know.

Donna put her hand to her mouth and giggled. "Flower store maybe? *Petal Pushin'*?"

I nodded, but the name didn't ring a bell. I felt like an idiot. I hadn't seen Alice in fourteen years, and her first impression of me was . . . that I was forgetful.

It's a dream, I reminded myself. *It isn't real. You're making this whole thing up from your memory.*

But it seemed painfully real.

"You're such a goof," Alice replied. "We've got time. We'll get them on the way."

Alice spun around, modeling her outfit. "Do you like?"

"Very . . . nice."

Alice frowned good-naturedly. "Nice?"

"I mean . . ."

"Look at the boy," Donna grinned. "He's speechless."

"Was it too dazzling for you?" Alice said. She winked at Donna.

Both girls laughed. In melodramatic fashion, Donna grabbed my left arm, and Alice slipped hers through my right.

"Hey, Stephen," someone yelled from behind us. It was Chris. Smiling, and out of breath, he ran up to us, holding out his hand. Instinctively, I accepted what he was offering: car keys.

"You forgot these, ol' sport."

Donna chuckled with his usage of her Gatsby appellation. Alice touched my chin, lifting it gently before nodding with satisfaction. "The head is still attached, folks."

"Good thing," Donna said, catching my arm again. "C'mon, we're going to be late."

I turned to see Chris waving good-bye, then giving me the thumbs-up.

"Do you know where the car is parked?" Alice giggled.

"*I* remember," Donna replied. "Even if he doesn't."

I responded to her lead, and somehow we found the light blue Volkswagen. Donna crawled into the backseat, and Alice sat in the front with me. As I started the car, I began thinking furiously. *Where is Petal Pushin'?*

It came to me. Forty-eighth, just down the street. I turned left at the next intersection, heading south. Two blocks away, I double parked and told the girls to wait. I burst in the door, startling the young lady in a green smock behind the counter. "I need two corsages. Under Whitaker."

The lady searched a notebook and shook her head. "Are you sure you ordered them?"

Oh no. This wasn't the place.

"You're in luck, partner. We've got extra."

She disappeared into the back and returned holding two white boxes, each covered with clear cellophane. She rang them up. "That'll be twelve-forty."

Twelve-forty?

I was confused with the price. "Did you ring 'em both?"

She nodded, and then I remembered. Things were cheaper back then . . . now . . . whatever.

Instinctively, I reached for my back pocket, then slapped my shirt pockets again. *Nothing.* My heart dropped. I'd forgotten my wallet. Someone touched me from behind, and I heard a whisper in my ear. "I thought you might have forgotten." It was Donna.

"Here," she said, offering the woman a credit card. She winked at me. "Our little secret."

Embarrassed, I muttered, "Thanks."

Back in the car, I gingerly pinned the corsages on my dates—first Donna, then Alice. My eyes glistened as I manipulated my girlfriend's dress, the feel of silk reminiscent of the day she died.

"Beautiful," Alice replied. "You have good taste, Mr. Man."

I leaned back, stared at Alice's corsage and shuddered.

What have I done?

"What?" Alice frowned. "Crooked?"

I looked over at Donna's corsage.

They were white.

"We're running late," Donna announced. "I don't want to miss the opening remarks."

This was Donna's evening, I remembered. We were her "entourage" attending the lecture of a famous author, whose name I couldn't recall. In the car, on the way north—heading somewhere I couldn't recall—I remember hearing the song "Blue Sky."

"Our theme song," Alice announced.

"Turn it up," Donna said, leaning forward.

Alice did so, and the moment she did, time seemed to speed up, then slow down. My peripheral vision wavered. Like many dreams, one minute we were sitting down in a large auditorium, the next we were standing up, clapping. Then suddenly back in the car. Later, after we'd arrived on campus, Alice grabbed an innocent passerby. He snapped a picture of the three of us in front of the Clock Tower.

I remember thinking through my pasted-on smile: *You can't take this picture! The corsages aren't blue!*

More vague images followed as the dream shifted in and out of clarity. I remember hugging Donna briefly in front of the dorm, watching her enter the building, leaving me alone with Alice, then kissing her good night. I remember walking back to my dorm room, then reciting the evening for Chris's benefit. The "wavering" of my vision increased until I sensed a kind of flickering light as if a light bulb was about to go out.

Everything finally went black, and when I awakened I was lying on the couch in my house. I looked at the clock. It was seven forty-five in the morning. The *next* morning.

Chapter Thirty

Rubbing the sleep out of my eyes, I pondered the strange quality to last night's dream—so real and vivid, as if I'd actually *lived* it.

I stumbled to the phone and dialed Sally's number. Donna answered and I asked for Alycia.

"She's off to school," Donna said.

I glanced at the clock. *Of course.* I inquired of Alycia's mental state, and Donna sighed. "Blacker than I've ever seen. I almost didn't let her go."

Donna asked about my mother again, and I told her what little I knew. Encircled by close friends, Mom was doing as well as could be expected.

"How are you holding up?" Donna asked.

I gave her the usual assurances, then hesitated, wondering how much to say. Eventually she would know everything about Larry and probably ask me why I hadn't been up front. The authorities would likely question her and wonder the same thing.

Our conversation turned back to Alycia. We discussed other options, such as counseling and medication, and Donna agreed to make an appointment with a local psychiatrist and I agreed to pay for it.

"In the meantime," Donna replied, "call Sara's cell phone."

"Sara?"

"Her best friend," Donna said. "Sara lets Alycia use it during school. They have nearly every class together."

We hung up, and I dialed Sara's cell, getting the voice mail. Most likely, the girls were in class and the phone was switched off.

After leaving a message and hanging up, I took a shower and grabbed a quick bite of toast. I drove to the corner grocery store and picked up an assortment of boxes. Back at the house, I continued organizing. With Donna's and Alycia's things gone, there wasn't much to pack.

Images from last night's dream continued to pick away at me, but at the moment, I had more important considerations. I needed to focus my attention on the matter at hand: *the money.* Two point four million phantom dollars sitting in an offshore account with my name on it.

Alycia called at nine-thirty. "Where were you?"

I apologized profusely and promised to pick her up after school. She didn't even bother to object.

"Three o'clock, Dad. Right in front. You promise?"

"I'll be there," I said, and we hung up.

I went to the living room, picked up the phone and dialed Donna's number again, hoping to alleviate her worries, but she didn't answer. Maybe she'd left the apartment.

I spent the remainder of the morning organizing and packing. At noon, I stuffed some more cereal into my mouth, and at about one o'clock, I tried the apartment again. This time, Donna answered on the third ring. I summarized my conversation with Alycia, and Donna seemed relieved.

After we said good-bye and hung up, I received the call that changed everything.

Cary Epstein, another high school buddy and the jewelry store manager across the street from the office, was concerned. There were two men rifling around in the office . . . and Cary wanted to alert me.

"Where's Larry, anyway?" Cary asked.

I promised to get back to him and promptly hung up. Sitting in the living room, I put my head into my hands and tried to think. My heart galloped like a gazelle being chased by a cheetah. The paper in my pocket had the account number and password. What if the authorities came now? What if they searched me?

Up in smoke, I realized. Two point four, gone, just like that.

Yet I still hadn't determined for sure if the money truly existed. Before I decided anything, I had to discover for myself the reality of the accounts. Then, and only then, could I plan my next move.

"They'll be here in days," Larry had said.

Missed it by a weekend, I countered.

If I used any of my computers, and if the money was real, I'd be finished. They'd find the evidence on my hard drive and seize the contents. Only one alternative remained. I reached for my cell phone and tried to call Alycia through Sara's phone, but neither answered. I put the phone in my shirt pocket.

For her sake, I told myself again, heading out to the car. In minutes, I was on Highway 12, heading east out of town. I glanced at my watch. In two hours, I'd be in Milbank, where no one knew me.

Minutes later, I called Alycia again. Still, no answer. As I drove, I kept trying. About three thirty-five, Sara finally answered and handed the phone to Alycia. My daughter's voice was ragged. "Where *are* you?"

I had to go out of town, I almost said, thinking better of it. "Something came up. Can we talk on the phone?"

"You promised, Dad."

"How 'bout seven? Can we talk then?"

"I'm meeting *him* at seven!"

Him? I didn't like the sound of that.

"Then right after?"

She didn't reply.

"Alycia?"

Silence. I almost hung up, convinced I'd lost the connection. Finally, she whispered into the phone, her voice flat and emotionless. "I'll call you."

"Where will you be?"

Again, silence.

"Alycia, please . . ."

No answer.

"Alycia?"

She was gone.

I'm doing this for her, I argued against the clamoring inner voices. *I can be back to see her before she leaves at seven.*

When I got to Milbank, I found the library, commandeered the corner public computer, and nervously typed in the address to the international bank Web site.

When the information flashed, my mouth literally dropped open.

The account truly existed. Swallowing hard, I navigated through a series of screens and located the account total. My body shuddered again.

Larry was wrong. There wasn't two point four million in this account. There was nearly two point *five* million dollars. More precisely: Two million, four hundred ninety-eight thousand, twenty-nine dollars, and seventy-two cents.

I stared at the number for a minute or two, waiting for it to suddenly disappear.

Stolen money.

Money earned by giving tax advice.

Illegal tax advice.

Money earned fair and square.

I quickly closed the screen. On my way out, the gray-haired librarian smiled cheerfully. "Did you find what you were looking for?"

"Yes, ma'am," I replied, averting my face.

I drove back to Aberdeen on Highway 12, my thoughts whirling.

Two point five million dollars.

I grabbed the phone from my pocket, redialed that cell phone number. No answer. I tried Sally's apartment. No answer.

I stepped on the accelerator, checking the rearview mirror. I had to get to Aberdeen and find Alycia.

As I drove, I created a mnemonic string of exaggerated mental images to help me remember the account number and password. I rehearsed it for nearly an hour until satisfied that I wouldn't forget, and then ripped the paper into tiny pieces and threw the evidence out the window. For the rest of the way back, I imagined every possible interrogative question, and then formulated and practiced reasonable responses.

I tried to contact Alycia again but still no answer. When the apartment phone rang without anyone picking up the receiver, I knew there was no point in going there to find Alycia.

I turned onto my street at six forty-eight, and my worst fears were confirmed. A nondescript white sedan was parked in the street, and the front door of my house was standing wide open. I parked on the street, took a deep breath, and got out. I strolled up the sidewalk, wondering, *Do I pretend surprise? Do I feign anger?*

Two men in dark suits—one was blond of average height, the other balder, shorter, stockier—appeared to be stunned when I walked in.

Having decided on a response, I did my best to appear aghast.

"Stephen Whitaker?"

"What have you done here?" I demanded.

"Would you please come with us?"

"You can't just walk into my house—"

One of the men flashed a piece of paper. A search warrant.

I glanced at the clock. 6:50. They watched me carefully, and I struggled for what I hoped would appear to be a believable length of time to recover my composure.

"May I make a quick call?" I asked.

The blond-haired agent in a black suit and striped blue tie smiled. "You're not in a position to be making requests."

He ordered me to raise my arms. I did so and submitted myself to the first legal search of my life. While he patted me down, I badgered him with questions to which I already knew the answers. Without responding, he removed my wallet, my keys . . . and my cell phone, and placed them in his pocket.

"They'll be safe with me," he said.

Chapter Thirty-one

With my hands handcuffed behind my back, the two men escorted me down my front steps, across the sidewalk and into the car.

We drove in silence to the sheriff's station, a small squat building off Main Street. As we drove, I mentally rehearsed the account numbers and password. In the backseat, I felt like a criminal, vulnerable to observation. *Play dumb,* I thought. *It'll soon be over.*

At the station, they led me up the sidewalk, in through the door, down a hallway to a folding chair, one of several lined against the wall in a roomful of desks. I searched for a clock and found one across the room. 7:35.

The blue-tied agent who'd searched me now changed my handcuffs to fasten me to the chair.

"Is this really necessary?" I asked.

He grinned, and when I requested permission to make a phone call, he only glanced at his shorter partner.

"Just give us a moment to get the paper work started."

Forty-five minutes passed, and no phone call. I sat there, alone, open to observation. Finally, the two men casually emerged from around the corner, uncuffed me, and led me to a small drab room designed for questioning.

I sat there for another fifteen minutes or so before the blue-tied man came in carrying a coffee cup. If I hadn't been so nervous, the whole thing would have seemed a little silly, as if they'd watched a few too many episodes of *Law and Order*.

"Can I get you something, Stephen?"

"How 'bout that call?"

He gave me a patronizing smile. "Who was it you wanted to call again?"

"My daughter," I replied.

He frowned. "Most people call their lawyers."

"I promised her."

He turned to his buddy. "Do *you* think he's calling his daughter?"

The other guy shrugged and flashed a perplexed smile. "Sounds like a story to me, Jake. Like maybe you're going to give someone a message or something."

"Please," I whispered.

Jake smiled. "Just tell us what we need to know, and I'll let you call anyone you want." He smiled at his partner. "He can even call the president if he likes."

His partner, the heavyset man, wearing jeans and a leather jacket, made a mocking frown. "I don't think the president would take the call."

Jake joined the frown. "Hmmm. I guess you're right." He turned to me. "You might want to keep your calls restricted to the kind of people who might actually pick up the phone."

"Two minutes," I whispered, startled by their level of sarcasm.

He shrugged good-naturedly, reached in his pocket, and removed my cell phone. He placed it on the table. "I'll make you a deal, Stephen."

My eyes darted to the phone and back to his face.

"Just tell me you have the money"—he snapped his fingers—"and you can make a call immediately."

I let out a deep breath.

He raised his eyebrows. "Seriously." He picked up the cell phone, extended it to me, and I reached for it. He withdrew it at the last second but kept it poised within reach. "So tell me, Stephen, do you have the money?"

I hesitated. "What money?"

"The money that disappeared from your Wells Fargo account."

"Which account is that?"

He made a face: *Give me a break.*

Actually, I didn't know anything about the Wells Fargo account. It must have been secretly opened by Larry.

I placed my hands on the table. He extended the phone again, but I didn't fall for it this time. His voice came out mockingly innocent. "It's yours . . . right now . . . if you just tell me . . . the truth."

He dangled the phone in front of my face again, just inches above my hands.

"You promised," Alycia had said.

I swallowed. I was now breathing heavily, and the two men were enjoying my pain. They waited.

"I don't know what you're talking about," I murmured and closed my eyes.

Jake sighed, shrugged, and put the cell phone in his pocket. "That's too bad. You seemed pretty desperate there."

The other guy nodded. "Yeah . . . well, maybe not desperate."

Jake agreed. "Eager, then."

"Yeah . . ." the other guy echoed. "Eager."

Jake stepped out of the room for a moment, then came back, sitting down on his side of the table. He opened a thick file and proceeded to study it. A few minutes later, a female office worker delivered a box of donuts. She set a cup of coffee in front of me. I took a sip.

Jake winked. "Good, eh?"

The formal interrogation began.

"Your partner wasn't exactly low-profile," he began. "We've been watching him for months."

"We have witnesses who recall seeing you and your partner at the Steak House, just before he disappeared."

My gut clenched.

"What did he tell you?"

I did my best to fudge, but they weren't buying my ignorance.

More questions followed. I told them everything, exactly as it happened, except for one tiny important detail—the detail they wanted.

Finally, a short man came in with a sheet of paper—a transcript of Larry's bank accounts. The two men examined the paper and then frowned at me. The sarcastic smiles were gone. We'd come back to the crux of the matter, the aspect of the case that would determine their own personal failure or success.

"So . . . where's the money?"

"I have no idea," I lied.

They asked the same question again and again, only in different ways. I answered again and again, over and over, until Jake announced, "You're not even a good liar."

They have no proof, I reminded myself.

"So where is it?" he asked again.

The phone rang. *My phone. In Jake's pocket.* They looked at each other and smiled. "Could that be for you?"

A trickle of sweat slid down the side of my face. "It's my daughter."

Jake pulled out the phone and squinted at it, reading the caller ID. The phone buzzed again.

He glanced at me. "I'm thinking she'll call again."

My eyes watered. "Please . . ."

Another ring. They watched me. "Where's the money, Stephen?"

I blew out a breath.

He extended the phone to me, I reached for it, and once again, with a quick flick of the wrist, he withdrew it at the last moment. He raised his eyebrows. "Are we talking yet?"

"Please."

He shrugged. "She'll call again."

The phone stopped ringing. "Sir . . . I need to speak to her."

Again, that maddening smile. Jake raised his eyebrows in an unconcerned manner, and turned to his buddy. "Is that our problem, Hal?"

Hal shook his head. "Not our problem, I'm thinking."

My blood boiled. Jake placed his hands on the table and leaned in. "I'm good at spotting lies, Stephen. And I'm spotting a big fat one. See . . . all you have to do is tell me the truth. Why is that so hard?"

I swallowed again; my rage was building.

"Where's the money, Stephen? Oh, and while we're at it, where's your buddy?"

The phone rang again. My body shuddered, and they smiled. Once again, and with dramatic flair, he withdrew the phone from his pocket and looked at the ID. "It's for you, I think."

I leapt out of my chair and lunged for the phone. Jake jumped back, grinning, and I lost it. Without thinking, I went after him, but Hal grabbed me just before my fist connected. Restraining my arms, he pulled me back, then pushed me against the wall. I hit it hard.

Hal put his forearm against my neck. I couldn't breathe. I glanced at Jake across the room and watched with horror as he answered the final ring.

"Hello?"

He listened, and then: "Just a sec." He raised those eyebrows again. "She wants to talk to you."

"Please . . ." I gasped.

Hal pressed against me. "Don't you have a question to answer?"

My resolved buckled, but I didn't answer. Jake spoke into the receiver. "Your father said he's too busy." He snapped the cell phone shut just as I screamed. "Okay! Okay!"

They smiled triumphantly. "Okay what?"

"I have the money," I said. "Now let me call her."

Jake looked at Hal. Lowering his forearm to my chest, Hal turned to Jake. "I wonder if he's just saying that."

Hal nodded. I struggled again, and Hal pressed harder against me. I was dumbfounded with fury, but no match for Hal. "You promised," I hissed.

Jake nodded. "Give me the name of the bank, the number, and the password, and we've got a deal."

He pushed a notebook and pencil across the table, and Hal released me with a warning in his eyes—*are we cool?*

Gasping for breath, I sat down and clutched the pen with my shaking right hand. Holding the paper with my left hand, I wrote the name of the bank. And then swallowed. *What was the number?*

Jake smiled. "Cat got your brain?"

I saw images of scrap paper flying into the wind.

Unbelievable. "I can't remember."

Jake shrugged, putting his hand on the doorknob. Hal joined him by the door. "Knock on the door when you do," he said. "And then you can call the president if you want."

Hal slapped his back. "I think you forgot, Jake. He doesn't *want* to call the president."

"Oh that's right," Jake said, "I did forget. Thank you for reminding me."

"You're welcome. Any time."

They pushed out of the room.

For three long hours I sat there, and although I finally remembered the password, without the number it was useless.

Alycia's fine, I consoled myself. *She'll understand.*

When they returned at last, I changed my story. "I was bluffing."

They didn't buy it, and I didn't care. When I demanded to speak to my lawyer, they finally relented. Sitting on the table, Jake dialed the number for me, and when my lawyer answered, Jake handed me the phone.

Frustration shuddered through me as I realized I should have demanded Stan immediately, and then he could have called Alycia.

She's fine, I reminded myself.

Stan the Man was a brusque, no-nonsense type who liked to cut to the chase. He was good at what he did and borderline ethical at best, which is why Donna never got near him during our class-action-suit defense.

"I've been waiting for your call, Stephen," he said. "News travels fast. So what's up? What've you done now?"

I explained the situation as briefly as possible, and the more I talked the more animated he became. "What did you tell them?"

"Nothing."

"Good boy." Stan chuckled. "So . . . Larry actually skipped town . . ." He exhaled into the phone. "Well, if that don't beat all."

"I didn't have a clue what Larry was doing."

He harrumphed. "I don't care about that stuff, and if you do know anything, don't say a word. *I* don't even want to know about it."

"They want the money."

He laughed. "Don't we all?"

When he asked to talk to someone in charge, I extended the phone to Jake who sneered with delight.

Chapter Thirty-two

It was midnight when a sheriff's deputy, no older than his early twenties, drove me home. Before I was released, they'd given me my personal effects in a large envelope and made me sign a form.

In the backseat of the car, and like a thirsty man in the middle of the Sahara, I pulled out my cell phone, noted Sara's number on the ID and redialed it. Apparently, Alycia had borrowed it for the evening.

The voice mail service clicked in immediately.

I tried again.

Nothing. I dialed Donna's number and Sally answered. I asked for Alycia. After a long wait, Donna got on the phone, her voice sleepy. "What is it, Stephen?"

"Where is Alycia?" I asked.

Donna was confused. "Why . . . sleeping, I'm sure. Why are you calling?"

I resisted the relief that easily could have washed over me. "Please check on her."

I waited as Donna walked across the apartment, then I heard her gasp. When she spoke into the receiver again, her tone bordered on panic. "Oh, Stephen—she's not here!"

The deputy dropped me off at the sidewalk in front of my house, and I ran to the front door. Considering the damage, getting in wasn't difficult. In the kitchen, the main phone blinked to a staccato rhythm. I grabbed the receiver, dialed the voice-mail number, and listened. My mind raced. My throat went dry, and my heart beat violently. I punched in the retrieval code, got it wrong, cursed in frustration, and started over. I tried again and again, until finally I got it right.

I shoved the phone to my left ear. *You have three unheard messages . . . first message . . . left 8:20.* It was Alycia. "Dad, why aren't you answering your cell phone? Call Sara's number."

The phone beeped.

Next message, left . . . 8:31.

Alycia again, same number, her voice high-pitched and desperate. "Are you there? I think someone else has your cell phone."

Silence. The phone chirped again. The recorded voice continued again, *Next message, left twenty minutes earlier . . .*

Twenty minutes earlier! Hope burst through my veins. I pressed the button. Alycia again. Her voice was calm. I sighed in relief. Whatever her problem was, she had solved it without me. "I love you, Dad. It's okay. I forgive you. Tell Mom I'm sorry."

I felt my body decompress. She was safe. I dialed her number. *But what did she mean? Tell Mom I'm sorry?*

One ring. Two rings. Three rings.

No answer. I dialed again.

Panic consumed me.

"You two are communicating on a deeper level than the rest of us," Donna had once told me.

I punched in Alycia's friend's cell number again and waited.

Same response. *The party you have called is unavailable at this time . . .*

I hung up and tried again. One ring. Two rings. Three rings.

Again: no answer. Had she shut off the phone?

I lurched around the room looking for my keys. When I found them, I staggered to the front door, then remembered the cell phone I'd left on the couch. I changed course, lost my balance, nearly falling into the couch. Grasping the phone, I headed for the door again.

Once I reached my car, I tried, in vain, to fit the key into the ignition with my shaking hand. My cell phone rang.

Please let it be her, I whispered.

"Stephen? Did you find her?"

The car roared to life.

"Where does he live?" I demanded.

"Who?" Donna asked.

I was already speeding down the street when she sighed with anguish. "Oh no . . ." She hesitated, then whispered the words. "On Merton, I think . . . uh . . . end of the block . . . uh . . . white house, black shutters."

"Okay . . ."

"Stephen?

"Yes?"

"Please don't hang up."

We continued to compare notes about her recent behavior until Donna asked me the question I'd feared. "Did she call you?"

I told her everything as I sped down the back streets of Aberdeen. Well, nearly everything . . .

She was dumbfounded about the office disaster. "*Our* Larry?"

Yes, I thought. *Our Larry.*

"They think you have his money?"

"Yes," I replied without elaborating.

"Where are you now?" she asked.

I was one block away from the address she had given me. The moon flickered through the bare trees, and in my state of mind, they looked like skeletal monsters. I parked in front of the house and jumped out of the car. The lower window was brightly lit. I mentioned this to Donna.

"Good!" she whispered. "Maybe she's there!"

Without ending the call, I put the phone in my pocket, pounded on the door, then rang the doorbell.

Lights flashed all over the house. I heard footsteps from within.

The door curtain slid open, revealing the face of a startled man whom I took to be the boy's father. I forced a smile and tried to appear harmless.

The man opened the door.

"Where is your son?" I asked.

The man frowned. "What—?"

I gasped out an explanation. "I'm looking . . . I'm looking for my daughter . . ."

"Well . . . Sean's in his room . . . downstairs."

I prevailed upon him to let me in. Together we descended the steps to the basement, crossed the darkened cement floor to a room with bright light leaking below the door.

The father knocked on the door, "Sean!"

Sean opened the door, looking bewildered and wide-eyed.

"Where's Alycia?" I asked, peering around to his bed. By now, I'd assumed the worst, but Alycia wasn't there. Which meant something even worse.

Sean didn't even try to lie. He'd taken Alycia to Melgaard Park hours earlier—several blocks away—and then she'd jumped out of the car.

"Jumped out?"

"It wasn't moving," he shrugged. "She was ticked."

I asked him what they'd talked about, but he only shrugged. "Just . . . stuff."

He was holding back. I could tell by the look in his eyes something very serious had happened.

"What did she tell you?" I asked. He looked away, his face suddenly pale.

I didn't have time for his guilt excursion. "Where did you see her last?"

"She kept running," he said. "She wouldn't let me take her home."

I gave his white T-shirt a quick tug, and he and his father followed me upstairs.

"Find the girl," the father demanded, handing him a coat. Sean shoved on a pair of tennis shoes and followed me outside. I was ten paces ahead of him.

Getting into my car again, I reached over to unlock his door and realized the cell phone was still in my pocket. Donna would have heard everything.

"Are you there?"

"Stephen, please . . ."

"I'm on my way," I assured her.

Sean jumped into the passenger side of the car, slamming the door shut.

"Take me where she got out," I demanded, and his chin stutter-nodded, his eyes glassy with fear.

Donna spoke into my ear. "Sally's been calling Alycia's friends on the other line. Sara hasn't seen her."

I raced to Melgaard Park. When Sean guided me to the exact spot where he'd last seen her, I shoved the gear into park and got out. A thick new blanket of snow had covered the area, but I was able to make out some tennis shoe tracks. Maybe they were hers, maybe not. I followed them for a block until they led back to the road.

Best guess, Alycia had begun walking home. It wasn't far, less than a mile. So where was she?

I turned around and took in the recent snow. It reminded me of Alycia's love of blankets. She liked to bury herself under layers of warmth. She liked to be warm. She liked to be covered. That's why she always took baths: She loved the warmth of the water covering her.

A gasp escaped me, and my body shuddered, as if I already knew. I spoke into the phone, "Donna, have you been to the bathroom?"

"What do you mean?" She paused. "Wait. No. Not the main bathroom . . ."

The sound of her breathing increased—the unmistakable sound of rising panic—as I heard her race across the apartment floor.

Why hadn't I thought of this? I thought. *Maybe I could have saved her. . . .*

I was still staring out over the landscape of frozen snow when the phone clattered and Donna screamed.

Chapter Thirty-three

I went insane.

I had a vague sense of what had happened, but I was drunk with grief, utterly incapable of grasping reality. My brain became a broken record, the same thoughts playing repeatedly. That superstition about "threes" had lodged in my brain, and I couldn't give it up. *Someone's lying. This makes four,* I thought. *And four is one more than three.* Therefore, Alycia was alive. Case closed. Any moment she would call, "Hey, Dad. What's a girl have to do to get ice cream?"

I awakened that afternoon in the living room, peaceful in my delusions. I sat up on the couch, breathing in, breathing out. My brain was on the fritz, but, as usual, my body knew something was wrong. I trembled uncontrollably as if standing outside in subzero temperatures.

Bits and pieces came back to me. I'd raced to Donna's apartment. The police and an ambulance were already there. Flashing lights reflected off the houses of the entire neighborhood. Families huddled together in their doorways. My car had squealed to a stop in the middle of the street, and I'd barely pushed the gear into park. It *thunked* into place.

Maybe it's not too late!

I leapt out of the car, sprinted for the ambulance, but someone grabbed me just as they were rolling the gurney up to its open doors.

I reached for Alycia, but they pulled me back. "Can't let you do that, man!"

When I saw that her face was covered, I staggered and groaned.

She's just cold, right?

I tried to reach her again without success. I began yelling, *Alycia! Alycia! I'm here, sweetie. I'm late, but I'm here. . . .*

They held me back, and I fell to the ground, kneeling in the snow. I felt hands underneath my armpits, helping me to my feet.

Someone's voice, "Mr. Whitaker?"

I tried to speak, but my throat had closed.

"We're sorry, but she was gone when we arrived."

"What do you mean?"

"She was gone, sir."

I grasped hope. *Gone isn't dead, is it?*

I must have blacked out, because I couldn't remember anything after that, not even how I'd gotten back home.

Now sitting on the couch, I clasped my hands.

Where is Larry? Normally, he'd be with me now.

Gone.

And Paul?

A flutter like birds' wings passed through my imagination. I was driving back from Milbank. I threw the papers into the wind because I'd memorized the password and account number. And now they came back to me, every number, and every syllable.

I shuddered. I truly was insane.

The phone rang. I examined the Caller ID, and my heart leapt.

It's Alycia, I thought. It was just a joke. She's teaching me a lesson. *Good one, sweetie.*

I grinned through the tears. *Got me good.* Frantically, I grabbed the phone. The voice on the other end felt like a thud against my soul. It was Sally.

"The funeral is Tuesday, Stephen."

Funeral? Why?

She gave me further details, but none of it registered. She hung up without saying good-bye.

The phone rang again. I wouldn't have answered it, except I thought Sally was calling back. But it was Susan who sounded frantic. "Oh, Stephen, I just heard. I'm just back from Minnesota. Are you okay? You're not alone, are you?"

I mumbled something incoherent.

"You *are* alone?" she asked. "Do you want me to come over?"

Why bother? I thought.

When I hung up, I closed my eyes and tried to remember what I'd said. I then shut off all phones in the house, including the cell.

Finally a sliver of reality broke through. Alycia was dead. I was never going to see her again. She was dead, and it was all my fault. I'd reached for the money and cut her off the face of the earth. I'd killed her as if I'd slit her wrists myself.

What now?

My mind lurched at the money again, and my soul filled with disgust. Two point five. A pile of dust in the wind. I couldn't even give it to Donna. Too many Feds wearing blue ties. Too many Feds holding cell phones. I thought of Jake and my blood boiled.

Larry was right. Good ol' steak 'n' potatoes Larry. *"Next thing you know you'll be trying to start a car in a closed garage."*

It suddenly dawned on me. *Why not?*

I'd been required by a court order to maintain a hefty insurance policy to the tune of half a million dollars. Donna was still the named beneficiary, and by now the suicide clause would have passed the required time limit.

"You're worth more dead than alive," evil Potter had told George Bailey.

I closed my eyes. *No.*

I'd caused it, and I wouldn't take the coward's way out. For the rest of my life, I would face my mistakes, and pay for it through sheer regret.

Alycia's voice whispered in my ear, *"You saved my life! I'm serious!"*

Just before she'd left our home, Donna had stood in the hallway, taking one last look at what had been—what might have been. I went to the hallway, steeling myself. *My favorite isn't up here anymore,* she'd said.

I removed Alycia's nine-year-old photo from the wall.

See? She's alive.

Clutching the photo in my hands, I descended the steps, gripping the railing tightly, heading to my office. The phone rang, but I ignored it.

Inside, I sank into the couch and peered at my daughter—she was full of hope, and fully alive. Memories of our life flew tumbled through my mind, and I remembered the day I'd met Donna at the airport. At the time, we'd been grieving for Alice, devastated by her loss.

I thought of Donna's love of literature, especially the tragedies I remembered kidding her about it. She'd smiled wryly. *"I love tragedies because I never stop believing that* somehow *everything can be solved. Even at the worst of moments, I imagine the characters finally coming to their senses, imploring God to save them from their foolish thoughts and choices, and then I imagine God . . . in His brilliant power and majesty snapping His fingers and . . . Poof! All solved!"*

Alycia's picture slipped between my fingers to the floor, and I buried my head in my hands. Donna's words continued echoing in my mind: *"God can do anything."*

Looking up again, I caught a glimpse of the Clock Tower photo on the desk, remembering a time when our lives literally dripped with hope. Donna wearing her white corsage. Alice wearing her own white corsage. And me in a black tux.

My head grew more fuzzy.

Give me a second chance, I whispered, a foolish prayer indeed.

I reached for the Clock Tower photo and gazed at the past. *Let it go.* I turned the photo over on the desk and sank back into the couch.

"You can save me, Dad!" came her familiar voice.

Something wasn't right.

The door bell rang.

I considered ignoring it, but then wondered if maybe Susan had dropped by as promised. I rushed upstairs to the front door and opened it, only to find Mrs. Saabe, the elderly white-haired neighbor from across the street.

She stepped in closer. "Stephen, I just heard about Alycia. Oh, you poor dear . . . you and Donna!"

I opened my arms and allowed her to hug me.

"What a wonderful girl she was," she said, sadly. "What a terrible tragedy!"

I nodded into her shoulder and released her, but she held on to my arm.

"If you need anything, you let me know," she said. "I'm just across the street."

I forced a smile. "That's very kind of you."

"Are you hungry?"

"Perhaps later?"

"Good!" She finally released my arm. "I'll go fix you something."

"Uh, thanks, that would be nice," I said.

She trotted back across the street. I watched her for a moment, and then it hit me.

White roses.

Impossible, I thought.

I descended the steps again, nearly bumping my head on the stairwell ceiling. In my office, I placed the photo under the light, and studied the tiny corsages.

White.

I blinked rapidly, clearing my vision, and pushed my nose to within centimeters of the photo. No question about it. The corsages were white miniature roses. Could they have lost color with age? But the rest of the photo, including the girls' gowns, was color perfect.

You ran out of time, remember?

"That was just a dream," I whispered. "That's not what really happened."

Look at the photo, ol' sport. You never gave her the blue rose. You ran out of time. You even forgot which flower store. You went to Petal Pushin' instead.

"That was a dream," I whispered again.

The cell phone was lying on the couch. Donna would remember for sure. *No,* I thought. *I can't call her about this.*

Ignoring my better judgment, I picked up the phone, turned it on, and dialed Sally's number. A very testy voice said "Hello?" like a question.

"May I speak to Donna?"

"Oh, Stephen . . ." Sally muttered.

"I won't say anything to upset her," I promised.

"*You* will upset her."

I hesitated and considered a white lie. "I just remembered something she'd want to know."

"She's grieving, Stephen! What could she possibly want to know?"

"Please put her on, Sally."

"No, Stephen," she said. "And I'm hanging—"

I heard Donna's voice in the background. A muffled discussion ensued. Donna came on the line. "What is it, Stephen?" Her voice sounded very far away, very tired.

"I need to ask you something."

"I told you she was fragile, Stephen," she said, her voice breaking. "Do you remember that?"

"Yes . . ."

"I warned you, didn't I?"

"Yes."

She choked a sob. "What can you possibly say to me now?"

I knew she was about to hang up, so I went for broke. "Were the roses blue?"

Silence at first, and then an incredulous: "What?!"

"Was your rose corsage blue?"

Another hesitation. "What are you talking about?"

"The night of the banquet," I said. "The picture in front of the

Clock Tower. Please answer me and I'll never bother—"

Donna expelled another tortured breath, her voice now breaking. "How can you even be thinking of this?"

"Please, Donna. I'll never bother you again. Just answer the question—"

Her words were harsh: "Our . . . daughter . . . just . . . *died.*"

"Donna, please—"

"You forgot, Stephen!" she exploded. "Doesn't that ring a bell? You were late and you forgot. I even paid for the corsages! How could this possibly matter to you now? We just lost our daughter!"

I was stunned into silence.

"Are you satisfied?" Donna said, her voice suddenly reduced to a weeping whisper. "Let it go, please. . . ."

The handset was muffled. "We're hanging up, Stephen." It was Sally. "Get some help before you hurt someone else!"

The line went dead. I pressed the off button to the phone. Donna was wrong. The corsages had been blue. Not white. Not *ever* white. Not until the dream. I paced the room. *What does it mean?* I asked myself. But I knew, didn't I? A white rose meant I could still save Alycia.

The doorbell rang. I went upstairs and opened the door. It was Mrs. Saabe, holding her casserole dish, covered with aluminum foil.

She smiled sadly. "You won't be alone much longer, will you?"

I shook my head, took the dish from her, and she bade me farewell. "You just call if you need anything."

I thanked her as politely as I could manage and watched again as she descended my steps. She turned one last time and gave me a kindly wave before crossing the street. I wandered to the kitchen and placed the casserole on the table.

Downstairs, I picked up the photo again and stared at the roses, as if they might have changed back while I wasn't looking.

What if things like this could happen? What if Paul's celestial wormholes truly existed? What if people sometimes fell into cosmic rabbit holes? What if folks sometimes had strange dreams that took them into a special kind of past where things could be changed for real?

A glimmer of something eased its way into my skeptical soul. For the last time, I stared at the photo, and I *knew* without a doubt the roses had been blue. I decided to take a giant leap of faith and let the chips fall where they may. As I did this, the moment I decided to believe, that burning, overwhelming grief began to be pushed aside. I was now a father determined to save his daughter.

But how?

I picked up the photo of Alycia. Memories of a happy past came roaring back. I closed my eyes and allowed myself to let them in, fully living each one. "Please God," I whispered, ignoring the curtain that still seemed as dark and as impenetrable as the day Alice died.

Hours passed as I sat there, reliving our life, waiting to fall asleep, waiting for one final chance to save my daughter. The last time I glimpsed the clock, it was after four o'clock in the morning. By the character of the dark beyond my window, I could tell dawn was near. My eyes were slowly drooping closed. My conscious thoughts mingled inexorably with unconscious memories. I fought the loss of awareness, determined to awaken within my dreams.

Eventually, I must have slipped away . . .

. . . and awakened to the scent of vanilla mingled with pizza. It was like waking up at the bottom of the ocean, within the murky darkness, struggling for the surface. I fought the impulse to slip back into the dream, fighting for the surface of my consciousness, determined against all odds not to let it slip away, and then . . .

. . . I opened my eyes and looked around, expecting to see the framed posters in my downstairs office, but instead . . . I saw a roomful of young people sitting at booths. The radio was playing in the background, and I recognized the tune.

It took a few moments to put it together. Obviously, I wasn't in Aberdeen anymore. I was back east in college, sitting in the Soda Straw. I was awake and yet dreaming.

But something had gone terribly wrong.

I looked across the room and saw Nina smiling at me. She wandered over and giggled with delight, staring at something in my hands. "Well, that's gonna look good on my finger!"

I looked down and saw the ring. Startled, I dropped it to the table as if it were a giant spider.

Nina frowned. "You okay?"

"What day is it?" I blurted out.

"Day?" She looked mildly entertained. "Stephen, you've been studying way too much. It's Friday." She twisted her wrist. "And it's quarter to four." She smiled humorously. "You want the date too?"

I smiled, playing along. She gave me the date. May 12. I was waiting for Alice. I was about to propose.

"You okay?" Nina asked again.

I closed my eyes tightly, took a deep breath, and opened them again. Nina sat across the booth from me. "You don't look good, Stephen."

I shrugged, trying to clear my head.

"Stephen?" Nina's voice rose.

I twisted in the booth and looked over toward the entrance. In fifteen minutes, Alice would come walking in that door. And when she left—if I didn't stop her—she would be hit by a car.

Nina patted me on the hand and rose from her seat. "Pull yourself together, partner."

I barely noticed her slip away. I tried running at it again, like a mathematician recalculating his formula, but no matter how many ways I figured it, the same result glared back at me. I'd thrown myself into a paradox.

Alice was about to die. Could I let that happen? But if I saved Alice, I would never marry Donna, and therefore Alycia will have never existed.

I would kill my daughter . . . forever.

I looked at the ring. I had to follow the first script. I had to do everything the way it happened fourteen years ago. When Alice left the room, I had to let her die.

My soul shuddered. How could I do that? How could I let her die . . . all over again?

I had no choice.

I looked at my watch. 3:55. There had to be a way out of this.

My brain twisted like a pretzel. I'd spent a lifetime longing for a second chance to relive this day, and here it was. Alice was alive. Any minute she'd come walking through that door.

I heard the squeal of brakes, the sound of a muscle car turning the corner. Just like before. Nina stopped by my table again. "You still don't look good, Stephen."

Nina glanced toward the door. "Well, look-ee here."

I turned to see her—Alice was descending the steps into the restaurant. She smiled, but it wasn't very bright.

"Pull yourself together," Nina said again.

Alice was beautiful, just as I remembered. I stood up. Alice reached for me, and I hugged her back, holding her physical form in my arms. Her perfume mingled with her own scent, and I kissed her.

She broke away, holding on to my arms, "Stephen, are you okay?"

"I'm just so happy to see you," I replied.

She kissed me again. I touched her soft cheek and gazed into her eyes, and she winked. "You act like you haven't seen me in a while."

"It's been . . ."

"Twenty-four hours?"

"Too long," I said.

As she settled into the booth across from me, her brunette hair shimmered in the light. The moment she sat down, a shadow descended across her face, just like before. I reached for her wrist and felt her skin beneath my fingers.

"You seem troubled," I began.

Alice shrugged. "It's . . . nothing."

Nina came over, meeting my eyes with a knowing smile. Alice

ordered a soda. She grinned at me. "And Stephen will have a lemonade."

I glanced at my watch: It was 4:05. Fourteen years ago, we had talked for nearly fifteen minutes before she'd rushed out of the shop.

I could barely concentrate. The question churned within me: *Can I let her go?*

"Are you okay, Stephen? You look a little pale."

I pulled at my collar. "You know . . . I am feeling a little . . . strange."

She touched my hand. "Where's Donna anyway? Did she say something to you?"

I glanced at my watch again. It was way too early for Alice to ask this question. Somehow, the script had already changed.

Alice hesitated. "Well . . . maybe that's a good thing because . . . I did something terrible."

My heart slammed against my chest, and she fixed me with a guilty expression.

"What is it?" I asked.

"I found it . . ." She hesitated again, and I braced my hands against the table, ready to leap after her.

She shook her head, sighed loudly. "I have to show you. . . ."

I was already slipping out of the booth when I realized that Alice hadn't budged. Instead, she'd reached into her purse and removed a diary. Donna's diary.

"Where are you going?" she wondered aloud.

I sat back down across from her. "It can wait," I croaked out.

Alice looked at me strangely as she clutched the diary. An image of the contents in Donna's memory box came back to me. Her leather-bound diary had been nestled in it with the rest of her items.

"I was going to leave it in the car, but I couldn't," Alice told me now, tears slipping down her cheek. "I shouldn't have been snooping, but . . ."

She looked away, then wiped her cheek.

What had she read?

When she looked up again, her eyes locked with mine, and something shuddered through me. She seemed suddenly different to me, as if I were now looking at her through the eyes of a thirty-six-year-old man. I remembered what Donna had said to me the day of our divorce. *"She was exotic. You wanted her life."*

I reached for her hand, to console her, my mind swimming helplessly, trying to determine how to proceed. Sensing my reticence, Alice expelled a breath and grabbed her purse. "I shouldn't have done this. I'm so sorry. I have to go, Stephen."

I stared in disbelief as she slid out of the booth. I glanced up at the clock. Exactly fifteen minutes had elapsed. Although our conversation had somehow veered from the original, the moment of her leaving was exactly the same.

Desperately, I reached for her, but she broke free, muffling a sob. By the time I could slide to the edge of my own seat, she was halfway across the room.

"Alice, wait!" I shouted.

Let her go! something screamed within me.

I couldn't help it. I leapt to my feet, headed for the door, and ran smack into Nina, who was balancing a tray of plates on her upraised arm. The plates went flying, and I grabbed Nina to keep her from falling. By the time we recovered, Alice was already at the door.

"Alice!" I screamed just as she slipped out. I raced up the steps to the door, narrowly avoiding another waitress, twisting in between a group of students. I reached it and frantically pulled on the door handle.

Let her die!

Reaching the sidewalk, I glimpsed her at the curb preparing to cross. She stepped down and took several steps. I continued screaming.

It happened within seconds . . . the squeal of brakes that seemed to last forever . . . racing across the sidewalk between the door and the street . . . Alice's forward movement even as she was turning toward me . . .

This time, however, I reached her, grabbed her slippery blouse with every ounce of strength, pulled her toward me, hoping against hope that the material of the blouse wouldn't rip . . . feeling the whisk of air . . . the brush of a car speeding past us . . . breaking through the space that had been occupied by Alice a split second earlier . . .

My shoulder hit the pavement, and she fell on top of me, and I held on to her. I heard the squealing stop, and at first, neither of us moved. I felt her body twist in my arms, her chest breathing in and out, the stunned and incredulous tone in her voice: "Stephen? What happened?"

A small crowd was forming around us.

"Are you okay?" Alice said, sitting up. I just lay there, breathing heavily. When I finally sat up, Alice hugged me tightly. "How did you know?"

Someone touched me on the shoulder. "Dude . . . you're a hero."

After fully appraising my surroundings, I helped her to her feet. I was still catching my breath, unable to let go of her blouse. More people had gathered.

What have I done? I thought.

"I'm okay, Stephen. You saved me."

My vision wavered.

"Stephen?" Alice asked. "Are you hurt?" Her face came into focus for a split second.

I was speechless. She hugged me again. "I'm sorry, Stephen. I'm sorry I ever doubted you."

The flickering continued.

Alycia was gone forever.

Everything went black.

Chapter Thirty-four

I awakened slowly, slipping in and out of consciousness. Hazy images danced in the back of my sluggish mind. I heard a muffled *whooshing* sound in the distance. It seemed to increase in volume just as it receded. Alycia's voice echoed in the back of the whooshing: *"I need to talk to you, Dad. Do you promise?"*

An image of a blue rose crossed my vision. I opened my eyes and looked at the ceiling first, a spackled popcorn texture. *Where am I?*

I looked around the brightly lit room, and not until that moment did I recall fragments of the latest dream. *The Soda Straw. Nina, the waitress. And Alice. Dear Alice.*

I'm sorry I ever doubted you, she had said.

This room appeared to be a large bedroom. On the opposite wall was a dresser and mirror above it. Slightly to the left an arched entryway to another room. Apparently the bathroom. I heard the trickling sounds of what seemed to be a shower. To my right, curtains twitched with a subtle breeze. Radiant light struggling at the edges, and I heard that strange *whooshing* again.

Glancing back to the left, I heard the sound of humming emanating from the bathroom—a woman's voice. I flung the covers off and swung my legs over the bed, hoping that a sitting position might jog my memory, then noticed my attire. Pajamas.

I touched the speckled cut-Berber carpet with my toe, expecting it to give way, but it didn't. I pressed down harder, but the floor was solid. I stood up, slowly making my way to the beige curtains.

Taking a deep breath, I grasped the inside edges and pulled them apart, squinting into the light. Beyond the patio door was a wooden deck, and beyond that . . . miles and miles of distant, cloudy blue horizon. I grabbed the patio door handle, but it resisted. Fumbling for a lock, I pulled it open.

The sounds came alive—sea gulls, the roar of the ocean, the salty wind against my face. I tested the floor and found myself standing on the wooden deck, about ten feet by ten feet. I went to the railing and stared out into the blue-green of light-dappled waves washing against a deserted beach, part of a protected cove with the shore curving away on both sides. I took several deep breaths of the salty ocean wind. Images flickered at the edge of my mind.

I breathed deeply, struggled to remember, and the entire dream suddenly came to me: *I had saved Alice.*

And now . . . this.

I took another deep breath and turned toward the room, taking in the full scale of the beachfront home—the kind of house associated with the very wealthy.

Remembering the woman humming in the shower, I cautiously entered the bedroom, feeling the plush carpet beneath my feet, aware of the Mediterranean design of the room, the broadly textured walls, the vaulted ceiling, the elaborate built-ins.

I heard the humming again.

How old was I? And where was this? California? I went to the mirror and stared at my reflection. I appeared to be in my mid-thirties. My hair was shorter, closely cropped, and I had the vestiges of a one-day beard.

I opened the armoire cabinet and found a TV. Searching the room with my eyes, I saw the remote on the nightstand. Grabbing it, I thumbed through the buttons until I found the on button.

The woman was humming again. The shower water continued. Any minute it would stop.

The TV blared to life. Flicking through the stations, I found the Weather Channel. In the lower panel, the local weather was scrolling—Connecticut. I flipped through more channels and found another local station, a news announcer: *Here in Southern Connecticut, it appears the rains have subsided. . . .*

Humming came louder from the bathroom.

In the upper corner, the date seemed familiar. It was November.

I slumped down onto the bed again. Alycia was gone. I couldn't even mourn her "death." No picture of her existed. In this world, no one would understand. How could I explain the "death" of someone who was never born?

And who was the woman in the shower? Alice?

The shower stopped, and I prepared myself. I wiped my face and practiced a smile into the mirror, one that turned out to look rather ghoulish. More humming, clearer this time, familiar somehow.

As I quickly dressed into the only clothes I could find—khaki shorts and a white-and-blue Polo T-shirt—I was startled by the sound of stomping, beyond the closed bedroom door. The frantic twisting of the doorknob. Locked. Frenzied knocking. "Dad! Open up! She's finished!"

A horrified moment passed. I'd had another child. Such a thing hadn't even occurred to me. Of *course* Alice and I would have had children—maybe several.

"Dad! Hurry up!"

I rose and went to the door, twisted the lock, gripped the doorknob. I pulled it open, bracing for the worst—the physical reality of a child I didn't even know.

The door burst open. I jumped backward, and a brunette girl leapt into the room, her face beyond my vision. Her head was turned away from me toward the shower area. She whipped her hand behind her to grab my hand, whispering frantically: "C'mon!"

With my hand now in hers, she was pulling me out the door and down a hallway. "That was close, Dad!"

I tightened my grip, resisting her forward momentum. I hadn't gotten a good look at her face. She twisted around and faced me. "Dad! C'mon, we have to get in place!"

Alycia.

She frowned. "What?"

Speechless, I stared into her face.

"What's the matter, Dad?"

My throat closed up. Instinctively, I reached for her and pulled her to me, hugging her near, and reluctantly she hugged me back. "Da-ad! We don't have time for this!"

She fit in my arms just as I remembered. She'd never gone to Melgaard Park to meet Sean. She'd never cut her wrists in Sally's bathroom.

She pushed away from me. "Dad . . . are you okay?"

Swallowing, I nodded. "It's just so good to see you, honey."

"Parents are so weird," she muttered with some expressive eye rolling. "You'd think I died or something."

My grin felt wobbly.

"C'mon, Dad, we have to go!"

I released her, and she gave me her *get-it-together* expression.

"She'll be walking out any minute," Alycia whispered urgently. "You left the note, right?"

"The note."

She stopped. "You forgot the note?"

"Uh, I don't remember," I said.

"Da-a-ad!"

"Sorry."

Her mouth was working vigorously from side to side. "Okay," she said, heading back through the hallway. "No problem. I've got everything under control."

I watched her sneak to the door. Slowly she pushed it open, then peeked inside again. She glanced back, and made a *so-far-so-good* face. She slipped inside.

I waited, and it seemed to take forever. Looking around, I noticed the balcony railing, the elaborate windows. Leaning over, I noted the entryway, just downstairs. Glancing to my left, I saw a large framed print, a Broadway poster of *Titanic, the Musical.* A brunette woman stared rapturously into the face of another man.

Only his love could save her . . . the headline intoned.

The woman was Alice.

Suddenly, Alycia burst out of the room, her face ablaze with excitement. She giggled loudly and grabbed my hand again as she passed me, as if my hand were a baton. "C'mon!"

This time I went willingly. She pulled me down the steps, and when we reached the bottom, a hardwood floor, she turned to me, "Mom was dressing in the closet. I wrote it on the mirror!"

"The mirror?"

"It was foggy. C'mon, Dad, keep up."

She took me around a corner, released my hand, expecting me to follow, and headed through another door. We ran down another set of stairs, and when we reached the bottom, Alycia giggle-sprinted across the darkened room and disappeared behind a long wooden bar.

I hesitated. Was I supposed to follow? A tiny whisper erupted from the darkness. "Oh, Da-a-ad. Over here."

I followed and, despite the blackness, spotted her leaning against the wall. She held up a small electronic device that resembled a TV remote control. "I programmed it," Alycia whispered. "When I press this button . . . *Voila!* . . . the lights come on."

She rubbed her hands together. "This is going to be *so* cool," she said excitedly. "So she really thought we forgot?"

"What?"

"You didn't *tell* her, did you?"

"No," I said, still unsure of the occasion.

"Are you sure?"

"Positive."

"Stick a needle up your nostril?"

"Uh . . . yeah."

"What's the matter with you?"

"I'm old," I whispered.

"No kidding, but that's nothing new."

"Sorry."

"Apology accepted," she said, and then tensed. "Did you hear that?"

"No."

"Are you listening?"

"Of course."

A moment of silence passed. "You forgot the presents, didn't you?"

I had to think fast. "No . . . but I forgot where I hid them."

Alycia sighed with supreme exasperation. "In the downstairs closet?"

"Well, then. They must be there."

She expelled a breath. "What's wrong with you?"

"I guess we were up late."

My eyes had acclimated to the dark, and I saw her eyebrows merge into a frown. "Oh, gross. Information overload."

"All I said was—"

Her hands flew to her ears. "Ewww. La la la la . . . I can't hear you . . . la la la la la."

She dropped her hands. "You and Mom have been married for fourteen years, you know. That stuff should be old hat."

"What stuff?"

Hands to the ears again. "La la la la." Her eyes widened. "Did you hear that?"

"How could I?"

She plastered her clammy hand against my mouth. "Sssshhhh."

We listened but heard nothing.

She turned and frowned at me. "Why do you keep staring at me like that?"

"I like your face paint."

She frowned. "Oh yeah. The makeup. You actually like it?"

"Of course not, but you did a good job. You know. For a kid."

"I'm not a kid anymore, Dad. Acclimate."

She reached for me, but I grabbed her hands with one of mine and tickled her. She sputtered a giggle before snatching her hands away and slapping her mouth shut with both. Through her muffled hands, she sputtered, "D-a-a-ad! Look what you made me do."

The stair squeaked loudly, and we both heard it. Alycia sucked in a breath. "Did she hear us?"

I hope so, I thought, grinning like a fool in the dark. The ability to process this, to make heads or tails out of what was happening, would come later. In the meantime, my daughter was still alive.

"Are you ready, Dad?" she whispered.

"Ready for what?"

"She's standing in the hallway!"

I heard repeated clicking of a wall switch by the stairwell entrance. "That's strange," someone murmured. "The light must have burned out."

The voice was familiar, and by now I was dying to stand up and yell, "Surprise!"

"Are you ready, Dad?"

"Roger, dodger."

"We need to buy you some new lingo."

"Someone down here?" That female voice again, so familiar.

Alycia grasped my hand. "Ready?"

"Say the word."

"Now!"

Hand in hand, Alycia and I leapt to our feet and yelled "Surprise!" at the exact moment the entire downstairs was engulfed in lights and I heard the blaring guitars of rock music, which I immediately recognized as the Beatles' rendition of "You say it's your birthday. . . ."

The room exploded with illuminated balloons and streamers and banners, and across the room a woman squealed with delight. I didn't recognize her at first—for a completely different reason than someone might suspect: because this woman wasn't Alice. Not even close. I watched her, now ecstatic with delight, twisting around and around, taking in the entire room. "You guys, you guys, what did you do? I thought you forgot my birthday!"

Alycia squealed, and by now the woman had crossed the room and was reaching for me. Holding out her hands, she grabbed my waist, and by then there was no doubt in my mind.

Donna kissed me sweetly on the lips, and then squeezed my cheeks. "Hey, Lover Boy, when did you plan all this?"

Chapter Thirty-five

This was not the Donna I remembered. Her hair was cut chin-length with loose bangs. She was wearing white shorts and a loose-fitting blouse with pink and yellow stripes. Her entire frame was thinner somehow, but shapely all the same.

"No more kisses, okay?" Alycia said, her eyes wide with insistence. Donna embraced me again. Alycia slapped her hands over her eyes. "Okay, okay, I see no evil."

With melodramatic gusto, Donna kissed me again.

"This is *not* working out according to plan," Alycia complained, coming over and grabbing our hands. "Time for presents."

Donna caught my eye. "There's more?"

"Always," I whispered, but my words were coming out like echoes, as if I were talking in a tunnel.

Donna swung her hair from side to side to show off the earrings twinkling in the overhead lights. Alycia reached a closet and gave me a warning look, which I took to mean: I'd better have remembered. She poised her hand on the knob and gave me another look. I shrugged and waited, hoping I hadn't blown it. She pulled open the closet like a magician revealing the lady who had been sawn in half. "Voila!"

There were two large gift-wrapped boxes with silver bows sitting on a small stool. Alycia flashed me a quick, *well done* smile.

I felt proud. Donna squealed again and wrapped my arm into hers. "Oh, Stephen . . ." she whispered, giving me another peck on the cheek.

"Let's go upstairs," Alycia muttered. "Before things get out of hand!"

Alycia loaded up my arms, and I carried the presents to the living room. Cathedral ceilings and tall windows overlooked the sandy beach leading to the cove and the ocean beyond. I put the gifts in a leather chair.

Donna was now standing in front of the windows. She caught me looking at her, and I smiled, embarrassed. A glint of curiosity crossed her features.

Taking a deep breath, I got up and went to the windows beside her. Together we looked out beyond the deck and watched the foamy waves surge against the shoreline.

Moments later, Donna opened my present first, and I wondered what I'd gotten her. It was a framed print. I took a closer look. It wasn't a print. It was an original. Donna grinned. "It's beautiful!" She winked at me, and in a humorous tone, designed to sound slightly melodramatic, she exclaimed, "What did I ever do to deserve you!"

Alycia broke in. "Are you kidding, Mom? He's lucky to have *you*."

I forced a laugh. Next Donna opened Alycia's gift. It was a purse.

"I remember looking at this at the mall," Donna exclaimed.

"I paid attention," Alycia replied in a matter-of-fact tone.

"What did I do to deserve *you*?" Donna said, getting up to hug her daughter. Alycia shot me a warning glance, designed to intercept any potential sarcastic repartee.

Donna came back over and promptly sat in my lap.

"This is so totally getting out of hand," Alycia said, jumping up. "I'm going into the next room now, and when I return, you two had better be all finished with all this kissy stuff."

"Then you'd better be gone for a while," Donna chuckled.

"Oh, gross, Mom," Alycia whined. "TMI!" She headed around the corner.

Donna kissed me tenderly and began running her fingers through my hair. "You seem . . . a little distracted, Stephen. Everything okay?"

The whole thing was already unraveling.

She whispered into my ear. "You and Alycia, and your birthday surprises. I can't keep up with you two."

I took another breath.

"Am I too heavy?" She grasped my cheek lightly, peering into my eyes. "Sure there's nothing wrong? You're looking a bit partly cloudy."

I stared into my former wife's eyes.

"Wanna go upstairs?" she asked.

"You know . . . actually, I'm not really feeling that well."

Donna frowned thoughtfully. "I didn't think so. You shouldn't pretend, you big-strong-he-man type. Can I get you something?"

"Uh . . . like what?"

"The pink stuff? Was it something we ate last night, maybe?"

Last night? "Maybe."

"Maybe you just didn't sleep enough," she said and nipped my ear.

I shivered and she pulled back.

"Did that hurt?"

"No, of course not."

She frowned and stared at me curiously. I almost expected her to say, *You're not really Stephen, are you?* The moment she would begin asking me questions, I would be finished.

"I think . . . I need to lie down for a while."

"Okay," she said, and for a moment I thought I saw the old Donna, the one who carried a glint of hurt behind her eyes.

She was getting up when I pulled her back to me, and she giggled playfully. She looked at me expectantly. "We might do a little shopping? Alycia and I? While you rest."

I nodded, and she got up again. I began walking across the room with renewed effort to appear confident. I was halfway up the steps when I noticed her looking at me curiously. She smiled again, but that questioning in her eyes persisted.

I ascended the remaining steps, past the giant poster of Alice. The moment I was behind the closed door to our spacious bedroom, I let out a sigh of relief.

I leaned against the door, staring around the room with continuing disbelief, waiting for it to suddenly waver into oblivion, after which I would awaken in some asylum ward somewhere.

I could almost imagine someone whispering in the background: *Poor man, lost his mind when his daughter committed suicide. Thinks he's fallen down a rabbit hole.*

I wandered about the room, touching things, testing the sense of physical solidity as if that would convince me one way or the other. I handled the comb on the dresser. I ran my fingers along the bedspread, feeling the carpet beneath the soles of my feet, closing my eyes and opening them again. I even tried the old standard: pinching my arm.

In the bathroom, I continued to look for anomalies, little clues that would tell me the truth. The shower was still moist. The fog on the mirrors had evaporated. The beige tile felt cold beneath my touch.

Back in the bedroom, I sat on the bed.

What would it take to fully believe? To fully give myself over to this? I didn't know, but if the hours turned into days, and the days turned into weeks, surely it would sink in. Eventually it would seem like home. *Wouldn't it?*

How was I going to function in a world where I couldn't remember the past fourteen years? I had to learn the past in a hurry. I had to ask carefully worded questions. Until I got up to speed, I had to keep faking it. Somehow I had to survive in this reality without letting on. I had to learn who I became, and then become that person.

I considered another alternative. What if I came clean? I could face both Alycia and Donna and tell them the truth.

I almost laughed. They'd surely think I was crazy.

"What happened to you, Dad?" Alycia would ask. *"Did you hit your*

head or something?" And then she'd begin looking at me from behind scrutinizing expressions.

No, I had to play along.

First order of business—study the past fourteen years. Eventually, all my questions would be answered, including what actually had happened between Alice and me. *Actually?* I chuckled briefly at the irony.

I got up, went to the dresser, and pulled out the top drawer. Nestled in with spare change, pens and pencils, was a black leather wallet. The outer flap displayed my driver's license: South Dakota.

Strange.

I heard a gentle knocking on the door.

"Come in," I called.

The door opened, and Donna and Alycia appeared in the doorway. Alycia was wearing a Patriots baseball cap.

"Are you feeling any better?" Alycia asked. "We're going out. Wanna come?"

I considered her offer. What if they asked me to drive? What if we met people I was supposed to know? What if Donna and Alycia embarked on conversations that contained recollections I couldn't "remember"?

No, I couldn't risk it yet.

I gestured for Alycia, and she came to me, grasping my extended hand.

"You're growing up so fast," I said.

Alycia rolled her yes. "Oh boy, the parental-walk-down-nostalgia lane. Twice in one day."

"I love you, honey," I said.

She nodded, smiling sweetly for me. "I love you too, Dad."

Donna lingered by the door, observing us approvingly.

"So . . . are you coming or not?" Alycia asked again.

I shook my head. "Not this time."

Alycia shrugged. "We'll be gone for a while. Mom wants to go to

Essex. And you see . . . that works out just perfectly for me, because I just want to shop!"

I looked at Donna, and she chuckled. I turned back to Alycia.

"Neat baseball cap," I said. "It reminds me of when you joined the boys' team. Remember how we worked for months?"

Alycia frowned. "Joined the boys' team? Ick. When did I do that?"

"Just kidding," I replied.

"Dad, your stories are getting weirder and weirder."

I thought of her ears. "Lean over."

She did, pushing her hair out of the way. "They're looking good, huh, Dad?"

At first I felt relief, believing that something of our past had remained, but Alycia quickly clarified the situation. "The miracles of modern surgery, huh?"

Of course, I realized. *In this reality, we could afford to pay a surgeon to flatten her ears.*

Donna wandered into the room and stroked her daughter's back. "We'd better go."

"I challenge you to a rematch," Alycia said. "When we return."

"You're on," I said, although I wasn't sure what game we'd be playing.

Donna leaned over and kissed my cheek. "Get some rest, sweetie. And thanks for everything."

I nodded. They lingered at the door, waved, and left me.

Chapter Thirty-six

I began by going through every drawer in the master bedroom. I worked my way through the spare rooms, doing the same, until ending up on the lower walk-out level.

In a downstairs closet, I caught a break. I found another one of Donna's memory boxes, this one loaded with photo albums and diaries.

I was surprised to see them. Previously—in the other life—Donna had stopped keeping a diary after college. A full thirteen years passed with barely a mention of her thoughts and dreams.

I flipped through them, reading the dates, then recognized the one from college. I opened that one first, flipped through it, and felt a flicker of guilt for invading her privacy.

Sitting on the floor, leaning against the wall, I opened to the earliest diary—the *pre*-Alice record—and began reading from a past that had occurred long before I'd lost—or saved—Alice. Since it wasn't relevant, I nearly set it aside and went to the next diary, but a single line grabbed me. *Dear Diary, I've fallen in love with Stephen Whitaker.*

It took me an hour to read the rest of it, and in spite of everything that had happened, in spite of saving Alice in a dream, and somehow waking up and finding myself in a strange future—where my daughter was alive and Donna and I were still married—I was transfixed with Donna's narrative of the past. No wonder Alice had been so upset.

When I was finished, I leaned against the wall and tried to digest what I'd just learned.

Six months before Alice transferred to our college, I first saw Donna in Lit class. As an accounting major, I hid in the far back, the farthest row to the left. Donna sat three rows over, six chairs up. She liked to wear jean skirts and yellow or blue blouses, and I remember thinking she had nice legs. She also had an untouchable demeanor: *Keep your distance!*

Along with this, she never spoke in class unless called upon, and she never raised her hand. Even so, Professor Smith deferred his probing questions to her. After the entire class would weigh in, he'd often ask her, "And what do you say about this, Donna?"

You could sense the class crouching closer: The Queen of Lit was about to hold forth. After her reply, the prof would invariably say, "Exactly what I was looking for."

Despite the praise, Donna loathed the attention, and she especially did not relish being the teacher's pet. One day, she walked into class early, offered her hand to me, and said, "Hi, I'm Donna. Can we trade chairs?"

While our seats weren't assigned, our usual spots had become established through routine. Knowing full well why she wanted my seat and feeling feisty, I smiled. "What's it worth to you?"

"I'll buy you lunch," she surprised me by saying.

"Lunch?" I asked. "That's it?"

"And dessert. That's the deal."

Humored by her silly desperation, I replied, "I was thinking something more like help on the essays."

Her face fell. "I won't help you cheat, if that's what you want."

I opened my mouth to correct her impression, but she was already walking away. She got situated in her vulnerable seat, opened her book, and waited for class to begin.

Afterward, I approached her in the hall. "Is the offer for lunch still good?"

She frowned. "You didn't keep your part of the deal."

"There are three months left."

Reluctantly, she agreed, and as we walked across campus, I attempted casual conversation.

"What's your favorite classic?" I asked her.

She answered rather grudgingly, as if telling me would make it less significant. *"To Kill a Mockingbird."*

"Why?"

"If you have to ask, you haven't read it."

"Touché," I admitted.

Our short walk was such a disaster that by the time we reached the lunchroom, I expressed polite reservation. "I was just kidding. You can have my seat. We don't have to go through with lunch, and I certainly would never ask you to cheat for me."

"So why did you say it?"

"Because 'help' means 'help,'" I said with exasperation. "And because I don't read much."

Wrong answer, her expression said.

"I mean . . . not fiction."

"So what do you read?" she asked with little enthusiasm. We were standing just outside the door, both of us obviously looking for the appropriate parting words. While she was annoyed with my literary ignorance, I was annoyed with her elitist attitude, and I said what I hoped would offend her the most: "I read Christian books."

My answer had the opposite effect. Her mouth dropped open. "What kind of Christian books?"

I named some titles and her expression melted. "Wow, and I thought you were a jerk."

"Well, you're still a literary snob," I shot back.

She bit her lip and swallowed. I said good-bye and made to leave with a semblance of dignity when she grabbed my arm. "Stephen, may I buy you lunch to apologize?"

Lunch lasted three full hours. Once we got to talking, we couldn't stop. She barely made it to her three o'clock Advanced Comp class, and I didn't tell her until much later that I'd skipped my two o'clock General Science.

We had everything in common. Both of us were born and raised in small Midwestern towns, both to poorer families, and both of us made it to college by the skin of our teeth.

I told her about my rabbit-field prayers, how the sense of God's closeness was unlike anything I'd ever experienced, and she seemed awestruck. "I've sometimes struggled to believe God would answer my prayers," she admitted sheepishly.

I nodded. "But sometimes . . . God gives a sign."

She was surprised. "He does? How?"

That was difficult to say, other than it came with a sense of peace and confidence—a clicking into place.

In spite of our inauspicious introductions, we became instant best friends, which was all I had remembered about those days until I read her diary.

"My favorite picture isn't up here anymore," she'd said on the day she packed up and left me, and I now remembered what she meant. Two nights before Alice's celebrated recital, I took Donna to a French restaurant. Donna wore the only nice dress she owned at the time, the powder blue gown, and I wore the only suit in my closet.

Only faintly do I recall the meal, but I do remember the waitress. She was surly and abrupt, and despite the dominant theme of our discussion—*Christian love*—Donna became increasingly annoyed with the level of service. When we politely asked the waitress to snap our picture, she grudgingly agreed. Finally Donna could take it no longer. "Let's just go, Stephen. We can talk back at the dorm."

I remember smiling and saying, "Let's do something radical first."

She frowned.

"'Bless those who curse you,'" I said cryptically.

"You're kidding." She sat back in her seat and looked at me.

"Okay," she replied. "Let's tell her we forgive her for being such a lousy waitress."

She watched as I removed a twenty-dollar bill. Her eyes widened. "What's that?"

"Our tip."

She looked incredulous.

"Maybe she's had a bad day," I said. "Regardless, all waitresses work for tips, and, besides, we can leave a little note."

"Like what?"

"Like . . . we're praying for you, or . . . we could write a Scripture verse or something."

Her expression soured. "If we really want to do the right thing, we'd tell the manager and he'd fire her and save future customers."

I shrugged. "I suppose that's justice."

"You bet it is." She let out a breath. "Fine, Stephen. Do what you want. But I still think you're being naïve. God doesn't expect us to be stupid."

"Call it an experiment, then," I said, inserting the twenty beneath the water glass along with a scribbled note, hoping the next day would be better and we'd be praying for her.

Donna's diary explained what happened next:

Stephen and I were just leaving the restaurant and I felt terribly frustrated. I was also frustrated with myself because I couldn't feel anything but anger with this woman for ruining a perfectly good date, but mainly I was disturbed with Stephen because he was acting self-righteous (although I know he didn't mean to). We were interrupted by the sound of a woman's voice calling to us from behind us, and we turned to see our waitress standing by the door, hugging herself in the cold. Despite the dim light, we could see she'd been crying. We approached her, and she could barely talk. She mentioned the note and the prayer, and gasped out an apology for her behavior. She told us that her family was falling apart, that her father had left her mother.

I wanted to crawl under the cement sidewalk, but Stephen reached for her hand. And then he prayed out loud and afterward said something like: "There's always hope. Don't give up believing God is on your side." The waitress nodded. "Meeting you two has been a gift from God . . . to me."

As Stephen walked me back to my dorm, neither of us spoke. When we reached the glass door, I turned to apologize, but he placed his finger against my lips. He told me he'd been just as shocked as I was at the waitress's response.

We talked until three in the morning. When we parted, Stephen kissed me on the cheek. He told me he couldn't believe time had gone so quickly.

And then I said something wrong. "Meeting you has been like coming home." His expression dimmed slightly, and I could have kicked myself. I'd forgotten that home wasn't all that happy a place for him.

I feel like we're beginning to fall in love, but I have the impression Stephen is fighting it. Either that, or I've been wrong all along.

So, Dear Diary, here I am. In spite of my lifelong determination to stay single, I'm crazy about the only person who's ever given me any sense that God could love me. I like who I am when we're together, and if I can't have someone like Stephen, I don't want anyone. At the same time, I'm angry with myself for caring this much for him.

In her diary, Donna wrote this months later: *Unbelievable. I've just lost Stephen to Alice, and I never even had him. Then again, should I be so surprised? Why would someone like Stephen even want me? I must have proven to him that I'm not worthy of his love. Even his faith is beyond me.*

The remaining diary entries—one every two weeks or so, were filled with continuing details about classes, Alice, school, prayers to God, and occasionally . . . her unrequited love for me. While she'd gotten over the initial frustration, the sadness seemed to linger.

Two weeks before I proposed to Alice, Donna wrote: *I know that Stephen and I are supposed to be together, Lord, so why did you take him from me? I know Stephen loves me. Do something, Lord!*

That was her last college diary entry.

I placed the diary on the desk and leaned against the wall, closing my eyes.

"It seems you've forgotten everything," Donna had once told me.

I finally reached for the next diary. Two hours later, I was still alone. I'd read nearly five diaries and perused seven photograph albums. I'd received all the answers I needed. I now knew what had happened after I'd saved Alice, and if I hadn't read it for myself, I wouldn't have believed it.

Two weeks after that close call at the Soda Straw, Alice and I had taken a long walk around the campus. According to what I'd told Donna later, I had come to grips with my true feelings. *I've fallen in love with Donna,* I told Alice, and unbelievably, Alice hadn't protested.

"I always suspected that you two belonged together," she told me. And then she said something shocking. Her association with Donna had reconfirmed her faith in Christ. In fact, several nights earlier, Alice had knelt before God.

"I'll find a church in Manhattan," she told me, laughing. *"I'll be the only Christian on Broadway."*

At the end of the walk, I kissed her on the cheek.

"We'll always be the Three Musketeers, right?" she asked me, her eyes glistening in the dim light by the girls' dorm.

I hugged her quickly.

"Maybe I can be Donna's maid of honor someday?"

"Of course. And I'll always care for you, Alice," I said.

Knowing what I meant, she smiled at my choice of words. "Ditto."

I married Donna two months later. And in March of the following year, our dear Alycia was born.

Surprisingly, in *this* life, I had never lost faith in God. I turned down the Wall Street job—Larry had already called me with his business idea—and we'd moved to Aberdeen. Together, as a family, we attended church, and my habit of daily prayer continued. Every night, I committed my ways to God and asked for divine direction as a husband and a father.

On the other hand, Alice went on to New York City. She became a leading star in various musicals, and Donna's albums were filled with photos of the reunited Musketeers. But Alice made a few poor choices. She began taking uppers to stay on top of things, and then consumed downers to fall asleep. Her career faltered. So had her faith. She became bitter and disillusioned. She even spoke openly of her scorn for religion.

Physically, she fell apart too. In her thirties, she had gained a hundred pounds over five years. Her personality changed with her growing addictions to a multitude of prescription drugs.

She divorced four times and married five—each husband a product of an affair, resulting in another broken family.

And then . . . one night after learning of her latest husband's plans to leave her, she slipped into the bathroom and OD'd on a prescription drug. She died the next day.

I closed the diary, my heart pounding.

What have I done?

I wandered out to the balcony of our summer home in Connecticut and stared at the ocean as the sun slowly set. The horizon mixed a brilliant display of oranges and purples, but to the west, gray clouds threatened. The weather report had called for severe thunderstorms by evening.

I watched the slow-building storm and realized that I'd been in love with Donna from the beginning. I pondered the diaries I'd read, and remembered Donna's poignant statements to me on the day of our divorce. She knew the truth. She knew I'd been allured by Alice's exotic lifestyle and wealthy family, and then, after her fatal accident, I'd been blinded by the past. My persistent lack of faith had thrown me into a tailspin and interrupted the true course of my life.

Standing on the balcony, I felt a wave of loneliness. Donna and Alycia were still away, and I hoped they would return before the storm. I couldn't wait to see them again.

I had what I wanted, didn't I? Alycia was alive! Donna, the true love of my life, was my wife. I was wealthier than I would have imagined! I was standing at the edge of the beautiful ocean. Everything was perfect now.

And . . . who was I kidding?

The more I'd read of Donna's diary, the deeper the truth sank in. I was an imposter. A fake. On top of that, Alycia hadn't remembered any of our shared events. The ones that seemed so important to me had never happened to this Alycia. My wife and daughter didn't truly know me, and I didn't know them. This was not my world.

Sure . . . I could exist here, living with the kind of affluence I'd always craved, but I'd be living a lie till the day I died. I could never tell them who I really was, and, through no fault of their own, they would always be partial strangers to me. Worse, saving Alice had ruined her soul.

I stared into the water for a while longer. Later, I went downstairs and retrieved a cell phone I'd seen earlier. I navigated through the old phone numbers, found Donna's, and called her.

She answered cheerfully. "Hi, Stephen, feeling better? Looks like a storm coming in. We'll be home soon."

"I miss you," I said.

"I miss *you,*" she replied.

"Please come home," I whispered.

"I'll see you soon," she said, hanging up.

I went upstairs again and stared at the ominous storm. The rain came so suddenly the beachcombers had to run for cover. I took a deep breath and closed my eyes, feeling the rain spatter against my cheek, and the wind rushing in my ears. *God, no matter what, I'll serve you for the rest of my life. Please forgive me for a lifetime of foolishness.*

Slipping back in, I closed the sliding glass door and paused at the window, waiting for the downstairs door to open. Instead, the phone rang. It was Donna. "Stephen, we got caught in the rainstorm. We're now sheltered beneath a bank drive-through."

"I'll be waiting for you," I replied.

"I can't wait to get back, to be with you," she said, her voice low, as if she didn't want Alycia to hear. "You made my birthday so special!"

After hanging up, I sank to the floor, as the reality of it fully sunk in. They were strangers to me. And I was a stranger to them. *My* Donna and *my* Alycia were gone . . . forever.

An hour passed as the storm buffeted our house. I waited for my new family, and despite the raging storm, my eyes closed, and I dozed off. . . .

CHAPTER THIRTY-SEVEN

I awakened in a dark room, to the scent of musty walls and the sound of a distant car muffler. When I could put it off no longer, I opened my eyes and glimpsed the clock first. 7:41.

There was a thin line of daylight piercing the boundaries of high curtains. I sat up and recognized the feel of the familiar cushions beneath me.

I looked around and took in my surroundings. I was downstairs in my office, sitting on the couch my daughter had sagged by virtue of her youthful energy. I was home in my office on Northview Lane. Above me, the floor boards squeaked. Someone was here. I got up and noticed my clothes. I was fully dressed. Had I slept in my clothes?

Confused, I tried to sort through the strange dream I'd just had. Images of a rushing ocean came to me. A brewing storm had developed on the horizon. Where? Connecticut? Alycia and Donna had been there, and I remembered something about a birthday surprise. More fragments danced through my foggy mind, an entire litany of disjointed memories, as if months had passed, not mere minutes.

The more I struggled to make sense of it, the more images broke through. Donna had divorced me. My father had died and I'd lost everything. Larry had skipped town. Worst of all . . . my daughter had killed herself. But just before the ocean fragments, I'd had that dream again, like a dream in a dream, the one where I rush across the room, only this time . . . I'd actually *saved* Alice.

I shook my head, as if to clear it of the vivid mental pictures. *Just a dream,* I thought, and then my entire body shuddered.

Filled with a sudden sense of urgency, I headed out of the room, then paused halfway through the furnace room. Something wasn't right. The room was filled with Donna's things. I stared at the boxes, trying to put it together. Had she forgotten to pick them up? Why hadn't I noticed before?

She hasn't left yet.

I headed through the door and up the steps. I took them two at a time and bumped my head against the low part of the ceiling, something I hadn't done in years.

"Ouch!" I yelled, crumpling against the wall, holding my forehead.

"Stephen?" A voice from the living room.

Rubbing my head, seeing stars, I righted myself and took another step. The door opened, flooding the stairway with light.

"Are you okay?"

Still holding my head, I looked up and saw a shadow in the light.

Donna?

I quickly continued climbing the steps. Startled by my exuberance, Donna retreated, her eyes alarmed.

Reaching the top, I stopped at the edge. "You're here. . . ."

Her eyes squinted with curiosity. "I haven't left yet. Are you okay?"

I chuckled breathlessly. "It's nothing. . . ."

"Mom?"

Alycia? I twisted around, and there she was, standing just outside the screen door.

"Are we ever going? I have to meet Denise."

"Just a minute, honey," Donna replied softly.

I struggled not to rush across the room and scare *her* to death. Alycia cast me a sad look and headed outside.

Turning to Donna, I took a breath and let it out. She frowned again. "Are you sure you're okay, Stephen? I was looking at the pictures when I heard you—"

"I remember," I said softly. "Your favorite isn't up there anymore."

"My favorite?"

I nodded. "The French restaurant?"

Donna stared at me in astonishment.

"I remember when we took that picture. We talked until three in the morning. Surely, you remember the waitress, don't you?"

Donna nodded, her eyes little circles of unbelief. She motioned toward the door. "Alycia's waiting. I need to get going."

She moved past me, but I reached out and touched her arm and it felt as if electricity sparked between us. She turned suddenly.

"Don't leave," I whispered. "I want you to stay."

She seemed confused again, as if not sure whether to keep walking or stare at me. She stammered, trying to find her next words. "Oh, Stephen, I can't. . . . I mean . . . we shouldn't . . ."

I edged closer, reaching for her left hand. Looking down as I grasped it, she let me hold it for a moment before pulling away. Clearing her throat, she turned on her heels and headed for the door again. And then, as quickly as she got to the doorway, she stopped in her tracks, her face a mixture of defiance and curiosity. "We made a mistake, Stephen—"

"No, we didn't."

She frowned.

"From the very beginning it was you, Donna. I was just too foolish to see it. And maybe someday you'll forgive me. Maybe someday I'll earn your love again."

Perhaps I laid it on too thick, but frankly I was so overwhelmed by the sight of her, I couldn't help myself. But Donna looked absolutely horrified. She shook her head again, "I can't do this, Stephen, not anymore." She turned toward the door again. This time, without saying good-bye, she rushed out.

I went to the door and watched her back out of the garage. At the same time, I caught a glimpse of my daughter in the car. The car backed into the street and lingered as Donna switched gears, then traveled several yards. I stepped out on the concrete stoop and waved to a very confused Alycia in the passenger seat.

It was all I could do not to chase them down the street. The car reached the end of our block and then stopped. For a full minute it didn't move, and I could just imagine the conversation within.

"Are you kidding, Mom?"

And then . . . the car began backing up. It reversed all the way to the front of our house. Another pause, and then Donna got out of the car, crossed her arms, and just stood there beside the engine hood.

I grinned like a fool. Across the yard, as if traversing years and years of misunderstanding, and mountains of my own foolishness, our eyes met. I took the steps slowly.

With her arms still folded protectively, Donna worked her way around the front of the car, and when she reached the edge of the sidewalk, she smiled the kind of smile that said, *I can't believe I'm about to do this. . . .*

Eventually, Alycia got out of the car. She hugged herself as well, glancing about the neighborhood. Being this vulnerable to the neighbors' prying eyes must have been sheer torment for my socially conscious daughter.

I met Donna halfway down the sidewalk, and she gazed into my eyes. "Why should I stay?"

"Because you belong with me," I replied. "And I love you."

Donna's eyes narrowed, as if trying to solve a mystery. "You've never said that to me before," she said, and she was right. At least not like that.

The first tear slipped down her cheek. Blushing with embarrassment, Alycia refused to look at me, but I didn't care. I reached out for her shoulder, and she reluctantly allowed me to touch her. I wasn't worried. I'd seen this before.

"Dad . . . please . . ." she whispered, but her eyes melted.

She paused for a moment, and then, as if she couldn't wait any longer, she sank into my waiting arms.

"You can't lose her," Donna had once said to me.

And this time, I wouldn't.

Epilogue

Alycia came home from college the other day, her boyfriend tagging along. From the looks of things, they seemed pretty serious. I was glad to see that Doug was a clean-cut kid, blond hair, rather good-looking, well-mannered and respectful.

After the introductions, Alycia held out a dried flower. "You'll never believe where we found it."

I did my best to act surprised, but I wasn't. The rose was blue, the color of the sky. I'd heard for years that botanical scientists were close to changing the genetic structure. "I guess they finally did it," I said, marveling at the beauty. "They're doing amazing things these days."

"Nope," she replied, grinning from ear to ear. "We just happened to find it along the Connecticut coast, hidden among the other wild red roses."

I grinned back, thinking of all the *Ripley's Believe It or Not* tales Paul and I had read as kids.

For a split second I actually believed her. I caught my daughter's eye, and she twinkled at me. "Gotcha, Dad."

I chuckled. "Got me good."

"Actually they're doing surprising things with spray color," she giggled.

I was tempted to chase her around the house, maybe tickle her to death, but . . . not in present polite company.

Doug seemed chagrined, if not downright apologetic. "I told her not to do it."

I only laughed. "Practical jokes are our bread and butter," I said, and he looked relieved.

Needless to say, the passage of years has yielded some profound changes. Somewhere around the time Alycia became a freshman in high school, Donna and I moved to a new home, a rather modest rancher, northwest of our previous house, roughly five rungs removed from my childhood Uglyville.

Then again, Uglyville doesn't scare me anymore. Sometimes, in fact, I take the long way home just to drive by my old neighborhood and recall the days when I talked to God in the rabbit fields beyond the Whitaker house. I now look at it with profound nostalgia.

Several days after Donna nearly left me, I'd called my father.

"Busy, Dad?"

"What's that you say?" he spluttered.

"Mom says you got a new computer."

"Uh . . . well . . . can't run the blasted thing."

"That's what sons are for."

"Come again?"

On Tuesday, after work, I drove up to Frederick, and within a few hours, got the thing up and running. The old mental tapes were still playing, of course, and it wasn't easy to be with Dad, but I persevered. Weeks later, I sucked up my pride and invited him over to watch a Vikings game with me on a Sunday. He accepted. During halftime, while my mother and Donna scrapbooked in the dining room, Dad and I tossed a football in the front yard. This time, he lasted more than five minutes. I even had to talk him into quitting for the third quarter.

Two weeks later, I accompanied him to see the "local deity" he'd been avoiding. After he submitted himself to a series of tests, I pretended surprise when the doctors caught my father's aneurism in time. His opinion of the medical profession softened after that, and it gave us a few more years to watch the Vikings on Sunday afternoons.

"How did you know?" Donna asked me, and I was tempted to explain but didn't. She wouldn't have understood. I'm not sure I understand it myself. Even now.

Two years after our close call, I persuaded Donna to return to school. And two years after that, she received her master's in literature. She then accepted a position as an assistant professor of literature at Northern State College, and she's never been happier. For her classes, *Mockingbird* is required reading, along with *The Great Gatsby.* Unfortunately, she took to calling me ol' sport again, not that I mind too much. I tried talking her into dropping *Gatsby* for *Ender's Game,* with little success. Strangely enough, she saw Paul more than I did, rubbing shoulders with him in the faculty lounge.

As for myself, I got back into the stock market, but took a lesson from my father's playbook. Instead of trading, I *invested.* This time, a different outlook, a more realistic goal, and starting each day on my knees, made all the difference. Most important, I abandoned the notion that the market could make me whole somehow, and eventually, my father and I repaid the debt we owed to members of our community.

Changing the course of my life wasn't easy, however, and I would be remiss to suggest such a thing. There were countless temptations to fall into my old habits, and sometimes I did. Fortunately, I was able to correct my course quickly enough. I'd seen the future, after all.

In truth, I suppose we all have second chances if only we'd observe the history of our own lives. Life seems to repeat, and for most of us, I'd venture a guess there's still time to change what often seems inevitable.

I invited Paul to dinner on a regular basis, and we enjoyed many a lively discussion, made less painful by the solidarity that Donna and I now shared. We also invited Susan over sometimes, and she became one of Donna's closest friends. Occasionally, much to Susan's consternation, we extended invitations to other young men—the "clean-cut" variety—to dinner as well. In fact, I was sitting across from the very Mr. Boring who eventually became the love of Susan's life. A year after their meeting, Donna was the matron of honor and I was a groomsman in a wedding I had once found difficult to imagine.

Sadly, Donna and I were forced to engineer Paul's intervention for alcoholism, but Paul wasn't ready to hear of it, and he didn't speak to us for years after. He eventually lost his job, and I reached out again and convinced him to give therapy a chance.

He did, but it never took. In spite of our best efforts, and a mountain-load of prayers, Paul died at the age of forty from liver failure. Sometimes seeing the future isn't enough to stop it, and sometimes even second chances aren't enough. He did "chuck it all" and turn his back on his old ways, however, somewhat late, but then again, in the grand scheme of eternity what is "late"?

I've missed him terribly, and I grieve with his mother, but I suppose the prospect of seeing your loved ones again is ultimately what matters.

Donna and I renewed our vows on our twentieth anniversary, in the rose arbor of a botanical garden in Connecticut. She held a spray of blue roses, dyed of course, to match her pale blue dress. Larry was my best man, and Alycia stood proudly next to her mother, who looked absolutely stunning at forty-two.

When we visit New England, as we do nearly every fall, Donna and I stay in a humble cabin a couple of blocks from the ocean. It's all we can afford, but it's plenty. We walk the beach at night. Occasionally, the weather is a little brisk, but the colors are stunning, and with my arm around her, I whisper sweet nothings in her ear, and she whispers them back. We're like new lovers, making up for so many lost years.

In spite of our vacations, I look at Aberdeen differently these days, and I can't imagine leaving my hometown. It's become comfortable, like an old blanket or comfortable shoe.

Needless to say, Larry was shocked when I confronted him with his illicit tax avoidance schemes. Due to a generous plea bargain and an agreement to surrender unduly obtained funds, Larry served two months of a six-month sentence. I never told him how I knew, but he wouldn't have believed me anyway.

"I'll be waiting for you," I told him. "We're partners, remember? For better or worse?"

Finding Jim, now in his late seventies, retired on a farm just outside of Aberdeen, was easy. Persuading him to talk to me wasn't.

"I don't want no Whitaker in my house!" he shouted through the screen door, balancing himself on a rickety wooden cane.

I finally prevailed upon his wife to let me in, and Jim cowered in the corner as I explained my intentions. While they lived in rather poor means, I was glad to have the opportunity to change some of that. When I wrote out a check for what he'd lost with my father, plus five percent a year retroactive, Jim's attitude changed.

"I was wrong about you, kid," he said to me. "I hope you didn't take it to heart."

I patted his shoulder and winked. "I didn't give it a second thought, Jim."

"Good," he nodded, seemingly relieved.

Like I said, nothing came easy for us, including Donna's spiritual struggles, but, again, I know it's helped her to have a partner in faith at last. Most important, Donna has truly forgiven me for the years of neglect, which is, perhaps, the greater miracle, and for which I'm most thankful.

I haven't given my "dream" experience more than casual reflection as the years have passed. I'm not certain what really happened, and how such a thing fits in with God's universe, but it doesn't matter.

Sometimes, Donna awakens to find me on my knees beside the bed, tears streaming down my face. Seeing me like this usually moves her to tears as well because she still remembers the old days when praying rarely crossed my mind except in panic circumstances.

In the end, Alycia married her "best friend," and it was a memorable wedding ceremony. I remember tugging on my ears moments before she said "I do," and she cast me a knowing squint—recalling an event a few weeks earlier.

We had been sipping ice tea on the back porch. Doug stepped inside the house to retrieve another helping of Donna's potato salad. I took this opportunity to inform my daughter of what I really thought. "I've enjoyed getting to know Doug," I said. "He's friendly. Intelligent. Responsible. But . . ."

Alycia rolled her eyes in anticipation.

". . . his ears are a little big."

Alycia squirted ice tea through her nose. "They are *not,* Dad! Take it back."

Donna grinned. "Better take it back. I think she means it."

"Well . . . maybe it's . . . the contour of his entire face, then . . ."

"Dad . . ."

"I'm just glad he's found someone who loves him—considering the ears and all."

Alycia put her ice tea on the table. I knew what was coming next. "Take it back." She rolled up her sleeves, raised her eyebrows, and wiggled her fingers. "I'm much bigger now. I have lo-o-o-ong fingernails, and my vicious temper hasn't improved much."

"Good point."

"Dad?" she said meaningfully, prompting my apology, her fingers still outstretched, poised to pounce. She turned to her mother. "Mom, make him."

Donna smiled. "Yeah, Stephen, you better say you're sorry."

"Mo-o-m! Try to sound convincing!"

"It's all I can do not to laugh, honey."

"Mo-om!"

"I'm concerned for your future children," I continued. "I mean, although we flattened them with a pin, genetically you still have protrusive ears. And with Doug's big ears, well . . . I hate to think of it." I faked a shudder. "My grandchildren's social lives will border on disaster. You might want to consider home-schooling them. Or . . . you might consider giving up on having children altogether."

"Dad . . ." She flexed her pinchers. "We're getting our marriage license tomorrow, and there's nothing you can say to stop me."

"I'd wear hats to the courthouse," I suggested. "Otherwise, in the interests of preserving our flat-ear society, they just might deny your application."

"Last chance, Dad." She flexed her fingers, long nails poised, within an inch of my nose.

I was undeterred. "In fact, we may be dealing with a birth hazard."

"Huh?"

"The baby might get stuck . . . if you know what I mean."

Alycia grabbed my nose. "Excuse yourself, or lose a part of yourself."

Donna chuckled, "You're in for it now, Stephen."

I frowned thoughtfully, and my words came out sounding like Daffy Duck. "Hmmmm. Maybe I am wrong. I mean . . . I could give it some further thought, perhaps change my opinion."

Alycia nodded, pleased with my abdication, and released my nose. "Smart move, Dad—"

I squinted thoughtfully and rubbed my damaged body part. "Then again, maybe it's the eyes . . ."

"Dad . . ." This time she picked up her ice tea as a warning.

"They're somewhat close together. And that makes his ears—"

She drenched me from hairline to chin. A tickle fight quickly commenced. Even Donna got in on the action—against me. Doug was back by now, and stood smiling in the doorway, but looking just the tiniest bit perplexed. I lost the battle in short order, taking everything back—everything and more. But for years later, whenever we got together as an extended family, I caught my daughter's eye, and tugged on my ears just to get in the last word.

"Dad . . ." she'd complain.

"What? They itch."

A few weeks after our twentieth anniversary, as Donna and I were getting ready for bed, I casually mentioned the diary to Donna. Her face turned pale, but I took her into my arms and nuzzled my face into her neck. "There's something I'd like to read to you."

"Alycia!" Donna chuckled under her breath.

Sitting next to my wife on the bed, I opened her diary—with her permission, of course—and flipped through the pages.

I know we belong together, she'd written years ago, and I now read it to her.

Donna smiled wistfully, expectantly.

I gazed into the eyes of my beloved wife. "And to think I almost missed out on you." I took her chin gently in my hand and gave her the most passionate kiss I could manage.

"Wanna fool around?" I whispered.

She smiled dreamily, and I kissed her again.

And again . . .

Acknowledgments

I wish to thank my wife, Beverly, for invaluable suggestions, Carol Johnson, my editor, for ceaseless encouragement, and Rachell Henderson, for essential medical descriptions. Special thanks also goes to Bill Johnson.

About the Author

DAVID LEWIS is the collaborating author, with his wife, of the bestselling novel *Sanctuary.* A former piano instructor, he loves books and music, and enjoys traveling to the Oregon coastline in the summer and visiting New England in the fall. He and Beverly make their home in the foothills of the Rocky Mountains.

More Heartwarming Stories from Bestselling Novelist DAVID LEWIS

Coming Home
by David Lewis

David Lewis's first solo novel is a beautiful heartwarming story of one woman's return home and the spiritual journey that follows. More than a decade after tragic separation, childhood friends Jessie and Andy are brought together again in search of the truth about Jessie's family. As his feelings for Jessie begin to grow beyond friendship, how will Andy ever manage to protect Jessie—not from her past . . . but from her future?

Sanctuary
by Beverly Lewis and David Lewis

After a mysterious phone call, Melissa James abruptly leaves her family and the life she has known to take refuge in an Amish community. Compelling and inspiring, *Sanctuary* is a love story that depicts the power behind revenge, the price of freedom, and the solace found in friendship. It portrays characters, both tender and flawed, whose search for meaning brings them to a moment of shocking and profound truth.

BETHANYHOUSE